THE COMING FIRE

GREG MOSSE

MOONFLOWER

Published by Moonflower Publishing Ltd.
www.MoonflowerBooks.co.uk

1st Edition

1 2 3 4 5 6 7 8 9 10

Copyright © Mosse Futures Ltd 2025

ISBN: 978-1-916678-05-7

Cover design by Jasmine Aurora

Printed and bound in Great Britain by Clays Ltd, Elcograf S.p.A. Suffolk, UK

Greg Mosse has asserted his right to be identified as the author of this work. This is a work of fiction. All rights reserved. No part of this publication may be reproduced, stored in any retrieval system, or transmitted, in any form or by any means, electronic, mechanical, photocopying, recording or otherwise, without the prior written permission of the publishers.

Moonflower Publishing Registered Office: 303 The Pillbox, 115 Coventry Road, London E2 6GG, United Kingdom

MOONFLOWER

For Moose, Martha, Felix, Ollie, Finn and Lily

PROLOGUE

September 2037

Seated in a motorised wheelchair in his control room on the Caribbean island of Haré, Aurélien Castile contemplated the progressive failures of his previously impeccable global information network. In particular, he was piecing together sparse information from Mali in West Africa, from Paris, the capital of France; from the Saint-Médard valley in the Pyrenees; and from southern Egypt.

It was entirely foreseeable that someone, someday, would have the ingenuity to breach the Aswan High Dam and allow the dynamic erosive qualities of its vast weight of trapped water to do the rest, leaving nothing but misery and ruin.

Aurélien was the brutal intelligence behind the Darkness and the Storm. Far from the action, he had relied on the communications infrastructure of the mid twenty-first century to remain up to date. Due to the actions of his associates, in September 2037 that infrastructure was crumbling.

A shame – I would have liked to observe my enemies' doom.

From the Caribbean to Aswan, there was no line of sight. The two locations were ten thousand kilometres apart, obscured from one another by the curvature of the Earth. Communications relied on undersea data cables and signals bounced off satellites. In the campaign he had named the Darkness, Aurélien had planned for the destruction of both, but Alexandre Lamarque had defeated those plans.

Inevitably, he will be coming for me now – unless my son has persuaded him that there might be a better path.

Aurélien had lived an extraordinary life, cosseted by money and influence, determined to outlive humanity's traditional span. But life had insisted on teaching him that, as in many other areas of life, a minor chink in any defensive structure – say, a person's immune system, or a crumbling, badly maintained hydroelectric dam – could easily lead to complete and catastrophic collapse.

The Storm has been successful, unlike the Darkness. Both of Lamarque's closest allies – Mariam Jordane and Amaury Barra – must surely be dead. Is there a chance, now, that I can turn him from my enemy to my friend?

Aurélien's mind, once so sharp, wandered into a daydream, a near-future in which humanity endured the shock of a *tabula rasa* and emerged reborn, the slate wiped clean, a chance to begin again.

No one – not even Alexandre Lamarque, with his uncanny ability to predict future events – can have foreseen the Coming Fire.

PART 1

AFTER THE STORM

1

September 2037

Okay, Alex thought. *There's a single way to be right but there are many ways – almost infinite ways – to be wrong.*

Alexandre Lamarque, an officer with the rank of captain in the French Directorate General for Internal Security, was a tall man with dark hair and kind eyes – but his face right now was drawn in an expression of worry and tension. The door to the flight deck of the needle-shaped Ae4 superjet was locked against him. The holographic interface popped out from his comm-watch was unfamiliar and the pre-programmed autopilot seemed to be fighting back. Down each side of the passenger cabin, an array of real-time screens showed him swamped land, high seas and threatening skies – his only view of the world outside.

Buffeted by the winds, Alex heard his prisoner cry out in frustration and, perhaps, pain from the tightness of his bonds. At the rear of the passenger cabin, Alex's would-be kidnapper, Davide Castile, was securely strapped, face down, on one of a pair of luxurious leather flatbeds.

Unexpectedly, the control holo suddenly offered a strong connection to a French naval frigate, identified as the *Roussillon*, part of a hurricane relief effort, standing a few kilometres off the Haitian coast. Alex put the jet into a holding pattern of steeply banked circles and instructed the Ae4 to open a channel of communication, sending his trilog call sign in reply – *constant-certain-connu*.

For a few seconds, he had hope – that he was no longer alone, sole possessor of vital knowledge that needed to be shared, acted upon; something he couldn't do himself, in imminent danger of falling out of the sky at six hundred kilometres per hour.

Alex received a trilog reply and tried to open an audio channel – instantly losing his ability to maintain virtual control of the locked flight deck.

Are those two things connected?

He felt the aircraft veer away to resume its flight-plan towards the island of Haré, skirting the northern edge of the island of Hispaniola, overflying the airport of Cap-Haïtien International. It seemed completely out of action – not even an automated warning from the control tower.

Is that hurricane damage or is there another problem?

Re-establishing virtual control, he realised that the extreme weather might turn out to be an advantage.

The French relief forces will be accompanied by marines.

He succeeded in taking the aircraft down to the minimum safe altitude, getting a better sense of the terrain from the external cameras. He wanted to swing south for an alternative landing strip. The best option would be the capital, Port-au-Prince. But, try as he might, it seemed impossible. He could only just maintain an erratic eastern trajectory while, several times more, the on-board software attempted to wrest back control.

If he couldn't reach an airport, a narrow strip of tarmac would do, as long as it had two thousand metres of straight run through the dismal felled woodland and scrubby undergrowth of the Haitian hinterland. Alex's eyes remained fixed on the fuselage-screens. Thanks to years of training with the French army and secret service, he had a highly developed sense of space and speed, so he judged he must soon be approaching Haiti's land border with the more prosperous Dominican Republic.

They might fire on me as an unlicensed incursion.

The Ae4's nose camera revealed a highway that straightened out as it left the twists of the hills. He flew over a small convoy of two fuel tankers and what looked like an accompanying security vehicle. Though the narrow strip of tarmac looked marginal, he felt he no longer had a choice.

The controls might eventually become unresponsive and that uphill incline should help with deceleration.

A bell icon in the holographic controls notified him that the Ae4 had just received a data drop from the *Roussillon*. Desperate for news, he wanted to open it straight away but resisted the temptation, in case launching the file entirely disabled his commands. It was hard enough keeping the aircraft level as he descended a kilometre or so ahead of the tankers.

Unable to judge the last few metres of altitude with any precision, he touched down with a sequence of four or five percussive bounces. With each impact, his prisoner cried out once more.

All might have been well but, as he fired reverse thrust to bring the Ae4 to a safe halt, he felt the starboard undercarriage catch and jam in a pothole, maybe where some ancient gnarled tree – too twisted to be useful for construction, too iron-hard to be cut up with hand tools to serve as fuel – had been toppled by high winds, tearing out its roots and a section of the road.

Strapped into his expensive leather seat, Alex felt the Ae4 skew round, the metal and plastic groaning and shrieking. Extraordinary shearing forces bent, creased and then split the aircraft into two pieces. Damp outdoor weather suddenly rushed into the air-conditioned interior.

Alex was wildly shaken as his portion of the Ae4, including the nose and flight deck, went rolling and tumbling, spinning and flipping, then abruptly came to rest on its side against some irregularity in the landscape. The remainder of the fuselage – containing his prisoner – was gone, ripped out of sight, leaving him shaken and alone, dangling against the safety harness.

His mind became blank as he slipped into unconsciousness.

2

Davide Castile was forty-seven years old. Once a fine physical specimen of middle-aged manhood, his health had been compromised by rash and unproven medical experimentation, ironically designed to prolong life – not his own. He had left the French army as a decorated officer with a 'mixed' disciplinary record and an intact pension. That wasn't important. What mattered to him was his status as sole heir to the extraordinary wealth of his family's energy company including massive intangible assets, plus cash cows in mining, solar, tidal, cleanburn waste disposal and much more.

Before the Ae4's catastrophic touchdown, foremost in his mind had been a dam at the head of a Pyrenean valley whose hydro-turbines spent every minute of every day spinning gold out of gravity, turning the weight and pressure of water into money, power and influence.

Or, rather, they used to.

The dam – if his accomplice, Léa Dujardin, had done her job – was surely gone.

And now, am I free?

Securely bound during the crash-landing, safe on the luxurious flatbed in the rear portion of the Ae4, Davide was buffeted but not injured. Stabilised by the wings, the section of fuselage he was in – torn away from the front portion that included Alexandre Lamarque's seat and the flight deck – had skidded along the tarmac before coming to an abrupt stop, shooting Davide out of his safety belt like a projectile from the barrel of a gun. Propelled across the carpet, he'd come to rest in a narrow space between the facing doors of the Ae4's two toilets.

After a moment to catch his breath, Davide tried to stand up. It was difficult and painful. His hands were tied by a strong dressing-gown cord behind his back. The medical port in his abdomen seemed to have shifted, leaving him with sharp, debilitating pain.

Pushing his shoulders against the toilet door, Davide forced himself to his feet. He looked out of the torn-open end of the fuselage, uphill on the lonely straight road, seeing desperate, degraded woodland punctuated by stumps that stood only a metre or so tall, from which hopeful buds and suckers were attempting to grow.

We are not on Haré.

At the top of the rise, maybe two thousand metres distant, he could make out the vague outline of a white-sided building, itself in the shadow of full-grown trees.

This is Haiti. Is that the Dominican border? Did Lamarque survive? And why was our progress so erratic? The Ae4's autopilot doesn't have any defensive protocols.

Davide stumbled towards the rip in the skin of the aircraft, his hands still tightly bound in the small of his back. The edges of torn metal looked sharp. He reversed against a suitable protrusion and – very carefully, so as not to cut his own wrists – started to abrade the dressing-gown cord.

3

Fierce winds whipped in through the broken end of the ruptured aircraft, rousing Alex from torpor, reminding him that he was in danger. But he found it hard to focus. The world was all odd angles. The repeated shocks of the successful but traumatic landing had winded him. Then the Ae4 flipping and ripping had rattled him around, leaving him dangling on his side, restrained by the four-anchor safety straps, one over each shoulder and one from either side of his hips, biting into his muscles.

He tried to change position, but the weight of his body against the belts made it impossible. His mind felt thick and his neck muscles were taut with fighting gravity. And he could smell some escaping volatile chemical.

Davide had told Alex that the Ae4 was powered with SAF, sustainable aircraft fuel. It might have been a self-justifying lie. Either way, there could soon be an explosion from escaping fluid hitting some hot flange of torn metal.

Am I injured?

His breathing was painful, but that was probably simply due to repeated surges of momentum abruptly arrested by the restraints. He didn't feel nauseated – which was a good sign – and all four limbs responded when he willed them to move. He had a taste of blood in his mouth and regretted not finding something to bite down on before attempting the emergency landing. It wasn't like in the movies. A vehicle highway was not a runway.

Exploring with his tongue, he found a place where the side of one tooth had cleaved away during one of the impacts, but it didn't seem to have exposed a nerve.

'Time to go,' he said aloud.

It was easier said than done. There was nothing he could get hold of to take his weight and adjust his dangling position.

Or is there?

Alongside his seat – and still intact – was a built-in cabinet for in-flight stowage. Its exterior was smooth, but he flipped open the lid and grabbed at the inner frame, getting some traction, pulling against his own weight, straining his bicep to relieve pressure on the safety harness. Meanwhile, with his other hand, he pressed the jammed button in the centre of the clasp.

Four tongues of polished steel sprung out, the straps instantly retracting into their housings. Alex tumbled to the floor – actually the wall – jarring an elbow to break his fall, coming to rest on the viewing screens that ran the length of the cabin. Winded, he lay in a heap. On the other side of the fuselage – now his ceiling – the screens revealed a straight-up shot of grey cloud, vaguely differentiated with a variety of threatening tones for incoming rain.

He sat up, the blood whooshing in his ears as it tried to reassert its habitual distribution through his body. It was good news that some of the screens were still receiving images from the external cameras, despite the fact that his fragment of the Ae4 was no longer connected to the superjet's engines. That meant that there was a battery back-up. He decided that the volatile chemical he could smell was simply spirit alcohol from broken bottles that had tumbled out of the fridge.

Another strong gust of damp wind came scouring in through the ripped fuselage, carrying wet leaves and a hint of hail. His mind began to clear. He checked his comm-watch and found no signal, neither ground relay nor satellite, but he clung to the fact that there was a power source of some kind on board.

He tried to stand but found it was too soon. His legs were undamaged but his balance was still impaired. Resting on his knees, impatiently, he ran through his priorities.

First, he needed to get in touch with Claudine Poiret, his ultimate commander in government, who he knew was aboard a French navy ship on a relief mission, standing off the coast of Haiti. Was that the frigate that had tried to contact him while he struggled to land the Ae4? He thought it likely. If so, was Poiret aware that he had passed within a few kilometres of her position before veering away?

She must have been informed of my call-sign. But I was flying too close to the ground to be accurately tracked by the Roussillon's *ship-control system.*

His second priority was to find out if Davide had also survived. In fact, that probably trumped getting in touch with Poiret. The man was his enemy – and the key to preventing further disasters.

4

On the island of Haré, Aurélien Castile – Davide's father – was on his circular terrace at the top of his castle-like home, at the centre of the island, looking out at the scudding clouds and the white-flecked, iron-grey sea. He could taste salt on his thin lips. From time to time, he waved a hand in front of his face to drive away the incessant flies, but his eyes remained fixed on the distant horizon.

The speck he expected to see against the grey skies had refused to appear.

Back in prehistory, tectonic forces had thrust the island's peak about a hundred and twenty metres above sea level, easily enough to cope with the rises predicted for his lifetime and for his son's. The island was fertile, a little over forty kilometres long and, at its widest point, thirty kilometres across, its geology honeycombed with crevasses, caves and pits. Aurélien believed he could rely on Haré's generous average annual rainfall – even in the age of ever more violent and less predictable twenty-first century weather – harvesting that life-giving precipitation into enormous underground cisterns, making his home immune from drought. The upper terrace that he was circumnavigating was one of the most important catchment areas.

He scanned the horizon.

Nothing, still.

Through his American agent, Aurélien had commissioned two parallel infrastructures for Haré Stronghold, one digital and one analogue. Aurélien knew that, when digital television and radio signals were first mooted, they were sold to the public on the strength of the improved quality of image and sound, easily perceptible to the human eye and ear. But it soon became clear that there was a significant drawback. In the digital world, sub-optimal performance was as good as useless – the image broken up into impenetrable blocks of shifting colour, the audio incomprehensible – while an unsmart analogue device operating at only forty per cent was still useful. A 'noisy' image or a muffled audio could still communicate.

Once Fire has destroyed the world's digital infrastructure, on Haré we will still be safe.

His motorised wheelchair sounded a timed alarm, encouraging him to move to improve circulation in his atrophying lower limbs. He drove to the parapet wall and dragged himself up, clinging to the white sandstone caps. Finding his balance, he trod gently on the spot, counting to sixty, one flex of each weak foot per second, then flopped back down, pitifully exhausted, brushing away a fly that wanted to drink the sheen of sweat from his damp and prominent cheekbones.

He mistimed the two actions. As his bony backside struck the edge of the seat, the wheelchair tried to scud away from under him because he had neglected to set the engine brake. His wiry fingers snatched at the armrests. His feet paddled on the smooth flagstones of the circular terrace, accelerating the thing backwards. Anxiety made more sweat pearl on his upper lip and forehead. Then the wheelchair struck the inner wall of the terrace, by the elevator, and he hung, ungainly and foolish, able neither to stand nor sit, teetering on the edge of a fall that might fracture his fragile pelvis.

Where are my servants?

His breathing came quickly. He tried not to give in to panic but each gasp was shallower and faster than the last. That was a part of his more general infirmity – the inability of his lungs to expel all the CO_2 created by the act of breathing. In the end, so the doctors said, it would be the act of breathing – essential to life – that killed him.

My arms are too weak to lift my own weight. I can't hold on much longer.

The elevator door opened. One of his domestic servants – carrying a tray on which was balanced Aurélien's frugal meal – immediately noticed his master's distress. He put the tray on the sideboard under the partial overhanging roof and leaned in, clawing his sharp fingers under Aurélien's arms and lifting him bodily back into the wheelchair. For a moment or two, Aurélien's face was squished against the man's pristine white uniform.

'Thank you,' he said, indistinctly.

'What happened, Chief Castile?'

'Nothing happened.'

'Should I call someone?'

'No. Just be quiet.'

Safely re-seated, his shoulders hunched and his head tipped forward towards his sternum, Aurélien's breathing slowed and he began to feel more in control.

In future, I will not exercise alone.

'I brought your meal, sir,' said the servant. 'Should I cover it?'

'Do so,' said Aurélien, shortly. 'Then go.'

The overhanging eave of the roof ran all the way round the circular terrace at the summit of Haré Stronghold. The servant moved back to the sideboard. From a deep drawer he took a large sheet of muslin, folded into a tight square. He transferred the tray to the table, shook out the muslin and draped it, half-concealing the meal of simple, local produce from the island itself, set out on fine bone china with elegant silverware and a crystal tumbler and carafe.

'Will there be anything else?' he asked.

'Leave me, I told you.'

The servant re-entered the elevator with his eyes down, as if forbidden to look any longer upon his master's frailty.

The elevator descended. Aurélien activated the motor on his wheelchair, trundling forward to the table. He could feel the bruises already forming where his servant's strong hands had grasped his frail flesh. He was fairly certain that his papery skin had split along the line of one of his prominent ribs – that he was bleeding.

No matter. I will call one of the nurses later on. There are matters to attend to, still.

The empty elevator returned, ready for its next use. Aurélien realised that the adrenaline of his almost-accident had – unusually – given him an appetite. He lifted a corner of the muslin cloth, taking a savoury *galette* from the bread basket, something like the consistency of a thick pancake or a soft Ethiopian flatbread. He spread it with creamy, two-day old goat's cheese. As he ate, he savoured the goodness – the fat in the cheese melting with the warmth of his mouth, coating his taste buds, activating his salivary glands.

Actual food was so different from the carefully prepared medicinal nourishment he had lived on as a younger man, when he had formed the idea of living well beyond a hundred years – a hundred-and-twenty or a hundred-and-thirty, who knew? At a little over half, the goal was unfeasibly distant.

Aurélien had been an evangelist for the 'enhanced human longevity' movement, inspired by one of its first gruesome experiments in which a pair of mice – one old and one young – were stitched together in such a way that the older one shared the younger one's blood flow. The 2005 results claimed that the older mouse became physically stronger and mentally sharper – significant evidence of de-ageing.

Not, however, a procedure that could be replicated in humans.

As an alternative, Aurélien – with a team of medical researchers whose research he funded – devised a program of plasma donation from his son, Davide. News got out under lurid headlines, 'Vampire therapy' and 'Living like Dracula'. It spawned several copy-cat start-ups, the best-funded of which folded in 2019 after the US Food and Drug

Administration declared that evidence of any benefit was statistically insignificant, while the risk for harm was substantial.

But Aurélien was undeterred. Continuing to inject himself with plasma from his son's blood, he entered into partnership with a canine researcher who claimed parallels between the ageing of dogs and humans. In the early 2020s, US regulators approved trials of the drugs they had developed, and he submitted himself in secret as a human candidate.

Was that the beginning of my decline?

Suffering from the first contra-indications of the experimental drugs – physical lassitude, muscle loss – he switched to a strictly managed lifestyle in which diet, exercise, sleep and so on were prescribed by an early medical AI that constantly monitored his health data. He exercised to an austere regime, forcing himself to wake and rest with iron-clad regularity, as if his human organism could be bent to his will.

That, too, was a dead end. At least I can once more eat real food.

More recently, Aurélien had attempted a number of transhuman biohacks, including slow-release medicinal implants under his skin, with negligible success. He had considered appending a stronger prosthetic hand to his own weak arm, like the one used by one his enemy, Alexandre Lamarque's friend and colleague, Amaury Barra. But his flesh was too fragile and slow to heal, and his deregulated immune-system made rejection inevitable.

Amaury Barra's youthful flesh accepted his prosthetic and made him stronger. But still, I managed to destroy him at Aswan.

Aurélien's most fanciful option had been to download his consciousness into a supercomputer or into the *de facto* supercomputer of the atomised World Wide Web. That was why, within the destructive vendetta of the Coming Darkness conspiracy, he had been attempting to gain sole control – through physical terrorism and viral attack – of a massive network of undersea data cables connected to Haré. Only the most massive synthetic intelligence could come close to mimicking the complexity of the eighty-six billion neurons of the human brain.

Lamarque put a stop to that. Maybe the answer was always obvious, in the Blue Zones, where centenarians are common: a Mediterranean diet and a placid existence, avoiding stress, accepting one's fate, like a dead-eyed sheep in its pasture.

Aurélien's diminished appetite was quite quickly satisfied. He left his second unfinished galette on top of the muslin cloth, gathering flies, as a kind of propitiatory sacrifice.

Let them feast and leave me in peace.

His mind returned to his purpose: the destruction of the hyperconnected world; the culling and fragmentation of human populations; the reassertion of differences between peoples; the preservation of the Earth's ecosystems from the pestilence of human reproduction.

I am so close.

But still, on the horizon, the fast-moving speck he was expecting – the Castile Energie Ae4 superjet – refused to appear.

5

Alex was feeling more alert but he was troubled by a deep ache in his left leg – maybe the mended hairline fractures in his tibia and fibula from the crash at Al-Jaghar in the defeat of the Coming Darkness conspiracy. But, having endured a tiresome convalescence, he wasn't sure if this new pain was an echo of previous damage or a fresh injury.

Standing on the inner wall of the tipped-over fuselage, the stowage alongside his seat was at eye level. He drew out his travel bag and opened the top flap, the fabric whipped out of his hand by a gust of wind.

Inside the bag were two changes of clothes, his gym kit – last laundered at the Hotel Etoile in the Malian capital, Bamako – and a few toiletries, though he had given up shaving in order to disguise his appearance as 'the man who saved the world'. In a side pocket was his Heckler & Koch .45-calibre pistol, a descendant of the first weapon he'd ever qualified for, back when he and Mariam and Amaury had embarked on their first day of training what seemed a lifetime ago.

He checked the mechanism, then concentrated on listening, wondering from which direction the new threats would come.

The dressing-gown cord finally gave way with only a graze to the back of one of Davide's hands, but the multiple turns still gripped his wrists with friction. He struggled against the severed bonds till they finally fell to the floor, then stood for a moment with his hands on his knees, an unpleasant stickiness on his abdomen. He pulled up his shirt and saw that the dressing on his med-port was weeping fresh blood.

'*Merde.*'

He wasn't losing a dangerous amount. The issue, as always, was the potential for an open wound to become infected. In the front section of the plane there were first-aid supplies, including synthetic skin spray and an antibiotic he could use as a prophylactic. The drug – almitidin – was one of the foundation stones of Castile Energie's wealth, before the company switched focus to energy generation and storage. Synthesised from a toxin produced by leaf scald – a devastating plant pathogen with the ability to destroy whole plantations of sugar cane in a single season – it was widely used in the treatment of hospital-acquired infections. Supply was closely monitored and regulated, to prevent E. coli and MRSA developing resistance to it.

I have my own personal supply.

But he was in the wrong part of the wrecked plane.

Perhaps Lamarque is dead. Perhaps he didn't have time to strap himself in for the emergency landing.

Davide stepped down onto the tarmac, his hair dragged across his scalp by the storm. Two kilometres up the road, there was movement at the border post.

Is that somebody on the roof, observing me through binoculars?

Warily, he doubled back round the wreckage to look downhill. The nose-portion of the Ae4 had come to rest on its side in the scrub at the side of the road. With just a hundred metres between them, he could see Lamarque crouching down with his back to the wind, looking through his travel bag, taking out a weapon, checking the clip.

'*Merde,*' Davide said again.

Just for a moment, he wondered if he could sneak down and take Lamarque by surprise, but soon dismissed the idea. Lamarque was younger, stronger, faster and better trained. Plus, Davide's physical attributes had been weakened by the medical experimentation designed to prolong his father's life and health.

He decided to slip away from the crash site and find somewhere to hole up until the radio frequency identification tracker under his skin brought help. The RFID was a passive device, needing no power of its own, energised by the electromagnetic radiation seeking it, without the need for line of sight. His father's people would soon be looking for him – would perhaps know the last location of the Ae4 before it went down, able to follow the aircraft's automated distress signal to somewhere close to this very spot. As long as the wild winds calmed down sufficiently to allow a rescue chopper into the air.

I need to be close at hand but not so close as to be within range of Lamarque's handgun.

He would have to take a risk with the delay and the damage to his med-port.

Or should I try and make it to the Dominican Republic border post?

He glanced up the road.

No, it's too far. Lamarque will hear my footsteps or the frontier guards challenging me.

He scanned the terrain either side of the road: wet dirt; hacked tree stumps; scrubby underbrush; a gully cutting into the hillside, providing cover.

Wherever I hide, I will need to be patient.

At the top of the rise, two Dominican border guards had climbed up onto the roof of their modest building, sharing a single pair of binoculars, their rain capes flapping. They were expecting the two tankers – returning empty as part of a relief scheme into Haiti agreed with the French relief agency – and had seen them in the distance, at the foot of the long straight section of climbing highway, arriving on schedule. Then they had observed the surreal emergency landing of the extraordinary super-jet, bouncing and flipping and tearing and breaking apart, with the tankers and their escort stopping further away down the road.

Wiping the lenses of their field glasses, they were, individually, each inclined to go and offer assistance. But they feared the arrival of one or another of the armed gangs that disputed the border lands, looking for equipment to salvage and sell from the wreckage.

So, they stayed where they were, waiting to see how events might play out, debating whether there was room on the narrow highway for the tankers and their police escort to squeeze past the jet's wreckage. That was the frontier guards' preferred outcome. Once the tankers were safe in the Dominican Republic, anything else was not their business.

'Or is there another way?' asked one.

'I am thinking the same thing,' said the other. 'Can we profit from this ourselves?'

On the far side of the crash site, the two fuel tanker drivers and their police escort were hanging back. They could see pieces of fuselage scattered across the landscape: the nose cone and a portion of the cabin on its side in the dirt; the larger rear section further up the road, its sleek starboard wing blocking most of the thoroughfare. They were out of their vehicles, leaning against the warmth of the first tanker's engine, raising their voices against the whine of the wind.

'How are we going to get past that?' said the first driver.

'Maybe there's just room?' wondered the second. He turned to the police escort. 'Do you want to go and find out what's happening there?'

The police officer shook his head. 'But maybe we can get assistance from the border guards?'

'I don't like sitting around, waiting for some bandit to come and hijack the tankers,' said the first driver.

'They're empty,' said the second.

'Your bandits don't know that. They'll shoot first and discover their disappointment later – probably take it out on us.'

'The tankers are valuable currency, too,' said the police officer.

'Thanks for that,' said the first driver, sarcastically. 'Very encouraging.'

Just then, they saw a dark figure emerge from the major part of the wreckage, furthest up the road. He seemed to stagger in the buffeting wind, a dark shape against the jagged white body of the devastated jet.

'Should we go help him?' asked the first driver.

Before either of the others could answer, the dark shape stumbled away and disappeared into a gully between the stumps of trees.

In the nose of the wrecked Ae4, Alex was just beginning to understand that he had twice been wrong about the smell of the volatile chemical. In a daze after the crash, he had worried that it might be SAF – sustainable aircraft fuel – bringing a very present danger. Then he'd surmised it was broken bottles from the fridge whose door hung open, the shelves sideways to the wall that had become the floor. But none of the bottles had broken. It was, in fact, the vodka that Davide Castile had served him – no doubt containing a fast-acting sedative – and then left, unstoppered, on the shelf.

Alex raised his gun and stepped out over the torn edge of the fuselage onto the tarmac. The wind blew his dark hair across his eyes, forcing him to twist his head against it. Leaning into the breeze, he made his way up the road towards the larger portion of wreckage, knowing that the storm would cover the sound of his approach.

Also – worryingly – any movement made by his enemy.

He reached the tip of one wing and placed a hand upon it to see if there were any vibrations from some mechanical or electrical element of the aircraft's technology that might still be operating. As far as he could tell, it was still and silent.

He followed the edge of the wing to the fuselage, putting his cheek against the white-painted steel.

Nothing – no sound, no movement.

He crept along the body to the torn end, preparing himself for swift action, leading with his weapon. He noticed some threads of torn fabric caught in the jagged edge of the rent metal. In a swift, silent movement, he took a fleeting glance into the cabin – less than half a second – then retreated with the image complete in memory.

Davide was definitely no longer tied to the flatbed, but was there anywhere for him to hide, crouched very small on the floor?

Unlikely.

Davide's broad shoulders and long limbs made it difficult to imagine that no part of his body would protrude.

For a second time, Alex swung round the torn end of jagged metal, this time planting his feet square, the Heckler & Koch in both hands, ready to fire. In the same moment he knew he was alone, feeling that special quality of absence in a place someone has recently left.

Was it the crash that freed him?

Alex imagined the abrupt changes of trajectory loosening Davide's bonds sufficiently for him to wriggle out. He inspected the flatbed. There was a smear of blood on the beige leather, just where Davide's med-port would have rubbed against it, still fresh.

How long ago? Minutes? Seconds, even?

Alex didn't know. He was unaware precisely how long he had dangled semi-conscious from his safety straps. Davide might be close by, or several kilometres away.

Or did he make for the Dominican border post?

He turned back to the threads caught on the torn metal.

Yes, that's the dressing-gown cord I used to bind his wrists.

Alex searched the cabin, opening the stowage, finding nothing of interest or value. He returned across the wet tarmac towards the nose portion, and clocked the three men, two hundred metres down the road, profiled against the engine of the nearer tanker.

If I go towards them, the wind will carry away my voice and I have no access to digital ID, no paper credentials to show them.

He clambered back inside, stepping awkwardly across the slippery wall-screens that had become the floor. He picked up a dozen miniature bottles of spirits and stuffed them into his rucksack. In the drawer above the fridge – now beside it – he found half a dozen packets of sweet-and-savoury nuts, so he took those, too, because a few handy boosts of protein and salt and sugar would always be valuable. And he found a med-kit in the foot of the wardrobe.

He tried the door to the flight deck, hoping that the armour might have been damaged by the crash, but it was as secure as ever. He began to formulate a plan to break in through the front of the glazed cockpit. It would be difficult – an aircraft windshield was made of high-performance laminated glass – but easier than trying to smash through metal.

In any case, one way or another, forced entry into the flight deck was his obvious next step – a place where he might be able to establish digital or even analogue radio comms with the relief frigate, the *Roussillon*.

6

Claudine Poiret, Alexandre Lamarque's ultimate boss in the hierarchy of the French security services, second only to the president himself, was beyond frustrated. She contemplated the *capitaine de vaisseau* – the ship's commander – a heavily built man whose corpulence strained the buttons of his crisp white shirt. His epaulettes depicted his rank with a large anchor woven with laurel leaves and five bright bars, all in gold thread. He stood with one hand on the door frame of the comms office for balance.

'Have the winds eased sufficiently to send out the Guépard helicopters?' Poiret demanded.

'Not yet, Madame Poiret,' he told her. 'But the forecast says soon.'

'The moment it's safe, I want a team out there searching.'

'Do you think he's likely to have survived? It's a lot of resources, just to bring back a body.'

Poiret controlled her anger by balling up her fists.

'The moment the winds drop, scramble your pilots,' she told him, her voice tight. 'Dead or alive, I want Alexandre Lamarque on board this ship.'

The commander saluted and left. Poiret let her anger subside, silently promising revenge, then turned her attention to the bearded senior comms officer. He was unaware of her glance, wholly focused on his three screens.

The French navy referred to the *Roussillon* as a frigate, but France's allies considered its enhanced combat capabilities put it in the destroyer class. Launched in 2027, it was designed for anti-submarine warfare and land attack and had no hull number because, unlike most foreign services, the French had removed them to reduce potential enemies' ability to identify individual ships.

The *Roussillon's* principal weapons were surface-to-surface missiles in two six-cell launchers and vertical-take-off *loup de mer* – sea wolf – rockets with line-of-sight guidance, radar and electro-optic control, enormous range, infrared tracking and sensor fusion technology. In 2029, the *Roussillon* had taken shipment of two brand-new H160M Guépard helicopters – the very first in their class.

Like the rest of the ship's capabilities, the missiles and the helicopters were controlled by the SCS, the AI-driven ship control system, using high-performance processors and a double-redundant fibre-optic network, developed by the IT specialists at Bordeaux–Mérignac airbase.

All of it was now non-operational. The ship's software systems had been attacked by a suite of mutating viruses.

'Is this new?' she demanded. 'Or is it an extension to the attack suffered by our security databases a few weeks ago?'

'Different,' said the senior comms officer, a man with experience of hack-warfare. He was on his third reboot of the SCS. 'I've had to disconnect from all incoming comms and data. I'm sorry it's taking so long, madame,' he said, rubbing his hand across his beard.

Poiret nodded queasily, swaying with the motion of the ship on the rolling waves, the stabilisers out of action. 'Was the data packet safe to send?'

'I have no way of knowing, madame. And, had there been a reply, we might have risked re-importing the virus.' He made a dubious face: 'The Ae4 was out of control, going down. And if Lamarque survived, the news will be utterly traumatising.'

Poiret glanced at the epaulettes on the shoulders of the man's crisp white shirt – thick black cotton tabs decorated with twin crossed anchors and woven bars of white and gold – and thought about the news she had insisted the comms officer attach to their reply to Alex's call sign. It was all bad, starting with the destruction of the Pyrenean hydro dam in the Saint-Médard Valley and, with it, the almost certain death of Mariam Jordane. There was an incomplete news report from Paris of an evolving emergency at the home of Emmeline Cantor, an officer at the Directorate General for Internal Security. It had something to do with the late head of the DGSI, Professor Fayard, one of her closest collaborators and allies, whose loss a few weeks before she had not yet fully accepted.

Is there more to that than meets the eye? Could Fayard have deceived us all? Is he, in fact, still alive?

Finally, there was the unimaginable catastrophe unfolding in the Nile Valley – the breach of the Aswan High Dam and the indescribable carnage of countless tonnes of rushing, tumbling, destructive water, obliterating all before it, levelling towns and cities all the way to Alexandria and the Mediterranean coast.

Should I have withheld all that?

The answer was no. It was not for her to decide what knowledge might prove important. That was Captain Alexandre Lamarque's domain, the interpretation of disparate facts into a pattern.

Understanding is power – even of facts that it hurts to acknowledge.

She told him: 'Captain Lamarque needs to know what's happening.'

The ship's commander returned, shaking his head apologetically. 'You must understand, madame, that everything on board ship is interlinked and managed by the SCS. We're still bricked, like an electric vehicle on upgrade, inert and useless.'

'You can't launch the Guépards?'

'It's a question of safeguards. Without certain parameters being fulfilled, the SCS considers it too dangerous to put crew in the air and won't release the clamps, even if the weather were within operational parameters.'

'What specifically has to happen to release the choppers from their housings? Can't they be detached physically? There must be cutting equipment on board.'

'That won't help if the Guépard itself still refuses to fly.'

'Meanwhile Captain Lamarque is lost somewhere in the Haitian hills.'

'If he survived the crash,' said the commander, dubiously. 'If not, there's no particular hurry, is there?'

Poiret went to the porthole, looking out across the choppy waters towards the coast.

'You are dismissed,' she ordered, looking at her own reflection in the glass – the dark jacket of her trouser-suit with brass buttons, almost like a uniform, her pale face and severe haircut.

Is it possible Lamarque managed to land safely? If not, with Mariam Jordane, Amaury Barra and Professor Fayard all, more than likely, dead, that leaves only me.

7

With a hum from its electric motor, Aurélien Castile drove his wheelchair into the elevator and pressed the button for the control room. When the elevator came to a halt three floors down, he was obliged to reverse out, the space being too cramped to turn. Like so much connected with his physical infirmity, he found the action demeaning: the loss of independence; the forced intimacy with physicians and carers; the remorseless attention to bodily functions.

In the control room, he found two members of his staff present. One was a technician wearing the same pristine white uniform as the domestic servant who had saved him from a fall, perhaps from a serious injury to his osteoporotic skeleton. The other was Johnson Pederson, the man who – was it seventeen years before? – had helped him build Haré Stronghold. He was, as always, dressed like a mid-western farmer in jeans and a plaid shirt.

Both men stood up, Pederson stocky and confident, his face attentive, biddable, ready for instructions, the Haréan with a closed-off expression, as if his mind was on other things. Aurélien found this annoying.

'You, leave me.'

The Haréan's eyes revealed his sudden worry: 'Forgive me, Chief Castile. I didn't mean any disrespect—'

'Must I say it twice?' barked Aurélien.

The technician bit his lip: 'No, Chief Castile.' He crossed the control room, past half-a-dozen workstations, to a reinforced steel door that stood ajar on the stairwell. Before he disappeared, he hesitated and looked back. 'Please—'

'Go,' barked Aurélien. The technician left, looking slumped and defeated. Aurélien told Pederson: 'Delete that man's credentials and send him back to his *chefferie*. Any news of my son?'

'The Ae4 came within range but descended too low for us to track its final approach on Haiti.'

'Dangerously low?'

'Real low.'

'Have you sent out the K-Raptor?'

'The storm is still too fierce.'

Aurélien drove his wheelchair to a U-shaped desk with four screens connected to a seldom-used keyboard, a microphone for voice commands and a large touchpad for his thin right hand. Beside it was large-format, leather-bound notebook.

One of Aurélien's screens displayed the status of the digital operating system for the whole island, including a permanent evolving readout for virus protection. The system told him that everything was, for the time being, intact, that there had been no breaches to his firewalls – which was simultaneously logical and counterintuitive, given that Haré was the source of the new global infections.

Aurélien's chin sank into his chest as he pondered his next step. The viral attacks were designed constantly to mutate, seeking new ways to exploit new weaknesses. There was no way to tell the implacable artificial intelligence that Haré Stronghold's software wasn't the enemy. His coder, Todor Kaldonov, had programmed it to turn every digital command structure either to meaningless soup or suicidal, even the most protected fail safes.

For the time being, we remain operational.

Pederson was still waiting for instructions.

'You've been monitoring our firewalls?'

'I sure have, Monsieur Castile.'

'Any significant attacks?'

'What I want to call exploratory actions, as if the AI were probing for weaknesses.'

Aurélien lifted his hands from the armrests of his wheelchair, holding them out, flat but shaking.

'I almost fell. Look, I have a tremor, still. Is it adrenaline or is it a more general failure?' Pederson said nothing. Aurélien went on: 'The domestic servant on duty, he lifted me back into my chair. I believe I am bleeding from his clumsy fingernails.'

'Traces of blood have soaked through your shirt.'

'I need a nurse. The one who doesn't talk much, with the broken tooth.'

'Right away?'

'No, when I call. Deal with that other man first. And maybe it's nearly time to prosecute the cull. We have too many Haréans still. Double what we'll need – maybe more.'

'You want them off the island, I get that. But they deserve some kind of severance, like the previous tranches. Maybe a resettlement package and—'

'You've given me your opinion. I don't need to hear it again.'

The American's face flushed red, then he exited the control room, leaving the reinforced steel door ajar.

In the end, thought Aurélien, *Pederson is not on my side.*

Aurélien spoke a voice command.

'Energy analysis.'

On his second screen, a graphical display provided readouts from the different energy sources that powered the island: waves, wind, sun, oil. The first three all made significant contributions but their impact could not always be relied upon. High-carbon oil was the energy fail-safe.

Haré Stronghold needs another shipment from the shadow fleet.

Aurélien's thoughts returned to his brief argument with Pederson. The American's program of works on Haré had drawn huge immigration from Haiti, swamping the indigenous population, reaching a peak of a little more than two thousand in 2024. Subsequent waves of pathogenic infection had reduced numbers by twenty per cent. Then Aurélien had instructed Pederson to return some of the excess Haitians across the water, keeping only about twelve hundred in total, the majority in the two northern *chefferies* and just three hundred native islanders in the south.

One question remained.

How many humans are too many and how many just enough?

8

The rain had arrived, rattling against the torn fuselage. Because it was on its side, Alex lifted the door of the wardrobe like the flap of an enormous letterbox. It contained Davide Castile's outdoor clothes, meaning – wherever he was – that his enemy was still dressed in the soft pyjama-like suit he had changed into when they came on board in Bamako.

By Alex's feet was a glass tumbler that had somehow survived the crash. It was upside down and, trapped beneath it, like a dangerous spider, was Davide's *chevalière* ring – chunky gold with a secret compartment containing a dry, powdered poison. He removed the glass and touched the ring carefully with a fingernail to make sure the deadly powder hadn't escaped.

No, the cap on the secret compartment is secure.

He put it in his jacket pocket and heard several vehicle motors, made to seem distant by the buffeting wind and rain, but whoever was driving was gunning the engines and they were coming closer. It almost sounded like they were having to fight the storm.

Alex pulled on his rucksack and jumped down onto the road, seeing the two fuel tankers heading towards him, accelerating up the hill. One after the other, they veered to avoid some smaller wreckage, revealing a police car following them and, beyond that, a fourth vehicle, a camouflage-painted truck with a machine gun mounted on the roof of the cab. The machine gun burst into life, sending a wild spray of deadly projectiles skittering across the tarmac and wildly into the air.

Alex threw himself down behind the broken fuselage, not completely under cover but a smaller target, the gritty rain striking his cheek and the back of his neck. For a second, he doubted the gunner's competence, spraying their projectiles indiscriminately, then he heard the distinctive pop of one tyre then another as both the police car's rears were punctured. It lost traction and speed. Within a few seconds, the camo-truck was on it, ramming the smaller vehicle with its heavy front fenders, sending it spinning off the tarmac and flipping over onto the dirt verge, the roof squeezed down to the level of the dashboard, crushing whoever was inside.

By now, the two tankers were almost upon him. Alex saw the face of the first driver barrelling past, tense and set, as he swerved through the chicane of debris, followed by his colleague.

Alex knew what they were trying to do. They were making for the border, attempting to flee what was inevitably a lawless armed gang – one of the many that provided a kind of brutal atomised government across three-quarters of Haitian territory.

These are not people I want to meet.

The camo-truck roared by, chasing its prey. Up ahead, the first tanker's heavy right wheels were catching in the verge as the driver tried to squeeze past the tip of the wing of the rear portion of the Ae4.

He managed it, but the second tanker, following on, hit a tree stump, veering the heavy vehicle left into the protruding wing, rupturing the Ae4's fuel tanks. They immediately began spilling sustainable aircraft fuel across the road. Hammering along in pursuit, the camo-truck didn't slow or deviate.

Perhaps the driver hasn't noticed. Or perhaps he's simply an idiot.

A sustained volley rang out from cabin-mounted weapon.

The gunner, too.

The scorching-hot projectiles ricocheted through the spilt SAF, sending up a curtain of blue flame that chased across the tarmac, finding its way into the reservoir in the wing. Sudden combustion in an enclosed space caused an explosion that sent strips of scorched metal flying in all directions. The shockwave propelled the camo-truck off the road, all four wheels leaving the ground. It tumbled over twice, throwing the gunner clear, and came to a halt right-side-up. Surprisingly, the gunner was unscathed. Alex saw him land on his feet, contemplate the wrecked truck for four or five seconds, then run up the road towards the border post.

Alex skirted the wreckage for better cover. More shots were fired from the Dominican side, seven or eight projectiles, striking the tarmac not far from the gunner. He jumped to one side, veered away off the road, scampering over the damp ground, through the ragged undergrowth and out of sight.

Did the border guards shoot to kill or did they deliberately miss?
He thought the former.
What other rational strategy is there when a civilised democracy is confronted, across a porous land border, by a territory ruled by indiscriminate violence?

Alex scanned for the next danger. There were further fuel tanks in the port wing of the Ae4, yet to ignite and blow, but the blue flames were dying in the fierce wind and rain.

He jogged in a wide arc through the undergrowth to the right of the highway, coming upon the camo-truck from the side, approaching the cab with his Heckler & Koch raised and ready. The door swung open and the driver tumbled out onto the ground, dressed in ill-fitting fatigues, his face bloody, his nose squished from an impact with the steering wheel or windscreen. Seeing Alex, he fumbled a long hunting knife from a sheath on his belt. Alex stepped in and trod on his wrist.

'*Reste tranquille,*' he ordered.
Stay still.

The man writhed, grabbing at Alex's leg, saying something through gritted teeth in Haitian Creole that Alex couldn't understand. Then he reached out his other arm and grabbed a boulder about the size of a baby's head, ready to use it as a weapon.

Alex regretted what he needed to do, but had no hesitation in putting a bullet in the man's head.

9

In the control room in Haré Stronghold, Aurélien was still considering his energy reserves. Once the world descended fully into chaos, he wanted at least five years' oil supply on hand, in addition to the massive lithium battery arrays in another of Haré's many underground caverns. But the Caribbean hurricane season had gone on for so long that the island's aeolian generators had operated at barely five per cent capacity, for fear they would be destroyed by the fierce winds. Plus, the churned-up seas meant that most of the wave-driven generators were now awaiting repair. Meanwhile, the darkness of the skies over nearly three months had impacted the replenishment of the solar reserves fed by photovoltaic panels that stood on south-facing slopes of the craggy terrain.

Oil remains our best option.

Despite the advances in renewable energy generation and storage, still nothing rivalled natural hydrocarbons for the astonishing quantity of chemical energy trapped in every kilogram of fuel. Heavily taxed under the post-Paris protocols to inhibit consumption, there were legitimate suppliers – Saudi, Qatar and Iran, for example – and illegitimate ones, those that traded out of sanctioned regimes such as the squabbling Russian factions or the eternally failing states of Venezuela and Nigeria.

Because extraction and refining in the disintegrating renegade economies continued, there was product available to be sent out on the high seas. But only on-board a 'shadow fleet' of illegal tankers, operating without insurance or judicial oversight, without regard for industry regulations, hidden behind multiple changes of flag and complex layers of shell-company ownership.

It is a function of the modern world that the rule of law – whose purposes are safety and security – offers opportunities for rapid gain for anyone prepared to work outside the norms.

Wealthy beyond imagining, Aurélien had no need to buy crude at knock-down prices from the shadow fleet, but it pleased him to do so. It was another kind of disruption, a way of disavowing the futile efforts of fragile diplomacy to align the desires and actions of a global population swollen beyond reasonable limits.

Aurélien reversed out of his U-shaped console and crossed the control room to a desk that looked out of place, with analogue radio equipment and a set of paper charts. He picked up a plastic microphone-and-speaker handset, bringing it to his ear. Using a private frequency, he gave his call sign – 'Haré Stronghold' – then waited.

Time passed with a faint hiss of white noise, as if from a great distance, indicating that a connection existed. Then a voice responded with the name of the tanker.

'*Pablo Adisa*,' it announced.

'What is your estimated time of arrival?'

'Uncertain. There is a French destroyer in the area. We risk interception.'

Aurélien left a pause. It was true. The fact that France had sent substantial relief support to Haiti was an impediment to concluding his illegal resupply. He wondered if there might be another tanker in the region, one with a less risk-averse captain. It was unlikely. Since the peak of shadow fleet numbers in the mid-2020s at more than three hundred vessels, the figure had dropped to a few dozen, often swiftly impounded.

'When the time is right, I am prepared to double your price.'

'Money we cannot spend if we are in prison or dead,' replied the captain, a man of Spanish descent from the Philippines called Rodrigo Diaz.

'And provide you with asylum,' Aurélien offered, regretting his words the moment he had spoken them.

'From what?' asked Diaz, his crackly voice brightened with interest and – perhaps – fear.

'From the future,' said Aurélien.

After a second or two, the tanker captain replied, in a tone of agreement: 'Everything is falling apart.'

Aurélien sighed, accepting that circumstances were, for the time being, against him.

'Do not approach until you are certain that you can do so without drawing attention to yourself.'

'Understood.'

Aurélien cut the connection, hanging the receiver back in its cradle, and returned to his U-shaped station where he summoned a detailed technical specification for the tanker.

The *Pablo Adisa* had had four other names over its worryingly extended career. Rechristening vessels was a way to make them hard to trace. It was equipped for ship-to-ship-transfers, an often-dangerous process for both crew and environment. Delivery to Haré would resemble a ship-to-ship transfer in the sense that there was no fixed deep-water port. The tanker would be struggling for stability against the heavy seas.

We must be wary. An oil spill would represent a medium-term environmental problem, undermining food self-sufficiency in a future without imports.

Aurélien took the doorless elevator back up to the terrace and emerged, the electric wheelchair motor drowned out by the whistling of the wild winds, the clatter of rain. To avoid becoming drenched, he remained under the overhang, gazing out at the clouds.

He realised that he ought, by now, to have requested the attention of one of his nursing staff. The blood under his shirt was coagulating. If he let it bond with the cotton of his garment, it would cause more extensive damage to his papery skin when, finally, he removed it.

His eye on the horizon, he pressed a call button in the armrest of his wheelchair and waited.

10

There's always a trade-off. Doing the right thing is often not the same as doing the humane thing.

The latter was usually the harder option. Had Alex disabled the driver of the camo-truck somehow, prevented him from being a threat, he would simultaneously have acquired a burden.

To what purpose? In case there was useful intelligence to be gleaned from the man?

Alex thought that he knew what he needed to know: that he was in Haiti; that, if he was lucky, help from Poiret and the French navy might soon be at hand, if he could only make contact and communicate his location; that Davide Castile had escaped and was somewhere in the landscape, no doubt seeking assistance of his own; that there was still danger because the crashed Ae4 was a valuable technological prize that would soon attract more armed scavengers; that his ultimate enemy – the world's ultimate enemy – was to be found on the island of Haré, tantalisingly within reach, in a stretch of the Caribbean Sea protected from storms by the shape of the coast.

Compared to all of that, struggling to preserve the life of a murderous stranger was ridiculous. The trade-off, though, was one more tithe of toxic guilt and regret, settling like poison, deep in the reservoir of his memory.

Alex was now alone on the highway, protected from the wind by the cab of the camo-truck. The two oil tankers had made it to the frontier at the crest of the rise, the second one limping along, having lost pressure in several tyres. He'd checked that the driver of the upturned security vehicle was dead. Apart from the wind and rain, the lonely stretch of road was extraordinarily quiet, the landscape free of birds because all the trees had been cut down. There were flies, but there was little else to indicate that this had once been a fertile, tropical island, before the thirst for survival of a multiplying human population had depleted it almost to extinction.

Alex searched the pockets of the camo-truck driver's clothes, feeling the pulpy weight of his dead flesh, the slackness of his muscles. In one of the patch-pockets on the front of his fatigues he found a leather purse inside which were a handful of dusty pills – some kind of medication, perhaps? – and a key of the kind used for a small strongbox. In the opposite patch-pocket he found a photograph of a group of revellers, dressed in something like the phantasmagorical costumes of Haitian tradition. Several of them were masked and he found it impossible to work out which of them – if any – was the man he had killed.

Alex undid the driver's belt and sheath and put it round his own waist. He prised the handle of the long hunting knife from the dead man's spasmed fingers and slid it inside.

Hoping there might be a Citizens Band radio in the camo-truck, he climbed up to look. The cabin was sparse, just two uncomfortable seats bolted to the steel panels of the floor and the rudimentary controls characteristic of a cheap thirty-year-old internal combustion vehicle. A chunk of flesh from the bridge of the dead driver's nose still adhered to the steering wheel.

No radio.

Alex leaned across to look under the far seat. Maybe he would find the strongbox the driver's key belonged to.

Nothing.

He jumped back down and picked up the rock the driver had tried to use as a weapon. He weighed it in his hand.

Perfect.

To protect himself from any shards of glass, he pulled off the dead man's jacket and wrapped it over his fist. Then he went back to the aircraft's nose, lying on its side, set his feet solidly and began beating against the glass.

At the third blow, it crazed but remained intact. At the ninth, a sharp corner of the hard granite boulder penetrated the windshield. He widened the breach until he was able to fold his fingers through, protected by two or three layers of the heavy fatigue jacket. The laminated glass flexed like fabric. With two hands in the rent, he dragged an opening wide enough to climb up and slither inside, across the control panel, landing on the starboard wall, with everything tilted over by ninety degrees.

He stood up, evaluating his new circumstances. The Ae4's controls seemed mostly generic. Though he had never flown one, it didn't take long to locate the on-board computer, controlled from a large touch-sensitive tablet in the centre of the dashboard, within reach of both pilots – but there had been no pilots. Davide had programmed the flight plan on automatic.

Alex wondered if there might be useful information in the log, in addition to the unopened data drop from the *Roussillon*. He touched the control screen. No response. He ran his fingers round the black rim, looking for a power button, and found an almost-invisible depression that responded to pressure with a haptic vibration.

The screen came to life six long seconds later, resolving into a default readout of engine performance, fuel load, altitude and air speed. Touching a house-shaped symbol, Alex located the home-screen and navigated his way to the flight log. Scrolling swiftly back in time to departure from Bamako in Saharan Africa, he found the initial flight plan.

There was no need to make a mental note of the destination's GPS co-ordinates. That hadn't been a part of Davide's subterfuge. The landing strip even had an official three-letter airport code: HSX. He guessed it stood for Haré Stronghold, plus the letter X to distinguish it from dozens of other HS codes ending in different letters.

Alex scrolled on. He found a log of satellite pings, confirming the Ae4's location and altitude, crossing the Atlantic at its non-fuel-efficient maximum speed of Mach 1.6, burning up the seven thousand kilometres between Mali and Haiti. Then the log became confused, the GPS coordinates switching wildly from one geo-location to another.

Is that a satellite thing ...?

Alex didn't complete the thought. His eyes felt tired, his mind clouded with uncertainty and doubt. He took a few deeper breaths, wondering if he was suffering the after-effects of the drug Davide had used to subdue him, or the consequences of an undiagnosed concussion from the crash landing.

Both, probably.

He scrolled the screen up and down, trying to make sense of what he was seeing.

Taking control of the aircraft via the piggy-back tech on my comm-watch should have made no difference to the Ae4's ability to correctly log its location.

In any case, the point in time when the sat-pings became incoherent was the moment of receipt of Poiret's message and the data drop.

Dizzy and uncomfortable, Alex leaned against the starboard pilot's seat, wondering if he had drawn the wrong conclusion. He had assumed that the attempt to open a live channel to the *Roussillon* had overloaded his comm-watch's processor, making it impossible to remotely pilot the plane using the holographic gesture-controlled display. But what if it hadn't been that at all? What if communication from the frigate had contaminated the Ae4 with a software attack?

The kind of accelerating global attacks Poiret warned me about back in Mali and wanted me to investigate. But if they originated from Haré, wouldn't they have been able to make the Castile Energie Ae4 immune?

Paging through the Ae4's system, Alex found he couldn't open the data drop, but he was able to isolate it and move it out of the log to an external memory stick he always carried – with biometric protection from his own fingerprint. The filename extension identified it as an mp4. The transfer took almost a minute as the stick's in-built scanning sterilised the data.

The Roussillon *must run on a digital SCS. Poiret will be having troubles of her own. I may be on my own.*

Out of the corner of his eye, through the crazed windshield, he noticed a gap in the clouds and a bright corner of sky, away to the west, uncertain whether the weather was breaking or if he was now in the eye of the storm. He removed the memory stick and took a deep breath, fighting another wave of nausea.

Definitely a concussion.

Without properly thinking through what he was doing, he reactivated his comm-watch's piggy-back tech, connecting directly to the Ae4's digital operating system, intending to run an anti-viral program. Within seconds, in the top right-hand corner of the Ae4's control screen, a symbol began to flash. He tapped and it expanded to reveal a warning, indicating a deliberate rapid depletion of the reserve power supply.

Odd.

Confused, he switched back to the aircraft's log and found that a 'drain' command had been instigated.

Why would the Ae4 be deliberately – suicidally – running down its battery back-ups?

Fearing it must have something to do with his own actions, Alex spoke a voice command to his comm-watch.

'Stop program.'

There was no soft chime in response.

'Shut down.'

It was too late. The comm-watch screen was blank.

For a few seconds, Alex simply sat, aware of his error, but not yet aware of its repercussions.

What have I done?

Then a symbol appeared on the square screen on his wrist, like a figure eight, but geometric, with sharp corners, two triangles on top of one another, the inverted upper one's apex balanced on the point of the one beneath. Alex knew what that symbol meant.

Self-destruct.

11

After several minutes watching the forty-five-degree rain falling from the chasing clouds, Aurélien drove his wheelchair to the lee of the elevator building beneath the tall antenna array. The sky began to lighten as the precipitation moved on.

As every prepper knows, there can be no survival except in the places where raindrops reliably fall.

He continued his circuit. Twenty-odd kilometres away, he could just make out the outline of his two-thousand metre runway, suitable for the Castile Energie Ae4 jet. Beyond it were the two northern settlements for imported Haitian labour – human beings he no longer needed.

The indigenous people will be my people. I will be like a god to them.

He trundled on, thinking about the fact that the Haréans had inhabited the island for many thousands of years. On a fertile area of pasture on the south flank of the steep coastline was the ancient solar temple – damaged, yes, but that was only to be expected of a structure that had endured the storms of weather and time for more than three millennia.

Confined to his wheelchair, Aurélien was generally only able to see the solar observatory from one position. His terrace had a kind of promontory or belvedere, a viewpoint where the parapet wall was lower, allowing him to look down on the sheep and goats that grazed beneath the megaliths.

That, too, is something clean and immemorial – a co-existence.

The observatory was comprised of thirteen standing stones, aligned to provide a calendar, using the arcs of the sun and moon on rising and setting. Precise to within one or two days, even three thousand years later, it predicted and marked equinoxes – when the day lasts as long as the night – and solstices – when either day or night is at its longest.

Aurélien had devoted considerable energy to studying the megaliths' markings – carved inscriptions that he at first thought might be the names of the builders or what they had called this special place in some ancient version of the Nengone language of the Haréans, descendants therefore of the great explorers of the Indian Ocean. A team of archaeologists had judged the observatory to have been abandoned some time around the life of Christ. No human remains were found and nothing was discovered about the culture that produced them. Closely questioned, the Haréans disavowed any knowledge.

It is possible that the stones predate the arrival of the current inhabitants.

Anonymous and imposing, they seemed part of the natural landscape, as if grown out of the land, not imposed upon it. Their petroglyphs – images carved in the rock – had survived to be investigated like a secret code. That was an idea he enjoyed.

Have I not spent much of my own life attempting to retreat into the shadows?

Aurélien took little day-to-day interest in the Haréans who lived – literally – beneath him. He had a modest staff of overseers who kept him detached from administrative chores, trained by Johnson Pederson. He was more focused on the wisdom of the past.

It seems that, today, only I understand what the stones have to teach.

Unseen by Aurélien from his high vantage point on the belvedere, concealed by one of the mighty standing stones, Yeiwa Egesho was contemplating the choppy, grey surf and, inside her mind, a more immediate problem – a disturbing trade in female children.

Yeiwa was aware of the realities. The trade was a consequence of the harshness of existence for poor Haitian families, experiencing the devastating consequences of what the news streams euphemistically called 'extreme weather events'. Not far from Haré, across a narrow stretch of navigable sea, parents in marginal communities were under such stress that they offered girl-children – some only just past puberty – in marriage in return for cash.

For the distressed sellers, it was simple – though perhaps heartbreaking – economics. For the relatively wealthy Haitian immigrant workers in the northern Haréan *chefferies*, it was what financiers call an 'arbitrage opportunity': a difference in valuation of the same good across two different markets.

Of course, educated girls were less likely to be married off early, and more educated parents were less likely to marry off their daughters, but the school infrastructure in Haiti had collapsed.

The leader of the southern *chefferie* of indigenous Haréans, Yeiwa was unaware that the man her people referred to as Chief Castile was intimately connected with all of the very worst things happening across the tormented globe – events that impacted the poorest more severely than anyone else. But she had the wisdom to distrust him.

Because of its height above sea-level and the steepness of its coasts, Haré had proved immune to rising waves. Sheltered from hurricanes by the nearby coastline, it was well wooded, plus its extensive agricultural terraces produced sufficient food to allow an export surplus, in addition to meeting local needs.

The surpluses hadn't always been the case. It was the arrival of Chief Castile, purchasing the island with – apparently – a tiny fraction of his vast wealth, that had transformed its agriculture from subsistence to plenty: better water management; protection from soil erosion; vast quantities of imported soil improvers, well-rotted pig and horse manure, bat guano.

Yeiwa wondered what would happen, should the inputs from overseas – and, for an island, everywhere was overseas – ever stop.

Our population, swollen by more than a decade of Chief Castile's building projects, must vastly exceed what local food production can support.

Yeiwa Egesho was a woman of great natural authority, but circumstances had given her only a limited canvas over which to exercise her intelligence. She had been taught by her father to read the standing stones, like fortune tellers read their Tarot cards, their I Ching sticks or the lines of the palm. He had been taught by Yeiwa's grandfather, and so on, back through time.

An austere man, Yeiwa's father had died in the earliest days of the coronavirus pandemic, before Chief Castile's people brought the vaccines. He had seen his own death on the horizon of his existence and had asked his entire community to assemble in the circle of megaliths, expiring with a rattle in his throat and great lengthening gaps between each painful breath. Soon after, Chief Castile had come to question Yeiwa about the meanings of the petroglyphs carved in the smooth rock. Yeiwa had had no trouble convincing the incomer of her ignorance.

On this day, however, after inspecting the stones and the sky, she believed she knew what was to come.

I cannot say how or why, but there will be Fire.

Unaware of the unrest among people he considered mostly dispensable, Aurélien drove his wheelchair into the lift and descended to the control room, an alert to his armrest console telling him that his systems were under attack.

At his U-shaped desk, he discovered a cascade of minor failures in his digital systems, from which he deduced that the mutating viral contagion was finally breaching Haré's firewalls. With the winds at last subsiding, however, he gave the order for Pederson to despatch the K-Raptor fast helicopter to scan the last known location of the Ae4. Davide was chipped like a valuable pet with a remote-activated radio-frequency identification device that the K-Raptor's powerful scanners could search for and activate.

'I will go myself,' said the American.

Left alone, Aurélien briefly contemplated the possibility that his son might be dead.

No, Davide is a survivor with a tenacious, stubborn urge to cling to life.

He thought about his own botched medical self-experimentation.

Is Davide's thirst for survival a dangerous flaw, clouding his judgement on our greater goals? That same thirst will be my downfall.

Aurélien opened his large, leather-bound notebook in which he had meticulously copied the petroglyphs from the standing stones. His most recent studies had brought new and unexpected insight.

Aurélien felt a warm glow of achievement at what he had done, working long hours, comparing the petroglyphs to hi-res images of other picture-based languages from across the globe, in particular those from the Indian Ocean, the probable origin of the builders of the solar observatory. Just a week earlier, he had begun to crack the syntax and grammar of this unknown language, experiencing an unaccustomed emotion.

Profound contentment.

For perhaps sixty seconds, Aurélien had felt himself 'a new Champollion', the scholar whose genius and persistence had finally deciphered Egyptian hieroglyphs. In that moment, Aurélien had desired to embrace his son and tell him, just as Champollion had done in his moment of intellectual triumph: '*Je tiens l'affaire.*'

I've got it.

But Davide had been in Europe, putting in place the destruction of the Saint-Médard dam and, with it, the death of the troublesome Mariam Jordane.

What had Aurélien discovered?

That the predictions of the original Haréans – whoever they were and wherever they may have come from – culminated in destruction by fire. From what source, though, the carved petroglyphs could not tell.

Perhaps the ancient builders of the stone circle did not foresee me.

12

Alex frowned, staring at the comm-watch screen with its innocent-looking symbol. Who had chosen a geometric figure-eight to mean auto-destruction? He had no idea.

The device was getting warmer on his wrist. A countdown appeared inside the upper inverted triangle:

10, 9, 8 ...

He undid the strap and draped it on the armrest of the pilot's seat. He thought the heat was just the processor working hard, not because it would explode or burst into flames, but ...

... 3 ,2, 1.

The screen went dark. Picking it up again, he had the odd sensation that it had died. There was a faint odour, as if a physical burnout had irretrievably confirmed the data wipe.

Alex took a moment to consider his situation. He was lost somewhere in eastern Haiti with no means of contacting any allies. His prisoner had escaped. In the wreckage of the Ae4, he was sitting on a pile of treasure – but not treasure he could use himself, just a lure for the worst type of bloodthirsty scavengers. And his mind was clouded. It wasn't just that he thought he was suffering from a concussion, it was the fact that his ability to synthesise and interpret his circumstances seemed off-kilter, deregulated.

How many times had he been wrong since coming to his senses, dangling sideways in the harness of the Ae4's luxurious leather seat?

Three or four, at least. And, worst of all, he had failed to realise until it was too late that he ought to have been more careful in protecting the on-board equipment from cyber-attack. It was his fault that his comm-watch was dead, that the Ae4 had dumped all reserve power.

Alex unlocked the armoured door from the flight deck to the cabin – easily done from the inside. With the wreckage on its side, opening it gave him a horizontal slot to awkwardly climb through. Once on the other side, he took a clothes hanger from the wardrobe to hook over the door jamb and prevent it from relocking.

The fridge door still hung open. Its contents – including a few more miniatures – were canted over inside. He was tempted by the alcohol but knew it was wiser to drink something more wholesome, especially while he was potentially recovering from a brain injury. He chose a steel water bottle and drained it. Of the screens above his head – on the starboard wall – one persisted in showing a view of the sky from an exterior camera.

It must have its own internal power source.

There was no longer a vicious wind sweeping in through the broken fuselage. The screen showed the sky lightening, the clouds becoming ragged. He played his fingers round the rim, looking for a slot to connect his memory stick, and found one, bottom right.

Is this the right thing to do? Or am I about to destroy another valuable resource?

Alex thought not. He had confidence that the data on the stick was clean. And the screen was just a dumb device, a relay from the external camera completing a closed-circuit loop.

I need to know.

He pushed the stick into the slot and a touch menu appeared on the screen. He scrolled to the file folder where the download had automatically been stored and double-tapped. It began playing. He watched with his head tipped back.

The Ae4's closed-circuit screen provided no audio. The first images were from a neighbourhood of Paris that he didn't recognise. A human chain was working to pass chunks of hardened orange foam out of the front door of a bland ground-floor apartment, before being tossed in a heap at the side of the cobbled road.

He scanned the screen for anything that would help him identify the area, and spotted a road sign indicating the fourteenth arrondissement. Then the camera pulled focus on a young woman with flame-red hair – his junior colleague, Emmeline Cantor. In response to the journalist's unheard questions, Alex thought Cantor's lips shaped the classic non-committal reply: '*Je n'ai rien à dire.*'

I have nothing to say.

The camera swung round so the journalist could speak to camera. Again, Alex tried to make out what was being said by lip-reading. Among other disconnected words and phrases, he understood 'basement', 'trapped' and 'feared dead'. Then the camera took a prurient interest in a body being brought out of the apartment on a stretcher, without ceremony, bundled through as quickly as possible so as not to delay the human chain.

Alex touched the screen and activated 'pause' to look more closely.

Perhaps it was the water he had drunk or maybe time passing, but he felt his mind was beginning to clear, putting together the clues. He was looking at the dead body of another traitor from within the Directorate General for External Security. And there was some kind of rescue mission underway, to recover a person – or, most likely, a body, buried beneath …

What is that hardened orange foam? Where have I seen it before?

It came back to him – at the building site round the corner from his mother's apartment, at the headquarters of Tabula Rasa, one of the minor players in the Coming Darkness conspiracy. The building was being gutted and almost completely refurbished. Expanding orange construction foam had been used to secure new window frames in the stone openings.

But who could Emmeline Cantor have concealed in her basement, who was now 'trapped' and 'feared dead'?

Someone important enough for Emmeline to risk her life by giving them sanctuary.

The road-sign indicating the fourteenth arrondissement was a clue.

The man whose secret midnight burial in Montparnasse cemetery must have been a trick to allow him to continue his work in secret.

It had to be Professor Fayard, the supposedly deceased former head of the French secret service.

And, now, is Fayard dead 'again'?

Alex touched the screen to make the video resume, hoping for more interviews to interpret by lip-reading, but the footage abruptly switched to satellite imagery that, again, he found hard to follow without hearing the voice-over. It was a massive river flood, that much was clear. Then the angle changed to terrestrial and he was able to see half-drowned road signs with text in Arabic script.

A terrible sensation of dread took hold of him. Fayard in Paris. Amaury in Egypt. He wasn't supposed to know that was where Amaury was, but his friend had given him a cryptic clue.

The video switched to an aircraft or a drone, overflying a dam. From its height and vast size, Alex knew it must be Aswan. The channel of water rushing through a deep cleft in the wall looked almost insignificant from a distance, like the running of a tap, but Alex knew that it must comprise millions of tonnes of water every minute. And he knew that Lake Nasser was four or five hundred kilometres long.

The devastation must be unimaginable. We've failed.

The air-shot of destruction followed the path of the river – no longer a river, in fact, more a vast sluggish snake, sinuous and massive and brown, terrifying in its simplicity.

Amaury must be dead.

There was another abrupt change in shot to a new location and a second flying-eye. It was what Alex had feared the most when the shiver of dread had taken hold of him.

The new footage was another dam that he recognised – from research into Castile Energie – at the top of the Saint-Médard Valley, named after an early Christian bishop, the patron saint of storms.

Then, abruptly, without a warning or a countdown, the screen went dark and there was nothing he could do to revive it. The independent battery power had drained out.

Is that all?

He wondered, if he'd been able to watch a little longer, would he have found a lip-readable message from Poiret, perhaps, giving further details – that Mariam's drowned and battered body had been recovered from the Pyrenean flood?

Feeling a sense of desperation, he searched the cabin for another device capable of playing the mp4, re-checking the wardrobe, flipping open all the stowage compartments.

Nothing.

He slumped down, sitting with his knees drawn up. He was the target in all this, because of what he done at Al-Jaghar, preventing the apocalypse of the Coming Darkness conspiracy, saving the satellite network and keeping the skies free of the Kessler Syndrome of cascading destruction. He thought about how close the world had come to disaster from the God's Thunder orbiting weapons.

And, because I became a target, so did all those close to me. And now they're dead.

For some time, Alex simply sat, his mind wiped clean of hope, vaguely listening to the diminishing wind.

But it wasn't in his nature to give up. Almost involuntarily, his mind began searching once again for the pattern.

Soon after take-off from Bamako, Davide Castile had engaged him in conversation about global catastrophe.

What would happen next?

How would the world look like in the aftermath?

Who would the best prepared to manage survival?
Would it be possible to maintain order?

In reply, Alex had wondered aloud about circumstances – such as a nuclear holocaust – that might make life no longer worth living. Then, to Alex's surprise, Davide had revealed that he saw Alex as a potential right-hand man in the post-apocalyptic world, the authority of his triumph against the Coming Darkness conferring an aura of trust and integrity.

I want to offer you a job.
I have a job.
An escape route, then.
From what to where?
From the present into the future.

Alex's eyes narrowed.

Are these nightmares in Paris, Egypt and the Pyrenees all a part of that plan, a way of narrowing my options through the deaths of everyone I love?

He thought back to his last conversation with Amaury. His friend had been in bed, looking mentally drained by attending the official function celebrating the rebuild of the Cyrenian parliament building that had been damaged in the same fire-fight in which Amaury lost his right hand. Alex had asked how it went.

What can I tell you? They wish it was you but they're making do with me.

Looking back, Alex now wished he hadn't demanded to be allowed to step away from being the public face of triumph, leaving Amaury to endure protocol and photo ops and – finally, surely – death in the cataclysmic rupture of the Aswan High Dam.

He thought back to his last conversation with Mariam. No, not even a conversation. He had been driving back to Bamako from the southern mining belt, in a powerful rented electric saloon car, on a darkened road through the Malian hinterland. Just before the lights of the capital appeared on the horizon, Mariam had sent him an unexpected message – unexpected because he knew that there was no modern connectivity at her Aunt Sara's farm. The message was a pre-record, telling him the bare minimum of what she had been doing, asking if they could speak in the morning when she would be able to use a live sight-and-sound connection belonging to the protestors up by the Saint-Médard dam. He remembered his dismal, workaday reply.

Yes, either before nine my time or maybe after eleven.

Was that it? Was that how everything they had meant to one another – everything they had achieved together – would end, with a bland, emotionless invitation to a routine work catch-up?

He tried not to let himself believe it but felt another stab of anxiety at the thought of what might be happening in Paris. Twice, already, his mother had been the victim of insidious attacks, simply because of what he, Alexandre Lamarque, represented. He drew his knees up further, unconsciously self-protective, his back propped against the bulkhead.

Is Maman dead, too?

Out of nowhere, Alex remembered something he and Professor Fayard had agreed upon.

All of life is six-to-five against. For every five times you win, you lose six. Eventually your stake dwindles to nothing.

Was that what had happened? Had Alex's 'stake' – the people that gave his life meaning – dwindled to nothing?

13

Claudine Poiret had no life outside of her work, a state of affairs that she accepted. Her responsibilities were immensely wide-ranging and required her to stay briefed on a preposterously broad range of topics.

Before setting out on the Haitian relief mission, she had been studying the French navy's development of hypersonic weapons – ship-to-ship or ship-to-shore missiles capable of travelling at Mach 5. They had been designed in a cross-Channel collaboration to replace the British Harpoon and French Exocet. They had come on-stream in 2031. There was even a more recent version carried by hypersonic glide vehicles way up into Earth's upper atmosphere, using gravity to achieve more extreme speeds.

Contemplating the strategic implications of this hard-to-track potential first-strike weapon, Poiret had pondered once more the illegal orbiting monstrosity *Tonnerre de Dieu* – God's Thunder. The official line was that its three lethal platforms had been propelled out of orbit into space, never to be seen again. Poiret had felt the need to verify this through her second-in-command, Marthe Hidalgo, putting her in touch with someone high up in the French Air Force Command. A dove not a hawk, who could confirm or deny.

But she had run out of time. The need to act on the humanitarian disaster in the Caribbean and then the multiple disasters of the Coming Storm – including, it seemed, the loss of her closest allies – had monopolised her attention.

And now she was completely out of the loop. The *Roussillon* was barely able to maintain its position against the swell and the currents, relying on makeshift engine controls devised by the chief engineer to bypass the failed digital SCS.

Plus, Claudine Poiret felt – she wanted to say – 'like death'. But she couldn't. There was too much death. It would sound like selfish hyperbole.

'Are there any anti-nausea drugs on the ship?' she asked.

'There's a medical facility aft on this deck,' said the bearded comms officer.

'I can't move right now,' said Poiret, feeling her face must be turning green. 'This is awful.'

'I'll go. Would you excuse me?'

He left her with his assistant, a younger woman who looked tired and unhappy as she flipped a switch on her console. A light came on, projecting a horizontal blue line on the wall of the small room.

'Keep your eye on that fake horizon, Madame Poiret,' she said. 'It may help to stabilise your inner ear.'

Wordlessly, Poiret leant back against the wall by the door, doing as she was told. At first there was no difference, but she persisted. After a couple of minutes, she realised it was beginning to work and she felt halfway normal. Without the overwhelming nausea, her thoughts began to clear and she felt a need to act.

'What technology do we still have?'

'The SCS is still down. The engineers have rigged alternative manual controls for propulsion where they can. But the stabilisers and several other sub-routines are co-ordinated by algorithm and they …' The woman's face was pale and drawn. She seemed incapable of continuing, making a helpless gesture. 'I'm sorry …'

'Have you never seen active service before?' Poiret asked.

'*Oui, madame.*'

'Under fire?'

'*Oui, madame.*'

'Then what's happening in your head?'

'I don't ...' The woman almost choked on her suppressed emotion. 'Everything is falling apart.'

'Everything's always falling apart,' Poiret snapped. 'There are always huge risks coming into focus, being dealt with by people like me.'

'But there's nothing you can do.'

The comms major re-entered with a blister pack of anti-nausea drugs.

'Take one of these, Madame Poiret. And our spotter has more news.'

A junior seaman followed him into the cramped space. Poiret ignored the medication.

'What is it?'

The spotter told her: 'I was on duty at a fixed binocular station on the bridge. There's a K-Raptor, outbound from the island of Haré towards Haitian territory.'

Poiret took a moment to allow several threads to weave into something sturdier in her mind.

We received Lamarque's call sign, so we know that he was aboard that Ae4, a superjet registered to Castile Energie. That's the same company that owns the Saint-Médard dam where Mariam Jordane recently died.

'Communicate this information to my office in Paris. Do we know who's on board the chopper?'

'How could I know that?' protested the spotter, weakly.

Poiret frowned, telling herself that, for the first time, there was a chance that her ultimate enemy had revealed himself.

Breaching the Saint-Médard dam fits the pattern of self-sacrifice and suicidal destruction from the Darkness and the Storm. And Lamarque was in Bamako with Davide Castile.

Poiret felt a surge of adrenaline – the possibility of action.

Haré is where the Castiles must be based. That's where I need to get to.

'Take the K-Raptor out. Shoot it down.'

'It may already be out of range,' began the comms major, 'and our missile capabilities remain compromised—'

'Get me the ship's commander,' barked Poiret. 'I want that chopper down and I want to set course for Haré.'

14

How much time had passed, lost in contemplation of his solitude and failure, Alex wasn't certain. He felt foolish, selfish even, thinking about his own losses when so many people must have died: Mariam's aunt and cousin in the Pyrenees; the security detail he had insisted should follow her; at Aswan, a collection of honoured guests, dignitaries that might even include the inspirational prime minister of Cyrenia, Souad Mourad, with her compelling vision of a better future and a fairer world.

What a disaster that would be.

But, in the end, none of that mattered. There were only three people he deeply cared about: his mother, who might or might not be safe at home in Paris; Amaury, his closest colleague, a kind of head to his tail, utterly different in personality and patterns of thought, but steadfast and true; and Mariam, without whom …

Alex considered his options. He could stay where he was, giving in to despair, losing the will to act, or he could allow himself to hope.

No contest.

It would be the latter, obviously. But summoning that will was painful and conflicted.

You don't know for sure. They might all be safe.

He adjusted his position and was briefly dazzled by the reflection of a sunbeam from a shard of broken glass. He raised his eyes, taking in the improvement in the weather, the patches of blue sky, the milder air, and heard a thrumming in the distance, the rotors of a fast chopper. He forced himself to stand.

His face set, Alex walked the length of the torn cabin and climbed down onto the road, picking up his heavily laden rucksack, verifying the presence of his handgun. The sun was surprisingly warm, melting some of the tension that had built up in his muscles. Shielding his eyes, he picked out the chopper, maybe five kilometres out, like a black insect against a patch of stark blue, tracking from east to west, then west to east, sweeping the land below. As it came into profile, he identified a double top-rotor, a perpendicular fan-rotor on the tail, plus a pair of missile launchers slung beneath.

Clearly not Haitian military.

There was no possibility that the impoverished Caribbean state could have equipped its armed forces with the cutting-edge technology of a K-Raptor, available to buy for around sixty million euros a piece. Abruptly, it sank down into the landscape, out of sight between the hills.

That's Davide's rescue. If the K-Raptor is in the right spot, he's less than an hour's hike away.

Alex felt a surge of frustration. Somehow, Davide had succeeded in signalling for help, something Alex was unable to do himself. Had he not been stunned by the crash, he could easily have followed and overpowered his prisoner.

Masked by a cleft in the landscape, the thrum of the chopper's engines and the whooshing of the rotors didn't entirely cease, then they regrew in intensity as the K-Raptor rose, turning on itself until its nose pointed directly towards where he stood. Time slowed as Alex saw in his mind's eye what was about to happen, narrowing to a point of decision, of fight or flight.

The K-Raptor lurched with a fire-flash from one of its underslung missiles. Alex pushed his arms into the straps of his heavy rucksack with no time to properly close the top flap. He ran, his mind calculating how much time he had: the chopper about five kilometres away; the missile travelling at around three-hundred kilometres per hour. The maths was weirdly symmetrical, the answer precisely one minute. How far could he run in that time, laden by his cumbersome rucksack full of useful supplies. Three hundred metres, maybe?

The direction he had chosen was uphill. Until this moment of crisis, he hadn't wanted to approach the border post. He thought it likely the Dominicans would shoot first and ask questions later – questions he wouldn't be able to answer to their satisfaction because he would be dead. But he pounded on, past the rear section of the Ae4, hoping it would provide some kind of cover from shrapnel and from the shockwave of the blast.

The missile struck. With a glance over his shoulder, Alex saw it was a direct hit – no mean feat, fired with aerodynamic interference from the throbbing downwash produced by the paired main rotors. The explosion propelled the remains of the Ae4's nose cone up into the air and dug a crater in the tarmac, but he was – for the time being – unharmed.

Ahead of him, he calculated he had cut the distance to the frontier post by two-thirds. He was just aware, in peripheral vision, of the K-Raptor adjusting its approach, angling its nose to fire again on the rear portion of the Ae4.

He tugged the rucksack off his shoulders and threw it away to the side of the road. Relieved of its weight, he accelerated, like an athlete in the home straight – but an athlete weighed down by an accumulation of stress, concussion, shock, fatigue and grief, feeling exposed, an easy target. But he knew the reality was that he was invisible to the chopper pilot, still several kilometres distant.

He left the road, into the partial cover of a dip in the low undergrowth. Then, he heard the whump and the whine of a second missile launch.

Breathless and tiring, he ran on, his feet slipping on the damp ground, not glancing back until after the explosion, seeing the rear portion of the Ae4 blasted into a hundred torn shreds by another direct hit and a small lake of burning fuel that spread across the road from the remaining tank in the port wing.

Is there some special reason why the aircraft needed to be destroyed? Was there intelligence on board, secrets I missed or hadn't had the time or intuition to discover?

He thought not, though he didn't believe he'd been spotted, either.

The chopper pilot – maybe even Davide himself – fired on the wreckage to take me out, unaware of precisely where I am.

The K-Raptor was much closer, now, turning in a narrow circle. Alex remained crouched, out of sight in the scrub. To his surprise, a weapon was fired from the frontier post – probably a rocket-propelled grenade – not directed at him, but over his head. He saw the K-Raptor's air-to-air defences take out the projectile with a lidar-guided intercept pattern of tracer shells. The garrison at the frontier post launched another RPG and the K-Raptor took evasive action, banking away to the north, spraying its air-to-air defensive fire more wildly, some of the tracer shells biting into the dirt within metres of where Alex lay, defenceless and uncertain.

The frontier garrison must be under standing orders to fire. Or maybe they're kids, recruits with no tactical intelligence, overexcited and eager to engage, unaware that wisdom and common sense are always on the side of delaying the moment of actual combat.

The K-Raptor completed its banked turn and retreated, flying away towards the west where the sun was a diffuse orange glow, falling towards the horizon behind a thin veil of cloud.

They didn't see me. The shallow angle of the daylight was on my side.

Alex's jacket and trousers were wet all down one side from the soggy depression. Bent double, he crept back downhill, close to the road, towards the place where he had discarded his rucksack. It was lying under a spiny bush. Reaching it, he checked the contents. Most of his stuff was still inside but, at some point, his weapon had fallen out.

Merde.

Was it nearby, though? It had to be.

He took a chance and raised himself up to scan the damp tarmac, seeing a flattish black object, lying close by the exploded wreckage.

Should I wait for darkness before going to get it?

15

Alone in the control room, Aurélien was practising his brain exercises. The purpose of the puzzles – essentially encoding and decoding patterns of numbers, words and shapes – was to maintain his cognitive reserves. Science had shown that, even were his brain attacked by some form of dementia, he might protect himself by developing alternative neural pathways.

My mind will stay acute, even as my body rots around it.

He was finding it hard to concentrate, thinking about Davide calling him from the pilot's seat of the Ae4, just before lift-off from Modibo Keita International in Bamako.

While you are in flight, Davide, circumstances will be changing, deaths multiplying. Lamarque will be more alone. All this may play in our favour.

Is it certain that we need him, father? I have made every effort to become an acceptable figurehead.

His unblemished authority can help us in managing our futures, Davide.

If I can't persuade him, what should I do?

Bring him to me. Perhaps I will prove more persuasive.

The analogue radio Aurélien had used to speak to Captain Diaz aboard the *Pablo Adisa* crackled into life. He drove his wheelchair to the console and picked up. The connection was poor. He could just make out Pederson telling him that the chopper was in-bound with his son on board.

'He's dehydrated and hypothermic ... waiting for extraction and ... without shelter ... in-flight sleep suit.'

'And Lamarque?' Aurélien demanded.

'Survived the crash. Davide saw him. But we destroyed the wreckage.'

'What about Lamarque?'

'Unknown, repeat, unknown.'

Aurélien thought he had probably survived.

It is in the man's nature to find a way, to perceive danger and evade it.

How was that? What gave Alexandre Lamarque the ability to see patterns that others hadn't? Aurélien knew from information released to him by his agents inside the French Directorate General for External Security – men since branded 'traitors' – that Lamarque claimed to have no special skill, that all he did was 'pay attention'. Yet, he had uncovered the Coming Darkness conspiracy on the poorest of intelligence.

Any chief but Fayard would have told him to drop it.

Pattern-matching was, of course, an evolutionary imperative. Hunters became skilled at discerning the habitual activities of prey and predator. Gatherers recognised the seasonal ripening of wholesome and unwholesome plants. The weather's evolution could be predicted from studying the sky. Understanding those patterns conferred a survival advantage that could be passed on to descendants, multiplying the stock of knowledge, elevating humankind from being mere victims of circumstances to actively shaping their future and environment.

Aurélien was doing something similar. The part of Aurélien's brain that he was attempting to develop with his encode-decode exercises was the neocortex, the outermost layer, made up of countless folds of grey matter. The neurons in the neocortex could – apparently – rewire themselves to take account of new stimuli, new circumstances.

From the same 'traitors', Aurélien knew that Lamarque had attempted to resign, doubting that the orders he was given were benign. And Claudine Poiret had blackmailed him into remaining. That was why Aurélien had sent Davide to Bamako on the pretext of a carbon-sequestering project, to entice Lamarque out into the open and test his resolve.

Is Lamarque's brain 'plastic' enough to reshape itself to accept the consequences of the Coming Fire?

16

The K-Raptor was gone but Alex's ears were still ringing from the two explosions. Through his tinnitus, he was just beginning to make out the sound of vehicles approaching cross-country, gunning their engines and spinning their wheels. They emerged from the dip – a battered orange pick-up mounted with a mobile missile launcher and a lightweight jeep. They bounced up onto the tarmac.

The pick-up halved the distance to the border post, then made a sharp U-turn so its rear cargo bed was facing the frontier post. Two men jumped out. One climbed into the back to aim the weapon while the other held a megaphone to his mouth.

'*On cherche et on fout le camp,*' he shouted. '*C'est compris?*'

The words were a threat and a promise, directed to the Dominican border guards. The Haitian gang members wanted to search the wreckage of the Ae4 and then disappear. They didn't want trouble, but they wouldn't let themselves be interfered with, either.

Close at hand, four more Haitians climbed out of the lightweight jeep, all armed. Alex considered the options available to the Dominicans. They might be tempted to launch another few RPGs, but they were unlikely to score a direct hit on the pick-up before its missile launcher decimated their position.

It seemed the border guards understood. No answer came, but no attack, either. The gang members went about their business, looking for undamaged items of technology that could be recycled or sold for scrap.

They took a couple of surviving wall-mounted monitors and a heap of fragments from the flight-deck, ripping out looms of cable. The process was quick and violent. Then Alex watched the group of four get back into the lightweight jeep and pull away. The dark flat object he thought was his Heckler & Koch was still there, lying on the damp tarmac, halfway between his position and the remaining two gang members.

The gunner clambered down and was about to jump into the cab alongside his colleague when he saw it, crouching down, then holding the weapon up to the fading light. Alex flinched as the scavenger fired two shots into the air, his arm jerked upwards by the recoil, calling out to his companion, the driver: '*Ceci est pour moi!*'

This is mine.

He got back in. The pick-up bounced off the road and away through the martyred landscape of tree stumps and wind-torn vegetation, leaving Alex to contemplate his damp and defenceless solitude, beneath a sky that was just beginning to reveal its stars.

17

On board the *Roussillon*, the heavy seas were intimidatingly dark. Poiret ordered the spotter to take her to the bridge in person. Climbing the outdoor steps in the dusk to the glazed observation-and-control deck, she felt the seasickness fade as she sucked in fresh, outdoor air. Then, stumbling over the threshold, she repeated her order to take down the K-Raptor: 'Your spotter tells me it's now on its way back in to Haré.'

The corpulent ship's commander shook his head.

'The sea-wolf rockets can't be used while their guidance systems are offline.

'Do they not have manual infrared or line-of-sight?'

'Yes, but without proper SCS protocols it might not be safe—'

'The K-Raptor will soon be out of range again. Do it now. That's an order.'

His face set with resentment, the ship's commander lifted a handset, calling down to his gunners: 'Ready sea-wolf tube one, manual guidance.'

Poiret asked: 'What about the Guépard helicopters? Have they been freed from their anchors?'

'Not yet. There is only one cutting torch on board. Each bracket requires—'

'Never mind,' said Poiret.

On-board comms rang back with an old-fashioned bell chime, like a telephone. The commander picked up the handset. Poiret could hear the voice on the other end.

'We are standing by.'

'Fire,' said the commander.

There was a pause, a kind of stillness. Poiret looked for a flash of ignition and the missile screaming away across the darkening sky, but there was nothing. Then came a shocking boom from somewhere deep inside the ship, beneath her feet. The vessel lurched to port, throwing Poiret off her feet behind the command console. Two seconds later, there was another huge explosion, shaking the bridge and shattering the windows. Poiret had raised her hands defensively and felt a dozen impacts, each like a stinging bee. A siren began wailing, accompanied by a red warning light pulsing in the ceiling. For a few seconds, Poiret was unable to process what had happened. Then she worked it out with a deep-seated sensation of stupidity and guilt.

There's more to the viral attack than just disabling the SCS. We've been booby-trapped. The missile that I commanded them to fire must have exploded in its tube.

Grabbing the rail at the edge of the console, she dragged herself awkwardly upright, looking out through the ruined windowpanes into a new onset of sleety wind. Several decks below, she could see a tear in the side of the ship through which a torrent of grey churning water was tumbling.

A second siren began to wail.

'What is that?' she shouted against its shrill sound. 'Are we going down?'

The ship's commander was leaning against the wall of the bridge, a hand over the right side of his face.

'The bulkheads will hold, but you should go to your muster station.'

'I don't know where that is. Are we abandoning ship?' He dropped his hand and Poiret saw a gash from his temple to his nostril and a pulpy mess where his right eye ought to have been. 'You need medical attention.'

A marine commando wearing black fatigues entered the bridge, saluting respectfully.

'Should my men stand by the RIBs, sir?'

'Do it, Abadie,' replied the commander. 'And take Madame Poiret with you. She is your responsibility, now.'

Claudine Poiret's sedentary, stressful lifestyle as a senior civil servant had not equipped her for dynamic physical activity. She was strong, yes, but she was not agile or quick. And events were running away from her, like the deck of the *Roussillon*, that slewed and tipped with surprising speed, turning the staircases and walkways into death traps. Somewhere amidships, she and the marine – in his sinister black fatigues – hesitated as a further explosion rocked the *Roussillon*.

'What was that?'

'It came from for'ard again,' said the marine, Abadie. 'It may have been more ordinance exploding from the heat of the fire.'

'Where is the muster station?'

'Aft,' he told her, his pale face drawn. 'There are lifeboats port and starboard and our marine RIBs.' Seeing she didn't understand, he clarified: 'Rigid inflatable boats, two of them. Enough for my men and for you, Madame Poiret.'

He helped her to an external staircase, canted at an awkward angle by the tilt of the ship, and began climbing down to the main deck, making sure she was following close above, prepared to catch her if she fell. Poiret felt clumsy, landing awkwardly on a sloping outdoor passageway, grabbing at the rail and running her hands along the cold steel wall as she followed the marine all the way to an enormous open deck that included the helicopter landing area, an empty steel platform painted with a huge white H.

The exterior lighting came on, illuminating everything in stark white, including the opening for the helicopter lift, designed to raise the choppers from their garages below decks. It was stuck, with a top rotor and its heavy axle sticking out at about waist height.

With a lurch of the deck, even Abadie stumbled, grasping a rotor blade to avoid falling down into the bowels of the ship. Poiret did the same and saw, down below, two engineers who were still trying to release the chopper's landing gear from its automated chocks with the sharp flame of an oxyacetylene cutting torch.

'Leave that now,' shouted Abadie. 'Get above decks.'

The *Roussillon* heeled to port and back to starboard, then levelled out on the swirling sea.

'What's happening?' asked Poiret, her hands cold and her knuckles strained and white where she clung to the rotor blade.

'The water is spreading through the ship.'

'Are we safe?' Poiret asked. 'Are we not going down after all?'

'We're going down, but for the moment the ship is sitting more level in the water. We need to disembark before the aft sections below the plumb line fill up, lifting the prow.'

'How soon?'

'Minutes, maybe seconds.'

The pitch of the siren changed, layered with a synthetic voice:

Abandon ship.

Despite the terrible situation, Poiret felt more confident of her footing on the levelled deck. She and Abadie moved quickly past the helicopter lift to a railed area with four lifeboats port and starboard, ranged on white-painted booms. About a dozen crewmembers were busy struggling to release them from their mountings, watched by fifty or sixty others. More were emerging from two staircases, leading up from below decks, pushing their arms into lifejackets as they came.

Do I need one of those?

Abadie told her: 'It looks like the same problem as the choppers. The SCS has them trapped.'

'How will we get them into the water?' Poiret shouted.

The marine didn't answer. He was talking to the comms major whose white shirt clung to his flesh, drenched through with the spray, his dark beard dripping. Poiret realised that she was shivering, whether from fear or from cold, she couldn't say. Then, a warning cry went up as the first lifeboat swung out from its mountings over the churning water, dropping into the swell. The comms major shouted: 'First twenty.'

A score of crewmembers moved athletically to the rail, throwing themselves off the side of the ship into the rough grey sea.

The marine grabbed Poiret's shoulder, pointing to another stair that she knew led down to the aft deck.

'What about the lifeboats?'

'You'll have a better chance with me.' He shouted to the comms major: '*Bonne chance.*'

Good luck.

Poiret only managed to safely descend the final staircase because Abadie was supporting virtually her entire weight. She felt drained and disoriented, nauseated by panic and seasickness. They found the aft of the *Roussillon* running with water, sloshing in from either side as the ship tilted back into the swell, the prow rising out of the water, as Poiret's protector had predicted it would. She was too befuddled to count, but she thought there might be two dozen marines working to untie two rigid inflatable boats from the rails around the perimeter of the deck, working swiftly and efficiently in two teams, struggling with the movement of the waves.

To Poiret's eye, the RIBs looked too small to transport her and all the black-clothed commandos, each of them wearing a lifejacket and carrying a cumbersome rucksack with a short automatic weapon strapped to the outside in a waterproof sheath.

'Let's go,' said Abadie. He lifted her bodily over the rubber-tube hull. 'Take hold of these lines,' he shouted. 'Wind them round your wrists.'

The *Roussillon* made another lurch and the RIB slid across the aft deck, slamming into the rail, dragging the marines with it as they struggled with cold fingers on the cold ratchets of the retaining straps. Poiret found herself clinging to the nylon ropes, looking down at the swirling sea. Then all was movement as what seemed like far too many heavily-built commandos, male and female, leapt and tumbled in alongside her.

A new wave came rushing through and over the aft rail, lifting the buoyant RIB up off the deck, but not enough for it to escape the railings. Twice it butted against the timber handrail, making Poiret fear she would lose her grip. Then the wave withdrew and the RIB settled with a thump, banging her teeth together.

'Next wave,' shouted a voice close at hand and she realised that it was Abadie, alongside, with his left hand wound into the nylon rope and his right gripping her waist. 'The *Roussillon* is about to sink.'

To Poiret, it seemed to happen in slow motion, so heightened were her senses. The for'ard superstructure of the ship rose up as the aft dipped, tipping them hard into the handrail again, but the movement continued, the seas rushing in until the RIB was suddenly buoyant and free.

Poiret expected to hear a burst of life from the outboard, but the engine merely coughed, choked and unresponsive. Two marines got busy trying to reset some element of the ignition, each one held safe on board by a colleague grasping the webbing on their rucksack so they could use both hands.

Appalled, Poiret realised the other RIB was upside down, its crew in the churning water. Hers was, for the moment, clear of the doomed frigate but, though the initial movement had been away on the withdrawing wave, it was now being sucked back in. The huge grey hull, sinking down into the dark sea, was creating a kind of whirlpool, dragging them towards it.

Terrifyingly, above her head, Poiret could now see the antenna array and the bridge deck, preparing to crash down on top of them. She felt fear of a kind she had never before experienced, except by proxy, when sending her agents out into the field – despatching Alexandre Lamarque and Amaury Barra into the middle of the Cyrenian insurrection, for example. She had been aware of the risks they were taking, but suppressed her anxiety in order to be able to do her job. This was different – personal, immediate and very close.

Then the outboard motor suddenly coughed into life. The RIB bucked against the swell and they were away.

18

Alex judged it better if everyone – Davide Castile, the scavengers, the frontier guards – believed him dead. So he stayed where he was, crouched and uncomfortable, out of sight. Soon, a new bank of cloud rolled in and the darkness of the night – without moon or stars – became inkily complete, the air damp with a threat of more rain, the breeze chilly on his cheek. He crept out of his hiding place in the underbrush, his rucksack on one shoulder.

He had excellent eyesight but still found it difficult not to trip over the fragments of destroyed aircraft scattered across the tarmac. After a minute or so, he found what he was looking for; one of the flatbed seats from the rear of the cabin, more or less intact, a little scorched with a tear in the beige leather, but it would do.

It had landed off the highway, propelled by the explosion into the scrub, propped against a tree stump. He put it level on the ground and tucked his rucksack under it, then went to look for something to serve as a roof, quickly locating a warped and sooty panel from the nose of the Ae4, about two metres long, shaped like a gently curved hand.

In order not to make any noise, he needed to lift it up off the tarmac rather than drag it, but the torn edges were sharp. He protected his hands with scraps of leather from another seat that had been flayed from its frame by the explosion.

The nose panel was heavy and cumbersome. Soon, though, he had it in position, lodged on a tree stump at one end, the other pushed into the soft dirt. It created a kind of cocoon over the scorched flatbed, on which he could shelter and – he hoped – sleep.

He glanced at his wrist for the time, but of course his comm-watch wasn't there. He had taken it off when it overheated and never put it back on. It had probably been blown apart by the first missile impact.

He looked up at the sky. There was nothing to learn from the moon or stars, resolutely concealed behind cloud. He had only a sense of how much time had passed since the sun had set and what that meant in tropical latitudes in September.

Maybe half-seven or eight? When will daylight come?

The day in September would be a little shorter than the night. If he managed to sleep, he would need to wake before too many hours had passed in order to face the dawn and whatever new dangers it might bring.

He groped around the wreckage for a while longer, trying to find the remains of the wardrobe in which Davide had hung up his clothes before changing into his in-flight suit. The trousers had landed in a puddle a couple of inches deep and were no use. Davide's silver-grey jacket, though, was still on its hanger, caught as if draped for drying across a low spiny bush. Back in Bamako, Alex had noticed that the jacket was a little too big for Davide's broad shoulders, as if the man had recently lost muscle mass. Alex was able to pull it on over the top of his own.

Not far away, he located the bent and twisted shape of the wardrobe itself. In the top compartment were two light blankets, each tied with a length of silky ribbon whose colour he could not make out. Alex grazed his knuckles manoeuvring them out of their crushed and torn shelf-space.

He cursed and carried them back to his improvised shelter. By feel, he located the med-kit he'd salvaged earlier, in amongst the bottles and snacks and change of clothes in his rucksack. He used wound spray on the scratches, disinfecting and closing them with synthetic skin.

To give himself a perimeter of protection, he arranged a circle of bits and pieces of wreckage twenty metres out from his shelter, balancing them on top of one another. Had he been properly equipped, he would have set motion sensors to give an early warning of surreptitious approach. Without that possibility, his improvised alarms would have to do.

But, if someone gets that close, I'm already dead.

Alex ate some of the in-flight snacks he'd found – sweet-and-savoury nuts and some kind of trail mix – then tucked the remainder back in his rucksack underneath the leather flatbed. He lay down beneath his curved roof of scorched steel, awkwardly shaking out his thin blankets in the confined space, hoping they would be sufficient to protect him against the frigid night.

Satisfied at last, he became still and quiet, like a dead politician lying in state. He wondered if President Manouche of the Republic of Mali would have seen the time-delayed message that he had left in his computer system. It would be somewhere around midnight in Bamako right now.

Maybe he's already asleep?

The message was a request to communicate with Claudine Poiret, via the French embassy in Bamako, reporting on the terrorist attacks on the lithium mines in southern Mali and Alex's – highly prescient as things had turned out – uneasiness at being delegated to work with Davide Castile. It also contained a warning.

Remind Madame Poiret that she asked me to investigate the cascading digital failures. I haven't had time to do so, but my fear is that they are more than 'failures'. In my opinion, it is likely that they are deliberate accelerators of destruction. What she can do with that information, I'm not sure.

Alex told his brain to wake at five, before the dawn, then shut his eyes, hearing only the sparse noises of the night in the desperate landscape, shorn of trees, unable to sleep. He wasn't sure who would come. It might be more scavengers. It might be the Dominican frontier guards, if they received orders to conduct a night-time incursion and investigate. It might be Davide – or someone working for him – returning with different weapons to finish him off.

If they approach in a vehicle, the engine or the lights will wake me. But is this a mistake? Should I be trekking out of here?

The answer was no.

It's too dark. I could end up walking in circles or falling down some unseen cleft in the landscape, injuring myself more seriously than the wound spray can handle.

Lying motionless under his improvised steel roof, he wished he'd checked the contents of the med-kit more thoroughly. He was still troubled by the ache in the mended fractures to his left leg and the persistent damage to the medial collateral ligament that stabilised his knee.

There might be an analgesic of some kind.

And he felt a tingling from his fingers.

Is that an infection?

Danger came from pathogens that one's immune system wasn't used to. Among the first-aid supplies, there would almost certainly be an antibiotic – no doubt almitidin.

Alex decided that the tingling was merely the synthetic skin contracting and pulling on the hairs on his fingers. If, when he woke, he found himself developing a fever, it wouldn't be too late to start a course of antibiotic treatment. For now, sleep was the most important thing.

Counting his breaths, slowing their cadence, he willed himself to rest.

Amaury is alive. Maman is alive. Mariam is alive. All will be well.

Finally, undeceived, knowing how unlikely all that was, he slept.

19

Aurélien checked the analogue clocks on the wall, one for each of five major time-zones where Castile Energie assets were located: Greenwich, Manhattan, Seattle, Tokyo, Delhi. The K-Raptor had landed on the H-pad at the end of the two-thousand-metre runway, on the plateau at the northern end of the island, not far from the two larger *chefferies* of Haitian immigrant workers. Pederson had brought Davide in a buggy, like a golf cart, to the medical unit on a lower floor of the citadel. He was receiving fluids from an intravenous drip and being given attention for his damaged abdominal med-port.

I will let him sleep.

Aurélien had silenced the alarms from the digital systems, alerting him to breaches in his firewalls, but the screens were still active, displaying their pointless warnings.

Soon the global meltdown will be complete. A new age will begin. The only thing I need is the Pablo Adisa's *oil. And, perhaps ...*

Aurélien had put in place massive prepper stores, of course, but also knowledge, tools, seeds, all the rest. But Aurélien was aware that he and Davide would make for poor optics as surviving leaders of Haré Stronghold. If they were successfully to build their authority, they needed a better face than a prematurely aged man and a son whose own physical decline was a result of the same ill-judged experimentation.

If he is still alive, Lamarque might become the inspiring face of my leadership.

But if Lamarque was intransigent – if he preferred death or solitary anonymity to the chance of ruling at Aurélien's right hand – was there another choice?

What about Mariam Jordane? Might she be a viable alternative?

Mariam Jordane was probably dead, too, unless her native ingenuity had enabled her to escape the attack on the Saint-Médard dam.

But how likely is that?

And, even if she was still alive, Aurélien had no way of contacting her.

In imagination, he counted some of those who had fought and died in secret alongside him, sharing his purpose. There was the director of the data-and-energy relay at Kofinou, the junction of three continents, who hadn't survived the failure of the Coming Darkness. Neither had his allies in the Cyrenian armed forces. Nor either of his men, high up within the French security services. And a handful of others whose names he knew, plus many others that he had never troubled to learn, all gone in the service of the Coming Storm.

Were it not for Davide, I would be as alone as Lamarque.

Aurélien drove his wheelchair to another console where he could obverse the feeds from his network of internal and external closed-circuit cameras, a dumb system, wired, without comms capabilities. He found it was too dark to see anything in Todor Kaldonov's quarters, but Johnson Pederson slept with a nightlight.

Is that a throwback to an unhappy childhood, not wanting to wake in darkness?

Aurélien frowned.

He will fight me over the cull. He is too soft-hearted.

As a precaution, Aurélien used his remote authority to activate a mechanical servomotor and lock Pederson's airtight door. Briefly, he considered taking the elevator down to the medical floor to see his son, then decided against it.

The truth is, Lamarque might make a better manager than Pederson, a better son than Davide.

His mind began to drift, back to the near-future daydream, the clean slate and an atomised world, not the globalised, hyperconnected mechanisms of industrial-scale destruction and degradation, contempt for the individual, overpopulation and disease.

It is enough. The future needs the Coming Fire.

PART 2

EITHER SIDE OF DARKNESS

20

January 2018

It was at the 2018 edition of the Davos World Economic Forum that Aurélien Castile first began to visualise the *tabula rasa*, the reset, the 'clean slate'. In the luxurious alpine ski resort of Klosters, annually given over to a conference of governments, corporations, plutocrats and celebrities, enlightenment came by chance – as experience had taught him it often did.

The guiding principles of Aurélien's life, to this point, had been longevity and money. He was unimaginably prosperous and, because of this, extraordinarily powerful. But his attempts to bio-engineer and bio-hack his own fragile tunic of flesh had so far disappointed.

It would be fifteen years, however, before Aurélien confined himself to a wheelchair for his own safety. He emerged from one of the satellite events – a new investment opportunity into an underwater, volcano-dwelling cyanobacterium capable of converting CO_2 into biomass – carrying walking poles to make sure he didn't lose his balance on the slushy ground or the odd patch of icy tarmac. His hands were occupied, therefore, as a small group of protestors came bumbling up the centre of the street, singing in a language Aurélien didn't speak or recognise.

The protestors were dressed inadequately for the cold alpine evening whereas Aurélien wore four layers, his coat alone worth more than a thousand euros, designed for alpine sports in which he would never engage. It had reflective fluorescent panels sewn in to make him visible from afar, even in poor light.

He shrank back towards a darkened building, into a line of drips of melting snow from the eaves above. The protestors came closer and he found himself trapped on a rubber mat on the threshold of a locked doorway.

Just for a moment, he hoped he hadn't been seen. Then one of the protestors – with a broken front tooth and a Che Guevara moustache, wearing just a shirt and jumper, regular shoes, not even a scarf around his scrawny neck – caught his eye. The protestor broke away from his comrades, speaking in the same unknown language, then switched to imperfect French.

'You, too,' said the protestor, 'can be a part of our family.'

'I have my own family,' said Aurélien. 'Move along.'

'You must open your third eye,' said the protestor.

'What I see with my two eyes is quite enough.'

'Are you a part of it?' the man asked, the words slurred, waving a vague hand at the wealthy resort. 'You must be. You're here, aren't you?' Aurélien smelt the *gluhwein* on the man's breath, then the protestor stuck out a hand and pulled at the metal badge pinned to Aurélien's expensive jacket. 'And this gets you into places we cannot go.'

'Take it,' said Aurélien. 'Get yourself into the secret heart of the conspiracy. Perhaps you will see them remove their skins and reveal their lizard heads.'

The man laughed and Aurélien wondered if the protestor knew that all the venues had photographic databases, that a face on the entrance system had to correspond to the owner of the access badge.

'We don't want your credentials,' said the protestor, stepping in oppressively close. 'We want your mind.'

'Are you not cold?' said Aurélien, looking for a distraction.

'We all have a fire within.'

'Do you want money? I carry none.'

'The time will come when money means nothing.'

'I doubt it. You can have my coat. Leave me or I will call out.'

Aurélien saw, with relief, a pair of security officers on pedestrian patrol over the man's shoulder.

'I don't want your coat either.' The protestor glanced round, following Aurélien's gaze. 'You have nothing to fear from me. Only from the future you and your kind are creating.'

'Good luck to you,' Aurélien called out, almost shouting, to make sure the security officers became aware of him, stopping at the sound of his voice, peering towards the shadowy doorway. 'Leave me,' he hissed more quietly. 'Go on your way.'

The protestor pushed a hand into the pocket of his trousers, bringing out a folded sheet of paper.

'Promise me you will read this.'

'Of course,' said Aurélien. 'I will be glad to.'

The protestor slipped the paper into one of the patch pockets on Aurélien's expensive coat and leaned in, his mouth close to Aurélien's ear.

'It will open your eyes.'

Sickened by the scent of cinnamon and alcohol on the man's warm breath – and by the idea of the germs he might carry – Aurélien turned his head. The protestor stumbled away, heading for his fellows, a hundred metres distant at the well-lit entrance of an overpriced bar. One of them called out and the moustachioed man almost tripped and fell, replying in the unknown language. One of the two security officers helped him, taking an arm to lead him up the slope. The other approached Aurélien, recognising him.

'*Monsieur Castile, tout va bien?*'

Is everything all right?

'Will you assist me?'

'Of course, Monsieur Castile.'

The security officer – a well-built man with a dark beard and deeply creased eyes – took Aurélien's arm, leading him onto the main street and the lobby of the principal event venue. Aurélien sidestepped the queue at the main desk, using the priority channel where an ingratiating administrator also welcomed him by name. He made his way to a lounge accessible only to those with triple-A credentials. He sat heavily in a deep armchair, resting his walking poles in the gap between the cushion and the arm, then pulled off his gloves so he could retrieve the protestor's message. It took the form of an email, printed on standard paper.

From: info@opened_3rd_eye_now.com
Date: Mon, 1 Jan 2018 at 00:01
Subject: We are what follows the Darkness

Open your third eye now!

You are being lied to, poisoned, divided. The broadcast networks cast their nets and you become trapped. Their only purpose is controlling minds. They call it media programming for a reason.

What is their masterplan? Making us believe we are powerless. The one per cent hoard our money, commodities and resources while the rest of us spin the perpetual hamster wheel.

Wake up! Open your third eye now!

Time is ticking, bringing us closer to a worldwide event – a sinister agenda calling for massive depopulation.

You know this. The year 2030 is their deadline. Beyond that threshold, their covert attacks – the air we breathe, our food, our water, our medicines – will all have been contaminated beyond redemption.

You are not the problem. You are free. The divine spark of the Supreme Creator is within you. You can be redeemed. Power is in knowledge and in numbers and we have both on our side ...

The email continued in the same vein on both dense sides of the single A4 sheet. Aurélien's eyes unfocused as a germ of an idea began to burgeon in his imagination – a kind of solution.

If I cannot meaningfully extend my life's span, I can still extend Earth's. But to do this, I will first need to create chaos.

Aurélien felt an extraordinary surge of energy, as if his life had been building towards this moment. He glanced again at the subject line of the ludicrous pontificating email: *We are what follows the Darkness*.

On the contrary, he thought. *I, Aurélien Castile, shall become the Darkness – and the Storm and the Fire.*

21

January 2020

'Great wealth, in the end, brings only an illusion of power.'

Two years had passed. It was the third week in January 2020. Another World Economic Forum was coming to an end. Many of the major players had already left Klosters, on to other meetings in other places, using money to make more money, endlessly, beyond what any human being could ever hope to spend.

The speaker – a political theoretician – made a small bow and stepped away from the lectern, the PowerPoint slideshow behind him cross-dissolving into a photograph of him looking very much younger – alongside the URL of his podcast. Aurélien Castile turned to his son, Davide, who had attended in his French army uniform at his father's request.

'People without power,' he said, quietly, 'always want to believe that power is illusory. It isn't – not if you know how to wield and retain it.'

The venue was slow to empty. Using a walking stick, Aurélien led his son out of the main chamber, into the lobby to order coffee. While they waited for it to arrive, Aurélien took a stainless-steel pill case from his pocket and prepared seven different tablets and a capsule for his daily supplements.

'You seem worse,' said Davide.

'Time will tell.'

A waiter in a burgundy jacket brought them coffee in ugly mugs made from recycled plastic rather than china. 'Bring me a proper cup and saucer,' said Aurélien.

'Yes, sir,' said the waiter. 'And for you, *commandant*?'

Interesting that the waiter knows who we are, thought Aurélien. *Even down to my son's rank.*

'Whatever,' said Davide.

There was a commotion as some uber-famous celebrity from the entertainment industry entered the café area, bringing with them a bow wave of photographers and journalists and a trailing wake of groupies and hangers-on. A pair of PR reps in sky-blue suits attempted to persuade her to stand still for a moment in front of a conference banner that read:

Bringing together 3,000 participants from around the world, Davos 2020 will give concrete meaning to "stakeholder capitalism", assisting governments and international institutions in tracking progress towards the Paris Agreement and its Sustainable Development Goals, revolutionising discussions on technology and trade governance.

'Strange, is it not, that no one mentions what's happening in Wuhan,' said Aurélien.

'There are flu pandemics every year,' said Davide, dismissively.

'If that's what you think, you've not being paying attention.' The waiter returned with their coffee in fine china, the rims decorated with gold. Aurélien told him: 'I will need a second cup.'

Davide tried to hide his distaste as Aurélien began the laborious process of swallowing his supplements. A crackle of flash photography burst into brief life. Every head turned towards what was happening – automatic smiles and forced poses. Then, as quickly as it had begun, the commotion ebbed as the celebrity moved on through a door staffed by her own security into private rooms where global capitalism surfed the income from digital music and disposable fashion.

Pointless things for pointless people, made with persistent synthetic materials that will clutter the planet for decades, even centuries.

Aurélien had invitations to six official events that evening and could simply hobble into any that had failed to add him to their guest list. But he had no desire to sip overpriced wine with wary acquaintances while smooth salesmen pretended not to sell him things.

'What are we waiting for?' said Davide. 'I had to take leave for this.'

'You will soon be thirty years old,' said Aurélien. 'Your phase of adolescent impatience ought to have ended by now, don't you think?' Aurélien's second coffee came and he completed his methodical process, finishing with a tiny yellow-and-green capsule that contained, among other things, a stimulant. 'You know,' he remarked, 'in the British army, officers are required to demonstrate strong general knowledge. Candidates are asked questions to probe what they know of the world. The British are generalists. The American and the Chinese are specialists. What would you say of the French?'

'It depends on the individual, I suppose.'

'You "suppose". Can you not judge?'

'This is pointless,' said Davide, standing and straightening his uniform. 'We are expected.'

Aurélien watched his son's face. He knew Davide resented being tied to his father's personal projects and ambitions – and to those of the Castile Energie conglomerate. He knew, too, that one of the reasons was that he, Aurélien, had abused his son's trust in his quest for longevity.

The waiter in the burgundy jacket was standing nearby, ready to clear the empty cups. The expression on his face revealed that he had eavesdropped their conversation. Aurélien snaked out a wiry hand and grasped his wrist.

'I heard nothing, sir,' the waiter blurted.

'What is your name?' The waiter told him. 'I will send one of my security team to speak to you.'

'There's no need to—' the waiter began, a worried look in his eyes.

'I will decide what is needed.'

While his father hobbled away to the toilets, Davide took in the enormous lobby screen, displaying a sequence of extracts from the keynote speakers: a pointless barrage of self-aggrandisement from Donald Trump; an economist on navigating inflation; a general on tiny wars with the power to change the world; a futurologist on strategic resilience and geopolitical risk; a financier on a predicted surge in speculative investment; a doctor on extending the health-span; an ecologist on sustainable agriculture. Which of these did he, decorated soldier and sole heir of Castile Energie, believe in?

Not one of them.

Davide thought himself a pragmatist, anticipating a tomorrow always worse than today, one in which power would be essential, above all, for self-preservation. At the Saint-Cloud military headquarters, he had recently been interviewed for a new experiment in survivalism; a self-sufficient biosphere sold to the army as preparation for a potential Mars colony.

Davide didn't believe in Mars, but he was interested to know how people would fare – well-trained military personnel – in circumstances that mimicked the aftermath of disaster. On this, he and his father were agreed.

We need a stronghold.

The screen cycled through another batch of Davos panels and discussions. Contrary to what his father had said, the Wuhan flu did come up. Apparently, a social lockdown had been decreed that very day – a kind of stay-home quarantine for a population of eleven million.

Only in China, thought Davide. *But it's just flu, not ebola or the bubonic plague.*

He frowned, remembering his father's certainty.

Are we too late? Is disaster here and now?

Davide thought not. The structures of human existence remained sound, all the major players in business and government and the armed forces persisted in their interwoven common objectives.

His father returned, looking brighter and moving more easily, carrying his stick, rather than leaning on it.

'The supplements are helping?' asked Davide.

'The stimulant is working,' said his father with what looked like self-disgust.

Aurélien hated hobbling through the steep streets of the Klosters ski resort. They found the Chalet Caribe painfully slowly, about six hundred metres away, set back from the road by a pleasant garden of hardy plants capable of surviving being buried under snow for months at a time, though that sort of winter seemed less and less likely as the years went by.

The path to the front door was paved with ice-free bricks, presumably heated from beneath. Before they reached it – opaque smoked glass in a hardwood frame – the door opened, revealing the specialist real-estate agent, Johnson Pederson, in jeans and a plaid shirt, an all-American product of hormone- and steroid-enhanced milk and beef.

'Monsieur Castile, glad to see you again.' He held out a hand to shake. 'Commandant Castile, welcome. Johnson Pederson. I'm delighted to meet you. We can speak French. I had the great good fortune to learn from an *au pair* when I was a child.'

'No one else has seen this presentation?' demanded Aurélien.

'You requested exclusivity. Exclusivity is yours.'

'I have discovered that you have taken this chalet for the duration of the forum.'

'I have other plans, other complexes. No one else has had sight of the opportunity I've earmarked for you.'

They went inside, through a marble and gilt lobby, to a screening room at the rear.

'How quickly can we act?' asked Aurélien. 'Time begins to run short. Don't you agree?'

'I think that too. You'll have heard the news from Wuhan? Permit me to take you through my thinking, gentlemen.' The American beamed. 'All will become clear.'

Davide sat one seat away from his father in the front row of the screening room. Pederson's presentation began with a sequence of maps showing patterns of rainfall across the globe, evolving through time.

'The past is no longer a certain guide,' he told them. 'Change is too rapid. But climatologists can be confident of certain locations where essential fresh water will continue to fall from the sky to bless us. Putting this together with your requirements for pleasant weather and traditional outdoor agriculture, in addition to the indoor aquaponics, I've selected an optimum site.'

The next map showed the Caribbean Sea and its many islands, the southern coastline of the United States plus the Atlantic all the way to the African coast. It was striated with coloured lines, tracking west, traversing the ocean, then curving north – storms spending their last wanton energy on the American coastal states.

'Are hurricanes a concern?' asked Davide.

'There are options,' said Pederson. 'Let me talk you through them.' He pressed a concealed button on the lectern and the map closed in on three tiny land-masses. 'These are the ABC Islands, Aruba, Bonaire and Curaçao. They are out of the track of major hurricanes and they meet your requirements for sun and rain and mean temps, with protected marine parks and exceptional diversity. But they're pretty much impossible to buy into.' He clicked to another map, showing Barbados. 'Same problem.' He paged through several more close-ups. 'Saint-Vincent and the Grenadines. Trinidad and Tobago. Grenada is especially tough because it's backed by the US.'

The screen went black. Davide could only tell that it was still operational from the tiny 'Johnson Pederson Corp' logo in the bottom right-hand corner.

'But you have made a choice,' said his father. 'Show us your optimum, Mr Pederson.'

'Okay,' Pederson resumed, 'when I tell you the location is close to Haiti, you're thinking political instability, mismanagement, corruption and assassinations. Disease and poverty, too. And that'd be right. Maybe hurricane alley? But look at this.' A new slide came up, showing a narrower map of storms along the Haitian coast. 'This is the most recent annual data. I'm not hiding anything. Over a full twelve months, there was only one hurricane that came close, called Alpha, see? And it wasn't the strongest or the most dangerous. In fact, you might call it a "replenisher" for your fresh water cisterns. Once you've finished construction, above and below ground, a category five storm like Alpha could pass over your heads and you wouldn't even know it.'

Aurélien listened in silence as Pederson pursued his pitch. The island, named Haré, was privately owned, though it had an indigenous population with a habit of independent self-government. It was protected by nestling close to a curve of the coast. It was available at a price within the budget he had specified. Due to its special geology, Haré lent itself to underground water catchment.

Yes, this is a good choice.

'How quickly can we act?' he asked for a second time.

'I can have a meeting here, in Klosters, before the end of tomorrow. I just need to contact the seller's representatives and—'

'Who are the sellers?' interrupted Davide.

Pederson looked apologetic. 'That's not information I can share.'

'Don't be naïve, Davide,' said Aurélien.

'It is theirs to sell?' Davide insisted, 'Whoever they are?'

Pederson nodded. 'I can tell you that it was petrodollars that bought it in the late seventies when no one was thinking about finding themselves a "goldilocks island" as a refuge. Folks were simply looking for a tropical paradise.' He guffawed. 'That was when you should have got into this market, forty-five years ago.'

'Move on, Mr Pederson,' said Aurélien. 'What will we build there? Do you have an example from your portfolio?'

'Sure do.' He nodded to Davide. 'As a military man, Commandant, this will be of interest to you.' There was a pause while he switched out of one presentation to another, something more slickly branded, a real-estate sales pitch for a refuge that already existed, beginning with a massively armoured entrance in a dry hillside. 'This is the front door to the world's most sophisticated and luxurious private survival shelter, built into an abandoned US government missile silo, one of seventy-two built to protect our intercontinental ballistic missiles from disabling pre-emptive attack.' The American put his head on one side and, smiling, told them: 'This is a mission for me, gentlemen. I want in on the ground floor – which is a kinda funny thing to say when we're discussing underground skyscrapers. I went to the Pentagon and tried to dissuade them from their plan to blow up and bury a whole bunch of these useful silos, but I was not successful. Out of seventy-two, today there are only—'

'It doesn't matter,' snapped Aurélien. 'The silo is merely an example of what we might build. Move on.'

'Yes, sir. Sure thing,' agreed Pederson, emolliently. 'Time is short – for the world and for all of us. Let me tell you this. I have other buyers – and some of them will jump at this, whatever the cost.'

'We agreed a price.'

'Wuhan has changed that. And my other buyers maybe can outbid you.'

'You should think twice about going back on your word,' said Aurélien, coldly.

'That's not what I'm saying,' Pederson assured him. 'Look, I admire you, sir. You've made your money in trade and commerce. You haven't merely had the good fortune to find it under the sand beneath your feet.'

'Your other bidders are oil regimes?'

Pederson smiled. 'I didn't say that, did I?'

'No, not quite.'

'Anway, you've done something bigger and better, more real,' said Pederson. 'Like I told you, this is a life-mission for me. The bad times are coming and I have more than just real-estate experience that I can bring to the table. I want you to buy the island of Haré and I want to help you build the most resilient strategic stronghold on the entire face of the planet. Then I want to help you run it. That's my mission. I'm not just selling a place and a plan. I'm selling you me.'

22

Johnson Pederson wasn't certain how his offer had landed with the withered, prematurely aged patriarch and the wary and combative soldier-son. He fetched his guests some drinks, telling them: 'We'll be here awhile, if that's all right?'

Busy at the bar to one side of the screen, letting them talk, he thought about how carefully he had prepared his pitch, not intending to launch into such a heartfelt proposal quite so early. He had other options, wealthy clients – but whose expertise in the crucial areas of survival, energy generation, food security and military discipline were less developed. Haré was perfect and the Castiles were strong partners.

He served the drinks and Castile Senior told him to resume. He returned to the lectern, showing some of the facilities in the mid-western missile silo.

'There's a reverse osmosis filtration system capable of processing ten thousand gallons a day. That's forty-five thousand litres in European. On Haré, three cisterns will each hold twenty-five thousand gallons, accessed from the deepest part of your stronghold, level minus seven. On six will be the armouries, three of them, with separate coded access to each, including biometric. We'll include ARs, sniper rifles, APGs, night-vision helmets, gas masks, first aid kits, non-lethal pepper spray and rubber bullets. The idea is, though, that the armouries will not be needed. The island will be protected by a "ring-of-fire" perimeter of weapons installed in the landscape. Anyone comes messing with you by boat or by aircraft, you can mess with them, controlled either from the armoury deep underground, or from your absolutely secure control room, with no more threat to your person than playing a video game. Hell, if you don't want the hassle, you can set the ring-of-fire to automatic. Once you've repelled your first set of invaders, word will get around. People will learn not to mess with Haré.'

Pederson allowed the two Castiles to talk briefly to one another. He had the impression that the precise details of all this were completely new for the son, but not alien to his patterns of thought. The obvious antagonism between the two of them seemed to be diminishing.

'Okay,' Pederson resumed, 'life in the stronghold should resemble normal life. Survival mustn't feel like prison, you follow me? The food stores for general consumption will be laid out like a supermarket, replenished from secure larders, obviously, but also from the aquaponics, the plant-meat growers and the aquaria. Tilapia is the best food-fish, having no problem being bred in captivity. Their excretions make great fertiliser in the circular food economy.'

'What number of staff?' asked Castile Senior, 'to service the complex.'

'Fewer than you think, maybe? But the outdoor agriculture remains labour intensive. We'll have to come back to that when I know how many people you intend taking in with you.'

'And who,' interjected the son.

Pederson paused.

Is the son thinking about a wife or a concubine or something? Does he have someone in mind? It would be useful to know.

'You won't be able to sustain multiple thousands on Haré,' Pederson told them. 'But hundreds? No problem.'

'Go on,' said the father.

'Okay, still on the psychological benefits, social scientists recommend you have swimming pools, climbing walls, games rooms, gymnasiums, cinemas. I guess you can't have a golf course, but you could install a virtual driving range—'

'Move on from the entertainments, please.'

'Sure.' Pederson nodded, flipping through a few slides, wondering about how hard it might actually be to work for this autocratic old man. 'Does it make a difference to your ideas what the cause of the breakdown will be?'

'Why would it?' Castile Senior barked.

'We can't know, right?' Pederson countered. 'We have to be ready for all of them. There's the current pandemic with its capacity to become a global threat. And all the little wars, wars for land, wars for water – did you go to that session? – that could easily join hands. I'm worried about a major government default within the interlinked OECD economies, leading to structural and societal collapse as all the imaginary money consigned in books and digital wallets goes "phut".'

'We must be able to manage several years without fresh-air agriculture,' snapped the father.

'Yeah, but if it's real bad, you might want to wait longer inside. I'm not arguing with you. I'm just asking you not to underestimate the psych impacts of the entertainments and so on. They might be crucial in maintaining your support population of staff and colleagues and family and friends.'

'Yes, I apologise,' said Castile Senior, unexpectedly. 'I am impatient. The build will take at least eight years, you said?'

'Maybe more. It depends on how effectively you can martial resources. I guess Castile Energie can provide expertise as well as funds.'

'Yes.' He turned to his son. 'I want you to manage this project, Davide. You understand that?'

'I want to experience the biosphere. For survivalists, that's important preparation, too.'

'Then we must make the calendars coincide. How long is the biosphere experiment due to last?'

'Six months,' said the son, 'with an option on three more, at this point.'

'That,' said Pederson with energy, feeling he was close to sealing the deal, 'would tune in nice. The initial groundwork would be under way, ready for the Commandant to come in and take granular charge. Shall I proceed? Are you both good? Do you need anything to eat?'

'If you are right,' said Castile Senior, 'and this is the place, we will call it Haré Stronghold.'

Davide realised he had been leaning forward in his reclining cinema seat and told himself to sit back. Pederson briefly restated his ideas about psychological welfare, referring to some of the US government's 1960s experiments with enclosed populations, going on to show examples of lighting that mimicked sunlight and other tricks that gave an impression of 'normal life'. He talked about the need for work to 'give the population purpose', that the best available data showed that four hours of labour per twenty-four-hour cycle was sufficient, perhaps optimal.

'Fake windows are a thing, to give the impression of a circadian rhythm of day and night. You may know the sad story of the ancient Cappadocians who built themselves troglodytic shelters three thousand years ago then went crazy in there.'

'Yes, I've read about that,' Davide told him.

'Do you gentlemen like paper books?' Pederson asked.

Because his father seemed lost in thought, Davide alone replied: 'I do.'

Pederson nodded, ingratiatingly.

'The best-educated people still want to hold the thing in their hands, like a discreet unit of learning. So, there has to be a library, and that's connected to a wider sense of responsibility.'

'What do you mean by that?' asked Davide.

'If you save yourself,' said Pederson, a serious expression on his face, 'shouldn't you also save learning? And maybe a seed store? And a lab with genetic manipulation capabilities.'

'For the good of humanity?' asked Davide.

'Yep.'

'Ecocide is overstated,' interrupted his father. 'Life finds a way. And the remedies you propose are insignificant.'

'How about we make sure there's wine,' said Pederson. 'I mean good vintages. Say, two bottles a week per person for five years in storage. Then it's gone. What about the skills and experience to make more. That's safeguarding, too, maybe of a kind that you can get on board with? It's a lot to consider, but the population that you're asking to serve you needs to feel their lives are worth living. There need to be good reasons for surviving—'

'Beyond the desire not to be dead,' interrupted his father.

'That'll get old fast. Most people want the feeling of doing something good.'

Davide was becoming more interested: 'Could you elaborate on that?'

'The bunkers I cut my teeth on, developing survival systems inside silos – they were not places that humanity could be proud of. They were weapons of war, the most destructive technologies ever created at that point.'

'Why "at that point"?' Davide asked.

'You've got to be aware of the French government's "God's Thunder" weapon?'

'We are,' said his father. 'There was an argument for placing nuclear warheads in orbit, but there was considerable opposition and, perhaps, the opponents were right – that the risks were greater than any dissuasive or tactical benefit.'

'And we come back to whether nuclear winter would leave a world worth surviving in,' said Pederson. 'Hence the idea of platforms carrying dense tungsten rods capable of accelerating to hypersonic speeds, hitting the ground with the energy of a nuclear blast, penetrating much deeper than a ballistic missile ever could, but without radioactive contamination.'

'The tungsten payloads would be incredibly expensive to get up beyond the atmosphere,' Davide said, doubtfully.

'But oh-how-powerful once there,' said his father. '*Tonnerre de Dieu*,' he added quietly. 'It will happen, I believe.'

'God's Thunder,' said Pederson. 'I believe it, too. Anyway, my point is this. We want a habitable world after. And – perhaps I'm a simple man – I like the idea of what I've done, retro-fitting ICBM bunkers for survival. I would like it even better to be part of a well-managed community of self-reliance – a safe, self-contained, sustainable experiment in a better way of living, based on co-operation and the preservation of human knowledge, the perpetuation of human ingenuity.'

'And being part of a benign but absolute authority,' said Davide, quietly.

'Very good,' murmured his father.

'Yes,' said Pederson. 'That – without doubt.'

'Because you are without hope that humanity can fix the current mess?' asked Davide.

'The scale of the mess is too vast,' said Pederson with a theatrical sigh. 'There's too much complexity. We need to narrow down. Maybe it's not just me. Maybe people aren't clever enough beyond a couple of hundred issues. Isn't the upper limit for a real community how many names you can remember and match to faces?'

'Because a human connection is essential?' asked Davide.

'Sure,' said Pederson. 'And, speaking of human connection, it would be good if one or the other of you could develop more of a profile, become known for philanthropy or the cure for the Wuhan flu or saving an orphanage from an erupting volcano or something.'

'Why?' snapped Davide.

'Because you'll want your survivors to believe in you – to idolise you in a way that goes beyond luck or power or managerial competence. There'll be widespread PTSD and psychological meltdowns and they'll need to trust in you – like folks idolise football stars or prophets.'

'It is about control,' said his father, nodding. 'Unfortunately, I don't believe I will be able to transform myself into such a figurehead.'

'You could become that global philanthropist, Commandant?' suggested Pederson.

'People,' said his father, brutally, 'don't take to my son.'

'Okay,' said Pederson, slowly. 'Then, in the fullness of time, you might need someone else to be the "teeth and smiles" of your project.'

'This is all very far down the line,' said Davide. 'But how would you maintain the idolatry while millions are left outside to starve or sicken or burn?'

'Good question, and I don't know the answer,' said Pederson. 'But that's why you need to be unimpeachable or to find someone unimpeachable.'

'Like a kind of moral superman,' said his father, with an edge of contempt.

'But you gentlemen and me,' said Pederson, 'we're the survivors, right? We're just reacting to circumstances. It's not as if we're intending to be the ones making the bad thing happen. We're just trying to live through it and rebuild something better.'

Davide looked at his father.

Making the bad thing happen. That's a question we have yet to fully discuss.

23

August 2028

By the midpoint in the Haré construction project, in the late 2020s, the astrophysicist Wael Al-Mesih had been appointed to the nascent French-Cyrenian space program. His parents had chosen his first name, Wael, for its traditional meaning of 'one who seeks shelter, who provides refuge'. His family name, Al-Mesih, came from the Christian tradition because his ancestors were Greeks settled in North Africa. It meant 'servant of the messiah' and Wael had always thought it rather a mouthful, so he encouraged his colleagues to refer to him by his nickname, 'Hubble', gained from the period in his early career when he had worked inside the team that developed the Hubble Space Telescope and, later, the even more impressive James Webb Space Telescope.

Moving on from pure observation, Wael 'Hubble' al-Mesih joined the team working on the Double Asteroid Redirection Test that cost NASA and the European Space Agency around €200m every year. DART was motivated by official recognition of a threat that didn't register with ninety-nine per cent of the world's population.

Launch took place on Thursday 25 July 2023 when an irregular asteroid – sixty metres across and a hundred-and-forty metres long – skimmed past Earth, missing by about one fifth of the distance to the Moon, a hair's breadth in astronomical terms. As it did so, one spacecraft impacted the asteroid and another measured what happened.

In the media, the event was compared with damage caused by another space rock, this one only twenty metres across, that exploded thirty kilometres above the Russian city of Chelyabinsk in February 2013, creating a shockwave that flattened forests, shattered windows and injured around fifteen hundred people. By comparison, the 2023 asteroid, had it struck, would have toppled whole buildings.

Wael calculated that there might be five million near-Earth asteroids like the Chelyabinsk rock with a once-in-a-century risk of impact. A smaller number of asteroids around a hundred-and-fifty metres across gave a risk-impact of once in twenty-thousand years, but each one would be capable of digging a crater a couple of kilometres wide and generating mass casualties. Collisions with bigger asteroids – those a kilometre or more across – were judged to be so vanishingly unlikely that they were discounted.

Wael thought this unwise and argued that some kind of 'kinetic impactor' was required for Earth's protection, but more data were required to carry the argument.

In the northern hemisphere autumn of October 2023, a capsule from Nasa's Osiris-Rex probe entered Earth's atmosphere at around fifteen times the speed of a rifle bullet, creating a visible fireball, but protected by its heat shield. Parachute deployment brought it to a gentle touchdown in the emptiness of Utah's West Desert, its extraterrestrial payload no more than a handful of dust retrieved from asteroid Bennu, a space rock with a diameter similar to the height of the Empire State Building.

The Osiris-Rex probe had been launched seven years earlier, eventually intersecting Bennu's flight path, spending two years mapping its target, identifying a suitable surface location for the retrieval of a few hundred grams of space gravel with a blast of nitrogen gas to separate it from the surface. Sample capture occurred in October 2020, surprising Wael, who was observing progress with a substantial time delay. The surface parted like a fluid into a crater eight metres wide.

Asteroid Bennu behaved like that because much of it is water, bound up with minerals of which more than ten per cent are carbon.

Water and carbon – the ingredients of life.

It then took three years for the probe to return the sample to Earth. Wael and his fellow scientists were immensely excited, believing the sample might answer a raft of profound questions. How did Earth become habitable? Where did its atmosphere come from? How were its oceans formed? What was the origin of the organic molecules from which life sprang? Were the ingredients for life delivered by asteroids?

As well as a potential progenitor, Bennu was considered, in October 2023, the most dangerous object in the Solar System. Based on his earlier prowess, NASA and ESA charged Wael with calculating Bennu's likelihood of Earth impact. He judged it around one in two thousand, about the same as the risk of a woman developing breast cancer before the age of thirty. The odds of survival were good, all other things being equal.

Other things, however, are often not equal.

This was especially true in circumstances where what the lawyers called a *mens rea* – an 'evil will' or 'guilty mind' – might be in play.

Would such a mind not turn its eyes up to the sky, to asteroids like Bennu, carrying ingredients essential to the recipe of life – but also a vast potential for destruction?

By August 2028, Wael had changed his mind and became a critic of the launch of ART2, a 'kinetic impactor' about the size of a full-body hygiene cubicle whose purpose was 'catastrophic self-disassembly through astral collision'. The impact was successful – in that it changed the chosen asteroid's trajectory – but it also generated lots of debris, most of which ended up in Low Earth Orbit.

Feeling out of place, Wael sought new employment with the nascent French-Cyrenian space program, based at the desert launch site of Al-Jaghar. Interviewed by a panel that included Souad Mourad, the prime minister of the new North African nation, he explained himself.

'It's the law of unintended consequences. We have demonstrated that we are capable of altering the course of an approaching threat, but we have also created a cascading slow-motion disaster.'

The issue was the Kessler syndrome, a nightmare scenario in which satellite constellations – essential for GPS, comms, weather monitoring and so on, even the planet's collision-warning system – would be destroyed by a cascade of unpredictable collisions, creating more and more debris.

'This will never happen,' a naïve member of the interview panel argued back. 'Fragments of broken satellite in the immensity of space are like dried peas tossed into the ocean – insignificant in the vastness.'

'Except,' Wael retorted, 'those peas will be sharp pieces of cutting metal, and there'll be an ever-growing number of them, and they'll be moving at thirty-thousand kilometres per hour and will never slow down because they'll be flying through a vacuum.'

Wael was surprised to receive the support of Prime Minister Mourad who sent him to argue his case at the International Space Agency where new laws were drafted that obliged satellite owners to de-orbit their constellations at the ends of their useful lives. Reporting back to his new patron, he told her bitterly: 'No one will take any notice, Madame Mourad. You heard it here first.'

24

JANUARY 2034

The new nation of Cyrenia was legally established in 2032. Exhausted by the punishing civil wars that had fragmented the previously prosperous North African nation of Libya, Cyrenia's neighbours quickly recognised the new country. Despite being on the 'wrong' side of the Mediterranean, Prime Minister Mourad was successful in obtaining associate membership of the European Union and increased French finance for the desert launch site at Al-Jaghar.

Mourad's successes made her a prize draw at the 2034 annual meeting of the Davos World Economic Forum, once more taking place at Klosters in the third week of January, with the headline theme: *Building a Shared Future*. Her idealism and communitarian vision stood in stark contrast to the pragmatism and avarice of many of the three thousand delegates from a hundred-and-fifty countries, including fifty-two heads of state or government. For Aurélien Castile, it was a kind of discreet pilgrimage, a spiritual summit where deals of vast magnitude could be done, blessed by the exquisite contemporary partnership of idealism and greed.

The mood at Davos, despite the headline, was bleak, dominated by a sense of things getting worse rather than better, accelerating into a dystopian future where ordinary people became poorer not richer, with increased inequality, robots stealing human jobs and fossil-fuel addiction screaming past several desperate tipping points while the

Ukraine war ground on. A health official from the UK announced: 'This year, the climate crisis will cause eighty-thousand extra deaths in the UK from extreme heat and tropical diseases. The Asian tiger mosquito, a carrier of dengue, Zika and the chikungunya viruses, is becoming established in the south of the country as I speak. Exacerbated by flooding, deaths will come disproportionately from the aged and the poor as climate risks continue to correlate with existing gradients in health and inequality.'

Aurélien found himself in tune with the pessimism, but he attended a few sessions that took the opposite view because, as he told Davide: 'I like to know what the other side are thinking.' These included an immensely technical presentation on artificial intelligence, claiming that it might play a crucial role in a number of areas: the development of new drugs; fighting global heating; managing resources more efficiently; helping battery vehicles achieve cost and power advantages over the internal combustion engine; novel green fertilisers. The session ended with a wish list of more fanciful future breakthroughs: fusion energy; quantum chemistry; alternative protein design.

At the end of the meeting, Aurélien spoke in stilted English to one of the three men on the panel, Todor Kaldonov, a disgraced coder in a creased grey suit whose work was associated with a number of high-profile operating system disasters. A Bulgarian national, his early career had been spent pursuing hackers and virus authors for whom Bulgaria was a hotbed in the nineteen-eighties and nineties.

'It is easy to find Chalet Caribe. I expect you in one hour?'

The man stroked his moustache.

'You are Aurélien Castile.'

'I am.'

'Then it is hard to say no. Will I be glad to hear what you have to say?'

'I believe, yes.'

Feeling reasonably fit, Aurélien's fluctuating physical condition allowed him to walk to the Chalet Caribe with a wheeled frame. He recognised the pleasant garden of hardy plants and the pathway paved with square bricks that, in 2034, didn't need defrosting by the heating elements concealed beneath. Johnson Pederson met him at the door, wearing his habitual jeans and plaid shirt, and served coffee in a plush front room, alongside an extravagant open fire.

'We are progressing well with on-island construction,' he said in his excellent French, giving Aurélien a satisfied smile. 'You will have seen from my report that phase four is complete.'

Aurélien had been involved in enough building projects not to be surprised that the eight-year timeline had stretched out well beyond a decade.

'Our next priority?'

'Remedial work on the depleted agricultural terraces, new dock equipment.'

'We don't want deliveries from the shadow fleet to be too visible.'

'Understood.'

'The organic soil improvers? Do we have them?'

'Three thousand tonnes of the finest manure and guano.'

'The Haréans are happy?'

'More than happy – likewise the immigrant Haitian workers. We still benefit from the goodwill from the coronavirus vaccines you sourced in 2021, ahead of widespread global distribution. Plus, the vitamin supplements program continues to achieve a 100% take-up in all three *chefferies*.' Pederson paused, then commented: 'You took my advice about public profile?'

'Davide is ostentatiously trying to do good, making it a kind of public theatre. Will it be enough?'

'Perhaps not. He comes across as a technocrat. That isn't what people want, even if they might approve of his actions. They need to be led by charisma, not competence.'

'People are fools,' said Aurélien, quietly. 'What about our Haitian neighbours?'

'A concern. The closest port, Saint-Just, is now run by gangsters. It's isolated by a rocky range of hills and poor as dirt. Even the gang leader, Papa Lace, lives in squalor. On the other hand, he has people to spare that I think I can train up to be your guards.'

'Do I need guards?'

'You might do.'

'Will the ATLAS system not deter attacks sufficiently?'

'The ring of fire is a strong deterrent and a powerful defensive force, but boots on the ground can be handy.'

'How many are you talking about?'

'Half a dozen?' said Pederson with an upward inflection.

'Is that a question or a reply?'

Pederson made a conciliatory gesture. 'Half a dozen will be a reasonable troop to keep on hand. In the meantime, they can perform other functions in the citadel.'

'Yes, all right,' said Aurélien who saw the logic of the argument. 'Train six of them to do useful tasks and, in parallel, drill them in suitable fighting skills.'

'Good,' said Pederson. 'One other thing.'

'Yes?'

'There have been two more viral outbreaks, probably originating from the Haitian mainland. I recommend that we install quarantine doors on all the quarters and dormitories. The cost increase is marginal in the greater scheme of things.'

'Cost is irrelevant. Get it done quickly.'

'Yes, Monsieur Castile. That's everything on my list. Did Kaldonov agree to meet? Do you want me to stay?'

'No, I will make the pitch alone.'

Pederson left the Chalet Caribe. Aurélien put a log on the fire, wondering if his optimistic American agent had asked himself why Haré Stronghold needed an AI specialist.

Todor Kaldonov arrived precisely on time. He was a tall man with shaggy brown hair that matched his moustache. He had changed out of his creased grey suit and was now dressed in khaki trousers and a green hoodie. Aurélien took him into the cinema where Pederson had made his real-estate presentation back in 2020 and talked him through some images of Haré, speaking carefully in clumsy English. Then he asked: 'When you write the story of Dark Revenger, he was the most powerful virus writer in the world?'

'That feels like pre-history, now.'

'You make him seem … What did you say? A "genius-sociopath".'

'He has since expressed remorse.'

'He loved his power?' Aurélien suggested, going to the drinks table. 'I could not source Bulgarian wine. This is Romanian. I hope you aren't disappointed.'

'Not at all.' Kaldonov sipped then ran his tongue along his moustache. 'This is delicious. But you are wrong to speak of power. Indiscriminate destruction is not power.'

'Perhaps power only seems indiscriminate,' said Aurélien, carefully. 'Tell me why Bulgaria was "virus factory".'

'Hyperinflation, crumbling infrastructure, rationing, blackouts, feral animals in the streets, the cognitive dissonance of Soviet socialism. It was a kind of adolescent rage. We made things that destroyed because we seemed to have nothing worth preserving.'

'I see that.'

'And our viruses travelled the world while we were trapped behind closed borders.'

Aurélien pondered his man, giving himself time to formulate in English the thoughts that came to him in French.

Is this the right thing to do?

Haré would, within eighteen months at the outside, be ready for the first members of its long-term survivalist population – himself, Davide, Pederson in administrative charge, the impressively independent indigenous Haréan community of the southern chefferie.

Others will come.

It would be up to Aurélien whether he allowed entry.

Do I want Kaldonov to be one of us? I need him – or someone like him – to accelerate the destruction.

'Today, Mr Kaldonov, what are your goals? You are sixty-three. That is a moment when people think: "One last job".'

'Is that what you're offering?' asked Kaldonov.

'In a way,' said Aurélien. 'And a new life.'

Kaldonov drained his glass and asked: 'How ill are you, Monsieur Castile? I saw you earlier, walking with a frame. But now you seem to move more easily.'

'I am in a better moment.' Aurélien refilled Kaldonov's glass, wondering if the man was psychologically equipped to imagine what was coming. 'Let me tell you what I have learned. You were a "white hat", yes? You fight Dark Revenger. Then he tricks you and you are criminal. For fifteen years, you struggle to escape, seven under house arrest. But your government allows you proper IBM PC hardware, not clones from Eastern Europe, then more modern equipment. You become expert in "self-replicating artificial life". Correct?'

'I call it "synthetic evolution".'

'Yes, good, that is different. You begin CAST, the "Computer Antivirus Strategic Team". White-hat again, making rich, very rich for Bulgaria. You publish warnings for malicious code, the kind that, as you say, evolves. Then … What is the word?'

'My career stalled.'

'Yes. Tell me why?'

'I became bored. AI is nothing more than statistical analysis. Provide enough inputs and it will give you probable average outcomes.' Kaldonov held out his glass. Aurélien refilled it. 'Artificial intelligence is not intelligent. It provides a regression to the mean. Would you call that intelligence?'

'And, last year, one of your creations escaped?'

'Yes.'

'You shut down air-traffic control in five different countries.' Kaldonov didn't answer. Aurélien went on. 'Your AI virus escape is like the Wuhan laboratory theory of the coronavirus pandemic? So, now, you are respected but unemployable. Your professional life is over. You are bankrupt and your future is a struggle.'

'Unemployable except by you, apparently.' Kaldonov held out his glass again. 'What do you want me to do?'

'You have a partner and a child. They will be welcome, too.'

'What do you mean, "welcome"?'

'In the stronghold I showed you – a beautiful stronghold – you and I and your family and some others will begin a new life.'

'How come?'

Aurélien thought back to his conversation fourteen years before, at first with Pederson and then – in private – with Davide.

'We will be reacting to circumstances that cannot be traced back to us because they will be generated by a living thing.' He saw understanding dawning in Kaldonov's eyes. 'An AI virus.'

'With what purpose?'

'To destroy, once and for all, the digital hyperconnected world.'

Kaldonov looked down at his topped-up glass. He seemed, abruptly, to have had enough.

'And for me and my family?'

'To live through it and build something better.'

'You say "live through it". What is "it"?'

Aurélien waited for him to raise his eyes, then held his gaze, revelling in the sonority of the English words: 'Darkness, Storm and Fire.'

25

May 2036

As the Haré Stronghold approached completion, behind schedule but to an enhanced specification, Aurélien Castile and his son Davide welcomed Todor Kaldonov to the island on a limpid Caribbean spring day, the air soft and warm, overnight rain lending a sheen to every leaf and stone.

Kaldonov, his partner and child arrived via the airport of the Haitian capital, Port-au-Prince, then drove across country to the dilapidated settlement of Saint-Just. From there, it was only a brief hop across the placid waters in a Castile Energie tender. Now mostly confined to his motorised wheelchair, Aurélien judged it would be pleasant for the new arrivals to get to know the steep-sided island from the water and, although the boat bobbed and dipped on the moderate swell, the newcomers enjoyed the vistas, in particular the grassy plain where the stones of the ancient solar observatory were clearly visible.

Kaldonov and his partner, Stoyan Dilov, were standing in the prow, looking down into the shallows, marvelling at the transparency of the water and the bright colours of the fish. Their son – a bright eleven-year-old – was listening, apparently gripped, to Aurélien's stilted description of the standing stones, the petroglyphs that marked their surfaces, his long struggle to decipher what they meant.

'One day,' he said to the boy, 'I will undo more code. That is my life, do you see? Your father is clever. He makes the codes. I decode. Do you know what I mean?'

'No, sir, I don't.'

Aurélien pondered how else he might put it, reflecting that – despite his attempts to become more fluent – his English remained clumsy and inexpressive.

'Tell your parents what I said. They can explain.'

Aurélien watched the boy insinuate himself between his two fathers, saw them wrap their loving arms around his shoulders and join together in a warm embrace that included the boy. He couldn't hear what they said, but the boy was pointing at the standing stones. Then Kaldonov turned his head towards Aurélien and called: 'Mitya says you are a very clever man.'

A jetty linked the grassy pasture to the water but, from there, access to the citadel was tricky, the stony path steep and uneven, no good for Aurélien's wheelchair. Davide drove round to the eastern coast where the docks had been built, including a boom for ship-to-shore oil deliveries. Three islanders escorted them onto dry land, flinging a gangplank across, walking fore and aft of Aurélien to make sure that he accomplished the short but nerve-wracking crossing safe and sound. The others followed.

'There is a path for a buggy to take us to the summit of the citadel,' said Aurélien. 'We considered a funicular.' The boy asked a question in Bulgarian and Aurélien assumed it was the unusual word that had thrown his precocious intelligence. 'A funicular railway is one that uses water and gravity for power.'

Kaldonov touched his son's shoulder. 'Like when we went to the ski resort, you remember?'

'When there was no snow?' asked the boy.

Kaldonov and his partner, Stoyan Dilov, laughed.

'I must stay and prepare for a fuel delivery,' said Davide. 'A tanker is expected.'

'The island uses oil?' asked Stoyan, looking confused.

'The renewables are not all on line,' said Aurélien.

'And oil reserves remain a part of the mix,' said Davide. 'No one knows how circumstances will evolve.'

The buggy took them swiftly on a curving path up through the agri-terraces to the main entrance, a cave-like garage space on a lower floor. From there, they took the lift all the way up to a beautifully landscaped upper platform, a wide-open space paved with marble, broken in the centre by a temporary structure made of scaffolding and tarpaulins. Aurélien drove round the perimeter in his motorised wheelchair, pointing out the airstrip, then trundling along to the narrow, half-finished belvedere from which they overlooked the solar observatory.

'Keep back from the edge,' he warned. 'There will be a little wall later on.'

'Stay close to me, Mitya,' said Kaldonov.

'Perhaps we go to middle for safety,' said Stoyan Dilov in his thick accent.

'There are more dangerous openings,' said Aurélien, trundling over, 'for the elevator shaft and for the light tubes, down seven floors. But it is protected by the ...' He waved a hand, not knowing what to call the temporary structure. 'By this.'

A rudimentary site-elevator came rattling up through the scaffolding, revealing a stocky man in a red-and-blue plaid shirt. He pushed open the low barrier and stepped out, holding out a muscular arm and a hand that showed that he was not a stranger to manual labour.

'Glad to see you again,' said Johnson Pederson. 'Welcome to Haré, Mr Kaldonov, Mr Dilov. And this must be young Dimitri.'

'You can call me Mitya,' said the boy, charmingly.

'Okay, Mitya, I will.' Pederson smiled, showing his dazzling veneers. Aurélien told him that the Bulgarians' luggage would soon be brought up from the docks. He answered: 'Sure. Will you go and sit in comfort on level minus three? The two sitting rooms and the games room have been signed off. The doors are sealed to keep out dust, but I can fix that.' Down on minus-three, Pederson called on a local labourer:

'Yeiwene, would you strip the tape from these doorframes?'

Mitya was delighted to discover the pool table and challenged his father Stoyan to a game. Aurélien and Kaldonov entered a sitting room in the very centre of the citadel, with a light-well from the platform above illuminating a flourishing garden of drought-resistant plants. Aurélien invited Kaldonov to sit, as always feeling a sense of irritation that, trapped in his wheelchair, he was prevented from engaging in that social nicety.

'This is very impressive,' said Kaldonov. 'Better still than the videos you sent us.'

'But you have a question? I see it behind your eyes.'

'I do,' said Kaldonov. 'Why so fast?'

'Were you at Davos this January?'

'No, but I read the transcripts.'

Aurélien nodded. 'People safe from struggle, they believe technology will save us. They think: "AI will save us." No. We have already gone too far.'

Kaldonov told him: 'There is an academic, a contrarian, you know? I don't remember his name. He has a wager that humanity will not, repeat "not", be wiped out by 2040, in three or four years. He made the bet against someone more pessimistic than he, paying up front, just in case. I met him. He hopes to collect his winnings – a gold doubloon – on the first of January 2041.'

Aurélien took a moment to catch up with some of the more unusual English words. 'And if he loses?'

'It will no longer matter.' Kaldonov laughed. 'He will be dead or living in a cave.'

'And you, Mr Kaldonov? Do you believe AI is our "intelligent" saviour?'

'Because it is evolving independent thought? Why would it? It will remain limited by finite programming and finite experience.'

'People say it has already made magic – new compounds in medicine, new materials in construction?'

'Mr Castile, I don't believe in great drama. The future is usually like the past. You agree with me?' Aurélien made a gesture for him to continue. 'Technology sometimes does extraordinary things, but putting humans on the moon hasn't had the same impact as, say, email. Years ago, everyone wanted to work in virtual reality. They believed the advertising promise that "all things are possible" and … What did they say? "The only limit is your imagination." Then it turned out that the choices available were what sort of clothes your avatar wore.' Kaldonov looked round the room, taking in the sleek matt walls and the pleasant, muted lighting. 'Mr Pederson has done well. This is a place someone could be happy in for months. Years, maybe.'

'Good.' Aurélien nodded slowly. 'But change needs to come. How is your work? Is it ready?'

Kaldonov put his head on one side.

'When you offered to take us in, me and my family, it was because you needed something from me and, I have come to think, because you intend to make change happen, but you have never told me when.'

'Preparations are already under way. It is a question of which side of the barricade you want to stand.'

'Meaning?'

'Safe or not safe.'

This was, for Aurélien, the moment of crisis. He was relieved when Kaldonov replied: 'I am here, Mr Castile. I have chosen.'

'Good. And what did you decide to call it?'

Kaldonov took a slip of paper from his pocket on which was written a single word in the Cyrillic alphabet.

Огън.

'Is this—?'

'As you requested,' said the Bulgarian. 'The name will be embedded in each mutating copy.'

'It was predicted by the stones,' murmured Aurélien. 'I am the Coming Fire.'

26

June 2037

It wasn't until midsummer of 2037 that Haré Stronghold was finally complete. All the underground levels were fitted out exactly as Johnson Pederson had described them. Whenever a question had filtered up from the site teams, Aurélien had deferred to his American project manager.

'Why try to become an expert when I already employ an expert?'

In the end, Aurélien had found himself convinced by Pederson's arguments about aesthetic judgements in maintaining a 'happy' population. Pederson had even persuaded him to install state-of-the-art counselling software with a range of friendly avatars in order to confront the future post-traumatic stresses felt by the indigenous island population and the half-dozen employees recruited from Papa Lace, the gang master in Saint-Just. Pederson had allocated them additional responsibilities according to their talents: labouring; medical support; catering; gardening; administration. All six became skilled in the use of the state-of-the-art hand weapons with which Pederson had stocked the armoury.

Aurélien had also bowed to the idea of preserving knowledge in forms other than digital, making investments in redundant data storage from some of the world's biggest and most prominent museums and libraries, buying up old microfiche databases – photographic miniaturisations –

together with the rudimentary optical viewers needed to consult them. They were housed on level minus six, like the seed bank.

Despite the exceptionally efficient rain capture, Aurélien had also greenlit mid-scale desalination using reverse osmosis to remove the salt and minerals that make seawater poisonous for human consumption, a process less costly than heating or freezing, but still energy and resource hungry. It wasn't designed to serve all the needs of the entire population, but to provide a back-up for any periods of prolonged drought, pushing saltwater under high pressure through a semi-permeable graphene membrane – a one-atom-thick material made of carbon – whose pores were too small for the dissolved solids to pass through. Aurélien had ordered a set of a hundred graphene membranes at extraordinary cost. They had not yet arrived but, when they did, Pederson promised that they would produce a cubic metre of drinking water for an energy input of only two kilowatts.

'We need a topping-out ceremony,' Pederson had added, 'the traditional master builder's celebration – a kind of blessing of the building.'

The ceremony was organised for early dawn. This made no difference to Aurélien who was just enduring a haphazard cycle of sleep and wakefulness. The month was June and sunrise was very early. Davide was also in a bad health phase, his balance disrupted. Despite pursuing a culture of physical activity, he suffered from muscle wastage. He, therefore, would not take an active part in the topping out. Pederson ruled himself out, too.

'I've never liked heights,' he told them, laughing. 'Why do you think I've made a living by refurbishing holes in the ground?'

Aurélien was surprised when Kaldonov put himself forward. Though well-built, Kaldonov was no longer a young man. In order to reach the highest point of Haré Stronghold and attach a bouquet of ceremonial flowers, it would be necessary to climb the antenna array. Pederson argued that they could create 'buy in' from the island population if they invited a member of the southern *chefferie* to accompany Kaldonov. Pederson chose a young man from an important island family whose first name was Yeiwene, after the twentieth-century independence fighter whose grave was still decorated by the Haréans on auspicious days. He had come to Pederson's attention because he was the brother of the female leader of the southern *chefferie*, Yeiwa Egesho, on whose land the solar observatory stood.

On the morning of the ceremony, the upper terrace was chock-a-block with a hundred or so observers, standing shoulder to shoulder beneath a chilly pre-dawn sky in the half light. Kaldonov and Yeiwene donned their climbing harnesses and began their ascent, beginning easily with a set of steps bolted to the wall of the elevator shaft building. From there, they continued vertically on a fixed ladder secured to the concrete antenna plinth, attaching their safety ropes one after another to the rungs above their heads, repeating the process as they climbed.

Kaldonov went first, illuminated by a faint luminescence on the eastern horizon. He had been involved with the assembly of the antenna when it had been laid flat on the terrace, awaiting erection, 'getting his hands dirty' as Pederson put it, working as a physical engineer as well as a software engineer.

Yeiwene followed, carrying the bouquet of flowers with which the ceremony would conclude, ready to be tied to the uppermost point they could reach, a couple of metres from the top of the antenna itself, the final portion being too frail to climb.

The flowers chosen were rhododendrons. Pederson told Aurélien: 'I like that we're putting flowers originally from the high mountains of the Himalayas on the topmost point of Haré Stronghold.'

The sun crested the horizon. Leaning back in his electric wheelchair, Aurélien saw Kaldonov and Yeiwene swapping positions at the base of the antenna, Kaldonov allowing the islander to move above him while he attached his lines to the stanchions of the junction box for the island's comms, seeming to have a difficulty in clipping the carabiners into the framework.

Then the islander, Yeiwene, mounted the last few steps on the tapering ladder, drawing the eye, a tiny man against the pink-and-orange sky, reaching up with his bunch of rich red blooms on their woody stalks, celebrating – though he did not know this – the completion of a refuge from wilful destruction.

27

August 2037

'So, things are changing,' said Todor Kaldonov in his native Bulgarian. 'It has begun.'

It was two months later and he was giving his partner, Stoyan Dilov, a rundown on everything he knew about the Coming Darkness.

'There has been a vast explosion on the dockside in Cyrene City. There is an insurrection and the prime minster has fled for France where the news is full of the unexplained child murders. Castile has been asking me to infiltrate the networks at the desert launch base at Al-Jaghar. The French have a weapon in orbit and—'

'I don't understand,' said his husband. 'What are you saying?'

'I'm saying that our time here is at an end.'

'But you said this was the safe place.'

'I know what I said.'

Kaldonov's eyes were on the internal window that separated him and Dilov from their son, conceived *in vitro* and gestated by a surrogate, mixing DNA from both of their bloodlines. The lights beyond the glass were bright, in comparison to their own room that Kaldonov preferred to keep gloomy, as a partial remedy to the tiredness of his eyes that spent long hours focused on bright computer screens.

In the adjacent room, Mitya was building a rocket out of cardboard, tape and wooden cutlery. On the table at the base of his rocket he had arranged a cloud of 'launch vapour' made from cardboard packaging granules the size and colour of monkey nuts.

The boy looked up and waved. Kaldonov smiled, giving him a jovial salute. The boy frowned, recognising that the smile didn't quite reach his father's eyes. Kaldonov indicated that he was busy and pressed a button, darkening the glass. As his image faded, Mitya innocently nodded in reply.

'Stoyan, it was a mistake,' said Kaldonov. 'Or maybe not a mistake. Just a gamble. He is …'

Kaldonov stopped, frowning. He wasn't sure how to share the decision he had come to.

'Who?' asked Stoyan.

'I thought there was a kind of logic or plan,' said Kaldonov. 'But there isn't. There's just destruction.'

Stoyan pursed his lips.

'You persuaded me we would be protected, here.'

'I know.'

'Now what are you saying?'

'I have made a new plan.'

In the control room of Haré Stronghold, Aurélien was watching a closed-circuit feed from Kaldonov's family's quarters. It was comprised of four camera angles, each lens cleverly hidden in elements of the décor: air con; lighting; entertainment devices. All the same, he couldn't see much. The room was dark.

That didn't matter, however, because the room was also wired for sound.

Aurélien had made no progress in his attempts to improve his English. It remained encumbered by what linguists called 'monitoring' – a stumbling self-consciousness in which he was unable to express himself without simultaneously judging whether or not what he said was accurate. It had briefly crossed his mind to learn a smattering of

Bulgarian, as a kind of mental stimulation, but that project had got no further than a few polite terms of courtesy.

Happily, his lack of fluency in English and Bulgarian was more than compensated by the vast reserves of statistical linguistic analysis in a large language model installed in an unconnected silo of the island's operating system. Even if Kaldonov and Dilov spoke to one another in Dilov's native North Macedonian, the LLM could digest and relay their words into French in real time.

'We must leave?' asked Stoyan. 'Will he oppose us?'

In the gloom, Kaldonov tapped his comm-watch, checking the time, considering the tides.

'As soon as possible. I have made arrangements for this evening when he is on his terrace for dinner.'

'Someone will help us?'

'Yeiwa Egesho, the leader of the native Haréans. And her brother, Yeiwene. He works in the control room.'

'They will not betray us?'

'They do not know our intentions. They believe the excursion is permitted. We will leave everything behind …' Kaldonov's voice faded. He approached the darkened glass that separated him from their son, putting his hand on the frame, checking the time once more. 'Once we are off the island, all will be well.'

Stoyan stood up and Kaldonov half turned. Doing so, the glow from his comm-watch bounced up off the darkened glass, into the vent of the air-con. Between the grey metal slats, an answering gleam winked back at him.

'Todor—' his partner began.

Kaldonov silenced him with a finger to his lips, bringing his face close to Stoyan's ear.

'Don't speak,' he whispered.

*

Aurélien recognised the moment when Kaldonov – who was an exceptionally intelligent person, after all – realised that he and his partner and child were under constant close surveillance. For the moment, that wasn't his main concern, however. He was thinking about a set of arguments that he had been rehearsing in the back of his own mind, about the future of Haré and what would – inevitably – be an almost-captive population of dependents. He intended to have a serious conversation with Davide and Pederson about authority and how it might be maintained. On reflection, he had been over-optimistic. His small force of six trained Haréans trained in the use of his armoury had begun to seem far too few. Kaldonov, Dilov and little Mitya were a case in point. The Bulgarian and the North Macedonian had been on the point of discussing the details of their betrayal and escape.

This evening when he is on his terrace for dinner.

Aurélien had to admit that he was disappointed. In a lifetime of cynical pursuit of money and advantage, he had never quite shaken off the idea that those he took with him into the post-chaos future should be grateful. He spoke the thought aloud.

'Clearly, I was mistaken.'

If they intended to leave with the assistance of unsuspecting islanders, that meant by small boat, probably from the southern beach, across the narrow neck of water separating them from Haitian coast.

The Atlas 'ring of fire' can just as easily destroy deserters as assailants. But I still need Kaldonov. Without him, no Fire.

Soon after, Kaldonov was surprised and fearful to be summoned to Aurélien Castile's presence.

It can't be pure chance that this coincides with the moment of our escape.

He thought about how hard he had worked to nurture close relations with Yeiwene Egesho.

We will miss our rendezvous.

Kaldonov made his way to the control room via the access stairs alongside the lift, entering through the armoured door, arriving a little out of breath.

No matter. There will be other opportunities.

He was surprised when Davide Castile closed the door behind him, locking the mechanism with a thumbprint.

'What has happened?' Kaldonov asked. 'Are we under attack?'

'Good question,' said Castile Senior.

While the son remained just a couple of paces behind Kaldonov's back, the older Castile was on the far side of the control room, his electric wheelchair drawn up to the nest of computer monitors whose displays showed, among other things, the island's security systems.

'I often watch you,' said Castile Senior, 'when I am awake and you are not.'

Kaldonov felt a trickle of fear, like a creature sliding down the back of his neck, under his clothes.

'Why is that?' he asked with assumed unconcern.

'Just in case.'

On the central screen of his security consoles, Aurélien could still see the bedroom shared by Kaldonov and Stilov, as well as the smaller adjacent antechamber where young Mitya was playing. In the lapse of time between Kaldonov noticing the camera concealed in the air-con vent and Aurélien making his decision, Aurélien had pondered the most effective method of leverage. Lacking in human empathy, he had only a theoretical idea of how a father and partner might respond to a choice of threats. He was swayed by the success of his theatrical series of child murders, dominating the media and distracting from the Coming Darkness.

Would that be a good strategy in this case, too? Or, in this case, are the bonds of adult love more valuable?

Kaldonov shuffled his feet, summoning Aurélien out of his reverie.

'Why did you summon me?' the Bulgarian asked.

'I have a question,' Aurélien replied, pitching his voice so it would only just be audible above the whir and hum of the air-con. 'If you had to choose, which one would you save?'

Kaldonov's mind was spinning. He felt actually nauseated, as if assailed by a surge of motion sickness.

'What have you done?'

'Nothing,' said Castile Senior. 'Not yet.'

From the control room, the two Castiles took Kaldonov up in the elevator to the terrace level. The evening was warm and humid. The father drove his electric wheelchair to the far southern end, to the promontory overlooking the solar observatory, stopping on the very lip, closed by a low parapet wall about knee high. The coast of Haiti was visible as a line of white surf, behind which the landscape was pocked with a few yellow specks of light.

That's where we ought to be, thought Kaldonov. *Anywhere but here.*

The combination of the great height and the fear in his belly made Kaldonov step away from the promontory, putting a hand to his brow, stumbling away to ground himself by placing the palms of his hands on the coping stones of a taller parapet. He heard Castile Senior's voice as if from a great distance: 'You wish to leave Haré Stronghold. I don't understand this. You know, as well as anyone, what is coming.'

'I …' Kaldonov began. He tried to pull himself together. The stone still held the heat of the sun, despite the late hour. 'I did not realise …' He stopped, fearing his words were pointless. Then, for a shameful minute, he debased himself, telling the older man how much he was sorry, how foolish he had been, but the words seemed to evaporate into the air. What was the point of talking to the father about human feelings? He addressed himself to the son: 'What will come after?'

'We will,' said Davide Castile, speaking for the first time.

Yes, thought Kaldonov. *Haré will survive, but at what cost?*

Involuntarily, his glance went up to the red beacon on the top of the antenna array, blinking against the night sky. The son's gaze followed and a quizzical look came into his eyes. Kaldonov swiftly looked down at the ground.

'Your work,' said the father, 'is not quite done, Todor Kaldonov. I will hurt your family if you do not complete it.'

'Yes,' said Kaldonov. 'I understand.'

'You will be obliged to watch them suffer.'

'There is no need,' Kaldonov insisted. 'I was confused. I began to believe …'

'To believe what?' asked Davide.

Kaldonov frowned: 'That there was an alternative.'

Castile Senior laughed and told him: 'There is none.'

28

August 2037

Yeiwa Egesho was standing within the circle of megaliths. A few days had passed since the Bulgarian had first mooted the idea of an excursion to the mainland of Haiti, communicating through her brother, Yeiwene. Now the night had come, Yeiwa wouldn't be particularly surprised if the Bulgarian didn't turn up for the proposed trip. It had seemed to her an odd request, though she had seen no reason to refuse it. Commanding in her dealings with her own people, she had accepted a habit of subservience in her relations with the island's European overlords.

In addition, she had her own reason for making the brief crossing. She wanted to visit Saint-Just on the Haitian coastline from which two barely pubescent girls had been promised in marriage to men from the two northern Haréan *chefferies*, child brides bought and paid for by wages earnt from serving Chief Castile.

Yeiwa was fiercely opposed. It didn't matter to her that the girls' lives might be materially improved or that their future husbands might be generous, warm-hearted and kind.

'People are not to be bought and sold,' she had argued, raising her voice above the hubbub at a recent meeting, bringing together senior members of all three settlements on the island. It had taken place, as was tradition, within the circle of standing stones. 'Remember Toussaint. What did he die for, if not that all should be free?'

Aware of time passing from the pattern of moon and stars speckling the evening sky, Yeiwa walked down the gentle slope towards the beach and the jetty. The hem of her long, sky-blue dress trailed on the dry grass. Her brother came running down the hill to join her, wearing his pristine white Castile Energie uniform, a broad smile on his vacuous face.

'I have been chosen to be trained for more responsibility,' Yeiwene told her, delightedly. 'It is more money.'

'The stones say a time is coming when money will have no more meaning.'

'Now is now,' said Yeiwene. 'Money means something today.'

A boat from the mainland came chugging in across the docile sea. As it came alongside the jetty, the two figures on board looped their lines around two wooden posts, pulling it hard against the boardwalk. Yeiwa took a last look back towards the citadel, making sure that the Bulgarian was not coming. She felt a vague sense that circumstances had changed in a way she didn't understand.

Perhaps, with Yeiwene becoming more important to Chief Castile, I might learn more.

'Are you coming?' asked one of the two Haitians.

Yeiwa and her brother climbed into the small methanol-powered boat. Above the splutter of the engine, the Haitians began excitedly telling her all about 'the noise on the news streams'.

'Papa Lace tells us what he learns, that the children are killed and no one knows why, that the world almost came to an end.'

'No, it would have been cloaked in darkness to blot out the sun.'

'Or something,' said the other.

'But it didn't happen because of a Frenchman—'

'Called Alexandre Lamarque—'

'And he saved us all and—'

'He is the man who saved the world.'

They talked for the entire crossing, only pausing as they approached the dockside. Once the boat was tied up, it dawned on them that they hadn't behaved with proper respect. One of them asked: 'What do you say to that, Mother Egesho?'

Yeiwa looked each one in the eye. They were young men, no more than children really, twins dressed in grubby t-shirts, woollen jumpers and ragged jeans but with leather skull-caps mounted with the horns of a goat. Their faces revealed a febrile thrill at the idea of global catastrophe, childishly convinced that avoiding it had always been inevitable.

As they tied up at the Saint-Just jetty, the second one insisted: 'Do you have no answer, Mother Egesho?'

'I say this,' Yeiwa told them, 'Time and the stones will answer.'

29

SEPTEMBER 2037

A month later, Marthe Hidalgo, Claudine Poiret's second-in-command in the presidential palace in Paris, found herself feeling foolish pursuing her normal routine of meetings and briefings. She knew – more than most – how close the world had come to disaster.

It was mid-September 2037. Dressed, like her boss, in a dark trouser suit, she assessed today's paperwork: a review of predictions of climate disaster from sixteen years earlier, looking forward to 2040 and beyond. Her hope was that evaluating past predictions would confirm or deny the accuracy of those to come. Marthe Hidalgo knew, however, that small changes can make vast differences.

Is that not the basis of chaos theory? And what are we living through right now, if not chaos?

One of the documents she was consulting, printed on paper because she preferred that to non-stop screenwork, was a special edition of the newspaper *Le Monde* from 2021, working with data from international organisations and the French weather service. The focus was Paris, though it was the same story as in so many of the world's great cities, built on coasts or waterways. Two degrees of global warming, the paper argued, would lead to once-a-century events becoming once a generation, cobbled streets under water, cellars of lovingly stored vintages of noble wines destroyed. The underground mass transport system had already proved vulnerable. In 2016, high water on the Seine had caused the first closure of a major tunnelled railway, an event repeated with increasing frequency in the two decades since.

Then there was the other side of the coin – and the predictions from 2021 were right again – annual waves of dry heat lasting from May to October, interspersed with brief punishing storms. *Le Monde* thought that the average of fourteen days per year above thirty degrees centigrade would climb to twenty-two days by 2050 and thirty-four in 2085. It had quickly turned out that those were underestimates. There had been thirty-seven in the previous twelve months.

Hidalgo flipped through the other documents, a litany of smaller details that would have been distressing had she not already become inured: deaths from heatstroke and dehydration; heart attacks; compromised sanitation. Particularly insidious was the contamination of drinking water from microbes that flourish at higher temperatures, as well as from leaks or overtopping when sewage-treatment works – traditionally built next to rivers – found themselves periodically underwater. There was a separate section detailing the stresses the city's electrical system was under, causing brown-outs in planned waves across the capital. Then, the catastrophic non-planned complete blackouts and the widespread purchase of oil-fired back-up generators, solving today's short-term problem but making tomorrow's long-term issues worse.

The final and most recent report, published in May 2037, compared the alarming drops in fauna biodiversity – an eighty per cent fall in bird numbers in Paris between 2000 and the present day, for example – with thriving bacteria and viruses:

Life will go on but, from a human perspective, the loss of our insect, mammal and avian companions will be exacerbated by a disastrous flourishing of microbial life, inimical to human survival.

As Hidalgo put the papers aside, she reflected that they should have given more space to violent wind storms, bringing with them damage to property and danger to life. But she had another document to read with a narrower focus and equally serious consequences. It concerned the likely impact of sudden disasters on the financial sector. It had been written just a few weeks before, inspired by the events of the Coming Darkness. The authors had considered damage to the critical physical infrastructure of finance, whether from accidents, terrorist attacks or climate-related events.

Hidalgo was trained in economics from her post-graduate studies at the Parisian school of political science, the Ecole Polytechnique. She was hyper-aware that, since the abandonment of the gold standard after World War II, all money had become imaginary. It was valuable only insofar as everyone chose to believe in it, not because the pieces of metal or paper – or the numbers in databases or books – had any intrinsic value.

Early in her career, Hidalgo had been professionally attached to the French treasury when Iceland had defaulted on a significant proportion of its international debts, deciding to unilaterally wipe the slate clean and start again. The northern island nation was threatened with all kinds of dire consequences, 'ostracised from the world financial community for a generation and more'. The people of Iceland began to imagine a future with no new imports, maintaining and driving their existing vehicles, for example, until they fell apart around them. The most pessimistic – given the sparse natural resources on Iceland, insufficient to sustain its population without international trade – imagined massive depopulation.

But none of that happened. Within a few short years, it was business as usual. The world's international finance community decided to keep believing in Icelandic money, despite evidence to the contrary. And, of course, less than a decade later, Iceland had turned out to be a viable potential refuge from climate change, with its northern latitude and endless geothermal power.

Hidalgo made herself a third cup of coffee – her limit for the day – and took it back to her desk.

Almost all the bad things she had been reading about had happened, more or less as the various report authors had predicted. What was new was the accelerating digital meltdown, possibly driven by the same artificial intelligence that so many optimists had proclaimed humanity's salvation, forgetting that even the most innocent tool becomes a weapon in evil hands.

Hidalgo sipped her coffee, remembering how AI evangelists had insisted that their technology would 'empower not control'. Instead, novel systems had been released without thorough testing, such as surveillance bots with racially biased facial recognition. Meanwhile, legitimate news sources had been swamped by a sea of mis- and disinformation, deep fakes and alternative realities.

Perhaps, in the end, the more insidious problem isn't so much that people believe counterfactual ideas. It's the endemic anxiety and depression that results from a resolutely pessimistic vision of humanity's future.

Hidalgo drained her cup and was about to shred the paperwork for recycling when she remembered the IT problems on the presidential palace network.

Will I be able to print it again?

She stood up and put the report in a seldom-used filing tray on the cabinet behind her, then remained where she was, a frown on her tired face.

How many people are out there, still on the side of Darkness?

Two days later, notice of a new threat landed in Claudine Poiret's inbox, for the attention of her second-in-command, Marthe Hidalgo. It concerned the campaigning organisation Tabula Rasa that, back in August, had only been able to pursue its catastrophic purpose because it had been sheltered from Alex's investigation into the Coming Darkness by a traitor within the Directorate-General for Internal Security.

Having a cell-structure with no central command and no database of followers, many Tabula Rasa adherents had not yet been tracked down – except for those Alex and Amaury had killed in self-defence. Apparently, a new Tabula Rasa campaign had burst into unwelcome life – the destruction of the capital city's surveillance network. The text read:

How is it we didn't notice when they called the invasive paraphernalia of the surveillance state 'Camera Control'? Why did that not set alarm bells ringing?

Cameras designed to Control!

But we don't want to be controlled. We want to be free. So, the cameras must die so that we can live free.

The campaign seemed well-financed, promoted through a dark website, offering cash prizes for 'incontrovertible date-stamped evidence of destruction', with additional bonuses for the use of 'explosive or corrosive attacks creating high-profile publicity, extensive damage and exorbitant cost of repair'. In the website gallery, beneath the destroyed surveillance cameras, solidified pools of molten metal could be seen, congealed and hardening on the pavement slabs, in the fourteenth arrondissement, around Emmeline Cantor's apartment. The favoured method of attack was thermite, a powder-mixture used in the manufacture of incendiary bombs, ignited by a strong heat source such as a sparkler to initiate the reaction.

Hidalgo considered the report, then began to draft a response to this 'coordinated vandalism', intending to run it past her dynamic and focused boss, Claudine Poiret.

The government is aware of the legitimate moral and legal concerns of those who question the passive intrusion of the capital's surveillance cameras in their daily lives. However, Camera Control has been responsible, over the last five years, for forty-two per cent of all street-

crime solves, many of them offences against the person, including mugging and a variety of sexual crimes.

The government hopes that all responsible Parisians will appreciate that legitimate questions around our valuable and effective crime-fighting infrastructure do not warrant indiscriminate destruction. Although the attacks are presented as a 'game', they are nothing of the kind. Although they are sold as a defence of liberty, they undermine the security of every law-abiding citizen.

Click through this link to give your anonymous tip-off and help keep our streets safe.

Unfortunately, Claudine Poiret had already left, to coordinate the Haitian relief effort on a French naval frigate more than seven thousand kilometres away in the Caribbean. For twenty-four hours, Hidalgo had had no meaningful communication with her.

That, too, may be more than a temporary problem.

30

SEPTEMBER 2037

The airbase of Al-Jaghar was located in southern Cyrenia, in the heart of the Great Sand Sea, about thirty kilometres from the closed Egyptian frontier. It had been seriously damaged by Captain Alexandre Lamarque's desperate mission to prevent the launch of a rocket with a payload of cluster bombs, designed to decimate the constellations of artificial satellites that circled the globe in Low Earth Orbit, provoking the Kessler effect.

Captain Lamarque had been successful, destroying the launch gantry and the control tower, toppling the rocket so that, when its powerful propulsion engines ignited, it scorched a path through one wing of the Great Solar Array before burying itself in the dunes. By chance, it ruptured all ingoing and outgoing wired comms. Immediately afterwards, because the entire Al-Jaghar air-force hierarchy had been killed, a civilian scientist – Wael Al-Mesih – took charge of the rebuild.

Trusted by the idealistic Prime Minster Souad Mourad, his promotion a just reward for a lifetime's work, Wael wasn't entirely happy. Arriving in the capital for a briefing with the premier, he was met by his good friend Faroukh Al-Medawi, a Cyrenian diplomat.

'Congratulations on your promotion, Wael. I have an invitation for you – an important ceremony at Aswan to celebrate the defeat of the Coming Darkness conspiracy. I am going myself. The Egyptian heroine, Zeina Yaseen, will be there.'

'Faroukh, I wish I could, but it's not possible. I am overwhelmed with building contracts, bills of supply, snagging lists and all the rest of it.'

Faroukh Al-Medawi took Wael to the parliament building within its celebrated rose gardens, riding in his official vehicle. Evidence of refurbishment from the damage caused by the insurrection was all around. Wael delivered a speech to a sub-committee of lawmakers, restating his concerns regarding the crowded skies, concluding: 'From the dawn of time, we human beings have looked up at the stars in hope of guidance, wondering what they might teach us. Many of civilisation's oldest monuments are observatories of the progress of these mysterious "lights in the sky". The presence of hundreds of thousands of reflective artificial satellites crowding Low Earth Orbit cuts humanity off from one of its sources of greatest wonder, from the most distant of timelines, and from evidence of the vast majesty of creation.'

After his speech, Wael was invited, without political fanfare, to a private meeting with Mourad. She welcomed him in her safe room.

'Is this,' he asked her, 'where you awaited the Frenchman's extraction force?'

'It is.'

'Your brief exile must have been very trying.'

'It was but, in Paris, I learnt of a new danger.'

Wael became more focused. 'I will do what I can to help.'

Mourad excused herself in order to respond to an urgent message that had come through on a tablet in her lap. Wael looked round the safe room. It was wood panelled with a heavy and intricately carved blast door, meaning very little sound could be heard from the building work just the other side of the reinforced walls. The prime minister was sitting in a leather armchair with a brass reading-light over her shoulder, dressed in her habitual 'robes of office', a long formal gown of ivory silk with vertical panels of burgundy embroidery. She completed whatever task the tablet had required of her and put it aside.

'Professor, I must first thank you, as a civilian, for taking control of the Al-Jaghar military base, as well as the scientific research campus and the Great Solar Array. You will always be able to count on my support. Faroukh Al-Medawi told me you were the ideal candidate.'

'That was kind of him.'

'Second, I need someone to locate God's Thunder,' she told him, abruptly. 'Do you know what that is?'

'I have heard rumours,' said Wael. 'I am at your command. I will do what I can.'

'Let me give you some history. For a long time, the fiercely independent French military remained at arm's length from international treaties, declining to join NATO for example. Out of this spirit of independence, they considered placing nuclear warheads in orbit. Deployment would have contravened international law, including the 2031 update to the Outer Space Treaty. I don't know if that would have prevented them. Other voices within their administration perhaps advised caution. In any case, what they did instead still contravened its spirit. France went to great trouble and expense to launch an alternative to a nuclear deterrent. They placed three platforms in orbit, launched from our facility at Al-Jaghar, carrying dense tungsten rods, each one what the strategists call a "city killer".'

'Three platforms?'

'Yes. Had Alexandre Lamarque not prevented the Coming Darkness conspiracy from launching its rocket, they would almost certainly have been knocked out of orbit, descending to Earth to do untold damage.'

'Perhaps even compromising the biosphere, like multiple massive volcanic eruptions?'

'That was the worst-case scenario. Two of the platforms were powered out of Earth orbit with great fanfare, aimed at the Sun, but one remains.'

'That "fanfare",' Wael suggested, 'was designed to persuade the international community that the threat was over.'

'Indeed.' Mourad stopped, perhaps seeing the look of concern in Wael's eyes. 'I do not want to use the weapon, you understand,' she reassured him.

'But you want me, potentially, to take control of it.'

Mourad became expansive.

'Cyrenia is a small country, a new country. Who knows what allies we may lose in the future, what enemies we may gain. I had high hopes of the thaw in relations with Egypt, that we might partner and become the centre of a new political block, but …' She stopped. 'I have not offered you any refreshment. How rude.'

'No, Madame Prime Minister. I do not need refreshment. But I do not wish to become a soldier, either.'

'Of course not,' she soothed. 'But will you accept to serve as my eyes and ears and report only to me – or to our mutual friend, the honourable Faroukh Al-Medawi of the tripartite presidential council?'

'Report what?' asked Wael, quietly.

'That remains to be seen. First there was Darkness. Faroukh tells me there is a threatened Storm. After that, who can say?'

'The conspiracy remains?'

'That is what is most infuriating. Neither I nor anyone else really knows. There are clues, but no pattern.'

Wael, a passionate believer in the hyperconnected modern world, told her: 'What is interesting is never the things themselves, but how they are connected, one to another and all to each.'

'But where everything is connected,' she told him, speaking very low, 'a small flaw can become a cascade.'

Wael returned to Al-Jaghar by fast helicopter, finding – to his surprise – that Mourad's words had placed a barb of doubt in his mind. Back in his office, he thought about the delays to the repairs to the cables connecting the airbase to the outside world and the increasing numbers of unexplained network failures across the globe. He sat down at his untidy desk, pondering a new pattern of thought, painful for one so advanced in years, with little time left and much still to achieve. He thought about his friend, Faroukh Al-Medawi, who had sacrificed his career to a population of ordinary people who expressed little by way of thanks and had endless energy for childish complaint.

Perhaps I should have devoted my life to the here and now, instead of riddling the ageless past, studying the ancient light of impossibly distant stars.

31

September 2037

Todor Kaldonov had no doubt that he had made a terrible mistake. Because of his own thirst for money and security, he had accepted the poisoned chalice of employment with Aurélien Castile and his unreadable son.

Now and then, he tried to tell himself that what was happening – what had begun in August with the Coming Darkness and was about to get much worse – was a surprise. He wished – as fervently as he had wished for Dimitri to be born safe and well – that he could believe the lie that he hadn't known the endgame to the Castiles' insane plan.

But that wasn't possible. With the tasks he had been set, it had become clear.

When they first arrived on the island in May of the previous year, he had worked almost exclusively with Johnson Pederson, devising and coordinating the digital systems that would make Haré Stronghold future proof, self-sufficient and secure. Little by little, the Castiles had then turned their attention to their weaponry and Kaldonov had felt unease when he was tasked with creating a native AI capable of managing the 'ring of fire' defences.

'No such system is ever foolproof,' he told them. 'Look at autonomous driving. It took thirty years for small fleets to become reliable – and only in major cities where their inboard systems are supported by on-street infrastructure.'

'The priority is our security,' Castile Senior. 'Don't you want that for your husband and for your son?'

His work then became focused on the creation of the self-propagating, evolving AI virus, code-named in Bulgarian as 'Огън', meaning 'Fire'. He tried to convince Castile Senior of the risks.

'The virus might compromise military failsafes, igniting a nuclear holocaust capable of destroying the Earth's biosphere, rendering Haré Stronghold pointless.'

'Then you must prevent. This is your job, not mine,' Castile Senior had barked in reply in his clumsy English.

It had been his most difficult coding task, devising mechanisms for the AI to recognise specific installations and respond accordingly. He ran thousands of simulation tests on his modelling systems and was, finally, convinced that he had made the program as safe as was humanly possible.

'But that is the problem,' he told Stoyan. 'My safeguards won't necessarily contain the evolving virus, once it's in the wild.'

Oddly, back then, Kaldonov's worries weren't shared by Stoyan or Mitya, as he liked to be called. They both enjoyed the mild weather and, intermittently, the exciting storms. The island was big enough to be hiked but not so large that they ever ended up too far from home. The geology provided easy climbing and safe caving. The sea offered a single sheltered beach on the south shore, below the solar observatory, where it was safe to swim – and Pederson had installed a shark net as additional protection.

This had all changed a few weeks ago, of course, when Kaldonov had worked out the level of surveillance that he and Stoyan and Mitya were under. Recently, neither he nor Stoyan nor Mitya had been allowed to leave the citadel. But that didn't mean that Kaldonov was powerless. Once Haré was disconnected from the web for its own protection, he was convinced the surveillance would be relaxed. And he had a plan involving the control box at the base of the antenna array.

Ever since Castile Senior had learned of Kaldonov's aborted plan to abandon Haré Stronghold, the Bulgarian had been playing a role. He thought he had managed it convincingly. He believed that he had persuaded Castile that he regretted his moment of weakness, that he understood that Haré meant safety and security.

Was there a value for the Castiles in him and his family being content to remain on Haré? He wanted to persuade them that there was.

Although the island's digital infrastructure would end up fried, its operating systems turned to soup, some channels of analogue communication would remain, including the radio set in the control room, receiving occasional crackly broadcasts from superannuated transmitters in Haiti, Cuba and Jamacia and – when they came within range – from passing ships. Plus, there were fixed lines between the citadel and the docks and the *chefferies*. In the future, he told them, he could be useful exploiting them.

Kaldonov went to find Aurélien Castile in the control room, asking him: 'Can I help you with anything?'

'What is left?' Castile asked. 'Your knowledge is overtaken.'

'I have been thinking about Haré Stronghold and an intranet.'

'It will fail. The AI viruses will circulate for ever.'

'I may be able to mitigate that. And the resource management between wind and solar and tidal and oil will be more efficient with a computerised responsiveness, making supply meet fluctuating demand. It could be a way to extend our independence.'

'You tell me this before.'

'We could use the fixed-line telephone system as a closed network.'

Aurélien laughed: 'You want to take us back in time?'

'It may help. I am grateful, Monsieur Castile, that you came to find me in Davos and gave me and my family a future.'

'Yes, all right. That you have said before also. Make your analysis and tell me what you find.'

32

SEPTEMBER 2037

Davide found his father in the control room, busy negotiating with the captain of a shadow fleet tanker via analogue radio. When Aurélien had finished, he said: 'I want to ask you something, father.'

'What?' asked Aurélien.

'Populations will survive,' Davide told him. 'Despite the destruction, there will be communities of people who will group together and potentially pose a risk to Haré Stronghold because people always want what they do not have.'

'And your solution?'

'I think we should recruit Alexandre Lamarque as our figurehead. He is "the man who saved the world", after all. We should bring him here. I've requested his presence from the French security services, accompanying me to a meeting with President Manouche in Bamako. They will not refuse. Once we are together in person, I will see if I can persuade him.'

'You seem confident,' said Aurélien. 'What about Mariam Jordane? If she is dead then he—'

Davide interrupted: 'The timing will be such that he will not know she is dead. The Saint-Médard operation will be delayed until he and I are in the air. He will believe himself on the way back to Paris before I make our offer. We will be alone on the Ae4, *en route* for Haré.'

Davide waited.

'It is worth trying,' said his father.

Davide took the elevator from the control room up onto the circular terrace. It was around the middle of the day and the sky was bright, albeit cloaked by thin cloud. His eye was drawn by the antenna array, reminding him of the moment when Todor Kaldonov had looked up at it, then quickly away, as if to conceal some secret knowledge.

There was a Haréan servant nearby, setting the table for his father's next frugal meal.

'You are one of our trained guards, as well as an attendant?' he asked. 'Which weapon do you prefer?'

'Excuse me, Monsieur Castile?'

'For close combat, which weapon do you prefer.'

'I prefer not to get too close to danger, monsieur,' the man replied.

'Good answer. But if forced to fight hand-to-hand?'

'The combat armour that has a glove with sharp metal knuckles and fits over the forearm like a sheath, incorporating an electric stun weapon.'

'I should have a look at one and see how it functions.'

'I would be glad to show you, *monsieur*.'

'What do you call it?'

'Er, well, it's silly …'

'Go on?'

'We call it a zombie killer, monsieur.'

Davide laughed and sent the man to find one. While waiting, he strolled to the southernmost point of the terrace, to the promontory overlooking the solar observatory. Although he felt he understood his father and shared his worldview, there was an aspect of Aurélien's personality that eluded his comprehension: his interest in the superstitions of the past, in particular the apocalyptic scenario Aurélien believed he had deciphered from the petroglyphs on the standing stones.

Almost by instinct, Davide looked up into the sky, as if that was where clues to the deadly future might be found.

'Monsieur Castile?' came a deferential voice from behind him.

Davide flinched in surprise, turning from the knee-high parapet, almost banging into the servant, his heart racing. He had almost overbalanced.

'What are you doing, creeping up on me?'

'I'm very sorry, monsieur,' said the man. 'Please forgive me.'

Davide was aware of his father's propensity for sacking members of staff on the slightest pretext. He disapproved. Such arbitrary behaviour was likely to breed resentment and the island population was a finite resource.

Or perhaps we will recruit from Haiti later on? No, there are already more than enough of them. In fact, too many.

Davide inspected the hi-tech arm sheath. The man flexed his fist, making knuckle blades protrude from the black-clad armour.

'Good. Thank you.'

Davide sent him away, then climbed the ladder up onto the roof of the elevator, the breeze tugging at his clothes. He continued on the second ladder, reaching the point where he remembered Kaldonov hesitating, swapping carabiner positions with the Haréan, Yeiwene.

What was he doing?

Davide swung open the metal door of the control box and inspected the contents: a mass of intersecting wires and, along the bottom edge, a row of capacitors or transistors or printed circuits.

It all looked honest, but he knew he was not really qualified to judge.

The control box door was awkward to shut, not quite aligned on its fragile hinges. He climbed back down and returned to the control room.

'What have you been doing?' his father asked. 'Time is short. The attack at Aswan can no longer be delayed.'

'While I am gone,' said Davide, 'you will watch over Kaldonov?'

'Of course.' His father narrowed his eyes. 'Have I missed something?'

Davide pondered.

Why did Kaldonov hesitate? Was it, perhaps, because he had just become aware of the scale of what they were about to do – the waves of disaster that the Fire virus would provoke? Or was it just the weary clumsiness of a man past his prime on a windswept ladder.

'No, there is nothing new. But I believe he will betray us if we let him.'

PART 3
MARIAM

33

September 2037

While Alex was overflying the western Atlantic, struggling to pilot the Ae4 via his holographic controls, Mariam Jordane was scaling a vertical shaft of rock in a cavern carved by a subterranean river in the Saint-Médard valley. The rough surface grated at her shoulder blades as she forced herself upwards, pushing against the opposite wall with her feet.

To get to the limestone chimney, Mariam had waded the chilly underground stream and her clothes were drenched. Her footwear was unsuitable for climbing – wellington boots a size too big, borrowed from her aunt, Sara Jordane, who would never need them again. Nor her son, Mariam's foolish cousin Benjamin, who had allowed himself to be duped by the journalist, Emily Olsen, inviting her up the valley to the isolated farm so she could ask Mariam once more what it felt like to have saved humanity from catastrophe, standing beside 'the man who saved the world', Alexandre Lamarque.

The shaft was about twenty metres in height and must have been formed by erosion – water finding a cleft in the mountainside and then running through the limestone for hundreds of thousands of years, its sides smooth to the eye but grating and painful on Mariam's skin.

She was halfway up and it was her only way out. The horizontal exit from the caverns, ten metres below, was still reverberating with the roar of untamed water released by the fractured dam, rushing past, dragging with it rocks and silt and fallen vegetation, bringing countless deaths to the Pyrenean valley that her family had, for four generations, called home. Of her undistinguished line, she assumed that only she remained.

Mariam took a break, wedged between the harsh walls, allowing her pulse to settle. She felt cold. The temperature in the caverns of the underground river was between twelve and fourteen degrees centigrade. In childhood, it had been a place to come when the sun became too ferocious on the mountainside. And it had been a source of fresh water, even when the *gave* – the mountain stream that, over millennia, had carved the Saint-Médard Valley – was reduced to a trickle by failing rains, the previous season's precipitation trapped by Castile Energie behind their hydroelectric turbines.

Mariam felt a shudder as her body tried to send blood to her chilled extremities. Just for a moment, it brought her a sense of warm physical relief, but she knew that it would not last, that the blood from deep inside her body would be instantly cooled before returning to her heart and lungs, only increasing the threat of hypothermia. With an effort of will, she roused herself into motion, squirming against the rough surface of the limestone, twisting her raw shoulders right and left, inching them up the surface of the rock, then stepping her feet up the opposite wall, like a kind of reverse abseil.

Again and again, closer and closer to the opening.

The sky above – seen as if through a small hatch where the chimney-like shaft narrowed to less than a metre across – was clear, without cloud.

Again, again.

At last, she reached the part where the shaft began to taper. The climb became slightly easier as she was no longer stretching quite so far. The walls began to provide a few cracks and clefts, useful hand- and footholds that permitted her to climb it more like a ladder, taking almost her whole bodyweight on the toes of her clumsy boots.

Then she was close, within touching distance of the outside, but still in the shadows, like a cold-blooded lizard emerging from hiding, desperate to replenish its reserves of animal warmth.

The opening was, as she had estimated, a little less than a metre wide, but narrower the other way, like a slot. She had to turn her shoulders through ninety degrees in order to squeeze through, and the last foothold was too low to do this with safety. If she fell back down the shaft, she wouldn't have the strength to climb it a second time.

She turned a foot sideways against the rock wall, contorting her body, trying to place the edge of the sole of her boot into a shallow crack. A thick root from a broom bush was just out of reach, beyond the outer lip of the shaft, in full sun.

If I push off with all my strength, I think I can grab it. But what if I'm wrong?

The answer was simple. She would she fall twenty metres and lie battered and broken and no one would know that she had lived. The storm of life would be over and she would never discover whether Alex and Amaury, scattered by the winds of disaster, had survived whatever calamities they had been destined to face.

Mariam took a deep breath, preparing herself. Her fingers on the rough handholds were tiring, losing their grip. It was now or never.

If they are still alive, will they come to the Saint-Médard Valley, in a kind of pilgrimage without hope, to see the devastated landscape where I died, not knowing that I had, for a little while, hoped I might survive?

She allowed her right leg to flex slightly, then pushed upwards, turning her shoulders into the slot, striking the side of her head, flailing upwards with her weaker left hand, desperately snatching at the root of the broom. She jammed her other foot higher against the rock wall, gaining a little extra purchase. Tensing her body like a spring, she used every last ounce of strength to launch herself upwards, folding her right hand over her left, hauling herself out into full sun, scrabbling with desperate toes against the limestone, heaving against gravity and weariness and cold, squirming left and right, like a snake emerging from hiding.

Then she rolled over onto her back on the wiry grass, beneath an indifferent sun, whilst all around her was disaster.

How much time Mariam allowed herself, she did not know. At some point, her comm-watch had been broken, the screen dark and cracked. As her breathing slowly returned to normal, she watched an ant climb a stalk of grass and detach a seed with its mandible, before carrying it away.

Life goes on – at least, some life goes on.

Mariam knew she ought to rouse herself and get her body moving, but it was so much nicer simply to lie where she was, feeling the delicious pressure of gravity, no longer a challenge or a threat, but comfortably pressing her down against the dirt and vegetation of her native valley.

After a while, she rolled over and pushed herself up on her knees. She heard a dog barking and saw it, an insignificant dot on the far side of the flood, jumping left and right, unable to understand the abrupt transformation of the landscape with its tiny canine brain.

Mariam could hardly comprehend it herself. The valley as she had known it was gone, replaced by a rushing torrent of water that had scoured out the soil and vegetation. High to her left, the damage to the dam wall made a tall, vertical cleft, through which the water gushed about a third of the way up, meaning at least two-thirds of the massive quantity retained in the reservoir had already escaped, dragging with it vast quantities of silt.

In the centre of the valley, the flood still ran about twenty metres wide, but the flow had clearly been much broader at first, as she could see from the shiny deposits of heavy wet mud that coated the land a further forty or fifty metres either side. And, right beneath where she stood on a shoulder of limestone, the rushing waters had scoured into the hillside and brought down a tumble of rock over the more accessible entrance to the underground river that had provided her with a way to cheat death.

Feeling a little strength returning, Mariam stood and followed the shoulder of limestone downhill, parallel to the flooded valley. She pushed through a waist-deep stand of broom bushes, their yellow flowers all gone over to brown. Beyond them was a small dip in which a few conifers had managed to take nourishing root in a pocket of deeper soil. She put a palm on each trunk as she stumbled through them, realising she was desperately thirsty and that there was an irony in that because the vast excess of destructive water was doubtless laden with toxins from the floor of the reservoir.

Beyond the stand of conifers, she found she could look down on the place where her aunt's farmhouse had stood, now just a few broken teeth of stone in the jaw of the land, not a single plant left standing in the carefully tended market garden, just uniform beige mud.

Beyond the torn foundations of the farmhouse, however, the barn remained intact, set apart on slightly higher ground, above the sweep of the valley, with about thirty centimetres of water lapping against the heavy doors. Mariam could reach it most of the way on dry ground. For a few seconds, she imagined her family finding shelter there, but she knew that wasn't possible. They had been higher up the valley, directly in the path of the sudden flood.

Before descending any further, she shaded her eyes, looking into the distance. From the shape of the land, she knew the location of the cemetery where she had so recently buried her sisters, but no visible evidence of it remained. Beyond that, the road had been peeled away and stretches of tarmac were piled randomly against knobs of protruding rock. At the limit of vision, Mariam could just make out the path of the flood, passing the small town of Saint-Médard, named after the patron saint of storms, no doubt taking most of the buildings with it, but leaving intact the church and a few other houses nearby.

Of course, in this place, a flood was nothing new. The inhabitants of the Saint-Médard Valley were all aware, through an immemorial oral tradition, of the likely path of any inundation from well before the era of the dam. Its eight-hundred-year-old church would have been built out of the path of disaster, thanks to the wisdom of even older generations.

Mariam felt a flicker of hope. Might her aunt and her cousin have leapt in the farm truck and, aided by the steep slope, managed to escape the flood, finding sanctuary behind the thick stone walls of the Norman church?

No, that was impossible, too. The wave came on far faster than any farm vehicle could outrun.

Mariam left the trees, navigating a path along the ridge, twice taking too much risk and almost sliding down into the rushing waters that had become a kind of oppressive white noise in her ears, a sound that she briefly thought would never end, a traumatic memory she would never fully digest.

The ridge rose again. Scrambling on all fours, she crested a lump in the terrain and found a path that led to the only remaining dry ground belonging to the farm, then she splashed through muddy water not quite overtopping her boots, but feeling the too-big wellingtons being sucked down with every step, clenching her toes to keep them on.

The heavy door of the barn was hard to open because the flood had deposited a pile of debris against it. Because it ran on horizontal runners, she was able to slide it just far enough to one side to allow her slim form to slip inside.

The sloshing water round her feet was eerily dark. She made for the rudimentary staircase – not much more than a ladder – to the first floor where smaller items of farm equipment and work-wear were stored on rough timber shelves. She found a decent pair of boots in a suitable size and a change of clothes. Leaving her wet things in pile that dripped down through the rough floorboards, making a ticking sound like a water-clock, she put on some winter long-johns and a set of blue overalls whose legs and sleeves she had to fold back to achieve a reasonable fit. The dry fabric irritated her wounds but helped her to warm up.

She went back to the ladder and looked down to the dirt floor of the barn. The sunlight through the slot she had opened in the heavy sliding door came in low, illuminating the timber walls, showing a dark line nearly a metre higher than the sloshing remains of the inundation.

She didn't want to climb down and get wet again, so she crossed the dusty boards, past a few bales of straw to the first-floor window. Built hard up against the hillside, there was a Mediterranean holm oak outside, its strong branches spread wide enough to push against the feather-edged external cladding. Mariam clambered up onto the window ledge, pushing aside the whippy twigs that scraped at her cheeks, launching herself out, through the thinner branches and towards the trunk, slamming in and wrapping her arms around it, smelling the distinctive aroma of its bark.

Winded by the collision, she paused before carefully climbing down to dry ground, half tripping as she stumbled out from beneath the lowest branches, almost on hands and knees. She emerged onto another shoulder of rock, peppered with tufts of rough grass, wincing at the coarse fabric of her overalls against the lacerations on her shoulders.

I'll make for the church and try and get through to Claudine Poiret's office. If Alex is alive, I want to be wherever he is.

34

Only part-way down the valley, keeping to higher ground out of the flood, Mariam spotted an inbound helicopter with military insignia. She waved her arms above her head and was gratified when it landed just fifty metres away on an area of flat ground. An airman jumped down. Mariam identified herself with her personal trilog – that he seemed briefed to expect – then he raised his voice to a shout: 'We've come to escort you to Bordeaux–Mérignac airport. Are there any other survivors?'

'Perhaps in the village,' she began, indicating the remaining houses clustered further down the valley, round the church.

'I mean military personnel – your bodyguard, for example?'

'Everyone who was in the valley is gone.'

He helped her on board and she strapped in. The distance to Bordeaux–Mérignac was about three-hundred and fifty kilometres, a little more than an hour's flight. On the way, she dictated a report on how the Saint-Médard dam had been breached. Then, she was given access on a tablet to a saved news report that showed her the traumatising catastrophe at Aswan, plus the information that Amaury had been there, standing in for her and for Alex at the important ceremony of celebration.

It's our fault he's dead, she thought, horrified. *He is only dead because he had to replace us once Alex and I became tired of being the public face of 'triumph'.*

'Can I see any more by going live?' she asked.

'There is currently no "live".'

The airman showed her how to open a terse official report, accompanied by embedded video-grabs, about the DGSI agent Emmeline Cantor's home in the fourteenth arrondissement from which the body of 'another traitor', André Chambon, had been recovered. She was appalled to learn of Professor Fayard's 'second death', smothered and crushed by expanding construction foam.

The ceremony in Montparnasse cemetery was a smokescreen. What a terrible death.

Mariam found herself overwhelmed.

So much death. I wonder what he was able to achieve in hiding.

On arrival, Mariam was delivered to the military wing of the airbase, protected by a double ring of steel, fences topped with razor-wire and surveillance cameras. She was encouraged to rest for a while in a rudimentary barracks dormitory designed for four but, in deference to her recent experiences, the space was all hers. In other circumstances, she might have spread her belongings across the quartet of narrow beds. But she had no belongings. Everything she owned that she had brought to the Saint-Médard Valley was gone – even the clothes she had been wearing when the dam ruptured.

A medical orderly came to clean and bandage her lacerations, then she lay down, finding herself in a daze of grief and loss, on a come-down from the overwhelming surge of adrenaline, leaving her body in a state of near collapse. After a while, another airman came to find her, knocking tentatively at the frame of the open doorway.

'Doctor Gabra is expecting you, Mademoiselle Jordane. I have been sent to accompany you.'

Mariam raised her head. It felt like she was wearing some kind of helmet, heavy and alienating, muffling the airman's words.

'Now? I just got here.'

'No, mademoiselle. You've been asleep almost two hours. I've been watching you.'

Mariam sat up. The airman gestured to a small chest-of-drawers under the window.

'I'm supposed to insist that you drink and eat first.'

'Can't we just get on with it?'

'I'm sorry,' said the airman, his voice soft with sympathy. 'I have orders.'

On a small tray was a carafe of water, a cheap glass tumbler and an energy bar labelled '20g of protein'.

'Pass it to me, then,' said Mariam, subsiding back onto the bed.

The airman put the tray beside her, pressing it down into the thin bedclothes for balance. He waited for a few seconds, then opened the packaging of the protein bar and put it in her hand. The knobbly surface was oily beneath her fingers with a faint odour of carob. The airman poured water from the carafe into the cheap glass.

'Perhaps if you drink first?'

Without a word, Mariam did so, then bit into the sickly snack, chewing reluctantly, but knowing her body needed the sustenance. At the same time, the suffocating weight of her grief and loss made it feel like trying to gnaw a pine cone or swallow a handful of sand.

The airman refilled the glass. She drank and pressed on, knowing that he would insist – that he was ordered to insist. Despite her status as a hero, it was not inconceivable that the authorities, in the person of the manipulative Damien Gerest, the head of French intelligence, might resort to force-feeding 'for her own good'. Finally, there was only a small bite of the energy bar left. She held it out.

'You finish it,' she said.

The airman made a hopeless, regretful face: 'You should try because—' He stopped, as if he had been on the verge of some indiscretion. 'You will need your strength.'

For the first time, Mariam made an effort to focus her gaze on the insignia on the airman's chest. He was not simply air force. He also wore the emblem of the Directorate-General for External Security. A name came into Mariam's mind.

'You're Paul Sanchez. I'm sorry, we've never properly met. Alex talked about you—'

'A great man,' interrupted Paul. 'And you, too – a hero.'

'Is there news of Alex? Why are you here?'

Paul looked pained.

'Mademoiselle Jordane, I have orders and … Please finish eating, then I will take you to the trauma counsellor. After that, there will be a further briefing.'

Looking at his serious, desperate expression, Mariam stood up, put the final piece of energy bar in her mouth and chewed. When it was gone, she opened wide to show him. He nodded.

'This way, please.'

Once Paul Sanchez had left her alone with the trauma doctor, Mathieu Gabra, Mariam wished she had insisted that the airman should tell her what he knew.

If Sanchez doesn't dare mention Alex, does that mean he's still alive?

Gabra spoke for some time without Mariam paying him any attention, his words like wind in the grass or distant birdsong, pleasant but devoid of meaning. She forced herself to concentrate.

'Your reluctance to eat and drink and sustain yourself – these are very reasonable reactions to the trauma you have endured,' said Gabra, a half-smile of sympathy on his face.

The 'trauma doctor' had dark curly hair, veering to grey, and a saggy, narrow face like a disappointed snake. His eyes were dark, too, and meant to be kind, but Mariam found their expression patronising. His hands were flat on the steel tabletop – the meeting was happening in an interrogation room – either side of a small tablet computer.

'Does that work?' asked Mariam. 'Do you have a connection?'

'Enough to wake it up but, the last time I did, the device became infected.'

'Show me.'

Gabra picked up his tablet and showed his face to its camera to wake it. The screen came dimly to life. Gabra turned it to show Mariam a black-and-white image of a sunrise – or perhaps a sunset – between storm clouds.

'Do you know what that is?' he asked. 'It wasn't there before.'

'It means we've lost,' she told him. She visualised the shrine her aunt had made for her twin sisters. She found herself describing the scene: 'Soapstone effigies, slightly sinister shapes in a burning bed of fragrant, aromatic wood – rosemary and sage and cedar, the scents of remembrance.'

Gabra told her: 'Ritual and ceremony are important as ways to digest trauma.'

'Why are you here, doing this? Why is it not an AI counsellor?' she asked him.

'Madame Poiret sent me here to be on hand after your sisters' funeral. She was concerned for your welfare.'

'I've read your book, "toxic" something.'

'I'm flattered. It was the publisher who wanted that title: *What Remains: the toxic legacy of distress.* I wanted to call it *The Healing Myth.*'

'Why?'

'Because we do not heal. We carry trauma with us and have to cope with that burden. Trauma is not what happens to us on the outside. It is what happens inside us in response.'

Mariam frowned, thinking about how evasive Paul Sanchez had been.

'Why am I here, exactly?' she asked.

'For me to help you.'

'Do what?'

'Begin to digest what has happened.'

'Is Alex dead or alive?'

Gabra didn't answer, asking her instead: 'You are aware of the catastrophe at Aswan?'

'I was briefed in the chopper.'

'And Montparnasse?'

'Some.'

'And, of course, you were there, in the Pyrenees. Civilian teams have been sent to the Saint-Médard Valley, though not as quickly as the military helicopter despatched to find you. It is possible that your aunt or your cousin survived, perhaps carried away by the flood, injured and isolated. If so, they will be found.'

'In your experience,' asked Mariam, 'is there a value to false hope?'

'Its value may simply be – I am telling you this in all frankness – to allow time to pass, to accustom oneself to the idea of loss.'

Mariam did not reply. She knew that, right now, she was doing what he described – allowing time to pass, breathing the stale air in the windowless interrogation room.

Why did I read his book? To prepare for the loss of my sisters. Did it help? I don't know.

'Back to Alex,' she insisted. 'You asked if I was briefed about Aswan and Montparnasse and you told me about the searches in the Saint-Médard Valley. You said nothing of Alex.'

Gabra held her gaze, evaluating, she thought.

He's trying to work out how I will react to what he has to tell me.

'Hope,' said the trauma doctor quietly, 'is sometimes harder than grief.'

The truth crystallised in her mind, without him needing to say it.

'He might be alive.'

Gabra was very still. 'There is a chance.'

'Where is he?'

Gabra looked pained. 'There is a protocol we must go through. I ought to have been more circumspect. I, too, feel the collective trauma of what has occurred, like an enormous cosmic cry of terror and distress. The numbers are so extreme, in Egypt above all, but also from the software failures. You know, there are entire wards of intensive-care patients whose AI-regulated medications have … have …'

'Simply stopped?'

'No, far worse. The progress of the AI viruses isn't simply to wipe out or erase. They are designed to create wild destructive swings – making vehicles suddenly accelerate or brake, driving climate control systems into excessive heating or bitter cold, administering overdoses and violent withdrawals of medication. The aim is chaos, not destruction.'

'Is there a difference?'

Gabra took her bitter enquiry seriously.

'It would depend on the time frame but, in the end, perhaps not.'

'So, before you tell me what has happened to Alex,' Mariam insisted, 'I have to prove that I can cope with the news, respond rationally, make myself available for further service?'

'In broad terms.'

'How long will that take?'

Gabra gave a small smile.

'In my judgement?'

'Yes.'

'We are nearly there.'

Mariam leaned towards him.

'You know, if you don't approve me straight away, I can easily reach across this desk and beat the truth out of you?'

'Yes, I do know that,' he told her, shrinking into his chair. 'Please don't.'

35

Mariam didn't reach across the steel desk and 'beat it out of' the trauma doctor. She endured the protocol. Ten minutes later, she recognised a tone of finality coming into Mathieu Gabra's voice.

'You demonstrate a normal human response to extraordinary circumstances and you are, in my judgement, capable of acting purposefully, responsibly. You cannot escape what is inside you, but you are equipped to recognise it and separate it from your logical, pragmatic mental processes. As an individual, you have a heightened – that is to say above average – level of compassion, including for people you have never met, making this difficult for you in the short term, but equipping you better than most as the initial acute empathic response fades. You are, through your work, acculturated to distress.'

'Is that a made-up word – "acculturated"?' Mariam asked.

'All words are made up, aren't they?' he quibbled. 'We say "chair", though it might be any other sound the human voice is capable of producing, as long as we all agree.'

'Fine, I'm "acculturated", like a lobster in a pot that doesn't know it's boiling to death. Is that what you mean?'

'Your behaviour is regulated, internally, by your will and, externally, by your sense of your wider responsibilities.'

'To my work?'

'And to your fellow human beings, in particular those who share your world-view and your goals.'

Mariam thought about the virally generated image on the doctor's tablet – the potential for chaos to give way to either a sunset or a sunrise through storm clouds.

Which is it? Sunset, surely. We've lost, but Alex might still be alive.

'In summary, then?' she prompted. 'I'm cleared to return to active duty?'

'You are. I just have to submit my report.'

'To whom?'

'Madame Poiret.'

Mariam frowned.

'How can you do that if all comms are disrupted?'

'We intend to try the analogue radio station. Would you like to come with me?'

The radio operator's room was not far, down a nondescript windowless corridor, then briefly outside, crossing the tarmac apron. Mariam and Doctor Gabra entered one of the ubiquitous air-force portacabins used as mobile accommodation or offices, stamped with the service's shield. Inside, a floor-standing air-con unit was whirring away, taking the heat and humidity out through an irregular hole that had been amateurishly cut in the wall, with yellow expanding foam holding the pipe in place. The sight of it gave her a flashback to what she had learned in the chopper about Professor Fayard.

The radio operator turned from the console – equipment that looked as if it had recently been assembled from cannibalised parts of other devices. It was Paul Sanchez once more.

This is a tight-knit operation, but that's not surprising. With so much treachery, it's the obvious thing for Claudine Poiret to do, to restrict those 'in the know' to the absolute minimum.

'Before I make my report,' Gabra told her, 'be aware that the psychological and emotional component can lead to physical symptoms. The mind and the body are not "connected". They are one and the same thing.'

'Sure.'

But there's almost no one left.

'Physical illness through inflammation or other causes,' said Gabra, 'is a natural consequence of distress. Because of your profile and experience and training, you may find yourself energised at first, but weakened later.'

'Weakened by what?'

'Intractable conditions whose risk factors are multiplied by trauma. Cancer, arthritis, addictive behaviours, mental breakdown—'

'Fine. I understand. I'll be aware.'

'We can meet again before you leave. I would like to give you the full benefit of my presence here.'

'You think a lot of yourself, Doctor Gabra,' said Mariam.

'Connection made,' said Paul, suddenly.

He flipped a toggle switch, pulled off his headphones, and a noise like hail falling on a tin roof filled the sparse room from an external speaker. Paul spoke his trilog call sign – a three-word identifier that would have been backed up by voice recognition on digital comms. No reply came. They waited. The hissing went on, unbroken.

'What's the problem?' asked Mariam.

'Maybe the storms in the Caribbean,' said Paul. 'There's atmospheric electrical activity.'

'Is that where Poiret is?'

'On the *Roussillon* with the relief effort. I've been in touch with her office in Paris on the wideband emergency channel. It's a coincidence, really.'

Mariam remembered Professor Fayard's oft-repeated words.

There's no such thing as coincidence, just undiscovered patterns of cause and effect.

'A coincidence connected to what?' she demanded.

'Captain Lamarque is there, too,' said the doctor, abruptly.

'Where?' Mariam asked. 'On board the frigate?'

'No,' said Paul. 'His whereabouts are unknown, but Madame Poiret's deputy, Madame Hidalgo, received information that the plane he was aboard came down near the border between the Dominican Republic and Haiti, that its final destination was the island of Haré.'

'Where is that?'

'Off the Haitian coast.'

'Which side of the border did he come down?' asked Mariam, knowing there was a difference – the Dominican Republic a functioning modern democracy and Haiti a failing state.

'Unknown,' said Paul. 'Too low to be tracked.'

'But he survived?' demanded Mariam. 'Don't we have black-box comms with the aircraft?'

'Not one of ours. It was registered to Castile Energie.'

'Have we been in touch with them?'

Paul nodded.

'A member of Madame Hidalgo's staff has been sent in person to their Paris office, but I don't know what they've discovered.'

'Castile Energie own the dam that was deliberately breached and killed my family.'

'Mademoiselle Jordane,' said Mathieu Gabra, 'remember our conversation. You are becoming overwrought.'

Mariam slapped a hand down on the desk, the draft of air sent a sheet of paper wafting to the floor.

'Tell me everything.'

'I can do that just as soon as Doctor Gabra's report is submitted,' said Paul, apologetically. He waved a hand helplessly at the pointless white noise that filled the room. 'But I can't get through. Until then—'

Mariam interrupted: 'Alex told me that the Bordeaux–Mérignac data systems constitute a closed intranet, only connecting to external networks for brief periods on a rolling schedule.'

Paul nodded.

'The software firewalls provided an instant alert when the intranet opened up for update, telling the technicians the base was under hack-attack, and they were able to isolate some of the kit, some of the databases.'

'So,' she asked, 'we're not completely on our own?'

Paul equivocated.

'The viruses are everywhere in the wild. Everything's connected and the only systems that are safe are those that aren't. We can't open up. It would just invite meltdown.'

Impatiently, Mariam insisted: 'Encode the doctor's approval on the wideband emergency channel and send it to someone else with authority. What about Damien Gerest?' she suggested, the civilian head of French intelligence.

'The director is under arrest,' said Paul, adding: 'Don't ask me why. I don't know.'

'Then Madame Hidalgo.'

'Doctor?' Paul asked.

'Go ahead,' confirmed the trauma counsellor.

There was a delay on the analogue radio channel as Paul confirmed his identity and status, then did the same for Dr Gabra. Finally, he was put through to a woman with a clipped Parisian accent who expressed her delight that Mariam was alive, extended sympathy for her losses and immediately reinstated her for active service 'on the authority of the office of Madame Poiret'.

'How do we get to the Caribbean, Paul?' asked Mariam, once the connection was closed.

Gabra put a hand on Mariam's arm.

'My goal, in all of my work, is freedom.'

'What does that mean?' Mariam demanded, impatiently.

'That we, victims of trauma, should not be played like puppets, dancing on wild strings of distress.'

Mariam left a pause, mentally unpacking the doctor's poetic summation.

'I'll bear it in mind.' She shook off his hand. 'The sooner the better, Paul, don't you think?'

Paul stood up and told her: 'There may be a way.'

Prepping the sole aircraft still capable of making the transatlantic flight took very little time. Paul took Mariam to a distant hangar on the perimeter, close to a fence, beyond which was grass banking. On the crest of the rise, beyond a second perimeter, a protest was going on – perhaps a hundred civilians and a couple of camera crews.

'What do they want?' asked Mariam.

'I have no idea,' said Paul. He steered their lightweight electric buggy inside the hangar where a bulbous aircraft was standing. They got out. 'Here it is.'

'What am I looking at?'

'It's a hydrogen BWB two-seater, a blended-wing-body plane.' He looked at her quizzically. 'Do you want to know more?'

'Go on.'

'It's a third-generation fuel-test prototype. The first version began flying in 2027 and progress has not been as quick as they wanted – for the commercial applications, I mean. But this smaller model performs well.'

'How do you know about it?'

'Since the Coming Darkness, I've been given more opportunities to fly. Captain Lamarque became "the man who saved the world" and Director Gerest liked to sell me as a hero, too. It's silly but—'

'I get it. Gerest is only interested in external optics and his own career. You said he'd been arrested. What's happened, exactly?'

'I'd tell you if I knew.'

'All right. Go on. This is a twin-seater?'

'Yes. Hydrogen combustion engines, advanced materials, load alleviation. The initial design idea was green, a CO_2 reduction compared with kerosene of up to eighty-eight per cent. The blended-wing-body design allows for the volume requirements of hydrogen fuel.'

'How come it's operational?'

'Not bricked, you mean? Because it's isolated as a test vehicle, not part of the fleet, and it was being serviced.'

'You mean there's something wrong with it?'

'There were faults indicated – you know, tell-tales on the control console – but I don't think they were serious.'

'You want us to cross the Atlantic in a plane that might be faulty?'

'Not mechanically faulty – structurally.'

'In what way?'

'You know about CNT and CNF construction?'

'I do not.'

'Carbon nanotubes and carbon nanofibers, hybrid materials, not as easy to monitor for integrity as the rivets and bolts and glue-seals in steel and aluminium.'

'So, we might fall apart in flight?'

Paul shrugged.

'This is all we've got.'

Another buggy from central stores arrived with a change of clothes – camo-pattern combat fatigues for both of them. There were also two FR-F2 rifles suitable for quick, mobile incursions, each with three detachable box magazines. They only weighed five kilos each and Mariam knew they were Alex's preferred weapon. The quartermaster's buggy also delivered two Glock Fr20 handguns.

Once these were stowed on board, Paul rapped on the door of a portacabin office. An older man emerged in blue air-force overalls. He and Paul embraced. Mariam went to join them.

'Mariam Jordane,' the older man said. 'You are more beautiful in real life than on the streams.'

'That isn't an appropriate way to introduce yourself, Papa,' said Paul. He spoke apologetically to Mariam. 'My father is of a previous generation. He doesn't mean anything by it.'

'It's fine,' said Mariam. 'Can we fly, Monsieur Sanchez, right now?'

'Good to go,' said Paul's father. 'But let me give you something.' He turned away to a small fridge tucked in an angle of the hangar's steel skeleton. From inside, he brought out a paper bag, thrusting it at Mariam. 'You don't want to get too thin.'

'Jesus, Papa,' said Paul.

Mariam thanked Sanchez Senior for the packed lunch and they climbed on board. Paul took the controls for take-off and he and Mariam were soon in the air because no other aircraft was in a position to use the runway. Once he had found a suitable cruising altitude with a helpful wind, Paul engaged the autopilot, saying: 'I need to sleep. I've been awake for twenty-four hours.'

Mariam was very tired, too, aching from the chill and physical challenge of her escape from the underground river. They both reclined their seats to their furthest extent while the sophisticated BWB aircraft ate up the distance.

The future, thought Mariam, *and the answer to the question of whether Alex is alive or dead, will only be resolved by time.*

PART 4
PARIS

36

A little over eight hundred kilometres north of Bordeaux, in the French capital, the emergency services had gone and the DGSI agent Emmeline Cantor was contemplating the fact that she was now homeless. It was obvious that apartment had been made uninhabitable by the insidious and unexpected assault on her secret house-guest, Professor Fayard. Before she had decided what to do, she received an in-person message from Gloria Lamarque's security detail.

'Captain Lamarque's mother sends her compliments.'

'She's out of hospital?'

'Yes, mademoiselle. She asked me to tell you that she saw the first reports on the news streams, before they began to fail. She wishes you to know that you will be welcome to stay with her.'

'I need to report to Damien Gerest.'

The security officer shook his head.

'Director Gerest is under arrest.'

'How come?'

'Above my pay grade,' he told her.

Emmeline and the officer took an autodrive taxi across Paris – an uncomfortable, lurching trip – with just a small bag of possessions and the clothes she stood up in, an athleisure track suit. Exiting her robot transport, the officer indicated the front door and its control pad, saying: 'Four-seven-four-seven.'

He crossed the road to the terrace of a nearby café. Emmeline entered the door code and pushed through into a large, cobbled lobby, designed two hundred years before to accommodate a horse-and-carriage. She made for the lift.

Gloria Lamarque lived in a generous-proportioned apartment in the Marais, on Boulevard Henri IV, a 'noble' street of six-storey houses built in the early nineteenth century in an area of – at that time – recently drained swamp to the east of the ancient city centre. Emmeline emerged onto the fourth-floor landing, knocked and waited. Her eye followed a trailing wire from a plug socket near the floor to a camera set in an angle of wall and ceiling: the in-building surveillance. She heard footsteps inside and a hand fumbling with a key. The door opened, framing Gloria Lamarque, dressed in a grey cardigan and tartan skirt.

'How are you, my dear? This is a great pleasure. Thank you for responding so quickly.'

'I ...' Emmeline began, then faltered.

What could she say? She carried an enormous burden of guilt. Why hadn't she perceived the threat? Why had she allowed Professor Fayard to persuade her to keep his presence a secret, even from those she would have trusted with her life.

'What is it, Mademoiselle Cantor?' asked Gloria, her head on one side.

'I tried to protect him. I thought ...' She screwed up her eyes. 'Should I have refused?'

'If you are speaking of the professor, it was inevitable that he would do something of the sort – a subterfuge in order not to be removed from the game. Even with the doctor's convincing testimony at the tomb in Montparnasse cemetery, I found it hard to believe that he was gone.'

Emmeline acknowledged that was true.

'And your son, Captain Lamarque, is there any news?'

'None. I hope he has colleagues alongside him should assistance prove necessary or useful.'

'Why would it not?' asked Emmeline, uncertainly.

'Assistance would be superfluous were Alexandre already dead, don't you think?' said Gloria.

There was a small pause. Emmeline was shocked by Gloria's matter-of-fact tone. She also knew she ought to enquire about Madame Lamarque's health.

'And you are—' she began.

'The recreational drug I was attacked with,' interrupted Gloria, 'has done me no lasting damage, except that the repeated hospitalisations have caused me to lose strength and puff. But here we are, still on the doormat. What am I thinking? Come in, please.'

Gloria led Emmeline to a large bedroom at the end of a corridor, with two tall windows overlooking the building's courtyard and several smallish paintings on the walls, all views of Paris. A wash basin was plumbed into one corner, with a patch of linoleum in front to protect the dark-polished floorboards. The small double bed was made up with a light coverlet and two sensible pillows, without fringes or lace trim. Beside the bed was a green-and-red rug with a pattern of roses. On it was a pair of hotel slippers.

'This is a wonderful room,' said Emmeline, distractedly.

'Thank you, my dear. Take a moment, then come and meet me in the front room where I have opened the windows onto the street. The air is dry today, not humid. You might enjoy the late-summer scent of the orchard down the centre of the boulevard.' Gloria sighed. 'Alexandre is – or was – very fond of the apple trees'

Gloria left her alone and Emmeline spent a little time just sitting on the edge of the bed, taking advantage of a few minutes of solitude – as Gloria had no doubt intended – feeling she had already proved herself a burden, allowing her raw emotion to spill out on the public landing.

After a decent interval, she found Gloria in the front room, drinking tea from bone china decorated with pale-blue flowers. Emmeline accepted a cup and saucer and sat down. Through the open windows, they could see the tops of the apple trees, their leaves turning russet and gold.

'We will not,' said Gloria, 'speak of the past. You understand? I am grateful for your company, but there is no point, I'm sure you agree, trying to anticipate and …' Gloria stopped, sighing. 'Oh, dear. I meant to make a coherent speech, but I find I don't have the energy. Perhaps you sympathise? Too much has happened – is still happening.'

'It's the opposite of my usual mindset, but yes, we should wait and see whether more information comes.'

'You are aware of the ongoing communications problems?' Gloria asked. 'Perhaps, with all the, er, drama, you have lost touch?'

'Things are getting worse,' said Emmeline, simply. 'It's a cascade.'

'You know,' said Gloria, 'I used to be able to contact Professor Fayard and even Madame Poiret in the office of the president. I have become concerned, though …' Her eyes scanned the room. 'There is a question, do you see, about whether such news as I might glean is safe to speak aloud? One never knows …'

Gloria pursed her lips meaningfully and waved a hand. Emmeline realised it indicated a suspicion that her apartment might be bugged. Emmeline felt a small surge of adrenaline. Here was something useful she could do.

'We have a system,' she said. 'A kind of sequence of checks we are trained to undertake.'

'You mean at the Directorate-General for Internal Security?'

'Yes, I do. Given you have twice been a victim of—'

'Yes,' interrupted Gloria, determinedly. 'I approve. Let us pursue your sequence of checks. I detest the idea that I might be spied upon, even more than I resent the attempts on my life and sanity.'

They shut all the doors and windows in order to make the apartment as quiet as possible, then stood, in silence, in each room in turn, listening for unexplained noises, turning off each of Gloria's own electronic appliances as they came to them. Once that was done, Emmeline found a stool from the kitchen and climbed up to investigate all the pendant light fittings, the smoke and heat and CO_2 sensors, checking for any signs of tampering. Finding nothing malicious, Emmeline asked Gloria to carefully re-assess the positions of her vases and knickknacks, her wall-paintings and hangings.

'Are any of them out of place or set at an unusual angle?'

'I don't think so,' said Gloria, uncertainly. 'But how would I know? I'm not house-proud to the point of mania like Alexandre.'

Emmeline nodded. It was true. There were books and papers on every surface, three computers – two portable and one superannuated fixed model – all manner of bric-a-brac. She crouched down on the floor and verified the power cables that trailed behind the furniture to make sure that each one was connected to an innocent destination, such as a lamp or other device. Again, all the wires came up clean.

Emmeline closed the curtains in all the rooms, then embarked on the laborious process of checking for lenses that might be hidden in cornices or in holes in the walls or ceilings, drilled through from the far side. She did this by activating the torch function on her commwatch and playing the bright-white light across the darkened rooms while holding a cardboard tube from a toilet roll over one eye to reduce her field of vision. Twice she located what she thought might be a lens, flickering in response to the torch, but both times it turned out to be a fleck of some innocent reflective material. She also used her torch on the two built-in mirrors, each one in a different bathroom.

'If the mirror is two-way, pressing the torch against it will reveal the space behind,' she said.

Neither mirror was two-way.

'Perhaps this is not necessary, after all,' suggested Gloria, sounding weary.

'We've started. I think we should finish. I'm going to look inside the light switches. Do you have a set of tools?'

Gloria found a suitable screwdriver in a toolbox in one of the kitchen cupboards. Emmeline conducted an efficient circuit of every light switch, loosening them and looking inside, before tidily refixing them.

'Okay,' she said, emerging from Gloria's bedroom. 'Nearly done.'

In each room of the apartment, Emmeline used her comm-watch to search for wifi, bluetooth and infrared signals that could not ordinarily be accounted for.

'All my communications with the outside world pass through cables,' said Gloria. 'That is something that Alexandre taught me many years ago, when he joined the DGSI, in fact.'

'What's this, then?' asked Emmeline, showing Gloria a strong signal, whose name was a long string of letters and numbers.

'I have no idea.'

To localise the device, Emmeline fetched a heavy cast-iron skillet from the kitchen and used it to create a signal-shadow. After a minute of trial and error, she identified the source as the ancient desktop computer.

'I haven't turned that on for years – a decade, perhaps,' said Gloria.

'Well, something's alive in there right now,' said Emmeline, looking more closely. 'There's dust on the top edge but here, where an access panel has been removed, it's clean.'

She unplugged the dusty desktop. The access panel was held in place by four bolts that had been screwed in only finger tight. Behind it, attached to the computer's internal transformer and power supply, was a printed circuit covered with microscopic soldered connections.

'Is that the bug?' whispered Gloria. 'What should we do with it?'

'This device doesn't have a power supply of its own. Because I disconnected the computer it's housed in, it's dead. It may have some kind of tamper-warning that automatically sends on disconnection. Whoever planted it may already know we've found it.'

'But the obvious candidates are both dead,' hissed Gloria, referring to the two known traitors within the security services.

'True,' said Emmeline. 'But neither was working alone. The best thing would be to send it to Madame Poiret at the office of the president.

She can ask her own technicians to try and find their way upstream to whoever's been spying on you.'

'Yes,' said Gloria. 'There is a security guard watching my apartment from the terrace of the café opposite, the one I sent to fetch you. He can take it.'

'You shouldn't have left yourself unprotected.'

Gloria indicated the surveillance device.

'I should have considered this sooner, shouldn't I?'

'Perhaps, but one can't think of everything.'

'No,' said Gloria, pensively. 'One can't.'

37

Marthe Hidalgo was shocked to take delivery of a surveillance device from the home of Gloria Lamarque. She sent it to the best 'guru' technologists in the president's back-office, tasking them with identifying the source by travelling upstream from the device to its controlling software, thinking it would be some time before they reported back. She took a meeting with the co-ordinator of the Saint-Médard investigation and clean-up, then, surprisingly, two technicians arrived at her door – an antechamber to Claudine Poiret's palatial office – looking confused and sheepish. One was young with thin, lined features, the other twenty years older, sporting an unbecoming grey ponytail.

'We had to come in person,' the younger one told her.

'We can't rely on any form of communication other than face-to-face,' said the older.

'What's happened?' she demanded.

They told their story badly, interrupting one another. The gist of it was that, to their great consternation, connecting the device had simply allowed a new, rapidly mutating virus to travel downstream and overwhelm their diagnostics, swiftly replicating itself, gaining access to their entire network.

'What have you done since then?'

'We had no choice,' said the thin-faced technician, apologetically.

'What does that mean?' demanded Hidalgo.

'Total shutdown of the entire Elysée Palace,' said the older colleague. 'Until we find some way to fight back.'

'Meaning?' asked Hidalgo.

'Meaning that everybody, including us … we're all on our own.

Marthe Hidalgo convened a meeting of senior staff. Because of the digital shutdown, everyone was free to attend and it had to be moved to the largest conference room. Several times, Hidalgo had to repeat herself as the place filled up. She had taken the precaution of bringing her experts so they could explain the scientific detail. The older man took the lead, sharing his words around the long conference table.

'Almost every computer chip in existence has two vulnerabilities. We call them "spectre" and "meltdown". Each one gives malicious code the potential to gain access to privileged information, maybe even bringing down a whole operating system.'

'Can you explain these vulnerabilities in simple language?' asked Hidalgo.

He frowned, tapping a nervous fingernail on the polished mahogany.

'Modern chips – I mean since around the millennium – use speculative execution as a way of speeding up processing. The chip "speculates" probable next steps, using past experience as a guide to extrapolate from current circumstances. And it can exploit the caching of data on the chip.'

'What's that?'

'Caching is another way of speeding things up, meaning the information doesn't have to be retrieved from elsewhere. On the hard drive, that data might be protected but, in the cache on the chip, it's exploitable. That's the "spectre" vulnerability, from "speculative execution".'

'Why is that bad?'

'I just said …'. The technician stopped, looking round the cabinet room at two-dozen frowning faces. 'Okay, it's bad because it's insecure to make predictions for data and outcomes for which the chip doesn't have permissions.'

'What's the difference between spectre and meltdown?' Hidalgo prompted.

'That's a good way to look at it,' approved the technician. 'Meltdown "melts" hardware security boundaries, effectively removing them. Spectre predicts data that should have been kept secret. The end result is the same, though. Bad things can happen.'

'Such as?'

'Self-destruct on a missile? Messing with automated medication? Crazy acceleration in an autodrive?'

'If these vulnerabilities are known – if they've been known for many years – why haven't they been fixed? What's the word – patched?'

'There have been hundreds of patches, maybe thousands. Modern chips are more secure, but do you know how many legacy chips are out there?'

'I don't.'

'Billions. More chips than there are people on the planet.'

'And these old vulnerabilities play into the current crisis?'

'They do.'

'And the current crisis – is it just malicious vandalism or is it something more?'

'Oh, God, so much more.'

'In what way?'

'You remember the 2028 wildfires – simultaneously in Australia, Europe and Canada? Like that, but not by chance – meant and everywhere.'

'Wildfires?'

'Software wildfires.'

'So, destruction?'

'No, I mean the software going out of control, like a wildfire, following its own path.'

One of the other department heads interrupted.

'Why are we talking in metaphors? How do we contain it?'

The grey-haired technician looked very serious: 'Not a metaphor. The mutating code has a name. It's called "Fire". And, as for how we contain it, we can't.'

A junior member of the Palace staff came nervously in and passed Hidalgo a note. She read it and invited the meeting to adjourn to the roof.

'What for?' someone asked in an impatient tone.

'You'll see. Be quick.'

The important heads of department and their aides left the conference room and climbed two storeys to a little-used access door onto the night-time roof terrace. As each one emerged from the landing, they gasped, exchanging words of shock and astonishment.

'The aurora borealis,' said the younger technician.

Hidalgo told them. 'I've seen it in Iceland, but this is so much more vivid.' After a pause, she asked: 'The aurora is created by the interaction of Earth's atmosphere with solar flares. Could that be the reason for the software wildfires? Is it connected to the AI viruses?' They began talking at once. Hidalgo held up a hand: 'One at a time.'

The older technician waggled his head from side to side and told her: 'No, it's this thing, "Fire".'

The younger one was enthused.

'The aurora is caused by a coronal mass ejection of charged particles travelling towards Earth from the Sun. So, normal. But did you notice it was right over our heads – I mean, we didn't have to look north for it. It was all around us. Somehow it travelled all the way south.'

'And that's unusual?'

'Very rare on the scale of one human lifetime,' he went on, 'but common when you take the perspective of all of human history. I have a picture on my wall, a reproduction, obviously, of a Japanese drawing showing an aurora seen at Okazaki in February 1872. The same storm was seen in Bombay and on the Black Sea, as well as recorded at the British astronomer royal's residence in Greenwich.'

'But I believe a flare,' Hidalgo insisted, 'can disrupt networks and power girds and—'

The older man interrupted in a decisive tone.

'We would all be better off if our problems were just accidental, but the digital destruction is meant.'

The remainder of the display lasted for another ten minutes. When it was over, Hidalgo stayed where she was with the two technicians. They seemed, above all, excited.

'Are you not worried?' she asked.

'The sun doesn't care about what's happening on Earth,' said the younger man, dreamily.

'Our situation is disastrous,' she snapped. 'Tell me what the repercussions of the solar flares might be. There's a web of telecoms infrastructure all across the globe. What about that?'

'It's physically fragile, too,' said the older man. 'In the past, even submarine cables have been affected.'

Hidalgo walked away from them, trying to formulate her thoughts, feeling lost, overtaken by events outside of her control.

If it's true that the solar storm has nothing to do with events on Earth – or, rather, is impacting Earth without—

'There's no point worrying about things you can't control,' said the older man.

'Solar flares, asteroid impacts, massive volcanic eruptions,' said the younger man. 'There are things that just happen and then we, humankind, have to make the best of it.'

'They're like,' said the older man, 'a definition of "acts of God", you know? Except there is no God, only cause and effect.'

She recognised, in the words they were using, a pattern of speech that she thought they had often rehearsed – not in the sense of preparing the words like actors, but because it was a set of ideas that they had previously discussed.

Are they right? Is there nothing I can do? Am I not important in any of this?

She returned to her office where one of the monitoring team on the wideband emergency channel was waiting with an urgent message from Bordeaux–Mérignac. Hidalgo followed the woman to an analogue radio station in one of the basements of the Elysée Palace and was delighted to learn that Mariam Jordane had survived the attack on the Saint-Médard dam.

Hidalgo expressed her sympathy and passed on the information she had received from the *Roussillon*, before comms went silent, about Captain Lamarque's possible location. Then the airman on the other end of the call abruptly cut the connection – or the signal was lost – leaving Hidalgo no wiser about what might happen next.

38

In 2037, the Paris Observatory was more museum than site of scientific inquiry. Founded in the mid-seventeenth century by order of King Louis XIV, it was built on a plot well south of the Seine, outside the city walls, bisected by the Paris meridian, predating the establishment of the Royal Greenwich Observatory by eight years. Famously, the celebrated English philosopher John Locke visited and commented in his journal: 'We saw the Moon in a twenty-two-foot glass, and Jupiter, with his satellites.'

Back in 1670, astronomers gazing up at the night sky were not inhibited by light pollution or smog from modern appliances. From the late 2020s, the gradual depopulation of the French capital – and legislation removing ninety per cent of internal combustion engine vehicles – meant the skies above Paris had cleared, except for during the long over-hot summers when thick sub-tropical cloud gathered in the bowl of land in which the city broiled.

Compared to modern imaging equipment, the 'twenty-two-foot glass' that so impressed John Locke was hopelessly primitive. But the technology of an earlier age was, at that moment, being used by an enthusiastic member of the museum staff.

Régis Petit had stayed late, in order to enjoy the latest in the sequence of light shows from the extraordinary 'season of solar flares'. Once the green pulsations had ebbed, he had remained transfixed by the heavens, helped by the fact that much of Paris was in blackout due to cascading failures in the electricity supply system, reducing light pollution.

That was why, to his astonishment, he saw something that ought not to have been there.

This is not possible. I have to tell someone.

39

Gloria Lamarque and Emmeline Cantor saw the extraordinary light show, too, because they had gone out for a walk in the quiet, unlit streets, followed at a discreet distance by the security officer. Not one of them knew that the aurora was another desperate thing they ought to be worried about. Then Gloria and Emmeline were distracted by the sight of an autodrive taxi, butting its nose against a granite bollard, over and over again.

Back at the apartment, the DGSI officer told them he was being reassigned.

'With the chaos everywhere, Madame Hidalgo suggests that you make your way to the Elysée Palace to join her if that's convenient?'

'Now?' asked Gloria.

'Or in the morning, if you prefer. I'd rather be at home myself. I have children.'

Gloria reassured him that they wouldn't be going out again as the hour was late. Back in the unlit building, she and Emmeline went together to the cellar in search of candles and found some in a crate alongside a rack of dusty bottles of vintage wine, colonised by spiders and insects. They toiled back upstairs, four flights on foot in the absence of the elevator, then lit three candles and uncorked a seventeen-year-old Burgundy – the 'coronavirus vintage' – and simply sat.

'I cannot stand this,' Gloria eventually said, putting down her glass.

'No, I know,' said Emmeline.

'Due to the subterfuge around the professor's fake funeral, you've been denied access to any information sources beyond those of a normal citizen?'

'That's right.'

'If you hadn't been stood down,' Gloria asked, 'what would you be doing?'

'It's hard to say. So much of my work relied on analysis of digital records and surveillance. Do you think all that is gone for good?'

Instead of answering directly, Gloria spoke of her own world of scholarly research, past debates she had been part of around the proper media for the preservation of historical documents.

'There is always a trade-off between convenience, reliability and cost.'

'What do you think Captain Lamarque would be doing, were he in Paris?'

'I think you could reasonably call my son by his first name, don't you?'

'What would Alex be doing?'

'Alexandre would be busy, ferreting away, taking long walks to mull things over, looking for patterns that others hadn't seen.'

'How did he learn to do that?' Emmeline asked.

'I have often asked myself. Perhaps because of a certain philosophical detachment, an absence of the desire to control. Most people are swayed by how they wish things were. Alexandre is – or was – very good at seeing only what is.'

Emmeline didn't answer for a while. She felt comforted by Gloria's confidence in her remarkable son.

'I wish there was something—' she began, then stopped, hearing a crescendo of shouts from the street, and the unmistakable sound of a single gunshot from a handgun. Gloria got up in order to move towards the window, but Emmeline was quickly on her feet, preventing her. 'Stay in the middle of the room. It's safer.'

'Could it be looters?' Gloria asked.

'I wouldn't be surprised. It happens every blackout, doesn't it?'

'What should we do? We are alone. The security detail went off duty.'
'Wait here.'

Emmeline left the living room, following the corridor to the spare bedroom she was using at the back of the apartment. Among the few possessions she had brought from her abandoned apartment in Montparnasse, she found her sonic immobiliser and a handgun. She returned.

'What are those appalling things?' asked Gloria.

Emmeline reassured her that she was well trained in the use of both.

'We should have left sooner. We'll take an autodrive to the Elysée Palace. It's better to be safe than sorry.'

40

The digital exchanges had failed. Even the telephone system was down. In the Paris Observatory, though, Régis Petit was in touch with a friend, a fellow enthusiast, via citizen's band radio, using an appliance from a twentieth-century exhibit in the museum.

'Have you seen it, Bertrand?' Régis asked.

'Yes, although my telescope isn't as good as the one in the Observatory. Have you been able to look it up?'

'No, but I've been observing it. I have an idea.'

'You know what it is?'

'Before the databases went dark, I was watching for 2037 AQ9. Do you know the asteroid I mean?'

'It was supposed to pass between the Moon and Earth.'

'Exactly. Now, I'm only working from memory but, if that's AQ9, it shouldn't be *there*. That's the thing.' There was a pause, filled with white noise from the grainy analogue connection. 'Are you still there, Bertrand?'

'Yes, I was just thinking.'

'About what?'

'About what would happen if AQ9 somehow found itself caught in Earth's gravitational field.'

'You know what would happen,' said Régis.

'Yes, but maybe I don't want to think about it.'

There was another pause. Régis asked himself who he could tell.

The police? They'll just laugh at me. The mairie – the town hall – of the fourteenth arrondissement? Would there even be anyone there on duty in the middle of the night?

'Hey, Régis?' said Bertrand, his voice tinny and distant.

'Still here.'

'What about the *fréquence d'urgence* – that exists, doesn't it?'

'I don't know what that is.'

'A wideband emergency service, you know, in case there's no other way of communicating.'

'What's the frequency?'

'It's in my CB manual. Hang on. Let me look.'

'Is it monitored, though?' Régis asked, but there was no answer, just the white noise. And it went on so long that Régis began to wonder if the connection had failed. 'Hello?'

Then Bertrand was back.

'Sorry, it took ages to find it. I'm quoting: "For wideband mobile emergency services, subject to Ministry of Defence agreement, the channel is 2340–2350 megahertz." What do you think?'

'What does "subject to Ministry of Defence agreement" mean?'

'I guess that you're supposed to have permission.'

'Screw that,' said Régis. 'I have to tell someone.'

In a little-frequented basement of the Elysée Palace, in the wing of the building used by the Ministry of Defence so that its officials could remain in close contact with the office of the president, was a corridor that led to a command-and-control bunker with its own independent power supply, air and water filtration systems, digital and analogue comms. It was staffed, for reasons lost to time, following the pattern of watches on board ship: from 20h00 until midnight; from midnight till 04h00; from 04h00 until 08h00; from 08h00 until noon; from noon to 16h00. Then, the early evening was divided into two 'dog watches' of two hours each, making an uneven number, so the rotating teams of watchkeepers weren't always on duty at the same time.

In the late 2020s, under pressure from cost-cutting at the Ministry of Finance, several command-and-control services were threatened with shutdown. But it turned out, in a world in which dramatic weather events just kept on happening, they were useful, after all. Among these services was the citizen's band emergency frequency, monitored by a staff member whose role also included maintaining a record of the location of senior government members.

The emergency frequency, though, was sometimes used by pranksters, meaning French emergency responders were taught passwords that they could use to confirm their *bona fides*. Régis had no personal or professional password, but he was insistent and, finally, persuasive. Plus, in a nation of sixty million people, he was not the only stargazer to have made the same deduction, to have tried to find someone in authority to tell.

So it was that a sceptical officer was persuaded to visit – for the second time that long day – the office of Marthe Hidalgo.

41

The Paris autodrive network included call-pads installed at street corners and in the lobbies of more prosperous buildings. They had been installed using the fibre-optic comms and entertainment network and were, it seemed, still in operation.

Emmeline and Gloria awaited the arrival of their robot taxi in the cobbled ground-floor lobby, sheltered from the commotion in the street outside by the heavy double doors, wide enough to allow a horse-and-carriage to enter, but locked and barred. The pedestrian door cut into the left-hand panel was equipped with a peep-hole and a fish-eye lens. Through it, Emmeline could see the dark pavement and road and the line of apple trees down the centre of the boulevard. Beyond that, shards of glass littered the tarmac from the smashed windows of the café-restaurant opposite. It looked like it had been looted. In fact, she could still see people inside, drinking and – preposterously – dancing.

An autodrive came into her field of view.

'Now,' she said, opening the door, stepping over the sill, almost stumbling over a bearded man lying on the pavement, blood on his forehead, his eyes vague and unresponsive. 'Be careful,' she told Gloria.

'We must help him.'

'No, we mustn't.'

Emmeline approached the autodrive, one of the larger models with two pairs of facing seats. Out of habit, she raised her comm-watch to confirm her identity to the on-board software, but her device was dead.

At some point, without her noticing, the screen had gone black. The door, however, opened when she applied her thumbprint to the sensor. She turned to help Gloria inside to find the older woman several paces away, bent over the man on the pavement, saying: 'He is my neighbour from the bar.'

'Come, now,' Emmeline hissed. She was aware that they had now been seen by at least two of the looters in the café-restaurant. 'We have to leave.'

'He's gone,' said Gloria, her voice thin and unstable. 'I was about to invite him to come with us.'

'Quickly,' urged Emmeline, not wanting to move away from the autodrive in case it assumed she had changed her mind, closing its door and driving away to a charging point. 'We have to leave.'

'We should have come out more quickly,' said Gloria, shaking her head. 'We might have saved him.'

Emmeline saw a man and a woman crossing the road, stumbling on the roots of the apple trees.

'Where are you going,' the man called. 'Can we share your ride?'

Emmeline evaluated them. They seemed jovial rather than threatening, but presumably they had smashed their way into the café opposite.

'Madame Lamarque, please get in,' she said, feeling the motorised door press against her body, trying to close. 'Now.'

The drunken couple came close, the woman's eyes vague and her gait unsteady. The man headed directly for Gloria.

'Ah, that's where he went,' he said. 'I guess he crawled. He didn't want us in his establishment.' The man laughed. 'But we changed his mind.'

Emmeline reached beneath her jacket for her handgun. The man was a murderer.

Gloria stood up and asked in a tone of accusation: 'Did you do this to him?'

'He'll be all right,' said the man. 'I just gave him a little tap.'

'He's dead,' said Gloria.

Emmeline wanted to take aim at the man, but the drunken woman was in the way. She spoke in a loud voice: 'Madame Lamarque, we must go now.'

'Madame Lamarque?' repeated the man. 'The mother of "the man who saved the world"?'

The drunken woman lurched over to him and took his arm, her voice slurred and wheedling: 'Come on, let's go back inside.'

The man shook her off and took a step towards Gloria.

'Stay back,' said Emmeline, levelling her weapon. 'Keep your distance.'

'Don't kill him,' said Gloria.

'Let's go, then,' said Emmeline.

The man lunged – what for, Emmeline couldn't say. Out of deference to Madame Lamarque's request, she fired a single shot, catching the man on the inside of his right thigh. He fell in a heap, crying out, his hands pressed against the wound. Madame Lamarque sprang back, within reach. Emmeline grabbed her hand, pulling her into the autodrive, jumping in after her, allowing the straining door to seal shut. The drunk woman banged on the glass, shouting: 'What have you done? Get help.'

In a clear voice, Emmeline gave a voice command: 'Drive.'

The vehicle pulled away with the familiar surge of torque from its four electric motors, one for each wheel. Emmeline and Gloria turned in their seats to look behind them, through the tinted rear glass.

'Thank you for not killing him,' said Gloria. 'There has been too much death.'

Emmeline didn't reply. She had aimed for the man's femoral artery. He would bleed out well before help came.

42

The autodrive began to behave strangely about the time Gloria and Emmeline crossed into the restricted heart of the city. The bollards just after the Tour St Jacques sank obediently into the cobbles but, for ten long seconds, the autodrive declined to move forward.

'Drive,' enunciated Emmeline. 'Drive.'

Away they went, accelerating unnecessarily quickly, causing the tyres to spin on the cubic granite blocks. Then, within fifty metres, the vehicle began to crawl at walking pace, several times scraping the kerb.

'Is this safe?' asked Gloria.

'I don't know,' said Emmeline.

At Place de la Concorde they came to a checkpoint controlled by human police, reinforcing the automated verification, the road blocked by a solid barrier that swung up out of the tarmac. The autodrive butted the yellow-and-black painted steel, quite gently, then again, rocking Gloria and Emmeline in their seats.

'Stop,' said Emmeline.

A police officer opened the half-door of his cubicle and approached, holding a tablet computer in his hand. He gestured for Emmeline to open the tinted windows. She tried to do so, pressing the button on the door frame, but they stayed where they were.

'I have no reading,' shouted the police officer through the glass. 'My tablet won't connect.'

'To what?' shouted Emmeline.

'To the database or to your vehicle. Where are you going?'

'To the Elysée Palace,' said Emmeline.

At that moment, the autodrive stopped oscillating against the tip-up barrier and the windows descended into the slots in the doors. The police officer looked in, craning her neck to get a look at the second passenger.

'Madame Lamarque?' she asked.

'Yes,' said Gloria. 'That's right.'

'We had word to look out for you.'

The police officer returned to her kiosk and the barrier descended into its underground compartment. Emmeline decided to try a reset.

'Stop journey.' The light in the roof of the autodrive changed from green to amber, indicating it was ready for instructions. 'New destination. Elysée Palace.'

The light went green and the vehicle pulled away, apparently reset, and it was no distance from Concorde to the Elysée Palace, a short hop up Rue Royale then left on Faubourg Saint-Honoré. The autodrive came to a halt at the gate but its doors failed to open. Emmeline felt a growing unease that Gloria clearly shared.

'I feel,' said the older woman, 'that events are leaving us behind, that our knowledge is incomplete. The connections are escaping us.'

In a slot in the door was a red hammer with a point of hard metal. Emmeline prised it out.

'Turn away,' she ordered.

Shutting her eyes, she struck the tinted glass in the top right-hand corner, making a tiny hole in the laminations that crazed out. She struck it again, more firmly. The glass flexed and dispersed the shock. An officer from the gate staff approached, brandishing a tablet computer with a look of frustration on his face, like his colleague at Concorde.

'Agent Cantor, DGSI, with Madame Gloria Lamarque,' Emmeline shouted, striking the glass a third time.

For no reason Emmeline could see, the door's mechanism suddenly sprang into life, swinging open, allowing the cool night air inside.

'Thank heavens,' said Gloria. 'I was beginning to feel this journey would never end.'

Emmeline got out and helped Gloria to follow. The older woman looked drawn and tired.

'This vehicle is faulty …' Emmeline began.

She didn't need to finish. The autodrive suddenly drove on, its doors still open, then slewed right across the road, crashing into the front door of a chic clothing store. Emmeline, Gloria and the gate officer exchanged glances.

'Do you know what's going on?' he asked, a deeply worried expression in his eyes.

'No,' said Emmeline. 'We don't.'

43

Régis Petit's persistence had paid off. He had travelled from the Observatory in the south of the city on his ancient unsmart mobike, seeing all kinds of evidence of decay and failure: stranded smart buses; road-traffic collisions between smart vehicles; jammed automatic doors; frightened passers-by. Jumping off on Faubourg Saint-Honoré, he clocked an autodrive that had smashed itself into the plate glass doors of a chic clothing store.

He was allowed into the Elysée Palace only when the gate officer was persuaded of his usefulness by telling him about the likely extent of the destruction from 2037 AQ9, that he had observed its changed trajectory using the 'twenty-two-foot glass' in the Observatory. Ten minutes later, having passed through metal detectors and a compulsory hygiene station, he was led down a set of dusty stairs to a grim corridor, several flights below street level, arriving in a communications suite where two women – one older and the other very striking, with flame-red hair – sat on polypropylene chairs. A third – pale in a starched uniform – was staring, horrified, at an old-fashioned radio set.

'Are you the person I spoke to?' asked Régis. 'My name is Petit. I called the emergency frequency about the AQ9 asteroid impact.'

'That's right,' said the operative. She put a microphone to her mouth, depressing a button on the side. 'They are all here, Madame Hidalgo.'

The woman with flame-red hair asked him a series of probing questions.

'Are you talking about an impact on Earth?'

'Yes,' he replied. 'Who are you?'

'If it's on a collision course, tell me why it's not been tracked.'

'It must be because of an astral event, you know, something outside the Earth's atmosphere.'

'What possible force could have deviated its trajectory?'

'Maybe the coronal mass ejections, you know, the auroras?' said Régis, tentatively. 'The CMEs are projecting incredible energy across more than a hundred and fifty million kilometres of vacuum. They could have nudged AQ9 into Earth's gravitational field.'

'Were you able to calculate its impact location?'

'I'm just a museum tech, at the Observatory.' He shook his head, looking apologetic: 'And the viral meltdown has—'

A brusque woman with a clipped Parisian accent arrived.

'My name is Hidalgo. I work with Madame Poiret in the office of the president. I can't stay. I've just come out of a meeting with him. Madame Lamarque, I am glad to see you've arrived safely. Madame Poiret left standing orders that I was to protect you. Did you have any difficulties crossing the city?'

'Not really,' said the older woman – politely, Régis thought. 'Thank you for your consideration. But I have a question.'

'Yes?'

'Is it really such a good idea for us to be underground?'

'These bunkers were designed to be proof against attack by some of the most powerful weapons ever created.'

'I realise that,' argued the older woman, 'but we are well below the level of the Seine, are we not? I feel – forgive me if this is a foolish thing to say – like a rat in a trap, with little to look forward to beyond being drowned.'

Régis reassessed the kindly looking woman, belatedly realising who he had been talking to.

'You are the mother of Captain Lamarque, the "man who saved the world". Where is he?'

'We don't know.'

'He is in Haiti,' said the brusque woman who had introduced herself as Hidalgo.

'Alive?' asked Madame Lamarque with a gasp.

'As far as we know,' Hidalgo replied, adding apologetically: 'Our last communication was some time ago.'

'Can he do something?' Régis added, hearing the naivety in his own voice.

No one answered.

PART 5
NORTH AFRICA

44

SEPTEMBER 2037

In Bamako, the dusty capital of Mali where Alex had been instrumental in dismantling a minor terrorist cell in the Coming Storm conspiracy, President Emile Manouche was eating at his desk.

President Manouche had a sweet tooth and had chosen a generous dish of *bouille*, a classic Malian dessert with a sugary biscuit-like crust and a custard filling. He had read the report on the terrorist attack on the lithium mine at Yanfolila and knew that one of the gang had been partial to *bouille* – up until the point when Chief of Police Konaré had him shot in the public square. Like the dead man, Manouche accompanied his *bouille* with a glass of *djablani*, made from ginger, lemon and mint, to cut through the stickiness.

In his open-air office, beyond the water garden that formed a centrepiece in the presidential palace, protected by a tented roof stretched across half-a-dozen angled poles, Manouche finished his sugary dessert and leant back in his office chair, thinking hard.

The previous week, he had taken a call requesting a face-to-face meeting from Davide Castile, promising the attendance of Alexandre Lamarque – 'the man who saved the world' – to sweeten the deal. Manouche had accepted. Castile's geologists had apparently been studying Malian territory using a sophisticated artificial intelligence, discovering an ideal location to sequester carbon dioxide in natural vaults, deep underground. Then, Castile had promised, his scientists would monitor these stashes of suffocating gas for all of time.

Ridiculous. Just another way for the developed world to exploit the developing world as its wastepaper bin. No, worse, its trash dump.

Of course, nothing was ever cut and dried in politics. As the great French socialist Pierre Mendès-France had pointed out: '*Gouverner, c'est choisir, si difficiles que soient les choix.*'

To govern is to choose, however hard the choices.

Castile's corporation, MaliLith, generated a substantial percentage of Manouche's nation's GDP. And MaliLith had many small shareholders, Malian nationals, drawn by the promise of wealth from the 'miracle metal' lithium, so fundamental to the hyperconnected world's mobile communications and transport technologies. But those minor shareholdings were a kind of smoke screen, many in number but insignificant in the overall scheme of things. Profit from the mines at Goulamina and Yanfolila were, to an overwhelming degree, expatriated to France or whatever pliant administrations Castile exploited in order to minimise or even wipe out his corporate tax bill.

Manouche touched a control panel, concealed in the surface of his iroko-wood desk. A screen came to life in the tented roof – a rectangle of light. It showed him a faltering news stream depicting the inconceivable cataclysm of the failure of the Aswan High Dam, bodies heaped in mounds by the flood. He averted his gaze.

Is it possible that the disaster was, in some small and unpredictable way, my fault? I sent my childhood friend, Major Chaka Kassam, as my personal representative to the Aswan ceremony with a substantial gift of lithium from the new mine at Yanfolila and ...

Manouche shook his head, like a horse bothered by a fly.

Is it possible that Chaka is a part of the Storm? Was it he who set the charges that caused the dam to fail?

Without the president giving an instruction of any kind, the cleverly disguised screen in his tented roof switched to his text-notes software, revealing a message from Captain Alexandre Lamarque, as if from beyond the grave.

Monsieur le Président, please forgive me for infiltrating your private network. You will only see this message if I am unable, for whatever reason, to access and delete it – meaning that I am in danger.

Please use your own diplomatic channels to contact Claudine Poiret in the office of the French president. I'm not certain what information will be important to share, but she will have her own ideas.

Explain to her that, with the assistance of your police department, we have dismantled another terrorist group in the lithium mining belt in southern Mali, but the investigation was a dead end with no leads beyond that local cell.

Tell her that it is not clear to me why Davide Castile requested my presence in Bamako, but I suspect that, in the near future, his whereabouts may be crucial. You, Monsieur le Président, might be able to localise him using information from air-traffic control at Bamako airport to whom he may have to submitted a flight plan. He is not to be trusted.

Furthermore, remind Madame Poiret that she asked me to investigate the cascading digital failures. I haven't had time to do so, but my fear is that they are more than 'failures'. In my opinion, it is likely that they are deliberate accelerators of destruction. What she can do with that information, I'm not sure.

Thank you.
Alexandre Lamarque

It took President Manouche a minute or two to piece together the likely sequence of events. He had welcomed Davide Castile and Alexandre Lamarque into the palace, instructing a subordinate to allow them access to the public wifi – the one used by journalists and visitors – trusting that his own official ring-fenced comms and data would remain secure.

Lamarque must have escaped the 'guest' IT perimeter that ought to have fenced him in.

Manouche acted swiftly, sending a courier to obtain the flight plan for Castile's Ae4, logged at Modibo Keita International Airport, named for Mali's first post-independence president, located about fifteen kilometres south of the palace. Meanwhile, a junior diplomat arrived to tell him about failures across the full gamut of Malian digital systems: email; EV charging; electronic point-of-sale; comms logins; road tolls; pensions and salaries. For all he knew, the same thing was happening across the whole world.

Everything is falling apart.

He tried to contact Paris via diplomatic comms, but it proved impossible. He sent the junior diplomat in person to the nearby French embassy.

The first courier came back with news that Modibo Keita International's systems were all fried. However, one of the air-traffic controllers who had been on duty when Castile's flight path had been logged was still on shift and remembered the unusual destination.

'A direct, supersonic flight to HSX.'

'Where is that?'

'I'm sorry, *Monsieur le Président*. I didn't think to ask,' apologised his courier.

'Then go and find out.'

Manouche wondered what else he could do. If Aswan had been – if only tangentially – his fault, duty compelled him to try. He knew, of course, the story of Lamarque's defeat of the Coming Darkness. Didn't everybody?

What am I missing? How did he do that?

Manouche had a moment of inspiration.

With the unexpected assistance of someone in the Cyrenian government.

Cyrenia was a trading partner with Mali, albeit a distant one, across the Saharan wilderness.

Is there something special about Cyrenia? Do the Cyrenians have a novel technology that might escape the meltdown?

The junior diplomat returned with an extensive formal apology from the French embassy, explaining that it was 'not possible at this time to accede to his excellency's gracious request'.

So, they have lost contact, too.

The subordinate who had made the dash to Modibo Keita International returned with the presidential pilot – a young man with an air of discreet competence.

'He knows where HSX is,' said the courier with relief. 'The island of Haré in the Caribbean.'

Manouche asked: 'Do we have an aircraft that can make the flight to Cyrene City, one that can fly without digital controls?'

The pilot frowned.

'No, sir, but the southern Cyrenian airbase at Al-Jaghar is a little closer. With refuelling stops *en route*—'

'Where, for example?'

'Niamey then N'Djamena,' said the pilot, naming the capitals of Niger and of Chad, countries with which Mali entertained amicable relations.

'Good. Make it so. Let me …'

Manouche printed Lamarque's message then hesitated, wondering what to add. Twenty-four hours earlier, it would have been easy to find the names of the key Cyrenian protagonists in the defeat of the Coming Darkness,

There was a member of their presidential council who played a crucial role …

He no longer had access to the constantly evolving web of the internet. Briefly, he wondered if all that was gone for ever. The viral infections – whatever their original purpose – had clearly become feral, loosed into the wild and out of control. All of that carefully archived information – the memes and the funny dances and the music videos and the crazed rants and the Ted Talks and the social media, the constantly expanding cloud-based back-up storage – turning to an undifferentiated soup of zeros and ones.

He pulled himself together, penning a brief note that explained the provenance of his information, folded the two sheets of cream paper in half and slid them into an equally luxurious envelope, printed with the presidential seal. In the absence of a name, he inscribed it: *A qui de droit*.

To whom it may concern.

He put the message into his pilot's hand and wished him good luck. The pilot and the courier left, stepping quickly across the stepping stones through the decorative water garden.

What else should I do?

The answer, thought President Manouche, was simple.

I should pray.

45

President Manouche's pilot's name was Tamba Dem. Enrolled in the military on the advice of a belligerent father, he was grateful to have ended up working for an air force that was not involved in armed conflict with any of its neighbours.

Aged twenty-nine, Tamba still revelled in the magic of flight, the extraordinary physics that kept the heavier-than-air contraptions aloft, from the earliest preposterous successes through to present-day superjets and near-space explorers. A practical man, his favourite was the modern-but-retro Aurora Propfan.

Just two weeks before, Tamba Dem had attended his eight-year-old daughter's school to address her class on a 'bring-a-parent' day.

'An aircraft rises into the air because the wing is curved on the top. Did any of you know that?' he asked the children. His daughter raised her hand. 'Any of you,' he said, smiling, 'who don't eat breakfast with me?' The children and their teacher laughed. 'As the wing rushes through the air, the bulge on the top makes the air above the wing move faster than the air beneath. That reduces the air pressure above the wing, so the air under the wing pushes up.' He made a gesture of take-off with his hand. 'If the engines stop and there is no more fast forward motion, the difference in air pressure fades and the aircraft falls out of the sky.' He made a crashing gesture. 'An aircraft needs two things to fly: a good design and reliable engines. And, of course, you need to know where you are going and why.'

With President Manouche's message in an inside pocket of his uniform jacket, Tamba was soon in the air, his Aurora Propfan eating up the distance.

He felt fairly confident. He had been to Niamey, the capital of Niger, twice before, delivering Manouche to a summit, received with honour by association with his boss. Those trips, however, had been planned carefully in advance. Today, he was flying almost blind, with only analogue radio as back-up. He hoped that he would encounter no opposition to bringing the unscheduled plane in to land.

I might, though. These are strange times.

46

Faroukh Al-Medawi, Mayor of Tobruk, member of the tripartite presidential council, personal representative of Prime Minister Souad Mourad of Cyrenia, was driving a stolen car on a dusty road. Accompanied by the 'accidental hero' Zeina Yaseen, he was heading for a road–rail junction west of Lake Nasser, a vast body of water five hundred kilometres in length, that was even now emptying itself northwards into the valley of the Nile, sweeping away people and property, trees and houses, cars and soil, coating everything in thick beige sediment.

Nutritious, no doubt, in years to come, but not now, while it choked the life from every living thing, human, animal or plant.

Al-Medawi knew what had happened, because he had been there, at the Aswan High Dam, as an important guest of the Egyptian government, representing the independent nation of Cyrenia, a beacon of charity and tolerance in the brutal modern world. As his fragile vehicle ate up the kilometres – not wanting to allow his thoughts to dwell on death – he was exploring more distant memories.

Back when Al-Medawi was a child, the prosperous, modernising socialist republic of Libya benefitted from sharp oil-price rises. He lived in the city of Tobruk, spoilt – but also neglected – by careless parents who loved music and entertaining, good food, ostentatious religion and their powerful new French car, imported from across the Mediterranean at great expense, the same model as the French president used.

They also had a colour television, bought soon after the World Cup of Football in 1974, broadcast in attenuated colours from Germany. It arrived with enormous pomp one Saturday morning, delivered in a civil service vehicle by two men who took payment in cash and seemed inclined to dawdle, wanting to observe the device in action.

The television, of course, refused to work until an aerial had been erected on the roof of the Al-Medawi apartment building and an antenna cable pinned to the brickwork and tucked in through a hole drilled in a window frame, the blinds pulled down to prevent the sun from bleaching out the convex glass screen.

Though the broadcasts were very limited in subject matter – and though transmission occurred during only narrow tranches of each day – the television became Faroukh's friend. His parents claimed they believed it educational, but he quickly understood that they were grateful no longer to have to entertain him themselves. His inquiring mind became fascinated by the news, dismaying his carefree parents who believed that other people's distress was not their business, prompting Faroukh to ask them: 'Why do some people have so much while others have almost nothing at all?'

His parents' answer was disappointing: 'It's the way of the world.'

Young Faroukh understood that. He wasn't stupid. But he also knew that the world was shaped by human action, that it wasn't compulsory to stand idly by and watch disaster unfold. One could be a 'man of action'. Unfortunately, young Faroukh also understood that he wasn't necessarily equipped to become such a man.

Small and wiry, he studied hard and, when bullies mocked him for his assiduity and for his respectful attitude to his teachers, he did his best to ignore them. When that strategy proved ineffective, he confronted them with stoicism and bravery, at the expense of black eyes, cut lips and dragged-down pants. Reporting these indignities to his parents, they asked him: 'But what did you do to provoke them? You must have done something to provoke them.' In this way, Faroukh learnt that people are willing to close their eyes to almost anything – even their own child's distress – in return for an easy life.

One evening, on his birthday, isolated in his family's ostentatious apartment, shunned by his classmates, he watched a news broadcast with black-and-white footage from China, interspersed with more up-to-date colour reporting: 'The coming of the River Dragon.'

It was the story of the Banqiao Dam, built in concrete and stone in the 1950s, later reinforced with bands of iron. When it failed, in August 1975, it released a flood several metres high that broadened murderously to an ultimate, devastating width of twelve kilometres, a tidal wave of life-giving water, sweeping away perhaps as many as a quarter of a million people.

Determined to make a difference in the world, Faroukh Al-Medawi qualified well from school, entering the civil service, like his parents. Unlike them, he remained uncorrupted, living simply and working for the common good. In his late twenties, his parents succumbed to cancers of the throat and lungs.

Becoming accustomed to solitude, Al-Medawi never married but, instead, developed into an increasingly significant cog in the administration of his home city of Tobruk. Buffeted by the whims of Libya's revolutionary socialist leader, Muammar Gaddafi, he maintained a steady course.

In 2014, civil war came. Now deputy mayor, he did his best to maintain the rule of law and the smooth operation of public services, despite plummeting city income streams as people and corporations began to neglect their taxes.

The conflict ground on. Trust in government began to fail. Faith in the bonds of shared community, too. More and more people chose to live for today, without a thought for tomorrow. In the mid-2020s, promoted for his austere competence, he became the embattled Mayor of Tobruk, and learnt of Souad Mourad's campaign for the secession of a new independent state of Cyrenia.

She argued that the prosperous eastern region should leave behind the war-torn rump of Libya.

Al-Medawi judged Mourad's plan to be a sad – but necessary – solution to the interminable civil conflict. He made it known through discreet back channels that he would be willing to 'make his own modest contribution'. Soon after, he was taken aback to discover that the new administration would be structured with Mourad as prime minister, overseen by a tripartite presidential council, made up of the mayors of the three most important cities – Cyrene City, Benghazi and Tobruk. He was, of course, willing to serve, but feared the possible inertia that shared power might bring.

As it turned out, he was wrong. Mourad's drive and vision carried the day. Very quickly, Cyrenia became a safe and reliable trading partner for the wider world; an associate member of the European Union; a haven for refugees from climate change, war, drought and hunger; a significant producer of renewable electricity from plentiful sunlight; even a pioneer, in a joint venture with the French military-industrial complex, in satellite launches and space exploration, based at the southern desert location of Al-Jaghar.

And now, fleeing the cataclysmic destruction of the Aswan High Dam, that was where Al-Medawi hoped that he was headed, the airbase and the vast solar farm in the middle of the Great Sand Sea – if he could only find fuel for the vehicle that he and Zeina Yaseen had stolen from the authorities at Aswan.

The Aswan disaster will end up ten or even twenty times larger and more deadly than the 'River Dragon'.

Al-Medawi could see Zeina asleep on the back seat, visible in the rear-view mirror, her abaya pulled over her face. He didn't know her well, but he was impressed by her resilience and strength of mind. She had been an insignificant labourer on the Great Solar Array before playing a small but crucial role in preventing the Coming Darkness.

He thought again about Aswan. Al-Medawi knew that the attack was part of a wider pattern of terrorist acts in different parts of the world, referred to by their perpetrators as the Coming Storm, in the fateful year 2037.

The fateful year ...

That was actually the expression in his mind as he relived scenes of fear that grew into panic and desperation and the incalculable hecatomb of the drowned.

But it was not inescapable fate. It was people – human beings without empathy or constructive purpose – who did this.

47

The approach to Diori Hamani International, just outside the urban area of Niamey, the capital of Niger, was easy to spot for an experienced pilot. After eleven hundred kilometres in the air, Tamba's fuel was seriously depleted. For the final ten minutes, he had been distracted by an amber warning on the control console.

He touched the St Christopher medal his daughter had given him for Christmas, pinned to his lapel, hoping that President Manouche's credentials would assist in replenishing his tanks and flying directly on to his next stop-off in N'Djamena, the capital of Chad, more or less due east. From there, if all went well, he would refuel for a second time and fly northeast to Al-Jaghar.

The runways at Diori Hamani International were oriented east–west. His approach followed the line of the mighty River Niger. He landed unopposed and was directed by military ground crew to taxi to a distant corner of the apron.

The situation in Niger appeared extremely nervous. One of the soldiers shared a rumour that the inexplicable software meltdown – that had grounded all air traffic out of Niamey – was an indiscriminate attack from rogue guerilla units, armed insurrectionists devoted to overthrowing democratic government. Tamba tried to persuade him that wasn't the case, that it was an international crisis over which no one in Niger had any control, but with no success.

Very quickly, an official-looking car approached and parked. A man with an air of authority emerged, in white-and-flowing traditional dress, carrying a small suitcase. Tamba explained his mission. The man directed the soldiers to summon a bowser and allow Tamba's aircraft to be refuelled.

'As fast as possible,' he told them, 'because, as your foreign minister, in the absence of other aircraft, I will be accompanying our visitor from Mali on his onward journey.' He turned to Tamba. 'There is room on board, I assume, and for my wife, as well?'

A woman emerged from the official-looking car, much younger than the foreign minister, wearing a slim-fitting western trouser suit. She, too, carried a small suitcase.

'Yes,' said Tamba. 'There are two seats behind.'

'Splendid,' said the man.

Tamba wondered if, had he said there was only room for one, the foreign minister of Niger would have left his "wife" behind. He had an idea the man was more focused on the contents of their two small suitcases than on his spouse.

Refuelling and pre-flight checks took only twenty minutes. Tamba taxied to the end of the runway, preparing to take off into the wind, so that nature could help with generating lift. He thought again about his daughter in her friendly classroom, nurtured by her devoted primary-school teacher, touching the tip of his right forefinger once more to his St Christopher medal.

An unhappy thought came unbidden into his mind.

Will I ever see her again?

48

Zeina woke and took the wheel, allowing Al-Medawi to doze on the back seat in his turn. But his sense of traumatic failure and loss prevented him from drifting into true sleep. Never would he be able to forget – or even digest – the horror of what he had seen.

The Aswan High Dam was designed to last – if not for ever – for as long as humanity endures. Except, it was entirely foreseeable that someone, someday, would have the ingenuity, cruelty and resources to breach it and allow the dynamic erosive qualities of the vast weight of trapped water to do the rest, leaving nothing but misery and ruin.

Al-Medawi and Zeina would have died in the flood, had they not been saved by Alexandre Lamarque's colleague, Amaury Barra, commandeering one of the service vehicles.

But Barra was then killed by the Malian officer. What was his name? Major Chaka Kassam. Did Barra's corpse, carried by the flood, make it to Luxor, to Cairo or even to the Mediterranean delta where innumerable bodies must surely be deposited in the reeds and mud-flats?

'We must stop,' Zeina told him from the driver's seat. 'There is a road block.'

Al-Medawi sat up.

'I will go and speak to them.'

He got out and addressed a junior officer, identifying himself as a visiting Cyrenian diplomat and explained Zeina's role – an Egyptian citizen – at the ceremony at Aswan. The officer, Lieutenant Rehan, was wary.

'Can you prove this?' Al-Medawi offered him some official papers he happened to have in his pockets. The officer complained: 'You have no proper credentials?'

'No,' said Al-Medawi, carefully. 'But neither do any of us while our devices are off-line.'

'One moment.'

The lieutenant walked away, towards a barracks building with a single lamp over the door. Zeina got out.

'What lights there are must be powered by generators, Monsieur Al-Medawi, sir,' she said. 'You can hear them, like a chorus of machines.'

'We have come this far together, please call me Faroukh.'

'I shouldn't—'

'I insist. It will allow me to call you Miss Zeina.'

'Very well, Faroukh, sir. What did you tell the officer?'

'That his commanders are all dead or, perhaps, if they managed to escape, lost somewhere in the featureless sands.' Faroukh's limbs felt stiff. He stretched, tipping his head back, seeing a shooting star, a comet of some kind, perhaps, on its own unknowable errand through the cosmos. 'By this time, how much water remains behind the broken dam?' he mused.

'I like numbers, Faroukh, sir. I saw the map in the observation room but I can't remember the dimensions,' said Zenia. 'Otherwise, I would try and work it out.'

They contemplated the neighbourhood. The barracks dormitory was on the edge of town, in a commercial neighbourhood made up of about two-dozen buildings, almost all of them engaged in trade on the trans-Saharan road and rail routes. In three of them, he saw lit windows, but otherwise all was dark. And, of course, he could hear the 'chorus' of generators thrumming away, providing energy that the hydroelectric facility at Aswan no longer could.

This is a disaster for isolationist Egypt. How will they cope when their meagre oil reserves run out and they have no foreign currency to buy more? They will broil in the day and cling to one another for warmth at night.

Then he reminded himself that the vast loss of life was the greater disaster, whatever the struggles of the survivors.

'We are running on fumes,' Zeina told him. 'We need to refuel.'

'I know, Miss Zeina.'

'We passed a service station. It was barricaded and protected by military personnel.'

'I'm sorry. I was sleeping. I didn't see. Perhaps I should have spoken to them, tried to persuade them.'

'For it to be guarded, there must be fuel in the underground cisterns.'

'Yes, and it is not far, now, to the western border. Then it will only be thirty kilometres to Al-Jaghar.

Faroukh flinched, startled by the silent approach of Lieutenant Rehan, a good-looking young man whose uniform was well-kept and fitted him nicely.

A survivor, thought Faroukh.

'What is your intention?' Rehan asked.

'We are expected in Al-Jaghar,' Faroukh lied.

The officer held his gaze.

'Then perhaps we should leave.'

Faroukh immediately understood the implication of the first-person plural 'we'.

'Yes,' he replied. 'Good.'

'Must she come?' asked Rehan, tilting his head towards Zeina.

'Brother, she must,' said Faroukh, deliberately appealing to the man's humanity. 'I told you, she is a hero and, even if it is not possible to protect everyone – every stranger in need – we still have an obligation to support those closest to us.'

The young man frowned. Clearly, he had expected Faroukh to jump at the chance of fleeing unburdened. He asked: 'Is it true, what they say, that all who come to the camps in Cyrenia will be welcomed and given a new start?'

'An opportunity to make a new start, brother,' quibbled Faroukh. 'It cannot be given, but it can be taken.'

Rehan scuffed a boot on the dusty ground.

'You will speak for me at the frontier? I have no permission to cross.'

'I will tell them that you have important intelligence to share in person with Prime Minster Mouad – that they must let you leave under my authority and supervision.'

He watched the man's face. There was indecision but, little by little, it was replaced by determination. Faroukh wondered if this new situation was one that could be safely managed.

A survivor, he judged. *But a dangerous one.*

'So be it,' Rehan said abruptly.

'Thank you, sir,' said Zeina. 'But we need fuel.'

'We will go to the service station,' said Rehan, gruffly. 'The men will obey my orders. If not, I will shoot them. I am the authority here. Obstruction would be mutiny.'

'It would be best,' Faroukh advised, 'if our departure was a discreet one.'

'It will be what it will be. No man can escape his fate.'

Lieutenant Rehan insisted on taking the wheel, with Faroukh alongside him in the passenger seat and Zeina behind, sitting prim and composed, the windows all open for the fresh evening air. There was just enough diesel still in their vehicle to drive through the dark streets. The service station was illuminated by a few weak points of incandescent light. A small queue had formed.

Honking the car's horn, Rehan wove onto the forecourt. Two Egyptian army grunts were on duty, one dressed in mechanic's overalls and the other in uniform, carrying a superannuated rifle. They were telling the first few drivers that their queuing was pointless, that there would be no fuel dispensed: 'Not this evening, not tomorrow morning – and perhaps not the next day, either.'

Two of the waiting civilian drivers wanted to confront Rehan as a queue-jumper. He got out and went to face them, shouting at them in a southern-Egyptian dialect that Faroukh found hard to follow, though its meaning was clear. His words – reinforced by the sight of his uniform and his hand on the leather holster on his hip – caused the civilians to back warily away.

Rehan gave the two grunts their orders. They moved aside an improvised barrier, created from a few empty oil drums and an outdoor bench. Faroukh scooted across to the driver's side to pull forward. Rehan fuelled the car to the very brim, depressing the trigger on the pistol over and over for the final drops, even filling the hose that led from the tank to the cap. Then he took one of the empty twenty-five-litre oil drums from the makeshift barrier, rinsed it with a splash of diesel that he tipped out on the scrubby verge, before filling it only three-quarters full because no one could find a suitable bung. Rehan sent the mechanic to the lavatories for a roll of toilet paper and, with that, he and Faroukh did their best to plug the jerrican, before wedging it in a footwell in the rear of the vehicle. From the rudimentary service station shop, Rehan appropriated a tray of bottles of water, putting them away in the shallow boot.

'It might be a good idea to show some generosity,' said Faroukh. 'You could give the order to reopen the pumps, perhaps even without payment, given the emergency and people's need to fuel their generators in the absence of hydro-electricity from Aswan. That will allow for many more vehicles on the overnight roads, making our departure less obtrusive.'

'Fine,' said Rehan.

He beckoned the two grunts. The nearest civilian drivers heard what was said and passed the good news back down the line, leading to a chorus of cheering as Faroukh drove off, heading west, away from the threat of the rising sun which – far too soon, he feared – would eventually appear behind him in his rear-view mirror as a bright orange crescent, promising a scorching Saharan day.

49

Tamba Dem's route from Niamey in Niger to N'Djamena in Chad was due east, overflying the rogue disputed territories of northern Nigeria, then a narrow neck of land belonging to Cameroon, finally bringing the Aurora Propfan down over the sadly diminished Lake Chad. From there, he simply had to bank south and follow another waterway, all the way to the capital.

Despite the noisy aircraft, Tamba heard some of the conversation from the seats behind. The foreign minister and his 'wife' didn't sound like a married couple. They sounded more like employer and employee.

Arrival was not very different from Niamey. They touched down on a strangely quiet apron and were directed by a military escort to a holding area well away from the control tower and official buildings. The response of the authorities was rapid, with a senior airport manager on hand in an army jeep within ninety seconds. He got out, revealing his flowing black robe with a bib decorated with geometric patterns of gold thread. On his head was a pill-box hat in the same design.

Tamba was sidelined while his male passenger – the foreign minister of Niger – spoke to the newcomer. After a while, with a shout of exasperation, the minster threw up his hands, returned to the aircraft and brought out a suitcase, propping it against a wheel and opening the lid. Inside, it was divided by zips into several sections. From one of these, he took out two thick wads of paper money – US dollars in high denominations.

Seeing these, the airport manager became very serious. Tamba could hear him demanding the minister gave him a rundown of all he knew about the progress of the meltdown and the disintegration of government and military control in Niger.

'It is no better in Chad,' said the airport manager. 'But the people don't seem to have realised how bad it will soon become.'

'Power blackouts?'

'Yes, but that is our normal in any case. If I give permission for you to refuel, where are you going?'

'To Al-Jaghar in southern Cyrenia.'

'Interesting. Why?'

'We have a message we must deliver personally from President Manouche of Mali,' said the foreign minister of Niger, slyly associating himself with Tamba's mission.

'And you think you will be safe there?'

The foreign minister nodded, indicating Tamba: 'This man seems a competent pilot. He is President Manouche's officer.' He put a hand on the airport manager's black-draped arm. 'These is one empty seat, usually taken by the co-pilot. It could be yours.'

The manager nodded and strode away to speak to his driver, sending the jeep back to the control tower, giving permission to bring a bowser for refuelling. The foreign minister climbed up inside the aircraft. Tamba heard him telling his 'wife' that all was well.

Reflexively, Tamba touched the St Christopher medal on his lapel, remembering his daughter's worried expression when he had told her that he didn't know when he would return.

50

On the majority of maps, both digital and physical, Faroukh had seen desert roads depicted as long straight lines. It made sense. There was an assumption that a 'featureless' landscape must allow a tarmac road to cross it without curves or detours. But, of course, it was a question of scale. Deserts were only featureless when viewed from afar.

A magnet for knowledge, Faroukh knew that the Saharan sands covered some of the oldest rock on the planet, part of the African Shield tectonic plate, forged by fire at the dawn of life, when the only living things were single-celled ocean creatures. The undulations of the dunes mirrored the irregular geology submerged beneath. And there were all kinds of impassable features, too, dry watercourses and stretches of rocky terrain too expensive to carve through with explosives or machinery.

All the same, the route taken was direct enough for him to feel that they were always heading in the right direction, even though they were sometimes obliged to creep along at only thirty kilometres per hour as the road – despite their headlamps – became invisible beneath the blown sand.

In the end, Faroukh thought, that wasn't a bad thing. Had they hammered along at top speed for too long, they might have overstretched the engine of the lightweight official vehicle whose previous service had never extended beyond the immediate perimeter of the Aswan High Dam.

Faroukh's communications devices – a simple smart watch and a tablet computer with built-in 'find me' – remained dumb. Zeina possessed no modern tech whatsoever. Lieutenant Rehan, however, was kitted out with a military-grade navigation unit capable – in theory – of identifying their location to within a couple of hundred metres, thanks to its wireless connection to unsmart ground relays on the line of the frontier, dumb devices without purpose beyond their location pings.

Theory proved inaccurate. The poor-quality Egyptian equipment brought them to the remains of the Egypt–Cyrenia border fence too far south and they were obliged to crawl northwards on a very poor track that began to strain the engine, a sinister smell of overheating making Faroukh nervous, especially because the cab was full of the odour of evaporating fuel from the inadequately plugged jerrican.

'It can't be far,' said Rehan, tilting his navigator this way and that.

'The temperature needle is in the red,' said Faroukh. 'We should refill from the oil drum and allow the engine to cool down.' Faroukh crept off the tarmac onto a rutted granite platform and cut the engine, turning off the lights. The sky was clear and the moonlight enough to see by. 'I will check the water reservoir and we will resume after half-an-hour. Agreed?'

'Fine,' approved Rehan, grudgingly.

'What has happened?' came Zeina's voice from the back, softened by sleep.

'We were overheating the engine. I am about to add more water.'

'Can I get out?'

'Of course.'

Faroukh opened the driver door and stepped carefully onto the hard stone, taking the keys to the vehicle with him, hoping it looked like a simple habitual gesture, though it was actually because he didn't trust Lieutenant Rehan not to jump across and drive away, leaving Zeina and himself stranded.

The night was chilly, the cloudless skies allowing the heat of the previous day to disperse. Faroukh rolled his shoulders to dispel the stiffness from tensely grasping the steering wheel. Zeina walked silently away with one of the water bottles from the boot, beyond a tall dune where, he supposed, she could squat in privacy.

'I am grateful for your assistance,' Faroukh called to Lieutenant Rehan. The officer grunted in reply. He was sitting grim-faced in the passenger seat, still attempting to encourage a stronger read from his navigator. 'I will do everything I can for you once we reach Cyrenia. A strong intelligent officer could become a valuable member of our armed forces, once refugee status is granted.'

Faroukh felt foolish, hearing his own flattery drifting weakly across the ridged granite. He saw a streak of light across the inky firmament from some falling object and wondered if it was connected to the comet he had seen earlier and if either or both were a part of the Storm.

There is not one of us who has the complete picture.

Faroukh leaned into the footwell to action the lever that opened the engine compartment. He topped up the water-cooling reservoir with two bottles from the trunk, then he walked away, placing his feet carefully on the rutted granite.

If we are successful in reaching Al-Jaghar, I will speak to Wael Al-Mesih and attempt to get in touch with Prime Minster Mourad in Cyrene City. Perhaps with the French authorities and even Lamarque himself? They, surely, will have more information on what happened at Aswan and what its consequences might be.

He heard the car door slam and turned to look at Lieutenant Rehan. The moonlight revealed a calculating look in his eye.

'I need to be sure, Monsieur Al-Medawi. I am deserting Egypt. But if I promise to serve Cyrenia … You can make this happen? You are a member of the presidential council? That is true? This isn't a trick?'

Moving carelessly over the deeply grooved granite, Rehan stumbled and cried out, his foot caught on one of the ruts. He toppled sideways and Al-Medawi heard the grotesque snap of a bone. Rehan screeched a second time as he hit the ground and his ankle joint dislocated.

Faroukh moved swiftly towards him, wincing as he saw the unnatural bend in the soldier's leg. After a moment's hesitation, he could think of nothing better than to lift Rehan bodily from the ground, holding him in a bear hug, his face in the taller man's chest, so as to ease the tortured break. Zeina came running to help.

'What has happened?'

'The lieutenant caught his foot in one of the gullys,' said Faroukh, his voice muffled, 'and fell against the break.'

Between them, to a background of Rehan's groans and cries, they helped the officer towards the car and leant him against the still-warm fender, balanced precariously on a single leg.

'Do something, for the sake of God,' he shouted.

'There is nothing we can do,' said Faroukh. 'We have no medical equipment.'

'I will look in the back,' said Zeina.

Rehan shifted position and cried out once more. Faroukh saw the soldier's dangling left foot move with the change in centre of gravity, as if it was now attached with only skin and sinew, not bone.

'I can't …' began Rehan, then he swore a stream of scatological, blasphemous curses.

Zeina returned with a med-kit containing a stretch-bandage. Faroukh pushed the wad of his handkerchief between Rehan's teeth, encouraging him to bite down and 'be brave'. Zeina crouched on the sandy rock to wind the bandage firmly round the ruptured ankle, but the fabric wasn't strong enough to stabilise the joint. Rehan groaned and whimpered at every movement.

'I have an idea,' said Zeina.

She went to the glove box to retrieve the vehicle manual, opening it wide and making a kind of tube that she wrapped round the shattered ankle joint, then she pulled her scarf from her head and wound that tightly over the top, creating a rudimentary splint.

It seemed to help. Once this was done, Rehan didn't fight them any longer as they manoeuvred him onto the back seat. The lieutenant leaned back, his features slightly less drawn, but still biting down on the wad of Faroukh's handkerchief.

Zeina took a couple of steps away and knelt down, rubbing dry sand through her fingers in mimicry of ablution. Then she bent her head to the rock in prayer. Faroukh watched her, feeling that time was suddenly against them.

He checked the comms on his simple smart-watch once more. To his surprise, he saw a faint signal, a dumb ping from Al-Jaghar. Zeina stood up and twisted her long black hair into a braid before pushing it into the collar of her jellabiya.

'I am sorry about your headscarf, sister,' came Lieutenant Rehan's strained voice from the back seat of the car.

'I hope you are more comfortable,' Zeina replied.

They set off, bumping from the granite verge, back onto the poor border track. Rehan groaned and flinched, reaching out an impotent hand to try and stabilise his awful wound beneath the makeshift splint.

'This will not be quick,' said Faroukh. 'But, by taking it steady, I hope to ensure that we make it.'

51

Zeina, Faroukh and Rehan arrived at the border post. It was a place Zeina knew well, having been her unexpected refuge when she had fled Al-Jaghar, in fear of being framed for the murder of the Cyrenian general whose body was in the trunk of her EV. At that point, she hadn't known that she carried with her information crucial to the defeat of the Coming Darkness conspiracy.

The border post comprised a mud-built cell, separated by a few metres of sand and rock from the frontier post proper – thirty square metres of cheap utilitarian accommodation, covered in corrugated aluminium siding, clearly visible in the light of their headlamps. Roused by the sound of their engine, two guards emerged, stumbling out, improperly dressed in fatigue trousers and vests.

Zeina stayed where she was while Faroukh got out and went to speak to them. She saw and heard him attempting to employ all his charm, the authority of his seniority in politics and diplomacy. The two soldiers seemed unconvinced, taking the papers he offered and putting them away in their own pockets, asking him in raised voices to prove that he was who he said he was, 'beyond these pieces of paper that anyone might forge'.

Zeina squirmed round to address the lieutenant.

'This is going badly,' she told him.

Faroukh had left the door open, meaning the cabin light was on. Rehan looked very poorly. His face pale had a sheen of clammy sweat.

Then Zeina noticed that the rear bench seat was soaked dark with his blood. She realised that, in their haste to stabilise his injury, they hadn't paid enough attention to the compound nature of the fractures. If a sharp fragment of bone had nicked an artery, Rehan's heart been pumping out his lifeblood ever since they got back under way.

We did our best. We're not doctors, are we?

'Lieutenant,' she called in a soft voice. 'Can you hear me?'

There was no answer. His face remained unchanged. His hands, resting in his lap, were slack.

Maybe he's in shock?

The border guards were shouting. Leaning between the two front seats, she managed to get her hands on the leather holster Rehan wore on his hip, undoing the buckle to release his weapon. She had very little experience of guns but the cabin light was good and the safety catch clearly marked. She released it and climbed out of the vehicle, concealing the weapon by pulling her sleeve down over her hand.

In the bright beams of the headlamps, twenty-five paces away, the two border guards were manhandling Faroukh. The Cyrenian diplomat was docile, clearly determined to endure mistreatment, hoping to achieve his goal through persuasion. Zeina did not think that was likely. She had been a prisoner in this place herself and knew first hand that the ill-educated drones that guarded the lonely frontier were not to be trusted.

'Excuse me, brothers,' she said, lowering her eyes so as not challenge or give offence. Through her eyelashes, she saw the border guards' faces reveal surprise and confusion. They exchanged a pair of foolish glances, as if each thought the other might know who she was and where she had come from and why she was there. 'All will be well,' she told them. '*Insha'Allah.*'

'Who are you?' one asked, wiping his hands on his vest.

She halved the distance to them.

'My companion, the honourable Faroukh Al-Medawi, is a member of the Cyrenian Presidential Council. In the car, we have rescued a wounded Egyptian soldier. He is badly injured and needs evacuation. The nearest medical facility must be across the border at Al-Jaghar. You will, no doubt, receive major military honours for bringing us assistance.'

'What do you mean, wounded?'

'See for yourself.'

Zeina gestured for the two border guards to walk past her to the vehicle. The lieutenant's pistol was heavy and awkward, concealed inside Zeina's sleeve. As they peered in, she went to stand next to Faroukh, speaking to him in a low voice: 'Can you fire a gun?'

'I never have,' he replied. 'But surely we can persuade these men—'

Zeina interrupted with a shake of her head. 'We cannot.'

'He is dead,' called the first guard.

'No, in shock,' Zeina called back, hoping it was true.

Concealed by her body, she showed Faroukh the pistol.

'This is not my way,' he told her.

Zeina sighed with frustration as the first guard called out again: 'He has no pulse. His blood is all on the floor.'

'Stand behind me,' she whispered to her companion.

'I don't know if this is the best strategy, sister—' Faroukh began.

'Move,' she insisted.

Zeina watched the two border guards converse together in low voices, overconfident, hatching their next move in plain sight, their expressions illuminated by the cabin light. Of course, they didn't know she had a gun and, luckily, neither of them was armed as they had wandered out to meet their unexpected guests in the middle of the night in their underwear.

They nodded agreement and moved round in front of the car, profiled into anonymous threatening silhouettes by the headlamps behind them.

'They mean to overpower us and lock us in that mud-built cell,' said Zeina, quietly.

'Let me speak to them again,' said Faroukh.

'It is too late,' whispered Zeina.

Zeina knew what she had to do and that, for the sake of accuracy, she should leave it as late as possible, until they were very close. She would fire multiple shots, attempting to keep her arm down, not allowing the recoil from the explosions to force the weapon high into the air.

Don't shut your eyes. Focus on what is necessary. You have no choice. You are so close to being safe.

'My brothers,' Faroukh began, stepping forward.

Zeina was forced to act. She had no choice but to reveal her weapon before the misplaced optimism of the veteran diplomat ruined everything by getting in the way. Out of some instinct that she wasn't aware that she possessed, she crouched down in the sand to give herself a more stable base. Her sleeve slipped back from the pistol, held tightly in her right hand. She grasped her left hand over the top, her wrists firm against her knee. The guards stopped, their shadowed faces unreadable.

Zeina fired – one, two, three, four, five – the sound deafening so close at hand, the recoil making the barrel dance, however hard she struggled to keep it level, her eyes closing involuntarily, as she had feared.

When she opened them, one of the guards was on the ground with two huge blooms of red blood on his filthy vest. The other was spinning around, grasping a torn shoulder with the opposite hand, blood seeping between his fingers, casting about as if looking for a weapon – perhaps a rock – to throw at her. And he was only three paces away.

Focusing on his belt buckle as the best way to centre her aim, Zeina fired again – one, two, three, four – then the magazine was empty and the trigger simply caused the hammer impotently to click. But she had succeeded. The second guard was face down on the sand with three exit wounds through the ragged vest on his back.

Zeina stood up, feeling numb. She dropped the spent pistol and lurched away to be sick on all fours in the sand. When she had finished, she saw steam in the beams of the headlamps and realised that some of her shots had gone past or through the two border guards, at least one of them puncturing the engine's water-cooling system.

'What have you done?' gasped Faroukh.

'What was necessary. Do you see that?' she asked, grimly. 'The car is no use any longer.'

'But these men—' began Faroukh.

'Trust me, they would have done worse. You must see that.'

'Yes, perhaps.'

'We cannot stay here.'

'Perhaps we can repair the vehicle? Do you know if there are tools in the frontier post?' he suggested, naively.

'There is no time. We must leave this place.'

'Or call for help?'

'No,' said Zeina, determinedly. 'That will only draw attention to our presence. This is the frontier. We are close enough. I know the way. We will walk.'

52

There was a road, but it was little used and the desert winds of the Great Sand Sea seemed determined to conceal it from human eyes. But, as she had said, Zeina knew the way.

In the aluminium border post, she had discovered a keffiyeh, left behind by one of the frontier guards, meaning she could replace her abaya. She and Faroukh each found, too, a small kitbag that they could commandeer. Before setting out, they sat down at the frontier post's dusty dining table to eat two filled flatbreads, cooked in their vacuum packaging in a rudimentary microwave. Then, enthused with the idea that their journey from the catastrophe at Aswan was almost at an end, they set out.

For a while, they walked with enthusiasm, talking of this and that. The road to Al-Jaghar ran due west and Zeina could feel it beneath her feet. When, on a few rare occasions, they accidentally left the moonlit tarmac, hidden beneath the veil of the shifting desert, she quickly corrected their path.

In a pause in their conversation, she fell to thinking about how she had become – briefly – a hero of the Coming Darkness. But, then, events had moved on, leaving her behind in misery and despair, only broken by the unexpected invitation to the ceremony at Aswan.

All those people. How many will be missed? Not many if they died with all their friends and families – everyone likely to remember them.

Without turning to look at her companion, she asked: 'What are we doing, Faroukh, sir?'

'We are going somewhere we may be useful, either with information or understanding.'

'Because are we sure that the destruction is wrong?' she asked quietly.

'How can you ask –?' he began.

'What if we simply let it happen?' Zeina insisted.

'This is foolish, sister,' said Faroukh. 'Your mind has been clouded by all you have seen. Do not celebrate death.'

'What is human life, though?' asked Zeina. 'A force that destroys all other life, a force that will not rest from pollution and exploitation while there is an advantage to be accrued, some kind of wealth to stockpile at the expense of others' misery.'

'It is true that humanity can do better,' said Faroukh. 'What is the point of Madame Mourad's new beacon of Cyrenia, if not to show that?'

They walked on another twenty paces, then Zeina blurted: 'But what if there are simply too many of us, breeding, multiplying, consuming, fighting – and not enough dying?'

'Human life is sacred,' protested Faroukh, his voice revealing the depth of his emotion.

'Every human life?' challenged Zeina. 'Even the ones that have caused this nightmare?'

'Sister, this is blasphemous.'

Zeina fell silent and walked on, a pace or two ahead. Time passed. Both periodically moved their kitbag from one shoulder to the other to ease the burden of the heavy water bottles they carried, a kilogram for every crucial litre, jostling against one another with each slowing stride.

53

Before leaving the tented office belonging to his esteemed boss, Tamba Dem had seen the message that he carried, a printout of a message from 'the man who saved the world', Alexandre Lamarque, and President Manouche's note, written by hand with a black fountain pen with a white star set into the top of its cap. It had meant very little to him. He knew he was just a cog in the machine, without any kind of authority or autonomy. His only concern was to do his duty – then find a way home.

How far from my daughter will I end up? Separated by about five thousand kilometres of forest, savannah and sand.

Before leaving Bamako, he had made some swift calculations regarding his likely fuel consumption in the Aurora Propfan on each of the three lengthening legs of his journey, Mali to Niger, Niger to Chad, Chad to Cyrenia. He knew that he would be stretching the operational parameters of his aircraft more and more, needing favourable winds. He had been comforted by the idea that he would have no cargo of any kind, not even a co-pilot. Now, though, he had acquired three passengers and two suitcases full of money and – maybe – hidden compartments of heavy jewellery or gold.

The last leg was almost over. Tamba had spent a lot of fuel finding a favourable wind. The Chadian airport manager was sitting alongside him and had hardly spoken, displaying the tense body language of someone frightened of flying. The couple he had picked up in Niamey, on the other hand, seemed much more at ease, almost excited.

'How far?' the foreign minister shouted from behind. 'How long?'

'We're about halfway.'

Because they were cruising so high, the land below was featureless. Tamba was navigating by compass, having taken a precise bearing before departing N'Djamena.

It's possible, but it'll be a close-run thing.

54

One of the peculiarities of the location of the Al-Jaghar base, in addition to its isolated position at the heart of the Great Sand Sea, was the fact that it was below sea level. Back in the mists of time, it would have been at the bottom of a long-dead inland sea. In the vast bowl of granite and sand, sound seemed disinclined to carry and the air felt oppressively still.

On their weary trudge, Zeina had taken solace in numbers. She knew how many motorised photovoltaic panels comprised the Great Solar Array, each one of them tracking the path of the sun across the sky for maximum efficiency. When it had been her job to clear the panels of wind-blown dust and sand, she had amused herself by calculating her progress: twenty panels per hour; one hundred and forty panels per day; seven hundred per week; about seven thousand before the events of the Coming Darkness overtook her and she had to flee for her life.

She and Faroukh stopped to drink. Zeina considered how many paces a hike of thirty kilometres must comprise. Her own gait and Faroukh's were similar, she thought – he was a shortish, unathletic man – at around eighty centimetres. That meant they would each need to take thirty-seven thousand, five hundred steps to reach their destination. If each step took half a second, they would need to walk for precisely three-hundred and twelve minutes and thirty seconds – or, say, six hours, given a few pauses on the way.

The performance of the Al-Jaghar employees had been tightly monitored so Zeina knew that a human being loses eight- or nine-hundred millilitres of water per hour beneath a forty-degree sun, perhaps two-thirds of that at night. The supplies in their rucksacks had seemed sufficient when they set out, six litres each. But, as their weary strides shortened and their kitbags grew lighter, their water supplies were diminishing much more quickly than their destination seemed to approach.

Zeina drained her bottle, just as the sky to the north began to pulsate with green light. The strange luminescence seemed to reveal, on the horizon, some human-made structures, blocks of blackness against the aurora.

'Do you see that? There, like a dark line? And a few points of reflected light. How far away do you think that is?'

'I have no idea,' said Faroukh, wearily. 'Is it even real?'

'It's the edge of the Great Solar Array.'

'We have arrived?' he asked, like a child being told that an interminable car journey was, at last, over.

'Not yet.'

Zeina knew the distance was much further than it appeared. But she didn't want her companion to lose heart. He was reaching the end of his strength.

'I'm not sure I can ...' he began, then his words faded away into silence.

'You're nearly home in Cyrenia,' she told him. 'You said there is work still for you to do.'

'Yes,' said Faroukh, vaguely.

Zeina opened her rucksack. She had half a bottle of water left. She realised her companion must have drunk all of his and discarded his bag at the side of the road. She shared what she had, then did the same.

'One final push, Faroukh, sir,' she told him.

They walked on. After a short while, Zeina thought perhaps she could hear an aircraft engine.

Or maybe it's the sound of the motorised stands of the photovoltaic array? No, they are too far, still.

She was about to mention it when, still trailing in her wake, Faroukh spoke, sounding as though sharing her last bottle had done him some good.

'I have been thinking.'

'About what?'

'We should make sure that we have no infected devices. We don't want to carry any viruses into the base.'

'I have none.'

'But I do and the precautionary principal dictates …' He looked around. 'Let us leave the road.'

To the left, a small distance away, was another rutted moonlit slope, like the area where Rehan had trapped his ankle and tripped. They carefully climbed the granite outcrop to a place with a few loose stones. Faroukh took charge of destroying his tablet and smart watch. The process reminded Zeina of her own behaviour on her escape from Al-Jaghar – was it two months ago? – when she had disposed of equipment belonging to the staff officer she had been obliged to kill in self-defence. She had done it in the same way, smashing the housings, removing the chips and crushing them between lumps of stone, driving the tip of her knife into the microcircuitry, leaving the valuable but broken kit as litter in the endless sands.

When it was done, Zeina looked west once more. Thanks to the green glow in the sky, the array was clearly visible from the slightly higher ground.

And are those headlamps?

Faroukh saw them, too.

'At last,' he said. 'Good news. Let's walk on to meet them.'

Zeina followed him back to the strip of sandy tarmac.

Since when, she was wondering, *has any news been good?*

55

From altitude, Tamba had an even better view of the night sky, throbbing with green pulsations. He feared he was irretrievably lost. His magnetic compass – that he had been relying on in the absence of any digital or connected equipment – kept spinning from side to side, unable to find north, incapable of providing a bearing. He had brought the Aurora Propfan down as low as he dared, out of the helpful tailwind, but the dark desert rushing past beneath his wings remained featureless.

'Is this the approach?' asked the airport manager, hopefully, from the co-pilot's seat. 'Shouldn't we be able to see lights?'

'Not quite yet,' said Tamba.

'How much range do we still have?' asked the foreign minister of Niger, his voice both angry and frightened.

'I'll tell you the absolute truth,' said Tamba. 'The tanks are so depleted that the console no longer gives a range.'

'Then what does it say?'

'That we should land at the first opportunity.'

'And when are we going to do that?'

'At the first opportunity,' Tamba repeated, grimly.

A warning began sounding from the dashboard.

'What's that?' demanded the airport manager, his voice tight with panic.

'It's nothing,' said Tamba.

'Don't tell us a high-pitched beeping is nothing,' said the minister. 'We're not fools.'

'Are we going to crash?' asked the airport manager in small voice.

'We're not going to crash,' said Tamba. 'We're low on fuel but we're nearly there.'

'How far? How long?' the minster shouted.

Tamba wondered if the man realised that he was repeating himself.

'Do you think,' he asked them, 'that I want to die? Trust me, I will do everything in my power to keep us alive.'

In truth, Tamba thought there was little he could do. The magnetic storm had disabled his only means of navigating an accurate course. Dawn was too far away for the light of the sun to help. He asked his passengers to be quiet.

'I need to do something.'

'What is it now,' asked the airport manager.

'I have to record a message.'

'Are there any parachutes on this aircraft?'

The Auroa Propfan was flying too low for parachutes to be of any use.

'No,' Tamba lied.

'Are there any other landing strips?'

'No.'

'Not even a road?'

'Be silent, I tell you,' he shouted. 'Let me concentrate.'

In case they had to ditch, Tamba had decided to make an audio recording of the message from Alexandre Lamarque.

We are not yet in radio range of Al-Jaghar but surely, we will be soon, though?

He locked the controls and took the envelope out of his pocket, sliding out the thick cream paper, silently reading it over. Then he held a microphone close to his lips and carefully enunciated every word, using Manouche's note as introduction.

Using the manual controls on the analogue radio set, he set the recorded message to broadcast on a loop. He heard it cycle three times through, then turned the volume down, preferring to think of happier things – going into his daughter's school to talk about his profession, trying to inspire the children with the mystery and magic of flight.

As the engines fire and the wing rushes through the air, the bulge on the top makes the air above the wing move faster than the air beneath. That reduces the air pressure above the wing, so the air under the wing pushes up.

That was okay as far as it went. It was the next bit that haunted him.

If the engines stop and there is no more fast forward motion, the difference in air pressure disappears and the aircraft falls out of the sky.

Thinking back to his basic training, he remembered advice he had been given about flying with the nose dipped down to encourage fuel flow from depleted tanks to the engines. But that would increase air resistance and, inevitably, cause his supplies to fail even more quickly.

He realised he was grinding his teeth with anxiety, then the engine coughed and he understood that that was no longer important. He tried to establish a glide pattern that might allow him to bring the aircraft down level and kind of bound across the dunes, like a skimming stone. But the final failure came suddenly and asymmetrically,

The starboard engine juddered to a halt, the loss of thrust causing the plane to slew round. The tip of the starboard wing dipped towards the sand and he called out: 'Brace, brace!'

Tamba's voice was lost in the wrench and grind of tearing metal and then the awful stomach-churning lurch and flip of the entire aircraft, turning a somersault and crashing upside down on a pan of granite, grinding along for what felt like minutes but which was probably only ten or fifteen seconds, shards of glass in the air as the cockpit windows shattered, the frame collapsing under the unusual pressure, folding in on Tamba and pinning him to his seat, so closely that he could barely take a breath.

Able to turn his head, though, he saw all three of his passengers, wrenched from their inadequate lap belts by the violence of the crash, piled like broken dolls.

His penultimate thought was another memory from his daughter's school.

An aircraft needs two things to work well: a good design and reliable engines.

Tamba wanted to touch the St Christopher on his lapel a final time, but he couldn't move his arms. Deprived of oxygen, his sight lost colour and definition. His final thought was an additional unspoken word of advice for his daughter.

And, of course, you need to know where you are going and why.

He died, suffocated by the collapsed fuselage. Meanwhile, the pre-recorded message continued to send.

56

The person who most needed Alexandre Lamarque's time delayed message was Wael Al-Mesih. He had gone to bed at his usual time, slept well for a few hours, then woken, his mind awhirl. He was now in his office on the edge of the Al-Jaghar science campus, three hundred metres from the perimeter of the military airbase and launch pad. A desk lamp on the sharp-cornered metal desk and a standard lamp beside the conference table were both reflected in the dark double glazing, like in a mirror.

The room was cool because Al-Jaghar still had copious renewable energy from its photovoltaics, so air-conditioning units continued to hum in every inhabited space. In a corner of the room, Wael's ancient analogue television set was silently showing a poor-quality overnight news broadcast from across the border in Egypt.

The AI driven digital meltdown is not a random event. It is meant. Thanks to luck and to me, though, this place remains secure.

As a response to the Storm, Wael had ordered a precautionary shutdown of all incoming digital data and comms, reinforcing the isolation caused by the destruction of the data and energy cables. But not before Prime Minster Mourad's office informed him that she was inbound by helicopter from Cyrene City as a precaution.

She is wise. Our isolation in the Great Sand Sea will keep her safe.

Wael smiled to himself, thinking about how the etymology of his given name seemed to have taken on a new significance: 'Wael, one who seeks shelter, who provides refuge.'

He crossed the science campus to the domed telescope room, settling himself in a reclining chair at the lens of the most powerful optical device on the Al-Jaghar base. Following Mourad's instructions, he had located the remaining God's Thunder platform. As he focused the telescope, he tried to put himself inside the mind of a terrorist, someone who wanted to destroy so that humanity should be forced to start again, but found it impossible. In any case, the deadly platform was currently out of sight, its orbit overflying the Pacific.

Wael yawned. Though he was stupidly alert, he was also tired, even though night-time had been his professional milieu since as far back as he could remember.

Am I now too old for this?

He thought about the reconstruction project and how that demanded a more regular pattern of waking and sleep.

I never wanted to be in charge.

He scanned the heavens, naming each constellation aloud. Then, like Régis Petit in Paris, in a patch of sky he knew well, he saw something that ought not to have been there.

Horrified, Wael moved away from the lens of the optical telescope to search a digital database at a non-networked terminal in the domed room, reviewing a sequence of images of the particular astral quadrant. He found the data he needed and, for ease of future reference, sent the images to an A3 printer.

'Professor, sir?' It was a member of the air-force overnight team, come to tell him that a dumb perimeter beacon had sent a ping, warning of activity on the road from the Egyptian border: two people, on foot. 'What should we do?' she asked.

'What would you have done before I was in charge?'

'Intercept if necessary.'

'Detain them, then. They may be infected.'

'Organically or digitally?' she asked.

'Either or both.'

'Yes, Professor, sir.' Wael turned back to the chuntering printer, just spitting out the final page, but the airman continued: 'Excuse me, Professor. There is one other thing.'

'What?' snapped Wael, his mind on the danger from the skies.

'The prime minister's chopper is on approach. We have been in radio contact. I can confirm that the pilot has disabled all digital systems, as per your orders. Should I wake some other officers for a guard of honour?'

'No, no. She's not like that. Thank you for notifying me.' He rolled up the A3 images into a tube. 'I will be in my office. Please take charge of her arrival, show her to the visitor accommodation, then escort her to me.'

Wael set off across the science campus towards his office, thinking about the threats prevented by the last-ditch actions of Alexandre Lamarque – the Kessler cascade and the potentially catastrophic deorbit of the God's Thunder platforms.

All three were supposed to have been sent out into space on a collision course with the Sun. One remains, however. Perhaps they tried? It is easy to assume the worst. If two platforms are gone, perhaps impulsion failed on the third. We had only the French government's assurance that it would happen, no evidence of any kind. And this new threat ...

A medical officer on overnight duty was out for walk between the utilitarian buildings. They greeted one another and she asked him about the reinstatement of connectivity. Wael told her they could discuss it the next morning in the regular status meeting.

'We would all be grateful for more news,' insisted the doctor with a worried frown.

'I understand,' said Wael, appealing to the woman's sense of solidarity. 'You and I must both remain patient.

He walked on.

This new threat ... It must have been the solar flares. The object's trajectory is decaying. I need to calculate its size and potential impact site.

He opened the door of his office, grateful for to be out of the chilly night.

But I, too, am limited in what I can do without reconnection. It is good that the prime minister is on her way here. If there was an impact in the Mediterranean, Cyrene City would be washed away.

He shut the door, seeing his own reflection in the dark double glazing.

Is there anything I can do? If anyone is going to give the order I am imagining, it ought to be someone with democratic authority, not an unaccountable scientist in his ivory tower.

57

Zeina and Al-Medawi chose to stand in the centre of the dusty desert road, their hands raised to the level of their shoulders so as not to appear in any way threatening. Squinting into the glare of the headlamps, they watched the vehicle approach, quickly at first, then more cautiously. Zeina recognised it as one of the small EVs used to buzz around the Al-Jaghar base, a Pratique. If they were both to get a lift, it would be a tight squeeze. Then she realised that there was another, larger vehicle coming up behind.

'I will announce myself and all will be well,' Faroukh told her.

'Best not to move, however,' Zeina warned him.

The larger vehicle – a small truck with yellow-and-beige desert markings – overtook the Pratique, coming to a halt about twenty metres away.

'My name is Faroukh Al-Medawi,' her companion called out, 'and I am a member of the tripartite presidential council of Cyrenia, Mayor of Tobruk. My companion is an Egyptian citizen and a hero of the Coming Darkness, Zeina Yaseen. Thank you for bringing us assistance.'

The passenger door of the truck opened and two men in uniform jumped down. They both wore gloves and face masks and were armed with handguns. One of them commanded: 'Keep your hands up and kneel.'

Zeina and Faroukh did as they were told. At the same time, a question came unbidden into Zeina's mind.

I have survived once more. Why, though?

58

Seated behind his desk, Wael was drinking filtered water from a paper cone, dispensed from a cooler in the corner of the room. Since his discovery in the telescope room, he had spent his time in frenzied calculations. Now, however, he was becalmed. The crucial moment for action had not yet come and, in any case, he wasn't certain how to broach with the prime minister what he had planned.

Mourad was sitting opposite him, having touched down on the air-force side of the base. She had briefly been shown her spartan visitor accommodation where she had changed out of her formal gown of ivory silk with vertical panels of burgundy embroidery and into a set of air-force fatigues.

Wael felt tongue-tied. Mourad had given him a rundown of the growing viral meltdown in the capital, Cyrene City, and beyond. The atmosphere was now subdued. Wael spoke in a series of incomplete sentences.

'I have been doing … Time is shorter than … Forgive me, I am processing a lot of data—'

'Clearly you have bad news to impart,' she snapped. 'What is it?'

'It's …' he began again, then floundered. 'I'm sorry. Could I have acted sooner?'

'Doing what?'

'Locating God's Thunder.'

'But you did so?'

'Yes.'

'And then what?'

'There is an entirely separate threat and there may be a way to … I feel I have to ask you—' he began.

'Professor,' interrupted Mourad, her voice businesslike. 'Your mind is not clear. Talk me through the sequence of events.'

'Yes, it will do me good to tell someone. Your propitious arrival …' He stood up and refilled his paper cone of water. 'There are two things.' He drank. 'The weapon, God's Thunder. I have located and tracked its orbit.'

'Where is it now?

He scrunched up his water cone and dropped it in a bin.

'On the far side of the Earth …' He frowned. 'Perhaps above China? It is …'

He stopped again. Mourad made an impatient noise and chided him: 'Come along, Professor. Put your thoughts in order.'

'Yes, I'm sorry. Right. Two issues – first God's Thunder, second … the asteroid.'

'The asteroid?'

'Yes.' He unrolled the tube of A3 printouts across his desk, arranging them so that the important quadrant of sky was visible on each. 'This is all quite new,' he told her.

'What are you showing me?' asked Mourad.

'These are sequential images of the night sky. Can you see the differences between them?'

'It is not important that I should analyse your images,' said Mourad, remaining seated. 'Tell me what they mean.'

'There,' he told her. 'That bright speck, it moves from frame to frame.'

'What is it?'

'That is the asteroid,' said Wael.

'How big?' asked Mourad.

'Yes, Prime Minster, that is the question. You get right to the heart of—'

'Answer my question.'

'Devastatingly big. And it is dangerously close to an Earth-impact trajectory, perhaps actually on track to … And I have been wondering, as I waited for you, here …' Wael paused again, then spoke quickly, spilling out his thoughts. 'What if we are the only ones who can do anything about it? If the meltdown is complete and no one is observing the skies and … But that's ridiculous. There must be many who, like me, have access to optical instruments. Many may be working half-blind, however. My own telescope is impeded by dust and weather. You know this site is below sea level. The best observatories are on mountainsides in clear air and—'

'What are you suggesting?' insisted Mourad. 'Is this another attack of some kind, like the Darkness and the Storm?'

He shook his head.

'No, that is vanishingly unlikely.'

'You say there is a threat of impact. But asteroids are all named and tracked. How can it be that—'

'Madame Prime Minister, are you not aware of the solar storms?' interrupted Wael, forgetting his manners. 'Vast coronal mass ejections have made auroras visible in temperate and even Mediterranean latitudes. Here in the desert, even …' He shook his head in disbelief. 'The CMEs represent vast quantities of energy projected out into the void.'

Mourad's eyes were sharp, her mind moving ahead of the information she had been given.

'You mean enough to deviate the path of an asteroid?'

'Yes,' said Wael, shocked at hearing the idea that was inside his own head pronounced aloud. 'And I have been wondering if we are perhaps the only ones who know what we know or, more importantly still, the only ones capable of taking action.'

59

In the back of the truck, Faroukh felt very weary, but he and Zeina were each given two small boxes of apple juice. Faroukh drank his, one after another, and felt the fructose go crusading through his bloodstream, bringing him gently back to life. Zeina, meanwhile, lay down on a hard bench, her breathing slow and steady.

They had only covered ten or so kilometres on foot, so it took fifteen minutes to arrive at the military-scientific campus in the depression at the heart of the Great Sand Sea. The masked and gloved officers took them to a hygiene station where a medical officer on overnight duty put them through a sequence of routine tests, including blood analysis.

Because the Egyptian border guards had taken his few official papers – and because he had destroyed his electronic devices for fear of bringing digital infection into the base – Faroukh was unable to confirm his identity. The doctor, however, was a refugee from Egypt and recognised her compatriot, Zeina, lending credence to Faroukh's story.

'And you have travelled here from Aswan?' asked the doctor.

'Yes.'

'How did you manage that?'

'Forgive me if I ask you to hurry. Professor Al-Mesih, your commander, is an old friend,' Faroukh told her. 'I need to speak to him at the earliest opportunity. Are the hygiene tests complete?'

The doctor refreshed her screen, consulted the readouts and pronounced them healthy. Faroukh noticed that the terminal was not connected, that its local area network cables were trailing, unplugged, on the floor.

'I saw Professor Al-Mesih a short while ago, going from the telescope room to his office. I have a buggy. I can take you. Would you perhaps like to shower and be given a change of clothes?'

'No, thank you. Time may be short,' said Faroukh.

'For what?' asked the doctor, looking worried.

'I wish I knew.'

The doctor drove them across the sand, under the dark night sky, unable to resist asking them a sequence of questions that Faroukh answered tersely but politely. Zeina remained silent. At the entrance to the administration block, giving access to the base commander's office, Wael met them at the outer door, embracing his old friend, wanting to know how he came to be there.

'This is extraordinary – and, perhaps, meant. We are in need of your counsel.'

'We?' asked Faroukh, feeling overwhelmed by the strange energy in his friend's manner.

'The prime minister and I.'

'Madame Mourad is here?' asked Faroukh, astounded.

'In person. Come.'

'Stay with me, Miss Zeina,' said Faroukh.

Wael led them through a deserted lobby into an antechamber with four desks that looked like they belonged to administrative staff. He opened a wide door into a much smarter space, with dark double-glazed windows beside a nest of sofas, a large conference table covered with architectural and engineering drawings, illuminated by a standard lamp, plus a more substantial desk with its own smaller light. A woman in fatigues stood up and turned to greet them. Though he had been told to expect her, it took Faroukh a few seconds to recognise the prime minister.

'This is the most remarkable coincidence,' he told her. 'Though it is also natural, given the circumstances in which we find ourselves.' He went on to formally introduce his companion, praising her fortitude and intelligence. 'Without Miss Zeina, I would be imprisoned in a mud cell on the frontier.'

Mourad demanded more detail and Faroukh gave her and Wael a succinct version of his and Zeina's flight from Aswan, including the crucial initial role played by Amaury Barra in helping them escape the flood.

'But he is dead?' asked Mourad. 'You are certain?'

'There is no doubt.'

She sighed and told them: 'He was there when the French extraction team snatched me from my safe room, saving my life from the insurrection at the gates. He lost a hand in doing so. What other news?'

'We know nothing except what I have just told you and—'

Wael interrupted: 'There is a more pressing question we must all face.'

'Yes,' said Mourad. 'I am glad you are here, Faroukh.'

'I am very tired,' said Zeina, quietly.

'Lie down, sister,' said Faroukh. Zeina did as he suggested, stretching out on one of the two sofas beneath the dark windows. Faroukh told Mourad: 'I am glad that I persuaded you to let me go to Aswan in your place. What else has happened?'

'What else is now happening is a better question,' said Wael. 'You are aware of the French weapon, God's Thunder? I have been tracking the third platform that remains in orbit. It presents an opportunity. There is a further threat.'

'What can that be?' asked Faroukh.

'There is an asteroid, 2037 AQ9 – that is its official designation – that ought safely to have passed by Earth between our orbit and the Moon's, but I believe the exceptional CME energies – the solar flares – have altered its trajectory. Prime Minster Mourad and I have been discussing—'

Faroukh interrupted: 'You are capable of sending God's Thunder on an intercept course?'

'That is very perceptive, my friend. I can try. And it may be possible.'

'And fragment the asteroid? There will still be impacts?'

'That is one outcome. They would be more minor and, as is often said, many may fall in the oceans.'

'I am minded to give the order to act, Faroukh,' said Mourad.

'What counter-arguments are there?' he asked them both.

'The additional impacts of the tungsten-rod payload on God's Thunder,' said Wael, 'but my idea and my calculations are designed to send both the weapon and the asteroid out of reach of Earth's gravity.'

'You believe you can do this?'

'I cannot be confident. But is it better to do nothing?' asked Wael.

Mourad made a sound of agreement.

Faroukh asked them: 'Can you discuss this further with other science establishments or other heads of state?'

'No,' said Wael.

'Of course,' he agreed. 'We are cut off.'

'And, as Professor Al-Mesih has explained to me,' said Mourad, 'for our own good, too.'

'Can I say something?'

They all turned to look at Zeina who had sat up on the sofa. Faroukh guessed her intention before she began.

'Sister …' he warned.

'If I have understood, it is an impact weapon. So is the asteroid. They will cause vast destruction, but will not leave a lasting toxicity. The consequences might be like pigs in an orchard, turning over the dirt beneath the trees, perhaps for better, not worse. Or, if they hit water, they will cause tsunamis to sweep over the surface of the planet. Death will come, yes. But think of all the terrible things that will be washed away, too.' Faroukh tried to interrupt, but Zeina continued. 'Humans are survivors. How many of us are needed for survival, if that is your concern, if survival is what we deserve? Not so very many, I think.'

'Zeina Yaseen,' said Mourad, 'you have played your honourable part. It is over. Now, I cannot stand by and do nothing,

'So, prime minister,' said Wael, ignoring Zeina's interruption, 'do you give me the authority to try?'

'You say there is urgency?'

'The relative trajectories will soon go beyond the point of opportunity.'

'After which it will be too late,' said Faroukh, pointlessly.

60

Wael took the prime minster and her closest counsellor into the operations room, adjoining his office, a space only six metres by five metres but containing, he told them, more computer processing power than every single NASA control room for the entire Apollo series from one to seventeen. They left Zeina to sleep in Wael's office.

Two technicians were on overnight duty, but Wael dismissed them. After they had left, he told his companions: 'The instructions are preset. I worked on them while waiting for your helicopter to land, madame. Can I ask you to confirm the order?'

'And if we do nothing?' asked Mourad, her voice uncertain. 'If we allow the disaster to happen?'

'The asteroid will strike, I believe, the northern French coast or maybe the Channel. Its impact will be devastating, with additional damage from pieces broken off the larger mass.'

'Will there be a tidal wave?' she asked.

'That depends on the depth of the water at the impact site, if it lands on water. But the force will almost certainly be sufficient to provoke a wave that builds.' He glanced at each of them. 'But we are safe, here, in Al-Jaghar.'

'What about Cyrene City?' demanded Mourad. 'Will any fragments fall in the Mediterranean?'

'I do not believe so.'

'Faroukh?' asked Mourad.

'As you said earlier, we cannot stand by. I agree.'

Wael nodded and Faroukh watched him access his computer control panel.

'This will only take a moment.'

Wael's fingers rattled the keys. A new worry came into Faroukh's mind. He began to speak: 'Is there—?'

Wael struck the 'enter' key.

'It is done,' he said.

'Good,' said Mourad.

'I was about to ask—' said Faroukh.

Just then, however, he was interrupted by one of the technicians, slamming the door back against the wall, a flimsy sheet of A4 paper flapping in her hand.

'Forgive this interruption, Professor Al-Mesih,' she said. 'The radio room has sent this over.'

'Is this from somewhere in Egypt?'

'No, Professor. It seems to be from President Manouche of Mali, but we have triangulated its source to thirty or forty kilometres west of Al-Jaghar.'

'What does that mean?'

'I'm afraid I have no idea, Professor. Perhaps a vehicle on the trans-Saharan trade route? Though the location isn't near any road.'

'Give it to me,' said Faroukh.

The technician looked to Wael for permission. He nodded and she handed it over. Faroukh read it through, stumbling over the imperfect transcription which included several spelling mistakes. He passed it to Mourad who, once she had perused it, handed it on, in silence, to Wael.

'You did well to bring this straight away,' Faroukh told the technician. 'Leave us now.'

Reluctantly, the woman left. As the door closed behind her, Mourad snapped: 'What does this mean?'

'I fear,' said Faroukh, 'that we have made the wrong decision.'

'Why do you say that?' asked Wael.

'Those last lines,' said Faroukh. 'Lamarque says that the viral contamination consists of "deliberate accelerators of destruction".'

'What has that to do with us?'

'You have just used your digital facilities to adjust the orbital plan for God's Thunder.'

'But Al-Jaghar is secure. We are entirely cut off from contagion.'

'I fear no longer.'

'What do you mean?' demanded Mourad.

'The weapon was retained by the French. Therefore, they will have some form of communication with it.'

Wael's face became deathly pale.

'So, the weapon itself may be infected?'

'And your new commands may be the spur for that "accelerator of destruction" to do its worst.'

Wael turned back to the computer console, reaching round behind to detach the cable for the local area network.

'Is that enough?' asked Mourad.

Wael didn't answer. Faroukh followed his gaze. The computer screen was flashing with a warning of viral attack, opening one pop-up window and then another and then another. As they watched, the cascade of graphical tiles jostled and crowded the monitor until every centimetre was overtaken. Then, abruptly, the device shut down.

Neither Faroukh nor Wael nor Mourad spoke, as if they all knew what was about to happen. After an ominous pause, they heard the brief chuntering of the hard drive as the computer restarted.

The monitor came back to life with a single word, blinking like a command in a sub-routine of code.

Fire.

61

Because Wael Al-Mesih had failed, in the sky above Earth's eastern hemisphere, a different kind of fire had come, illuminating the darkness of the night over Asia.

The asteroid designated 2037 AQ9 was travelling at about ninety kilometres above the surface in a decaying orbit, tracking from west to east at around twenty-two kilometres per second, meaning it was only a matter of time before it made impact off the north coast of France. Friction with the Earth's atmosphere was stripping away chunks of material. Every parcel was glowing hot.

At the same time, further south in the dark sky, the God's Thunder weapon had released its payload of tungsten rods, each about the size of a telegraph pole but shaped to be more aerodynamic and with far greater mass. They, too, were like streaks of fire, glowing hot, moving at about the same speed as the asteroid. The Fire virus – mistakenly uploaded as an 'accelerator of destruction' by Wael – had placed them on the most destructive trajectory possible, making landfall and seafall a little sooner than AQ9, about twenty-four degrees further south and sixteen degrees further east, in the region of the Canary Islands.

PART 6
FIRE

62

SEPTEMBER 2037

For Alex, the day of the Storm was at last coming to an end. He couldn't be certain that Mariam or Amaury or Professor Fayard were dead. He didn't know that President Manouche had given his time-delayed message into the hands of Tamba Dem and ordered him to overfly the Sahara. He had no idea that Al-Medawi and Zeina Yaseen were *en route* overland for Al-Jaghar. He was unaware that Gloria had invited Emmeline Cantor into her home.

Alex was generally able to sleep anywhere, any time: the upright front seat of a car; hard ground; a bench in a patch of shade at midday. It was a kind of superpower, Mariam told him, to be able to check out, to take a pause, to withdraw from whatever dramas were going on around him.

The improvised cocoon made from the wreckage of the Ae4 was comparative luxury, compared to some places he had been obliged to rest. Though not recently. It had been a couple of years since he had found himself alone and friendless in enemy territory. It was the hyperconnected world that did that. He was never alone, never out of touch, always contactable – rescuable.

Poiret knows I was alive before the crash landing. Why hasn't she sent help?

Rain began to fall, drumming on the fragment of nose cone. He tried to make a judgement on how much time had passed while he briefly rested. Maybe an hour, just enough to sink into a period of slow-wave sleep, profound and restorative, but not sufficient for the essential dreaming oblivion of rapid-eye movement. He felt slow and foggy, so he didn't at first process the noise he could hear. Finally, his mind began making defensive calculations.

How far exactly? And why so close without attacking?

The sound was away to the left, a ragged snuffling and something heavy but soft being shaken or tossed around. He leaned over the edge of the flatbed, groping for his rucksack. It was gone.

He sat up, taking care not to bang his head on the improvised steel shelter. It was very dark. He assumed the moon had set or was hidden by thick cloud. Disentangling his legs from the lightweight in-flight blankets, he slid off the edge of the flatbed onto his knees, feeling the moisture in the ground through the fabric of his trousers. He managed to stand without a sound, but his muscles were unresponsive and slow, bruised by the shocks of the emergency landing and crouching and running and crawling through the undergrowth, leaving him in need of a proper workout to metabolise the residual lactic acid.

He heard the noise again, about twenty metres distant in a slight dip in the land. At first, he could see nothing, then he caught a glimpse of two points of light, a hand's width apart, orange in colour – the eyes of a fox.

His vision began to improve as his pupils expanded, identifying the shape of the animal, a flash of white at the end of its tail, the lighter-coloured fur on its face. He ran and it ran, dragging the rucksack along in its teeth. Alex recognised the glint of glass from several of the miniature bottles of spirits as they tumbled out. Bending down, he found a stone the size of his palm and threw it, striking the fox on the rump. The animal tumbled forward, released the rucksack from its jaws and disappeared into the shadowy underbrush.

Alex followed the path the fox had taken, scanning the dark ground for his belongings, cursing his stupidity. He remembered eating some of the in-flight snacks before lying back, ready for sleep. And he hadn't finished them. He had simply folded the half-empty packets over and left them in the rucksack. The scent had no doubt drawn the nocturnal fox, perhaps from far away. Or maybe it had been his own human odour, warm and unwashed, that the intelligent scavenger knew to associate with waste food.

It was difficult to know whether he had found everything, but the rucksack felt more or less the same weight as it had before, so he retraced his steps, enfolded still by darkness, pulling off Davide's silver-grey jacket – that he had put on over his own for warmth – and stuffing it into the neck of the bag.

Abruptly, he was challenged by a voice speaking Haitian Creole. He ducked down. The challenge came again – unmistakable, though he didn't catch the precise words. Then it was followed by what he supposed was a translation into French.

'*Tiens-toi tranquille. On ne veut pas te faire de mal. Tu es un objet de valeur.*'

Stand still. We don't want to hurt you. You are a thing of value.

Pulling a cuff of his jacket down over his hand for protection, he pushed at the sharp rim of the nose-cone fragment so it toppled over, its heavy edge embedding itself in the wet ground, no longer a roof, now a defensive shield. He crouched behind it, listening for movement, needing to know how many, how far. To his surprise, a new sound came from the east, a vehicle of some kind, descending the highway from the frontier, without headlights but identifiable as an EV from the absence of engine noise, just the hiss of pneumatic tyres on the wet road. Then it stopped and its lights came on, brilliant white, making him feel like an unrehearsed actor or a trapped criminal, abruptly caught by a spotlight, not knowing what he should say or do.

Alex heard the doors of the Dominicans' electric vehicle open and the unmistakeable sound of the release of safety catches on weapons against which he had no defence.

Has Poiret managed to get in touch with the Dominican authorities, alerting them to my presence?

A shot rang out, striking the fragment of sheet steel from the Ae4's nose cone.

'*Reste-là ou tu es,*' shouted the same Haitian-accented voice as before. '*On va en discuter de la récompense avec les copains dominicains.*'

Alex heard soft footsteps pushing through the undergrowth, five or six pairs at least, making directly for the EV. He glanced round the edge of torn steel. They looked like silhouette puppets, meeting the 'Dominican friends' on the black ribbon of tarmac, in order to 'talk about the reward'. And, after a couple of minutes, they were laughing together and Alex concluded that a deal had been agreed, that the Dominicans were going to be cut in on whatever ransom deal the Haitians managed to strike.

You're wasting your time, he wanted to tell them. *There are far more important things happening.*

He saw a flare of light across the dawn sky, little more than a speck, but falling in a slow curve.

The AI viruses have reached the satellite clusters and they are losing velocity, dropping out of their degraded orbits. Poiret must be experiencing the same struggle for digital control of the ship's systems, undermining her ability to act.

Then he had another thought, remembering what had happened to his comm-watch and his warning about 'accelerators of destruction'.

Does a naval frigate have a self-destruct code?

Peering round the torn metal again, Alex could just make out a sequence of handshakes and the Dominicans getting back into their EV, making a tidy three-point turn and heading back up the hill to the frontier. The Haitians came towards him, fanning out, making it impossible for him to maintain his cover.

Maybe I want to be ransomed, brought to some kind of authority so I can share what I know about Davide and his father?

He felt acutely aware that he was behaving in a way dictated by the habit of survival and wondered what the point was, if everyone dear to him was dead or dying.

No, there is always hope, however foolish.

He stepped out into the open, raising his hands. The Haitian gang members surrounded him, haphazardly patting down his clothes, speaking to one another in Creole, failing to find the *chevalière* ring in the corner of his jacket pocket. They seemed each to be dressed in some kind of macabre fancy dress, except for their leader and a teenage boy who stood apart. The kid looked tense and jumpy with a mask lodged on top of his head, carrying a large hessian sack, in which one of the others placed the hunting knife and belt that Alex had taken from the dead camo-truck driver. The leader seemed confident and at ease in a voluminous rain cape, holding a handgun. When one of the others found the alcohol miniatures in Alex's rucksack, they all exclaimed in delight, but the leader forbade them to drink.

The leader in the rain cape pointed away towards the hills whose profile was just darker than the sky, adding: 'Come.'

'Where are you taking me?' Alex asked him.

They marched him three hundred metres away from the road to a dip in the ground where another battered truck was parked. Alex understood that he had been so tired and banged up that he had slept through their careful approach. He expected to be trussed and thrown in the back, but the leader invited him to sit up front. Surprisingly, the kid was driving. There was no cabin light.

'I will make sure you are well paid for delivering me safely,' said Alex. 'Can we go to the capital?'

'No, too dangerous. Rioting and looting. We go to Saint-Just.'

'I can get you a reward big enough to change all your lives, for every one of you, for ever.'

The leader nodded, slowly.

'That was in my mind, too.' The kid engaged first gear, then second, picking his way towards the road, the tree stumps starkly illuminated by the headlamps. The leader asked: 'You are a military man?'

'Yes.'

'What are you doing in Haiti?'

'I lost control of my aircraft and crash-landed.'

'Yes, that is what the Dominicans told us, but …' He stopped, the light of recognition coming into his eyes. 'You are Alexandre Lamarque. You are "the man who saved the world". The reward for delivering you will be great indeed. How did it feel?'

'How did what feel?'

'To do what you did?'

'It felt like duty,' said Alex, honestly.

'Yes. And people are grateful that you did your duty.' The truck picked up speed, following the straight run of tarmac, leaving behind the wreckage. 'The people do not do civil defence in France. You do not live in fear of invasion, of being forced into a life of resistance? When I was at school, it was something we were taught. There were classes in how to live on the bounty of the land, of nature, while preparing a counterattack.'

'Were you told who your enemy might be?'

'The Doms. Or you – the French. That is tradition, after all. Napoleon hunted the liberation army of Toussaint Louverture with dogs.'

'Many years ago,' said Alex.

'The ripples live on. In our classrooms, we pretended to be injured and tied tourniquets round one another's limbs. We trained with wooden rifles when the likely weapons of attack were long-range missiles.' He mimed such an attack, making a whistling noise between his gappy teeth and showing a trajectory with his hand. 'Then coronavirus, not missiles. We could not fight that with our guerilla training.' The leader shook his head. 'But none of it matters. There is only now and here, not before, not later, not elsewhere. What good to look back and say that Haiti was the first Black republic? What good to blame the earthquakes and hurricanes, Matthew in 2016, Antoine in 2033, or the failed governments and the men and the women of good faith who killed or were killed, because that was all there was – kill or be killed?'

'I understand,' Alex assured him.

There was a pause. The kid held the steering steady, following the slick, wet tarmac in the darkness. Then the leader suddenly declaimed – unexpectedly – in English:

'Though fallen Thyself, never to rise again,
Live, and take comfort. Thou hast left behind
Powers that will work for thee; air, earth, and skies;
There's not a breathing of the common wind
That will forget thee; thou hast great allies;
Thy friends are exultations, agonies,
And love, and Man's unconquerable mind.'

Alex heard voices from the back of the truck, joining in the last line like an invocation – the sounds of the words, if not their meaning.

'The English poet Wordsworth,' said the leader, 'mourning the tragic destiny of Toussaint Louverture, telling us that the "air, earth, and skies" will work to fulfil his – and our – dreams of prosperous statehood. I wonder, though, does the land really need people at all.'

Alex felt a shudder of unease. This was eerily close to the conspiracies he had been fighting, the idea that the modern human societies were the disease, that a world without people – at least, without a huge swathe of people – would automatically be a better place.

63

As the kid drove on, Alex scanned the dark terrain, concerned that they seemed very far from civilisation. He wondered who the Haitians thought they could sell him to. France had always taken an interest because Haiti had the potential to assume strategic importance in any regional conflict and – though this had yet to be categorically proved by exploratory drilling – sat on top of oil reserves that were rumoured to exceed even those of Venezuela on the far side of the Caribbean Sea.

The sooner we arrive at wherever the trade is destined to take place, the better. And in the meantime, best to keep them on side.

'You speak French extremely well. English, too,' he said. 'Where were you educated?'

The leader smiled his gappy smile: 'In the capital. I was a child of the administration of President Jovenel Moïse. My parents were both elected members of parliament. In different roles, they were involved with co-ordinating aid services provided by the United Nations and others, importing their cholera and their sexually transmitted diseases and their ignorance, along with their guns and ammunition and their frail survival tents.'

The road continued downhill.

'You say you were a child then? You must be thirty-five, forty, today?'

'I am thirty-two years old, but this body is worn and tired. I was a teenager in 2021 when President Moïse was assassinated. Perhaps my parents heard in advance? They sent me away.'

'They were killed?'

'Haiti was so poor. What use were we? What value was there in destabilising a broken nation further?'

'The oil beneath the ground?'

'Oil that international treaties on carbon reduction forbid us to exploit.' The leader shrugged. 'Moïse was accused of providing gangs with guns and money to intimidate his political opponents. Perhaps true. If so, he was an obstacle to prosperity which only comes with rule of law. And, today, prosperity is out of the question. We pick over the scraps of what is left, living for the moment. In Saint-Just, I am law.'

Alex changed the subject: 'Your companions are all wearing some kind of costumes. Why is that?'

'It is a carnival of my own creation. I made the characters out of tradition, but they are mine.' From beneath his rain cape, the man brought out a package of leaves tied with a natural twine. He carefully unfolded it, revealing a dozen smaller parcels, each about the size of a sugar lump. 'In these leaves there is "mad honey". Do you know what that is?'

'No,' said Alex.

'Many years ago, flowers came to Haiti, big leaves, dark and shiny, blooms in rich dark colours. They came from the Himalayas, which is a place I have never visited. Have you ever been to the Himalayas?'

'Yes,' said Alex, keen to build rapport. 'In the high mountains, you feel free, bizarrely free, but it can be a trick. At first, you think it's because of the majesty of the landscape and your own insignificance in comparison. Then you realise it's because you are oxygen deprived.'

The leader laughed and told him: 'That is very good. But the feeling of freedom is real, while it lasts? You experienced it, however quickly it faded. The explanation came later and did not change that moment.'

'We live in a state of constant reassessment,' agreed Alex, 'searching for patterns that reveal the truth of who we are, what our experiences mean.'

The leader's fingers played idly with the packages in his lap.

'The flower that came was the rhododendron, of course. It contains a poison, making it unpleasant for animals that would otherwise eat it. Animals who have not learnt this experience a racing heart, stumble and fall, vomit. But people use this poison in small doses for another purpose.'

'As a medicine?' guessed Alex.

'In a way,' said the leader, then he called out in Creole to his companions in the rear of the truck and they laughed. 'I told them what you said, that it is medicine, and they find that funny because it does not heal them but it does take them away from their troubles.'

'Is it a hallucinogen? Does it bring visions and dreams?'

The leader took Alex's chin in his hand, turning his head to face him in the gloomy cab.

'We did our search, but you are armed, still, with other weapons – intangible weapons – knowledge and experience and understanding. I can see them in your eyes.'

'You have knowledge and experience, too,' said Alex, resisting the desire to bat the man's hand away. 'And strength of body and mind. How else would you have survived?'

'Never mind,' he said, abruptly, releasing Alex's chin. 'We are here.'

The young man pulled the truck in to the side of the road, leaving the headlights on as they all got out, near to a ring of stones, a ceremonial meeting place. In the centre was a fire pit dug into the soft dirt, full of ash, soaked by rain. The leader indicated by gesture that Alex should take a seat.

In the glare of the headlamps, he could finally count seven adults, plus the teenager who just then pulled his mask down over his face, revealing it to resemble a lion. He contemplated the other costumes invented by the leader. The two immediately to his left wore leather skull-caps mounted with the horns of a goat or a ram, plus grubby t-shirts, woollen jumpers and ragged jeans. Beyond them was a very thin young man in close-fitting white long-johns and t-shirt, his dark face and neck and arms eerily daubed with white pigment. To Alex's right were, he thought, a man and a woman, wearing very baggy worn and dirty suits with cloth bags over their heads, with holes cut for eyes and mouths. Beyond them was a woman in a green hospital gown, her face painted in the same white pigment, a scrub-cap on her head, carrying a leather satchel daubed with a cross in ochre mud.

The leader was the last to take his position. Sitting opposite, Alex watched him pull off his yellow waterproof rain cape, revealing a dirty white dress that came down just below his knees, quite close-fitting on his strong torso but flared below the waist. The shoulders and hem were fringed with ragged lace. His handgun hung in a leather pouch that dangled against his chest. He folded himself cross-legged on the ground in front of his rock, using it as something to lean against, taking his time to sit as he was a tall man with long limbs.

A little way away, the boy fetched a battered plastic water container from the rear of the truck and put it in the leader's lap. Alex realised how very thirsty he was and hoped it would be passed round. He could hear a stream that ran noisily down a gully maybe a hundred metres away and wondered if it might be healthier to refill the jerrican with fresh. And there were water purifying tablets in the med-kit in his rucksack.

The leader was unwrapping the smaller leaves from the lumps of mad honey while the other Haitians – in their extraordinary costumes – were speaking to one another in the Creole he couldn't follow. To his surprise, the woman in the green hospital gown addressed him in broken French.

'I am Mama Cov. I bring death. You understand?'

'You play the role of—'

'I am Mama Cov,' she interrupted. 'Not play.'

Alex nodded: 'Mama Covid?'

She nodded, too: 'Cov is real. Virus real. Death come. There is no hide. Future come.'

'I understand,' said Alex, quietly.

Just then, the breeze picked up and a squall of rain came angling in out of the dark sky, illuminated like beads of crystal by the headlamps.

'Not here, then,' said the leader, gathering up the lumps of mad honey. 'It's a shame. This is a special place.'

He got up and they jostled him out of the ring of stones.

'Where are we going?'

'*Chez Papa Dentelle*,' said Mama Cov.

'The house of Papa Lace? Where is that?'

'*Chez moi,*' said the leader. 'My house. I am Papa Lace.'

64

Alex forced himself to remain alert as the long highway unfurled in front of them, hoping the teenager was a good driver because the rain persisted and the dark road began to twist and turn, first up into a range of hills, then down the other side through a series of switchbacks. At last, after maybe a couple of hours, they forked off onto a single-lane track.

The night was still dark with no hint of dawn. The teenager yawned and wound down his window, presumably to keep himself alert with the fresh breeze, allowing in a hint of salt air. The headlights scanned the landscape on the twisting road, revealing arid rock with little vegetation and no hint of rivers or streams.

Though clearly close at hand, the sea was not yet visible. The rain stopped as a set of blocky silhouettes came into view against the blue-blackness of the horizon. Alex deduced that they were approaching some kind of settlement, with one larger building profiled above the rest.

They came to the larger building first, surrounded by a corrugated iron fence, with a gateway made up of a couple of loose galvanised panels. The kid stopped the vehicle and the two gang members with horned caps jumped down from the rear to pull them aside.

Illuminated by the headlamps, the truck edged forward into the courtyard of a dilapidated nineteenth-century manor house where a smoky fire burnt in an oil drum. Alex saw a couple of smaller vehicles, a well and several untidy piles of scrap.

'The house of Papa Lace,' said the gap-toothed leader, rousing himself. He opened the passenger door and jumped down. 'My house.'

The courtyard was dry, indicating the rain had passed it by. The air was mild beneath thick cloud. They all trooped indoors to a large ballroom with an assortment of mismatched furniture arranged in a ring, reminiscent of the circle of stones at the side of the hilltop road. At a word from the leader, the young man in white tipped out the contents of Alex's rucksack, separating the med-kit and the clothes from the miniatures of alcohol. The teenage driver fetched the jerrican and removed the stopper so that the young man in white could pour in the contents of all the tiny bottles, nine or ten of them – vodka, whisky, brandy and gin.

Hopefully enough alcohol, Alex thought, *to neutralise any pathogens.*

Papa Lace gestured to everyone to sit down. He took the jerrican and drank deeply, then passed it to his left. Mama Cov drank, then the two Haitians in baggy, dirty suits. When it came to him, Alex tipped it up to wet his fingers with the alcoholic mixture and wipe them round the rim, hoping to eradicate any germs to which his immune system had no defence.

A murmur went up from his extraordinary companions, exhorting him to drink. He did so, tasting some kind of sickly natural fruit juice – maybe peach or apricot – fermented in order to produce an intoxicating mash, as well as the ghastly mix of spirits.

He passed the jerrican to the left and it was soon back with the leader. Papa Lace passed it over his shoulder to the kid, who lifted his lion mask onto the top of his head and drank, too. Meanwhile, Papa Lace placed the packages of mad honey on the dirty floorboards in front of him. The boy in the lion mask went round the circle collecting everyone's weapons, arranging them carefully against the panelled wall: three machetes; four knives of varying sizes; a length of plumbing pipe; Papa Lace's handgun. The leader laughed.

'Lion Boy will look after our weapons. Otherwise, who knows what our visions might make us do?'

There were eight tiny parcels on the floorboards, one for each of the Haitians and one for Alex, too, it seemed. Papa Lace raised his hands above his head, the sleeves of his dress slipping towards his shoulders, revealing his strong arms. The others all mirrored his gesture. Papa Lace pronounced a long string of Creole, incomprehensible to Alex, to which the others responded in kind. They stood up, each collecting a tiny green parcel of mad honey, removing it from its leaf wrapper. Then they placed the amber-coloured poison on one another's tongues.

Papa Lace crossed the room towards Alex.

'It is for you to place the mad honey in my mouth,' he said, 'and I will do the same for you.'

'I don't want to,' said Alex. 'It may do me harm.'

'It may do us harm, too,' said the leader. 'Mama Cov, the Fat Cats in their suits, White Zombie, the Goat Men. Only time will tell.'

'I mean you no harm. Do you wish me harm?'

Papa Lace shrugged: 'You are here. You must be a part of what we are. Then, perhaps, if all goes well, we will seek the great ransom together, the one you spoke of.'

'How long will it last, the mad honey?'

'What is time?' asked Papa Lace. 'A way of measuring what is past. Under the influence of the mad honey, there will be only now.'

Papa Lace opened his mouth. Alex thought of Professor Fayard and his habitual assertion that there would always be 'time enough'. Then he placed the sticky amber nugget on Papa Lace's tongue. The Haitian held it there, his lips drawn back and his gappy teeth bared, waiting for Alex to part his lips in his turn. Alex did so, allowing a nugget of mad honey to be placed on his own tongue.

Papa Lace began to chew. Alex copied him. The mad honey tasted bitter, like indigestible grass but with a faint sickly sweetness behind. It made Alex want to retch, but he thought that was perhaps a psychosomatic reaction. Papa Lace held his gaze then re-opened his mouth to show his parcel had gone. Alex swallowed and did the same, asking: 'Now what?'

Papa Lace returned to his position on the far side of the circle, adjusting his flared skirts and crossing his legs: 'We wait.'

At first Alex was aware only of the sounds of the others breathing and fidgeting. Little by little, though, time began to lose form and shape, like in a dream. He breathed deeply, hyper-aware of the air filling his lungs as if it was some viscous liquid. He experienced a flutter of panic at the idea that he was suffocating, but forced his rational mind to reassert control by standing up and stretching his arms up, expanding his chest, then his head began to spin.

Mama Cov came laughing over, taking his hand, leading him out into the courtyard, showing him the well with its battered bucket balanced on a rough wall. Even though Alex's rational mind knew that the drop to the water was only about three metres, the deep shadow resembled a dark crevasse opening into the bowels of the Earth.

Alex shook his head, trying to dispel the impossible vision. Then Mama Cov spun him round, looping the long strap of her satchel with its ochre cross around his neck. In the flickering light from the fire in the oil drum, the cross seemed to turn to liquid blood, as if the leather was living skin that had been sliced open.

Alex wrenched the bag from his neck and threw it on the ground. Out of nowhere, the Goat Men came and linked their arms through his, dancing him round, moving crablike, stamping and speaking in rhythm. Despite himself, Alex felt the desire to join in. He began mimicking the unknown sounds, copying them a little behind the beat.

The others all joined in and, soon, there was a circle of all eight of them, the rhythm of their chant matched by the pounding of their feet. Alex had a vision of a land being beaten flat by dancing feet through an eternity of days and nights of ritual. He had a blinding revelation that they were right, these Haitian revellers. They had found meaning where his life had none – and the meaning they had found was the dance. He broke away, knowing that what he was thinking was foolish, whimsical.

Or is it? Might it be possible that I have always, all my life, been mistaken, on the wrong path?

He fell to his knees, dry-heaving, but unable to be sick.

I'm dehydrated.

He groped for the well, imagining his insides withering like leaves in a drought, becoming brittle, veins atrophying and snapping, his arteries turning to dust. He felt his mind failing as if his brain had shrunk to the size of a small desiccated walnut.

Alex pushed the bucket off the wall into the water, hearing its splash from far away. Someone snatched at his clothes but he threw them off. The world had turned monochrome, a confusing whirl of dim greys and deeper blacks, as if he was the pivot of a grim zoetrope with each of his surreal companions a separate jerky image, stumbling and groping one another.

He hauled on the handle of the well, raising the bucket. When it came within reach, he drank desperately, clumsily, from the lip, sloshing water down his face and body, drenching his clothes. He staggered away, thinking he must be dying, which was stupid, because he didn't know what it felt like to die, though he had seen it many times, not least those people ground to nothing by the evil machinery of the Coming Darkness and the Coming Storm.

All the same, if he wasn't dying, what was this sensation of being out of breath from running, at the same time as fearing that the beating of his heart was slowing, the pauses stretching out into long silences without hope, coming closer to the final infinite silence?

He made a supreme effort to push himself away from the well, stumbling towards the front door of the dilapidated manor house, wanting to leave behind the debauched gang members, but he fell on the steps, tripping on the jerrican with its pungent cocktail of sweet fermented fruit and mixed spirit alcohols. He snatched it up, wrenched off the lid, then gulped like a drowning man coming up for air, until the Lion Boy pulled it from his weakening fingers.

For an unknown length of time, Alex lay on his back, looking up at the dark sky, before abruptly choking on a mouthful of acid bile. He rolled onto his side, coughing and spluttering, his eyes watering and his nose running, desperate to snatch inadequate breaths between the awful spasms of his stomach, trying to empty itself onto the damp ground.

At last, the heaving stopped and he lay, feeling compressed by gravity, but just about able to arrange his limbs into the recovery position so that, should he be sick again, he would at least not be suffocated by his own vomit.

Without a thought in his head, Alex felt consciousness leave him – not the gradual descent, deeper and deeper into sleep, but a sudden void, like snuffing out the only candle in a deep and shadowless cave, far underground, in pitiless isolation.

65

Claudine Poiret found the rigid inflatable lifeboat extremely challenging. She was sick over the side in the cold Caribbean Sea within a minute of the craft hitting the choppy water, clinging to a nylon rope looped tightly through handholds all around the inflatable hull.

Once the first malaise passed, she managed to sit up, more or less in control of her breathing and her digestion. The marine who had taken responsibility for her – Abadie – helped her into a lifejacket from a compartment under the nearest transverse seat. It inflated automatically and, for a panicked second, Poiret thought it would constrict her ragged breathing, already compromised by seasickness and fear. He tugged at the lower edge, resettling it away from her throat.

'*Je vous remercie.*'

Thank you.

The RIB seemed very crowded. She wondered if it was made for twenty and she was the extra passenger. But it sat quite high in the water. Despite her nausea, she began to feel more secure.

'Where are we going?' she asked.

'We need to make landfall,' Abadie replied.

At least, she thought he did. The noise of the motor and the wind made it hard to be sure.

He pointed and she followed the direction with her eyes. They were heading for a vague coastline beyond an area of sea that was broken and topped with white foam. In comparison, the stretch of water they were currently crossing was choppy but not dangerous.

They entered the area of white water and the lifeboat jumped and plunged as, by turns, they stalled and lurched and barrelled through the swell. The noise and stench of the diesel engine increased, now and then accelerating to a whine as the propellor left the water. Poiret lay her head down on her arms and shut her eyes, trying not to let her teeth bang together, attempting to slow the nervous rhythm of her breathing.

They hit a particularly awkward wave and she was bounced up into the air, losing her grip on the safety rope, landing in a heap between the transverse seats in a puddle of cold grey seawater that drenched her inappropriate formal clothing. Abadie helped her up, insisting she pin her arm beneath the safety rope, wrapping it over her wrist to give a firmer hold. He, like the other crewmembers, was wearing waterproofs over his uniform. Poiret wanted to thank him, but her gorge rose once more and she dry heaved.

Then the lifeboat, with its cacophonous gunning engine, passed some unseen change in the seabed and the water became much calmer.

'We're through into the shallows,' Abadie shouted. 'Over the coastal shelf. The wind was blowing the sea onto the rocks, churning it up. It'll be easier now.'

With the safety rope still wrapped around her arm, Poiret turned her shoulders to lean back against the inflatable rubber hull. She tried to catch a glimpse of any other RIBs or lifeboats, bouncing and dipping as they fought with the angry waves.

'Where's everyone else?' she shouted.

'There is no one else.'

'What do you mean?'

'The lifeboats were bricked by the SCS. They're supposed to auto-launch but …'

His voice faded on the wind. Beyond the reef of rocks, the aft of the *Roussillon* had slipped into the grey seas, while the prow was almost vertical.

'We thought that we were strong,' said Poiret, quietly.

'What's that?' shouted the marine.

'Tell me your full name.'

'*Victor Abadie, Madame Poiret. Commando marine, première classe.*'

Poiret wasn't concerned about his division or his rank.

'No one got away, Victor?' she asked, pitching her voice higher. 'Not even the lifeboats on the other side?'

'Maybe one,' he shouted in return. 'The chief engineer was trying to bypass the releases, taking the SCS out of the loop, but if the missiles self-destructed who knows what else …'

Abadie's voice faded again. Poiret followed his gaze to see the vertical prow sliding downwards.

'What will happen to the remainder of the crew?' Poiret insisted.

'Anyone who survives will use lifejackets and floatation devices – anything they can liberate.'

'Can they swim into shore?'

'The tide will be against them and there's a current,' said Abadie. He gestured to the east. 'It may take them within reach of the coast, but thirty kilometres away.'

'Will they survive that long in the water?'

'Some of them.'

Poiret followed his gaze back to the *Roussillon*. For five or ten seconds, it hung, upright, two-thirds submerged. Then, abruptly, the speed of its descent beneath the grey waves accelerated, plunging downwards as if dragged by some submarine monster. Poiret felt a sense of desolation.

Should I have anticipated this? It was I who gave the order to fire.

Then, within just a few heartbeats, the frigate was gone, leaving a scattering of objects littering the surface, too far away now for Poiret to see what they were, but some of them, she assumed, the remaining crewmembers who had not been able to access lifeboats to make their escape.

'A distress call will have been sent out?' she asked. 'They will all have tracking beacons?'

'We don't have any other ships in the area,' said Abadie. 'Maybe Dominican coastguards, but—'

Poiret completed his thought: 'The technology might no longer function.'

'*Qu'est-ce qui se passe, Madame Poiret?*' the marine asked.

What's happening?

'Keep your focus, Victor Abadie.'

They were now close enough to the coast for Poiret to make out features of the dark land: a broad stretch of gravelly sand; a steep rise to a grassy ridge; a few huts; pale blurs of goats or maybe sheep in a penned-off enclosure.

There was no more bouncing or lurching. The other crewmembers became busy with equipment in waterproof kitbags that they drew out from compartments beneath the transverse seating. Then there was the first grating of the rigid floor under the prow of the inflatable lifeboat, scraping on the seabed. A last surge propelled them up the beach, then the outboard motor was tipped up to get the mechanism out of the water so as not to damage the propellor by fouling it in the sand.

Four of the twenty marines jumped out into about twenty centimetres of running surf, grasping the nylon line to haul the lifeboat up onto the sand. They paused as the tide ran out, beaching the craft, then pulled again as another wave ran in, lifting the hull for a few seconds, allowing them to progress a few more metres. As the water withdrew, the rest of the crewmembers jumped out and formed a human chain, passing the waterproof kitbags onto a grassy hump of land about thirty metres from the surf. When all the kit was disembarked, six marines hauled the RIB further away from the waterline with Poiret and Victor Abadie still on board. He helped her to sit on the inflatable hull and swing her legs out and over towards dry land. Poiret realised she felt very cold now they were safe on the beach.

Abadie led her to where the kit had been laid out in neat lines. She asked if they had access to radio transmitters.

'Not with any significant range.' He indicated one of the other marines who had just opened up a bag that contained dry clothing. 'You must get changed, Madame Poiret. You risk going into shock or hypothermia.'

He turned away and Poiret realised that all twenty men and women had formed a ring around her, resolutely facing outwards, making a kind of human fence to protect her modesty, behind which she could undress. She had a sudden sense of the ludicrousness of her situation and had to stifle a laugh.

She hurried to remove her drenched suit, feeling the sting of the sand on her bare skin. The kitbag contained half-a-dozen navy tracksuits in a soft jersey-wear fabric. She found a 'large' and pulled it on, then found a jacket and trousers in a breathable but waterproof fabric.

'Is there any footwear?'

'*Oui, madame,*' said Abadie, without turning his head.

'I'm dressed. Carry on,' she said.

The ring of marines broke away and Abadie delved into another kitbag, finding some shoes with velcro straps across the top and round the heel, making them suitable for feet of different sizes. Before putting them on, Poiret took off and wrung out her socks, deciding she would do better to dry them off rather than wear them.

Where though? And how?

She dropped the drenched socks on top of her sodden navy-blue trouser suit and looked out to sea again. The litter of detritus from the *Roussillon* was barely visible in the swell.

The sea is a kind of desert, lifeless and vast. How many were sucked into the deep and drowned?

She asked Abadie. 'What's the tidal range? Do you know?'

'About a metre.'

Poiret nodded. Their improvised encampment was, therefore, on dry ground and would remain so. She assumed there would be tents in some of the other kitbags, but they might have to go further away from the beach to find firmer ground to erect them.

'Do we have any hard currency for emergencies?'

'*Oui, madame.*' Abadie took her to inspect a safe under one of the seats of the RIB, opening it with a four-digit code. It contained four transparent vac-sealed bags of bank notes. 'Euros and dollars, small and large denominations.'

'Good.'

A marine whose name she hadn't learned used a head torch to inspect the defensive wounds on the backs of her hands. Once she was satisfied that they were clean, she closed them with synthetic skin and stood back. Poiret realised that the marines had all accomplished whatever tasks their training had prepared them for. They had all formed back into a circle, but facing inwards this time, waiting – hoping? – for her explanation and her orders.

66

The sinking *Roussillon* created vicious whirlpools of choppy waves, sucking many of the crew down beneath the surface. All of those who managed get away from the undertow, with their lifejackets for support, were dragged away by an eastward current, through heavy seas. How many would ultimately make landfall, regrouping in the cold and waiting for first light to identify the nearest population centre, remained to be seen.

Just before the launch of Poiret's RIB, a dozen crewmembers had managed to get aboard the one lifeboat that had successfully detached, bobbing in the choppy water. They dragged one another on board and, with a viable motor, fought the current, making for the nearest coastline.

This was a reasonable thing to do. The lights of the modest dock on the eastern side of Haré were lit, despite the pre-dawn hour, and the shelter of a stone or concrete harbour wall was vaguely profiled against the grey sea.

When the lifeboat came within hailing distance, however, it was attacked by gun emplacements lodged in the steep terrain, strafing the sailors, slicing through the hull with explosive tracer shells, filling the water with splinters and blood.

The ATLAS ring-of-fire defences on Haré would normally have been set by Aurélien Castile to 'automatic' for just such a circumstance – an attack by night when neither of he nor his son nor Johnson Pederson and his team might be alert, in a position to activate their deterrent manually. But 'automatic' was no longer an option without the underlying AI that would prevent wild erroneous firing on seagulls. So Aurélien and Davide were both woken by a proximity alarm connected to the unsmart parallel island technology that didn't require a digital connectivity.

Davide was in the medical centre, so didn't have access to any controls. Aurélien was in his bed, with a touch-screen command pane within easy reach. He pressed a skeuomorphic 'fire' button and received a tiny vibration as a haptic response. Immediately, the angry, percussive sounds of the tracer shells from the ATLAS system became audible, even deep inside the citadel.

On the medical floor, Davide detached the drip from his canula and hurried upstairs. When he got there, he replayed the events on a screen, using video feeds from the defences, but was unable to pick out much detail in the darkness. A few minutes later, Aurélien followed him into the control room, accompanied by one of his Haréan staff – Yeiwene Egesho – dressed only in a towelling robe, his wasted calves protruding from its skirts. The Haréan carried a rug that he hurried to wrap round his master's knees. Once this was done, Aurélien told Yeiwene to wait outside, then asked Davide: 'Who were they?'

'I don't know.'

'Where did they come from?'

Davide waved a hand, gesturing towards the outside world through many metres of concrete and rock: 'Perhaps a sneak attack from a larger force?'

'An exploratory expedition?'

'Militarily, it could make sense – testing our defences.'

'Sacrificing how many lives?'

Davide returned his attention to the closed-circuit video from the gun emplacements.

'Hard to say …' He hesitated, winding the footage back through time, narrowing his eyes to pick out details in the splodges of grey, illuminated only moment-to-moment by explosions from the tracer shells. 'Maybe a dozen?'

Aurélien laughed. It was a cold, dry sound: 'Ridiculous.'

'Or it might have been a lifeboat from the French frigate?'

'Yes,' said Aurélien. 'Kaldonov's Fire virus will continue to self-propagate. Anything with the capacity to destroy itself will do so.'

'Leaving us,' said Davide, 'and our stronghold.'

'Exactly.' Aurélien tapped a thin finger on the arm of his wheelchair. 'It is perhaps time to proceed to a cull.'

'I agree. Have you told Pederson?'

'He is locked in his quarters. He argued with me. I am considering—'

Davide interrupted: 'His administrative abilities might be useful—'

'I will decide. There is no point questioning me, Davide.'

'No, father. What about Kaldonov?'

'His expertise might be valuable. For example, if we reboot the Haré Stronghold operating system, he will first install what he calls his "kill-switch".'

'What is that?'

'It can disable the AI viruses.'

'Do we want that?'

'The global devastation will continue but here we can begin again.' Aurélien tapped his fingernail once more. 'But we must act. There are far too many people on this island. Haré Stronghold was not designed to support such a large population. Pederson should have paid more attention to clandestine immigration from Haiti.'

'The simplest thing would be to cull entire villages.'

'I agree. The two northern *chefferies* represent more than three-quarters of them.'

'Consider it done, father.'

Davide opened the armoured door and found the Haréan outside.

'Remind me, what's your name?'

'Yeiwene Esho, Monsieur Castile.'

'I need you to accompany me to the water distribution station on level minus five. We're adding a med-booster,' said Davide, 'but only to the two northern *chefferies*.'

'Now, Monsieur Castile?'

'Because of my injuries, I will need your help with the canisters. It's part of the regular program of vaccines and supplements.'

'Are they expecting it?'

'It makes no difference. Delivered in their water supply, the med-booster will give them greater resistance to disease,' he lied. 'Their continued employment depends on it. I hope every Haréan and Haitian understands that.'

'And if my sister Yeiwa,' the Yeiwene asked, nervously, 'the leader of the southern *chefferie* – what if she wants to know why she doesn't have it?'

Davide frowned, thinking about how the surviving southern Haréans might react when they learnt of the northerners' deaths. It would be wise to delay that moment of crisis. He spoke very firmly: 'All three communities must remain isolated from one another for seven days, until everyone has established immunity.'

'A quarantine then,' said Yeiwene.

'A temporary one,' Davide told him.

'Understood.'

They took the elevator to the medical centre on level minus three.

'Additives to the water supply are stored in those canisters,' said Davide. Yeiwene transferred them to a small cart. 'Now, level minus five.'

Yeiwene called the lift and they went down two further floors, emerging into a semi-industrial space, full of pipes and pumps, with a wall of dials for monitoring the water supply to the three settlements and to the citadel. Davide directed Yeiwene to invert the two canisters, slotting them into brackets on two of the main supply pipes and opening the valves.

'Good,' said Davide. 'It is done. You are dismissed.'

67

Asteroid 2037 AQ9 crossed the eastern seaboard of the United States of America, passing between the flood-drowned coastal cities of Savannah in the state of Georgia and Charleston in South Carolina. The noise drew people from their beds to marvel and despair at the fire in the sky. The multiple objects – one central terrifying mass and dozens of outlying fragments – seemed already impossibly low. But, a minute later, it was gone, receding into the darkness above the Atlantic, tracking east-north-east. Not knowing what else she could do, a flood-watch employee at the city hall in Charleston set off the public alert siren. A security guard came to remonstrate.

'What the hell are you thinking? You want a full-scale panic?'

'It's my responsibility,' she protested, 'to warn people—'

'Of what? It's gone. There's no flood coming.'

'And when it hits the ocean?'

'Who says it'll hit the ocean. I wouldn't be surprised to hear it went all the way to Europe.'

'Even then,' said the flood-watcher, knowing she was right.

As AQ9 followed its path east-north-east, the God's Thunder platform had already fallen out of the sky, pieces of its carbon nanotube skeleton tumbling to Earth, cooling to no more than forty or fifty degrees as they fell into the Pacific and onto the rocky coastline of Washington state. The tungsten impactors flew on, however, following a deliberate, destructive bearing east-south-east, brightening the sky above Washington DC.

In several police stations, reports came in of people shooting at the sky, as if it was an alien invasion that could be repelled with bullets, rather than multiple human-made nightmares, hypersonically accelerated by gravity.

68

Dawn was breaking. Claudine Poiret followed in the rear as two-thirds of the company who had survived the sinking of the *Roussillon* – a dozen marines – fanned out into a defensive formation in order to advance on the shanty at the far end of the sweep of the beach. The closer they came, the bigger it appeared, extending beyond the few faint lights that had been visible from a distance, but disorganised and haphazard in dark silhouette against the sky.

Soon it was clear that the edge of the shanty was marked by a set of fish-drying frames. From the smell of them, Poiret assumed that a significant proportion of a recent catch had been allowed to rot in the rain.

A volley of barking split the silence and Poiret saw a dark shape come hurtling out from between the drying frames, heading straight for the frontmost marine. He took a knee and killed the dog with a single efficient shot to the head, punching the animal backwards on the gravelly sand.

The marine dropped into a prone position, hidden from the shanty by a dip in the ground, followed by all eleven others. Poiret copied them, anticipating more danger, new attacks. But all she could hear was the surf raking the shingle.

Victor Abadie was to her left. He rolled over onto his back. From one of the patch pockets on the front of his uniform he took out a small mirror on a telescopic handle, angling the glass to observe the shanty while remaining under cover.

'What can you see?' she whispered.

'Nothing. No one is moving. What do you want to do?'

Poiret had been thinking this through herself. The most decisive option would be to take the RIB and cross the narrow stretch of sea towards the island of Haré.

Who knows what defences they might deploy?

So, she had hesitated, hating to make any kind of move while a fog of unknown factors surrounded her. She had ordered the company to advance on the settlement in order to gather more intelligence.

But what if there's no one there who knows anything and we're just wasting time?

Her indecision was interrupted by her companion.

'Okay, someone's coming out.'

Poiret reached out for the observation mirror, rolling onto her back, finding the angle difficult, then locating a human shape that knelt down. She realised without knowing quite how that the person was mourning the dog. She stood up.

'Madame Poiret,' hissed Victor Abadie, urgently.

She paid no attention, covering thirty or so metres in just a few seconds, addressing the crouching figure.

'My name is Claudine Poiret. I am in charge of the French relief forces. How can we help?'

Without looking up, the figure replied with a strong Haitian accent: 'I could no longer afford to feed him, anyway.'

The miserable shanty was one of the saddest places Claudine Poiret had ever seen, the timbers and corrugated plastic of the bedraggled dwellings imbued with a multi-generational despair. There was no plumbing, no comms, no electricity. The lights she had seen were oil lamps, smoky and inefficient, barely illuminating the squalor, human waste mixing with discarded packaging and the bones of vermin that had been trapped and cooked for food. What looked like the entire population – perhaps forty people, prematurely aged by want and medical neglect – emerged, reaching out their thin, open hands as if for blessings but, actually, for charity.

Poiret instructed two marines to return to the RIB and fetch enough emergency rations to provide something for every distressed Haitian. Reassured by this evidence of support, the mood improved. Several people began lighting fires fuelled by what looked like crude oil, stored in open buckets and unstoppered cans, sending gouts of noxious smoke up into the air, mercifully dispersed by a stiff breeze. Poiret identified two seniors, sitting idly on an upturned fibre-glass dinghy while others brought them herbal drinks made from hot water and dried leaves.

'Do you know anything about that island?' she asked, pointing across the bay. 'And what happens there?'

'Why do you want to know?' asked one of the pair, a woman with a deeply lined face and grey hair that hung in ragged strands over her brow, half-concealing her eyes. 'What business is it of yours?' She pulled a threadbare blanket more tightly round her shoulders. 'You say you have come to bring "relief". Give it and go.'

The other elder – a man wearing a dark suit that had once been blue or black but was now an indeterminate brown – put a hand on the elderly woman's arm.

'Tell her what she wants to know. There is no harm.'

'Of course there is harm,' she spat back. 'They will interfere.'

'For the better,' said Poiret. 'And I am only concerned with what is to come.'

'Even here,' said the elderly woman, 'we hear stories of the end times.'

'You shouldn't believe all you are told. Do you trade with Haré? Can you help me get there in safety?'

Both elders looked down at the ground, as if ashamed. It took another ten minutes to extract the full story, culminating with a recent drama where, in return for supplies of oil and dried food, plus a small amount of money, two girls from Saint-Just had been sold to a pair of older Haitian men employed on the island. This had caused unrest and the woman leader of one of the island's *chefferies* had even made the trip across the narrow stretch of water to insist that it should not happen again.

'Which is easy to say when you are safe,' said the woman, 'when you live off the fat of Chief Castile's wealth.'

'Safe from what?' asked Poiret.

The woman spread out her arms, her rug falling from her bony shoulders, revealing the flaccid flesh that hung around the bones of her upper arms.

'From everything. From what you, the rich, have made of the world.'

The male elder repeated his calming gesture, bringing her frail arm back down to her side.

'This Frenchwoman,' he told the other elder, 'is here to help. She says she is not interested in the past.'

'When this Haréan woman,' demanded Poiret, 'this leader, crossed the water, who did she speak to? Where did she land?'

'There is a proper jetty in Saint-Just, a kilometre further on.' He made a rueful face. 'And cash-money shops, not barter shops. There is nothing for us there.'

He explained the parallel 'cash-money' economy, run by someone he referred to as "Papa Lace" with US dollars as a means of exchange, but entirely divorced from reality. A one-dollar bill in good condition was considered more valuable than a torn twenty.

'I have cash-money in good condition,' said Poiret.

He put his head on one side: 'And you are better armed than Papa Lace's people.'

'Can you show me?' said Poiret.

The elders climbed painfully to their feet and, accompanied by her remaining ten marines, Poiret followed them through the pitiful shanty to a ridge that looked down to a timber jetty and a boardwalk lined, as they said, with half-a-dozen commercial premises.

'Will anyone fire on us?' Poiret asked.

'My advice,' said the woman elder, 'is shoot first.'

'I am looking for someone,' Poiret told them. 'A Frenchman. His plane crash-landed on the island.'

'Ah, yes,' said the male elder. 'We saw this. Like a needle – going that way.' His arm indicated east, towards the lightening sky, beyond a ridge of hills, miming a wavering, unsteady flight path. 'It looked like it was fighting the air.'

'If he managed to land, where would he go?'

'To Saint-Just.'

'Why?' she asked, surprised.

'Papa Lace will find him and bring him, so he can sell him back to you.'

69

Alex was lying face down on a mattress that smelt of mould. His shoulders were stiff and his wrists sore because his hands were tied behind his back. He wriggled sideways so his legs slipped to the floor and he found himself kneeling. He tried to stand but was prevented by a tether attaching him to the heavy bed frame and tied around his waist. Then he realised he was kneeling on the rope and, shifting his weight, released it and managed to get to his feet in the grey light of very early morning.

His head began spinning with the after-effects of the mad honey and the bastard cocktail in the jerrican. He went a couple of paces towards the door before the rope stopped him once more. He listened, hearing two Creole voices in the corridor.

'I need water,' he called.

The door swung open and he was only just quick enough stepping back not to be knocked over. It was Mama Cov, her eyes very dark in her white-painted face.

'You sleep good?'

The young man in the dirty white long johns and shirt was behind her. The pigment on his arms and face had become smeared, revealing his natural skin tone. What had Papa Lace called him? 'White Zombie'. That was almost what he looked like, his eyes tired and bloodshot, his shoulders drooping.

'Can I have some clean water, please? Is the well-water drinkable?'

'Yes, well is good,' said Mama Cov. She turned to White Zombie.

'Go.' The boy slouched away. Mama Cov asked: 'You good, too?'

'I've been better,' said Alex, quietly: 'Where am I?'

'In Papa Lace house. At top. Look.'

She gestured to the window. Alex approached, able to get almost all the way to the sill. The window gave onto the courtyard three storeys below. The two Goat Men were lounging by the corrugated iron gate. The previous night's drug-fuelled debauches came back onto his mind. Then he saw White Zombie drawing water in the bucket.

Mama Cov asked: 'You hungry?'

'Yes,' said Alex, surprising himself. 'Very.'

'I bring bread.'

'Thank you.'

'After Zombie come back.'

'Sure.'

Alex went back to the bed and sat down.

Bread and water, he thought. *Traditional. Could be worse.*

Poiret was uncertain of her tactics. She had chosen to await the return of the two marines – that she had sent back for supplies for the Haitians – before doing anything else. Then she had chosen to wait a little longer so that the rest of her troop could relaunch the RIB and come into the jetty of Saint-Just from the sea, holding that position. From the vantage of the ridge, she finally saw them rounding the headland and knew it was time to move.

'Let's go.'

She led her dozen marines down the untidy slope of scrubby, sandy soil, Victor Abadie at her side. He held his weapon out in front of him, his eyes narrowed, looking along the barrel. With two hundred metres to go, the land levelled out. Along the squalid parade of shops, several outdoor barbecues were lit, each one producing noxious black smoke from burning heavy oil. No one was paying any attention to their approach.

What information will I find here? Am I simply delaying the inevitable, suicidal assault on Haré?

The perimeter of the settlement was protected by a fence of rusting barbed wire. They went a little way inland to find an opening, channelling them through a narrow gap, onto a path that led behind the shops into a cluster of unrendered breeze-block buildings and emergency tented accommodation, with washing lines strung between the eaves. Poiret saw a child of about six – or maybe an undernourished child of ten – playing with a dirty doll on the damp ground. She advanced alone.

'Where can I find Papa Lace?' she asked.

The child – a girl – looked up, her eyes cloudy and her expression vague. Poiret thought she might be blind. She repeated her question.

The child pointed inland, beyond the cluster of unhappy homes.

'Thank you.'

Poiret closed the girl's hand around a protein bar and led her troop on between the buildings, emerging from an alleyway to be confronted by a tall corrugated-iron fence, the panels attached by twists of wire to metal poles, set in rough concrete footings. She followed it to the right, turning a corner to a lower gate, staffed by two somnolent guards wearing bizarre leather caps, surmounted by animal horns.

Alex couldn't persuade Mama Cov or White Zombie to release his hands, so he had to allow himself to be fed like a small child, alternating solid and liquid. He ate an entire small loaf – a kind of rye bread, solid and sustaining – and drank almost two litres of water. Finally, he told them: 'Thank you. That's enough.'

Just then, there was a commotion of some kind, down in the courtyard. Mama Cov said something to White Zombie – presumably 'wait here' – and disappeared out onto the landing and down the stairs.

White Zombie went to look out of the window. Alex watched him, calculating the distance relative to the length of the tether round his waist.

*

Becoming suddenly aware of Poiret's presence, the two men wearing goat horns jumped to their feet and ran away into the compound, leaving the corrugated-iron gate ajar. They disappeared in through the front door of a nineteenth-century manor house, a remnant of the colonial era, in a state of collapsing disrepair. Poiret heard shouts of warning and complaint and instructed her marines to find cover and stay alert. They spread out, concealing themselves behind a large truck, two smaller vehicles, the stonework of a well, a heap of salvaged building materials.

A brief almost-silence took over, except for vague sounds from the tents and breeze-block homes beyond the manor house compound. Then Poiret saw several of the ground-floor windows swing inwards, revealing glimpses of faces semi-hidden behind the frames.

'I want to talk to Papa Lace,' she called out, her back to the fender of the truck.

Someone shot a single shell wildly into the air. A voice came angrily in response, demanding they hold their fire.

Good sign, she thought.

'I need information,' she said, very clearly. 'I can pay. I have cash-money, euros, US dollars.'

A loud, affected voice replied: 'What is this insolence, coming into my home uninvited with your guns? Send your people back outside. I will speak with you alone.'

She turned towards Victor, sheltering behind the rear axle of the truck, raising her eyebrows in inquiry. He shook his head.

'Come outside,' she called back.

'No,' came the voice. 'Send away the others and you come inside on your own.'

She peered round the fender as a body came smashing through a window on the third floor, flailing in the air and landing in a heap on the uneven ground with a sound like a slapped face.

70

The God's Thunder impactors, aimed for a worst-case scenario by the 'accelerator of destruction', the evolving Fire virus, struck the Canary Islands. The active shield volcano of Cumbre Vieja on La Palma suffered a series of huge landslips. A ruinous quantity of dirt and rock was also displaced from the western flank of Mount Teide on Tenerife. In addition, four of the impactors struck shallow water, causing ruptures in the submarine tectonic fault lines.

The cumulative effect was to create a dome of water that rose more than a kilometre above sea level, causing enormous loss of life throughout the seven islands of the archipelago. Within thirty minutes, it swamped the coast of Morrocco. More powerful waves still were radiated westwards across the Atlantic.

Almost simultaneously, Asteroid 2037 AQ9 and its attendant superheated fragments of space rock scorched through thin clouds covering the northern coast of France, the central mass hitting the ground at a velocity of 50 kilometres per second and an angle of 35 degrees, with a force of fifty-eight thousand megatons, generating catastrophic airblast damage as it approached sea level. The fragments struck across an area two kilometres long and one kilometre wide while the central mass carved a crater eight kilometres wide, generating more than a cubic kilometre of melted or vaporized material.

The asteroid impact generated another tidal wave. It crossed the Channel and swamped the south of England, washing miles inland, mitigated but not stopped by a range of hills called the Downs. It radiated east into the North Sea, drowning the low-lying cities of the Belgian and Dutch coasts, infiltrating the estuaries of the Medway and the Thames, causing appalling damage in London.

As it radiated west, the vast, growing wave travelled out of the Channel into the Atlantic Ocean, climbing on top of itself into a mountainous, devastating tsunami, merging with the waves from God's Thunder, rising to ever more vertiginous and deadly heights.

The tremors of the asteroid impact were felt two-hundred and fifty kilometres away in Paris, where Gloria Lamarque, Emmeline Cantor and Régis Petit still cowered in the impenetrable bunker of the Elysée Palace.

'What is that?' Régis asked.

'Something terrible,' said Emmeline.

'Something beyond our control,' said Gloria.

A little later, Marthe Hidalgo came to find them with news that the entire government had relocated to the subterranean corridors and conference rooms, that they were not to worry, that they were in no danger.

'Is that so?' asked Gloria.

'You are as safe as it is possible to be,' insisted Marthe Hidalgo.

'Not safe at all, then,' said the mother of 'the man who saved the world'.

71

On board the innovative, blended-wing-body aircraft, Mariam and Paul dozed until they were two-thirds of the way across the Atlantic Ocean, cruising at a fuel-efficient altitude, travelling east–west, keeping the sun behind them. Then they hit dirty air.

'Is this dangerous?' demanded Mariam.

'Hard to say. We don't have GPS, obviously, but turbulence can't be picked up by satellite anyway.'

The aircraft dropped and Mariam felt gravity lessen for a second.

'It's climate related?'

'Raised temperatures increase wind shear in the jet stream. I'll try and find something smoother.'

Paul was soon successful. Mariam opened the paper bag his father had given her. It contained two sandwiches and two energy bars like the one Paul had insisted that she eat back at Bordeaux–Mérignac, after her brief but desperately needed nap. Mariam passed one to Paul and ate her own.

'Where will we put down?' she asked.

'Wherever we can.'

'How will we swap call-signs and all that?'

Paul turned to face her, chewing.

'Depends where we're going, exactly.'

'I'm hoping we get an indication from Alex or from Poiret, maybe, when we're close by.'

Paul swallowed and asked: 'What else is there?'

'Two plant meat sandwiches, maybe some kind of faux-ham.'

'Great. I'm famished.'

Mariam passed him the bag and sat back, her half-eaten energy bar in her hand, looking out through the scratched glass at the dismal sky.

'How are we doing?'

'Good,' said Paul, his mouth full once more. 'Eating up the distance.'

'Are you getting any warnings for structural faults?'

He gestured to a panel on the control console where a set of picture-icons were displayed in three colours, green, amber and red.

'The amber ones indicate trouble from sensors on the carbon nanotube skeleton, but what choice do we have?'

'None whatsoever,' said Mariam.

72

Alex craned his neck to look down through the smashed window. Left alone with White Zombie while Mama Cov went to investigate the disturbance in the courtyard, he had waited only a few moments. White Zombie had been too interested in what was happening outside. Tethered to the heavy bed frame and with his hands tied behind his back, Alex had used the only tactic available to him, launching his shoulder into the small of the young man's back, propelling him through the window, doing so with such force that he had almost followed the Haitian through the smashed frame and glass into mid-air. But the tether had saved him, leaving him winded on the worn floorboards, the rope gathered tight like a corset round his waist, wondering what would happen next.

Alex sat up, making sure that he remained concealed. Now he was no longer under observation, it didn't take long to release his wrists and undo the tether, shaking his arms to return normal blood flow to his hands.

To protect himself from anyone coming into the attic room from the landing, he pushed the heavy metal frame of the bed against the door and retrieved his jacket from a hook on the back of the door along with the hessian sack containing his knife and belt. He put them on, arranging the knife on his right hip, then peered round the broken window frame. From his high vantage, he could see down into the narrow alleyways between the breeze-block buildings of Papa Lace's 'village', through which a small group of black-clad French marines were moving. Then he heard a strong, authoritative voice he recognised.

'Let me help you, Papa Lace.'

Claudine Poiret.

He felt an extraordinary surge of relief because now he would be able to …

To what?

He heard Poiret continue: 'If you don't let me help you, I will order my marines to shoot.'

'We can wait,' came Papa Lace's reply. 'And we are many.'

Alex knew that wasn't true, but he didn't want any more death. He shouted down into the courtyard.

'Madame Poiret, this is Alexandre Lamarque. I'm on the attic floor. There are only six or seven gang-members in the house, poorly armed.'

'Good,' came the curt reply. 'Are you injured?'

For a second, Alex considered how to answer. Physically, he was in poor but manageable condition. Psychologically, he was drowning, destroyed by drugs and grief.

'I'm fine,' he replied.

'Keep yourself safe,' she shouted. 'Take no risks.'

'Agreed.' He changed the tone of his voice, trying to express reasonableness and persuasion. 'Papa Lace, this is the deal you were hoping for. This is where you exchange me for money rather than dying.'

There was a pause. Alex wondered if he had found the right words.

'Yes, I have overplayed my hand,' Papa Lace at last called back. He gave some indistinct instructions in Creole, then shouted to Poiret: 'You are the masters, again.'

Poiret and Victor Abadie led the marines up the front steps of the dilapidated colonial building, into a deserted hallway.

'In here,' called Papa Lace's voice.

She followed the sound into a panelled ballroom with tall, dirty mirrors in dusty, gold-painted plaster frames. Papa Lace was sitting in a battered wooden chair, accompanied by half-a-dozen bizarrely dressed fellows.

'Is this all?' said Poiret.

'This is all,' said Papa Lace. 'Please remember, we looked after your man.'

'Victor, go upstairs and find Captain Lamarque.'

'You two,' said Abadie. 'With me.'

The three marines left the ballroom, leading with their weapons. Poiret contemplated Papa Lace and his companions: the two young men who had been lounging on gate duty in their horned skull caps; a woman dressed as a doctor or a mortician; two indeterminate figures in baggy suits with bags over their heads.

'How are you in charge here?'

'The well is clean water,' said Papa Lace. 'There are no rivers between the dry hills and the sea. Clean water is money. Soon, there will be a queue, like every day.'

Poiret heard footsteps on the stairs. The marines who had remained with her were well trained. They didn't turn their heads from Papa Lace and his crew. Poiret went out into the hall.

Stumbling on the half-landing above her, Alexandre Lamarque looked terrible. His hair was sticking to his forehead and his beard was greasy and untidy. Victor Abadie was offering to help him down the last flight of steps but he shook him off, pausing to get his balance, gripping the banister.

'You need medical assistance,' said Poiret.

'I need proper food and water, maybe a stimulant,' Lamarque replied. 'I was poisoned.'

'He told me you hadn't been harmed—' Poiret began.

'No, not maliciously. I interrupted their revels. It doesn't matter.'

Poiret watched as her prime operative carefully descended, placing each foot as if uncertain whether the treads would support his weight.

'We have hot food, nutritious food,' came Papa Lace's voice from the ballroom. 'Let us all breakfast together.'

Alex could tell that he must look worse than he felt. Though weak, he thought enough time had passed to metabolise the mad honey. He stepped off the final step of the stairs and, to his surprise, Claudine Poiret came forward, putting her hands on his shoulders and kissing his cheeks.

'I am glad to see you.'

'Likewise, but time is short.'

'Time is always short,' said Poiret.

'How many of you are there?'

'Twelve marines with me here, another eight at the jetty.'

'What happened?'

'The *Roussillon's* missiles self-destructed, blasting a huge hole in the hull. It was my fault. The ship went down incredibly quickly. Barely anyone got away safely – a lot of sailors in the water.'

'Did you approach Haré?'

'Not yet but I assume that's where we have to go?'

In a few words, Alex told Poiret the story of meeting Davide Castile in Bamako and the offer Davide had made, for him to be the figurehead of a post-apocalyptic world.

'This is all his doing?'

'His and his father's. They've turned Haré into a stronghold, like a super-bunker, so they can survive whatever happens next.'

Poiret told Alex what she knew about the widespread digital meltdown.

'That makes sense,' Alex replied. 'I was able to play your news download.'

They discussed the devastation in Egypt, Emmeline Cantor's apartment in Paris, the Saint-Médard dam.

'For the time being, nothing is certain, Captain.'

'Either way, grief or relief will have to wait.' Alex saw that Poiret was about to say something else – perhaps words of sympathy for the loss of those closest to him – but he went on quickly. 'Haré will be defended. If we approach in the RIB, we will almost certainly be taken out.'

'Come,' called Papa Lace from the ballroom. 'Let us conclude our negotiation.'

'What do you make of him?' asked Poiret.

'He is only strong because the people around him are weak. We should give him money and leave.'

'Pay him for poisoning you?'

'He kept me alive, in the end, and brought me here.'

Alex stayed in the hallway while Poiret went to conclude business with the gang leader. A marine with 'Abadie, Victor' on his name badge offered Alex a canteen of water. He drank it in two long draughts. Then Abadie gave him a soft protein bar that tasted claggy and over-rich after thirty-six hours of semi-fast.

'Lamarque,' Poiret called. Still chewing, he went into the ballroom. Poiret told him: 'Papa Lace says the island has defences, gun emplacements. The only lifeboat to successfully launch from the *Roussillon* was seen from the shore. It approached and was shot to pieces.'

'Like fireworks,' confirmed Papa Lace. 'Exploding projectiles. Nothing left but splinters in the water. You will need subterfuge. I can help you with that.'

Alex saw that the gang leader already had a wad of dollar bills in his hand.

'Get us to the island and there will be more money,' he said.

'More money,' mused Papa Lace, as if evaluating a novel idea. He spoke in Creole to his gang members in their surreal costumes. They all nodded and approved his words, the two in suits removing the bags from their heads. He turned back to Alex and Poiret. 'Perhaps we don't want Chief Castile on Haré any more than you do.'

Papa Lace's plan was simple. Alex and half-a-dozen marines would dress up in the Haitians' ceremonial costumes and cross the narrow neck of water to the beach below the solar observatory.

'This is a normal thing for us to do,' he told them. 'There will be no reason to suspect anything.'

'Is it possible to ensure we aren't fired upon?' asked Poiret.

'I will be with you. The machines know me. And I am a welcome visitor. I will stand in the prow. The facial recognition will disable the guns.'

'We won't be able to use the RIB,' said Poiret. 'Do you have a suitable boat?'

'Of course. A very good boat at a very fair price.'

73

The captain of the tanker *Pablo Adisa*, Rodrigo Diaz, was worried. Overnight, his vessel had been shadowed by what looked, from a distance, like a Dominican coastguard corvette. Then, for no reason that he could fathom, the corvette had burst into a fireball on the grey horizon.

Bad things are happening.

Diaz had promised Castile that he would make his delivery to Haré Stronghold as soon as possible, as soon as the weather allowed. Well, the skies had cleared and the winds, though significant, were no longer outside reasonable parameters.

Plus, the French frigate has disappeared from radar.

He wanted the business. He knew that other shadow tankers were capable of taking his place. And he had incurred a substantial risk with his current cargo, investing all his accumulated reserves, buying from an unlicensed Nigerian trader, crossing the Atlantic in a time of great upheaval, most of his crew appalled by the green, pulsating light-show from the unexpected aurora borealis, visible way too far south – a bad omen, they all thought.

It's a bad omen, too, to see satellites falling out of the sky.

Diaz was used to navigating by traditional methods: the gyro compass; line of sight; the positions of the sun and moon and stars; ocean currents; dead-reckoning based on direction, speed of travel and time. But he was in the habit of balancing these with the paraphernalia of the modern age: global positioning systems; automatic radar plotting; electronic chart display and so on.

In the hyperconnected modern world, these sophisticated contemporary navigation methods created a problem for someone who wished to pass unseen because they were all linked to the automatic identification system that was a legal requirement on any vessel above three hundred tonnes. Originally a network using VHF radio channels, AIS had been switched over to digital in 2032 and integrated with a directive from the International Maritime Organisation, identifying all large ships with a transponder – a device incompatible with discretion.

Diaz had hacked the *Pablo Adisa's* transponder. Each time he took the risk of connecting, it spoofed a new and fictitious ship's identity. On the most recent occasion, just an hour before, he had been surprised to find himself the recipient of conflicting data, placing the tanker in three different locations. Then, he'd had to countermand an automated course correction that he knew would take the *Pablo Adisa* onto a sandbar.

Rodrigo Diaz was not a fool. He had traded enough with Haré Stronghold to have guessed why Castile Energie had invested so much time and money in a goldilocks island off the coast of Haiti. But he had been shocked when Aurélien Castile had allowed himself to be perceived as desperate.

I am prepared to double your price.

Out of a habit of negotiation, Diaz had argued back: *Money we cannot spend if we are in prison or dead.*

Then Castile had said something very interesting, in a tone that suggested it was an offer that couldn't be countered.

And provide you with asylum … From the future.

Now, he had a chance to approach the docks and make his ship-to-shore transfer. While that was happening, he would disembark and speak frankly to Aurélien Castile, man to man.

He knows more than I do and, when bad things are happening, knowledge means survival.

74

While the BWB fuel-test prototype ate up the final kilometres over the vast indifference of the ocean, Mariam Jordane and Paul Sanchez were approaching the moment of decision.

'There are three options,' he told her. 'There's Cap-Haïtien International, Port-au-Prince or …'

He stopped, allowing Mariam to complete the list.

'We land on Haré itself. Enough runway?'

Paul nodded.

'If the Ae4 was going to land on it, we can.'

'Good.'

They flew on. The sun was catching them from behind, in the east. Mariam's mind created a sequence of possible futures, in none of which she dared fully to hope that Alex was still alive.

'We can't expect to be welcomed with open arms,' said Paul.

'Anti-aircraft defences?'

'Would you be surprised?'

'What chance would we have of avoiding them?'

'Zero. This bird only likes straight lines.'

Mariam felt their options tighten.

What are we trying to do here? Should we land elsewhere and take stock? But what if time is short?

'We couldn't land on Poiret's relief frigate?' she asked.

'Helicopter access only – it's not an aircraft carrier – if we could even find it without digital positioning, which isn't certain. It seems weird to say it, because a frigate is a substantial ship, but the ocean is more massive still.'

Mariam's eye scanned the control console.

'What about those warnings about the integrity of the carbon nanotube skeleton? If we land, that's when most stress is put on the aircraft. If a structural failure occurs, we'll be broken, stuck, unable to take off again.'

'Even if we manage to find hydrogen to refuel,' agreed Paul. 'Which is doubtful.'

Mariam nodded slowly.

'We go direct to Haré. We might be shot out of the sky but, if Alex and Poiret have survived and found one another, maybe we'll be sufficient distraction for them to do something more useful than we're able to achieve.'

'Hey,' said Paul, suddenly. 'Would you look at that?'

Mariam, who had cast her eyes down in thought, glanced up through the cockpit window. The northern sky was pulsing with undulating clouds of green light.

'Is that a problem?' she asked. 'It's electromagnetic, isn't it? Can you still navigate?'

'No problem for the moment, I think. We're still south of it, just about.'

For another couple of minutes, they flew on, Mariam found herself lulled by the thrum of the outside air over the bulbous BWB. After a while, she shared what she was thinking.

'Alex once told me that his entire life had been a mistake. He was the wrong person in the wrong role, called on to act and try and control events outside of his reach. Except that life kept bringing them within his reach.'

'I don't understand.'

'It's a stoic thing, a philosophical position that the only path to contentment is to cease worrying about things which are beyond our power to change.'

'Sounds Buddhist,' said Paul, indifferently.

'It was part of why he tried to resign.' She paused, then spoke her deeper thought. 'He wanted us to be content, together, the two of us. Did you know that he resigned, before the Coming Darkness? Then, he was blackmailed back into service with the promise of preferential medical treatment for his mother?'

'I didn't, no.'

'He and Fayard used to discuss classical philosophy together. Alex told me: "The universe is change. Our actions fit within it." I asked him if that made his decision to fight on, not to walk away, easier.'

'What did he say?'

'That the stoics were wrong, that the purpose of existence is moulding the future by how we live in the present.'

'So, he made peace with that?'

'No,' sighed Mariam. 'How could he? It was too much responsibility for just one small speck of humanity.'

'Was or is?' asked Paul, innocently.

'One or the other,' said Mariam. 'That's out of our control, too.'

75

Yeiwene Egesho, waking early after a poor and short night's sleep, felt unsettled, as if something bad had happened and it was his responsibility to fix it. He got up, washed and dressed and slipped out through the quiet staff accommodation to the garage. He briefly spoke to a couple of the Haitians trained for security, then took an electric buggy, driving north to the runway and the *chefferies* beyond.

Aurélien was still in his bed, thinking about his son, named Davide because King David of biblical Israel was a shepherd boy who rose to absolute power.

Aurélien was disappointed. He didn't believe that Davide had ever fully shared in his secret purpose: atomising the hyperconnected world; culling and fragmenting human populations; reasserting the differences between peoples; the preservation of the Earth's ecosystems from the pestilence of human reproduction.

What does Davide believe in? Anything at all?

For a minute or so, Aurélien thought about Davide's mother, selected from a range of potential surrogates, analysed from every parameter: health history; body mass index; age; pregnancy and delivery history; relationship status; IQ; lifestyle. His medical advisers also recommended that he should consider what they called a 'human connection'. Aurélien had dismissed the idea: 'Will the foetus be aware of my "human connection" with a mother it will never meet? A healthy outcome is all that I require.'

And Davide had served – a new life, genetically adjacent to his own, in order to further pursue his longevity experiments.

Now that all the possible futures have narrowed down to a single evolving present, why do I feel I have failed? Have I not achieved almost every part of the plan? Had it not been for Lamarque ...

He was unable to escape the idea that 'the man who saved the world' would have made a better son and inheritor.

If I could just explain to him, present him with the facts, with my reasoning, I could persuade him, I am sure.

Rodrigo Diaz signalled ahead via his analogue radio connection. Aurélien Castile answered, authorising his approach, confirming that the island's automated defences had been disabled. Diaz approached Haré from the north, grateful to steer the tanker into the deep-water channel on the eastern side of the island, in the lee of the steep hills, in calmer seas.

Approaching Haré with the help of a sympathetic, low-altitude tailwind, Paul brought the BWB in from the north, overflying a tanker on approach – the first land for nearly seven thousand kilometres.

'There's the runway. If this bird is going to fall apart, it's now,' said Paul.

'No one is shooting at us,' said Mariam. 'Maybe the gunners are busy with the tanker?'

'Or they're disabled to allow it to dock. We're coming in on precisely the same path.'

Mariam heard an ominous creaking from the BWB – not the aggressive noises of stressed metal, a more insidious suggestion of imminent failure. Three of the amber warning lights went red.

Aurélien's residential quarters were on the floor between the terrace and the control room, laid out with wide spaces between every piece of furniture to facilitate wheelchair access. The only other accommodation on the same floor was a kind of nursing station for his rota of attendants, always men because he felt more comfortable with what he believed was a masculine ability to disassociate from emotion.

His bed was a small double, with a medical mattress equipped with air pockets that gently inflated and deflated, in order constantly to adjust the pattern of pressure-points on his fragile flesh. His electric wheelchair was parked alongside in a charging station, meaning he had easy access to the comms incorporated into its frame – no longer the sophisticated holos and computing of the digital world, but wired lines connected in parallel with the charging point.

Aurélien had made a study of the restorative qualities of rest, as he had every other potentially 'hackable' aspect of his lifestyle. A proper sleep cycle comprised about ninety minutes in total: six or seven minutes of dozing; fifteen or twenty minutes of deeper rest; a period of slow-wave sleep; finally, more than an hour of the essential dreaming oblivion of rapid-eye movement.

He pressed a button and the alternating-pressure mattress flexed, gently raising his head and shoulders into a sitting position. He felt tired. When last in his bed, he had failed to sleep for a useful cycle. Now, he needed distraction to calm his thoughts.

He powered up a screen set into the wall beside him, thinking he would allow his mind to wander, observing the movement of the clouds or the closed-circuit video from the dockside, the gun emplacements and the airstrip.

The screen showed a password-entry system. Forgetting himself, he placed his thumb on a pad in the corner, but the biometric system was dead. He typed his recently amended password: *Fire*. The screen went dark, then re-opened on an array of choices from the island's management system, most of which were greyed out from the impact of his feral AI viruses. The closed-circuit video camera feeds, though, were active.

He touched the screen to select one on the dockside, watching four Haréan stevedores moving about in waterproof hi-vis jackets, getting ready to welcome the tanker. He tapped a right-hand arrow, paging through live views from each gun emplacement in turn. Then he chose a camera on one of the lighting stanchions round the H-pad at the far end of the runway.

To his surprise, he saw an aircraft, just a speck at first, then growing larger as it flew directly at the camera, as if on a collision course. He briefly asked himself why his ATLAS system of automated gun emplacement hadn't taken it down with explosive bullets, before acknowledging that his defences would, from now on, need to be staffed at all times by human controllers.

He pressed a button that would ring a bell in the dormitory of his control-room assistants.

The one on duty was named after the hero of Haréan independence, Yeiwene, thought Aurélien. *Perhaps, he will enjoy shooting at our enemies.*

Two-thirds of the way along the runway, Yeiwene forked off in his buggy to the left, to the smaller of the two northern *chefferies*, aware of an aircraft on approach above him – not the needle-shaped Ae4 he knew from previous experience, but an odd-looking bulbous plane.

He paid it no attention, driving on the short distance to the edge of the settlement, knowing he was doing something that Davide Castile had forbidden, that he shouldn't draw attention to himself.

The settlement seemed eerily quiet. The house had herb borders either side of the front door and was set a little apart, facing the dawn rather than its neighbours. He knocked and was greeted by a man he knew – a good friend and someone he would like to know better. His friend made his first coffee of the day and they brought the pot outside to drink, sitting on the front step, talking about the lights in the sky and the breakdown of media and internet reception.

'The aurora is beautiful,' his friend said, touching Yeiwene's hand.

Yeiwene had just refilled his mug. He was frowning and distracted, thinking about the unfairness of giving only the northerners the medbooster.

I could take a few bottles of water from here to Yeiwa for our family and those closest to us. The rest of our neighbours will get theirs in the fullness of time.

'Yeiwene?'

Realising he hadn't answered, Yeiwene raised his head to look into his friend's eyes. They were vague, his features slack. Yeiwene felt odd himself, as if drunk or half-asleep.

I must be protected, now. I'm drinking the treated water.

'I wonder ...' he said.

'What ... what do you ...'

'I saw ...'

Landing into a steady northeast wind, Paul lifted the nose very slightly so the rear undercarriage took the brunt of the impact. The BWB bounced twice, then began to decelerate with reverse thrust. For a few seconds, it looked like the K-Raptor helicopter, parked on the H-pad at the end of the runway, was coming too close too fast, but they came to a halt with fifty metres to spare. Paul shut down the engines.

'How much fuel did we have left?' asked Mariam.

'Four per cent.'

'What would you have done if we'd not reached the island?'

'We'd have reverted to landing on Hispaniola, in the Dominican Republic.'

'Leaving us a long way from the action. There's a kind of citadel. That must be where we need to end up. How far, do you think?'

'I'd say twenty or twenty-five kilometres.'

Paul completed the shut-down sequence for the hydrogen engines. Mariam opened the door on the port side of the cabin, slid her legs out, turned and lowered herself to the ground by clinging to the frame. Paul passed down the two FR-F2 rifles, then did the same. She showed him an ominous-looking crack where the wing met the bulbous body.

'Not a moment too soon,' he told her.

Aurélien's observation cameras were the best that money could buy.

My old-school, closed-circuit video images are not as clear as 4k or 8k digital, but what is the point of those formats if the human eye is incapable of discerning the difference?

In any case, he was able to zoom in on the face of Mariam Jordane, recognisable from the news streams and his obsessive research. Gazing at her perfectly symmetrical features, framed by the collar of her camouflage fatigues, he pondered his options.

Aurélien had been proceeding under the assumption that Alexandre Lamarque was alive, that it was a given that 'the man who saved the world' would try to save humanity for a second time, that he might, even now, be looking for a way to come to Haré. Davide had seen him at the crash site, apparently alive and well. But the unexpected arrival of Mariam Jordane was something new.

Could she be taken alive as a bargaining chip?

That would be another argument with which Aurélien could attempt to bring Lamarque onside.

If that does not work and they both prove intransigent, Davide can kill them.

Aurélien wondered for a moment if that was what he wanted.

Or perhaps she will be thirsty and drink the water in the close-by settlements at the northern end of the landing strip.

He sat himself up straighter in his bed, uncomfortable and still tired.

Where is that man, Yeiwene?

Neither Yeiwene Egesho nor his friend said anything else ever again. They fell asleep and, as the minutes passed, their sleep deepened to the point where it became unnatural, slowing their metabolic functions until their hearts stopped beating, their brains became starved of oxygen and they quietly died, culled by the Castiles' brutal logic – along with nine hundred and seventeen Haitian immigrant workers plus a few Haréans, their untidy bodies lying where they had fallen in their cramped dwellings and businesses, or out of doors, warmed by the pointless September sun.

76

Davide was down on the dockside, supervising the ship-to-shore transfer of crude, pumped out of the *Pablo Adisa* into huge sealed cisterns in the complex geology of the island. The tanker stood off, protected by the harbour wall but about forty metres from the land, like an enormous floating city block without windows or adornments, just a harsh flat hull, pock-marked with rust and age. He saw the ship's master, Rodrigo Diaz, coming ashore in a lightweight tender and decided to go down to the moorings to greet him.

The concrete hard standing was damp from overnight rain. The air carried the odour of hydrocarbons: the crude being pumped; the fuel in the engines of the tanker and the pumping equipment; grease and oil for lubrication of moving parts; acrid smoke drifting across the narrow channel from the Haitian coast.

Davide hadn't dressed for out of doors. He was wearing a lightweight tracksuit in a soft black fabric over his underwear and t-shirt. He asked one of the stevedores for his hi-vis jacket, telling the man to fetch another from the stores. Pulling it on, he thought about failure.

We wanted to remain in the shadows. It should all have happened without any connection to Haré or to us. Without Alexandre Lamarque perceiving the secret patterns, we might have succeeded.

He walked to the edge of the concrete and descended a few steps towards the water that sloshed against them, remaining just above the waves. He had a medical mask in his pocket and put it on.

Where did we go wrong? How did we become so visible. Was it simply bad luck?

The tender from the tanker was close, now, a tiny rowboat that would have been useless outside of the protected waters of the docks, sheltered behind the stone harbour wall. Rodrigo Diaz was alone on board.

No one need have known that it was our doing. Had it succeeded, Darkness would have been seen as the work of our allies in the French security services, what Lamarque called 'traitors'. Then the Storm was supposed to look like the work of others, inspired by Darkness.

Diaz came alongside, tossing a line to Davide, who wound it through a heavy metal ring set in the harbour wall, pulling it tight, thinking about appearing to be good while doing bad. He held onto the line with his left hand while reaching out with his right to help Diaz onto the damp steps.

'We haven't met,' he told him. 'My father tells me this is your third trip to Haré.'

'Yes, but I've never been ashore. You've built something amazing here.'

'We have. There are terrible people out there in the world. We wanted a place to feel secure and safe.'

'Can I speak to him?'

'I'm afraid not.'

'We communicated by radio. He invited me to—'

'It's bad timing. We have an outbreak of disease on the island, hence this face mask. My father is suffering. There's a quarantine in the northern villages. It's very unfortunate.'

Davide saw indecision in the tanker captain's eyes, wanting to insist, but Davide's reasoning was sound.

Diaz argued: 'If I come ashore alone, the crew can finish the transfer and stand off for a few days. I'm happy to wait.'

Davide shook his head, trying to put sympathy into his eyes.

'There are too many bad things happening. You must have heard. Who knows whether the *Pablo Adisa* itself is safe. Did you know a French frigate went down not far from here?'

'I'm nervous myself. I saw a Dominican corvette burst into a fireball and—'

'Precisely. We must complete the transfer, conclude our business and then you must go on your way.'

'On my way where?'

Davide was glad to be dominating the tanker captain, two steps higher on the damp steps.

'Are you asking my advice?'

'Yes, I suppose I am.'

'If I were you, I would make my way back to Nigeria for a new consignment. There will be customers keen to find you.'

'Did you know that your father offered me asylum?'

Davide forced his eyes into a smile above the close-fitting mask.

'He is badly affected, running a high temperature. I imagine he wasn't sure what he was saying. From what, after all?'

'That's just what I asked him,' said Diaz. 'And he said: "From the future." What do you think he meant by that?'

Davide mimicked concern.

'I'm sorry if you've been misled. He's an old man. Nothing is easy for him.'

'Look, Monsieur Castile, I'll say to you what I said to him. Everything is falling apart. It seems to me that you know why and how and Haré—'

'Captain Diaz, let me be quite clear,' said Davide. 'You cannot remain ashore. The quarantine forbids it.' There was a shout from one of the stevedores that the first cistern was full. 'You have already received a payment in bullion, have you not?'

'It was swung on board just before I came across,' said Diaz, looking uncertain.

Davide weighed the man up, glad that his expression was half-hidden. The tanker captain was a criminal businessman, but not a thug. He might be a useful ally at some point.

'You are right to worry for the future. Let me talk to my father. When you return with a new consignment, we can speak again about how things will have evolved. Perhaps the world will be a better place. Perhaps we will all be worrying less. If not, Haré will be grateful for your resupply. You understand me? It's bad timing, like I said.'

'Yes,' said Diaz quietly, grudgingly. 'Fair enough.'

77

Back in his control room in the citadel, Aurélien had been pleased to find that no one in either of the northern *chefferies* was responding to the calls he was placing over his landline network. On a screen on his desk, he could see that the gauges on the second oil cistern were rising steadily. By the time the transfer from the *Pablo Adisa* was complete, Haré would be energy-independent for at least three years, maybe eight or ten, given the drastic reduction in population. At that point in the future, it was uncertain if there would be any more deliveries from the *Pablo Adisa* or any other seagoing ship.

Despite Kaldonov's idea of reinstating computerised management of the island, Aurélien had come to the conclusion that neither Kaldonov nor his family were useful any longer, either for technological expertise or for leverage. He decided to remove the Bulgarian–Macedonian family in the same way that he had removed Johnson Pederson, locked in his quarters, relying on his parallel infrastructure of unsmart electronics, servomotors and practical locks.

He actioned the command, sealing all three of them in.

They cannot get out. Thanks to Pederson recommending we install airtight quarantine seals on all the dormitories, eventually their breathing will convert enough of the oxygen in their sealed rooms to carbon dioxide, so that they will lose consciousness and die.

*

When a very young man, growing up in Communist Bulgaria, Todor Kaldonov had become interested in technology from a practical point of view, making circuits with wires and batteries and tiny bulbs, connecting them with his soldering iron, going on to work with recycled parts from broken transistor radios. It was only later that his interests had narrowed to the coded world of software engineering. He had, therefore, an affinity with the parallel systems installed by Johnson Pederson on Haré and, ever since his abandoned attempt to flee the island stronghold, he had taken advantage of every opportunity that presented itself to learn the many pathways of the fixed-line comms.

That meant he had recently been able to make connections of his own, listening in on conversations that the Castiles, father and son, believed to be private. Now, he was wondering what to do about the awful information he had overheard.

There are far too many people on this island. Haré Stronghold was not designed to support such a large population. Pederson should have paid more attention to clandestine immigration from Haiti.

The simplest thing would be to cull entire villages.

I agree. The two northern chefferies represent more than three-quarters of them.

Then he had heard the armoured door open and the voice of the enthusiastic Haréan control-room assistant, Yeiwene Egesho, being given the task – though the young man did not know it – of delivering poison to nine hundred people through the water supply.

Kaldonov had felt the need to act, but hadn't known what to do. Early that morning, unable to sleep, he had slipped out of his quarters a little before dawn, leaving the pillows beneath the blankets in the darkened room to give the impression he was still there, alongside Stoyan. Once outside, he had found himself at a loss, but feeling the need to stay out of sight of both the Castiles and any of their attendants.

He had gone outside, taking a coat from the store near the main entrance to the citadel, on the level of the road from the runway. Looking up at clear patches of predawn sky, between sparse clouds, he had seen what looked like falling stars and made the obvious deduction: the satellites were falling because his Fire virus had gone beyond the atmosphere.

For a moment or two, he had enjoyed a feeling of satisfaction, a sense of pride in an extraordinary achievement. Then the reality had hit home.

Desperate to distract himself from the feeling of shame, he had hiked down from the citadel, through the gullies to the eastern side of the island. There, he had found a viewpoint overlooking the docks and seen the tanker come in to the sheltered waters of the harbour and the stevedores – tiny in the distance in their hi-vis jackets – connecting their pumps and cables.

Tired and hungry and cold, he had trudged back uphill, in time to see a lone figure driving away from the citadel on the road north. Not sure why, he had immediately assumed it to be Yeiwene and wished he had had a chance to talk to the young man, to ask him what he was doing, whether he was aware of the awful task he had been given.

Back at the main entrance, he was greeted by a pair of armed Haitian guards, imported from the gang leader in Saint-Just, both men he recognised as attendants on Aurélien Castile, one of them with medical training, the other a cook. Organising his features into a smile, he told them: 'It's the first nice day since weeks.' They both looked blank, not following his clumsy French, so he added a mime to assist: '*J'ai fait une promenade.*'

I took a walk.

They let him pass with a nod. He made his way to the dormitory floor, finding the door to his quarters locked. With a feeling of panic, he put his face to the corridor window of Mitya's room, just able to see his chest rising and falling in his three-quarter-sized bed.

Relief flooded Kaldonov's chest as he stepped back from the glass, pushing a hand into his trouser pocket, closing his fingers over the thumb drive with its executable 'kill switch' software.

After everything I've done wrong, this – perhaps – is something I can do that is incontrovertibly right.

Aurélien took the elevator to the upper terrace. Vitamin D synthesis with its myriad health benefits depended on him spending time outside. His breakfast was laid out under its usual weighted muslin cloth that hung over the edges of the small table. He drove his wheelchair in tight and his knees gently struck the frame, causing him to wince.

The morning was fresh so he activated the seat warmer in his wheelchair and told his attendant – who couldn't tell him where Yeiwene had got to – to fetch a wrap. The man found two in the sideboard and draped one over his master's shoulders and the other over his knees.

'Join the other guards. You are one of Papa Lace's men, are you not?'

'I am, Chief Castile.'

'Make sure you are all armed and ready. Seal the citadel. No one in or out.'

'Right away, Chief Castile. What danger is coming?'

'A plane has landed. Those on board are our enemies. They will no doubt make their way here. When they do, bring them to me.'

The Haitian left, using the elevator. Aurélien sat for a moment, his eyes half-closed so as not to be dazzled by the low sun. He felt a vague but insistent anxiety, as if something was coming over which – unusually – he had no authority or power.

It is not Mariam Jordane, nor even Alexandre Lamarque. There is something else ...

78

There was a settlement near the H-pad, a five-minute hike down a winding track that dropped perhaps eight or ten metres to a couple of hundred dwellings.

'I didn't except to see such a large population on this island,' said Mariam. 'Is it some kind of private army?'

'I don't think so,' said Paul, shading his eyes from the early sun. 'It looks like a workers' village.'

They entered via a tidy perimeter of white bungalows, each one equipped with both photovoltaic and solar-thermal panels, plus tri-blade domestic wind turbines.

'This is really, really quiet,' said Paul.

'We need information,' said Mariam. 'And transport to get to the citadel. We'll need a vehicle if we're to avoid a hike of several hours.'

'Agreed.'

They emerged from the residential bungalows into a wider street with a few shops down the shady side. In most, lights were lit, the characteristic white pinpricks of twelve-volt renewable supplies. The door of a hardware store hung open. Mariam approached, her Glock Fr20 in her right hand, her FR-F2 rifle on her back.

'Is anyone in?' she called in an encouraging voice.

No reply came. She approached the doorway on the angle, keeping herself in cover behind the right-hand side of the frame. Paul mimicked her on the left. She looked in, seeing a mug on the floor, lying on its side, with some kind of beverage spilled on the vinyl, as if someone had tripped just as they were unlocking.

'With me.'

She moved inside, through a narrow aisle and high shelving, towards a brighter light at the innermost end where she could see a portion of steel counter. Beside it, she saw a thin man of forty or fifty with a grey moustache, lying on the vinyl floor as if he, too, had been somehow spilt, like the unknown beverage. His face was peaceful but he was clearly dead.

Mariam and Paul left the hardware store and tried the next glazed door, a clothing and footwear shop. It was locked, but they could see two more Haréans slumped in a corner at the foot of a ladder, as if they had been restocking shelves together.

They walked the length of the high street to an open square with a memorial, decorated with cut flowers. A dedication was carved into the stonework.

To the memory of Yeiwene Tibo who died so that others might live free.

Next to the memorial was a dog bowl containing fresh water. Alongside that were two dogs, lying on their sides, their tongues protruding from their mouths.

Yeiwa Egesho, Yeiwene's far-sighted sister, knew that the oil tanker was in port because she had received a message over the old-fashioned fixed-line telephone system that linked the three *chefferies*, the citadel and the dockside. And someone had called from Chief Castile's med-centre, informing her of a seven-day quarantine – no one to leave any of the villages while the med-booster delivered to the northern settlements was allowed to develop immunity.

'Immunity from what?' she had asked.

'It's a part of the vaccine program.'

'And where is ours?'

'Your *chefferie* will receive it after the northern quarantine. It makes sense.'

It was true. It did make sense. But Yeiwa was unable to quell a sense of having missed something.

I wish I could ask the stones. Is it permitted for me to go down to consult them? Why not? I will meet no one there.

The morning was progressing. She spoke to her vice-leader, an elderly man called Bernard Boti who was already at work on reports of neighbourhood disputes in the council chamber.

'Try to speak to someone in the north. If you get no answer, send someone or go and find out what's happening yourself.'

Mariam and Paul took nearly an hour making a comprehensive search, but found no one alive to question, just a baby in a high chair in one of the many similar dwellings, crying because it had dropped its bottle on the floor. Paul picked it up and the baby drank greedily. The baby's parents were in an adjacent room, fallen in the process of dressing, the man with his trousers round his ankles, the woman with a dressing gown half off.

'This is like a nightmare,' said Mariam.

'Worse than anything I've ever dreamt,' he told her. 'What sort of people would do such a thing?'

'The same fanatics who destroyed Aswan.'

For almost a minute, they simply stood. Finally, Paul asked: 'Are we in danger, do you think?'

'It's not airborne.' Mariam indicated two cups lying broken on the vinyl floor. 'It was something in the water.'

'But the baby—'

'Premade formula, not mixed from the tap. You remember the Coming Darkness conspiracy planned to poison the Calais water supply? Alex prevented it, but this might be a similar policy.'

'Why, though?'

Mariam's mind had already imagined the likely scenario.

'Building the citadel and docks and runway and the agricultural terraces and so on would have required a large workforce, but now a smaller population is easier to manage?'

'Meaning these people became redundant,' agreed Paul. He moved the baby from its high-chair to its cot and left it there, safe but crying for its dead parents. Then he hesitated. 'I feel we shouldn't just leave,' he told her.

'We'll come back, if we can, or send someone. There's nothing else we can do here.' Mariam led him outside. The constant background hum from the small wind turbines on each roof was eerie and oppressive. 'We saw another settlement on approach, remember?'

'To the west of the runway,' he confirmed.

'Okay. We go there.'

Behind the hardware store, Mariam found an electric buggy without any security to prevent it being used. She and Paul drove out of the ghost village and up to the runway, then along to the fork that led to the second settlement.

Outside the first house they came to, they found the next victims slumped on the herb borders either side of the front step of one of the ubiquitous white-painted bungalows. They looked like brothers or, maybe, a couple, waking up together.

'Two more senseless deaths,' said Mariam, thinking with a deep ache of sorrow of her Aunt Sara and Cousin Benjamin. 'Among so many.'

Without hope, they set about another doomed search.

79

Poiret had insisted that Alex be thoroughly checked out by a marine with medical training. His cuts and abrasions had been cleaned, disinfected and dressed and he had taken advantage of the pause to trim his ragged beard. He mentioned that the tooth he had damaged in the emergency landing was giving him pain. The marine told him he had no dental skills but gave him two painkillers.

Alex returned to the ballroom. Papa Lace's companions had swapped out of their costumes and, at first, he didn't recognise Claudine Poiret dressed as Mama Cov, complete with white pigment on her face and hands. Alex and Victor Abadie pulled the baggy suits worn by the Fat Cats over their own clothes, holding the bag-masks in their hands for the time being. Two dark-skinned marines put on the jeans and jumpers and goat-horn skullcaps. A woman of smallish stature pulled on the long-johns and t-shirt of White Zombie, taking some trouble applying the white paste.

'I would prefer it if there were more of us,' said Poiret.

'You can give up your place for another marine,' said Alex, reasonably.

'No,' said Poiret. 'I want to be there.'

They trooped down through the miserable tents and houses to the jetty where Saint-Just met the water. The rank fires were still burning in the oil drums. People were milling about, doing meagre business, chatting, cooking.

Is Saint-Just the kind of future the Castiles envisage, subsisting from hand to mouth, poor life expectancy, filthy conditions, rule by violence, not courtesy, cooperation and law?

The jetty was poorly maintained, the boards patched with found timber, the footing uneven. Six or seven boats were moored alongside, plus a dozen more bobbing in the shallows close at hand. They headed for the largest, six metres in length with a proper cabin and wheelhouse, but the glass in the windows was gone, just a few shards still embedded in the rims.

'What fuel does this boat use?' Alex asked.

'Methanol,' said Papa Lace. 'An alternative technology project that we Haitians embraced. But the industrial production facilities no longer function.'

In high-tech facilities in France, Alex knew that methanol was produced from farmed anaerobic bacteria and phytoplankton.

'Where do you get it, then?'

'From burning the trees, but they are almost all gone. Some people call methanol "wood spirit". It can, of course, take away your cares by intoxication but also make you blind.'

'So, not enough wood?'

'Like the Easter Islanders, we have cut down all our trees.'

Alex climbed in. There was a hand's width of grey water swilling around beneath the seats. The French contingent had kept their own footwear, figuring that would remain unseen until they were on land. Papa Lace started the engine by touching two wires together.

'This craft was biometrically secured,' he said, 'usable only by its registered owner, but not any more.

The engine kicked into life, surprisingly loud with a kind of rhythmic boom from its pistons. Alex had a moment of nostalgia for his boat on the canal basin in Paris, for a life full of challenges but in a world that seemed fixable.

Among all their other crimes, the Castiles have undermined humanity's confidence in our shared future. Was that the point of the Darkness and the Storm?

He would have liked to discuss it with his mother. As a historian, Gloria would have had lot to say on the matter. Her patterns of thought – the analysis of continuity and change – had shaped his own.

We used to believe 'change' was a neutral concept. No longer.

They headed out. The water was choppy and the boat too small to mitigate the movement. Alex enjoyed the motion.

'I spoke to one of the families on the quayside,' said Papa Lace. 'They told me an aircraft came in to land.'

'When?' asked Alex.

Papa Lace shrugged and told him: 'Earlier. There aren't many clocks or watches in Saint-Just. They said it was fat like a pregnant cat.'

Alex looked round for Poiret but her eyes were down, leaning over the side of the glass-fibre boat. He wondered if she had been sick.

Victor Abadie told him: 'Could have been a BWB.'

Alex had flown in one from Bordeaux to Paris soon after the defeat of the Coming Darkness conspiracy.

'What would it be doing out here?'

'Our air force has been developing a long-range version,' said Abadie.

They were close enough now for Alex to pick out a ring of standing stones above the beach, with a figure standing in the midst of them, immobile. Then Papa Lace told him: 'Look, there is a gun emplacement over there, on the rocks to the right.'

Alex followed the direction of Papa Lace's outstretched arm, recognising an impressive piece of kit from the United States' Advanced Targeting and Lethality Automated System, originally developed as a small mobile autonomous tank, later revised to provide fixed gun emplacements. The rapid-fire projectile weapon was mounted on a steel frame, painted to blend with the landscape, with two belts of tracer shells protruding above. Equipped with its own operating system, it was supposed to acquire, identify and engage targets three times faster than a human mind and eye.

As Papa Lace had promised, the gun remained silent.

Is that because our subterfuge is working, or has the software meltdown reached Haré, too? It seems unlikely Castile or his father could have kept their own digital systems free of the viral tsunami they've unleashed on the rest of the world.

The marines in the Goat-Men skull caps prepared to jump out as Papa Lace gunned the engine. The fibreglass hull of the boat knocked against a well-maintained timber jetty. Everyone moved for'ard and jumped out onto the boards.

'As I promised,' said Papa Lace, smiling in the unglazed wheelhouse. 'But I will not stay here. There will be upset and, I think, violence.'

'Yes,' said Alex.

Poiret, looking green and unhappy, removed a tight roll of banknotes from beneath her Mama Cov disguise and gave it to him.

'I will leave you,' said Papa Lace. 'This has been a successful interaction, no?'

He gunned the engine, pulling away from the jetty.

'Thank you,' called Alex. 'Whatever comes next, good luck.'

On board his fibreglass boat, watching them hike up the beach, Papa Lace had a moment of doubt. On reflection, he didn't like the way Lamarque had pronounced the words: 'Good luck.' It had sounded as though the Frenchman didn't believe such a thing as good luck was possible.

Would I perhaps be better off with 'the man who saved the world'?

He let the engine die, watching them cross the sand to the rough fringe of salt-loving grass, then into the sweeter pasture. From the other side of the cove, he saw someone paddling out to meet him, making swift headway in a kayak against the shallow surf. The man came alongside and reached up a wiry hand, just able to grasp the timber rail.

'It's me, Amadou,' said the man. 'You recognise me, don't you?'

Papa Lace frowned. It was one of the six gang members he had sold to Chief Castile to be trained for his protection.

'What is happening?'

'I don't know,' said Amadou, his grey uniform darkened by seawater. 'There is upset and argument. No one knows what is coming. Chief Castile and his son are perhaps not in agreement. And there is no word from anyone in the north. Yeiwene went early this morning to speak to them and has not returned. It is as if all of them are dead.'

Papa Lace contemplated the man's desperate features.

'This is good to know. Haré Stronghold is no longer so strong. I almost made a terrible mistake.'

He reached over the side and wrapped his hands around Amadou's wrists, pulling him bodily out of the water and on board.

'Thank you, Papa Lace.'

'And, who knows,' said the gang leader. 'Perhaps when, on Haré, they have all killed one another, we can move in and take their places.'

With a smile of satisfaction, he touched the two bare wires together to fire up the methanol engine once more, setting a course for the safety and security of Saint-Just.

80

It wasn't far to the grassy plateau and the ring of stones. A woman wearing a long, pale-blue dress was standing in the centre of the circle. Alex, Poiret and the marines were soon close enough for her to see that they were not who they appeared to be – that they were dressed in the costumes of people she knew, but not those people after all.

'Who are you?' she asked. 'What do you want here?'

'My name is Claudine Poiret and I am a representative of the French government, in charge of the relief operation to Haiti and concerned at what has been happening here on Haré and in the rest of the world.'

'What do you mean, "the rest of the world"?'

'The Castile family,' said Alex, sharply, 'is at the heart of a global conspiracy of destruction. Do you know who I mean?'

'Chief Castile?' asked the woman.

'Who are you?' barked Poiret. 'What do you know about him?'

'Please believe me,' said Alex, 'when I tell you that this is extremely urgent.'

The woman weighed him up and found, he thought, in his favour.

'He has turned Haré into a stronghold,' she said. 'Have you come to take it from him?'

'What is your name?' demanded Poiret, impatiently. 'What are you doing here?'

'My name is Yeiwa Egesho. I am the leader of my *chefferie*.' She waved a hand. 'Over beyond that ridge there are three hundred people who look to me for leadership and guidance. I am here because I look to the stones.'

'What does that mean?' Alex asked.

'I told my brother, Yeiwene, that the stones say a time is coming when money will have no more meaning. I told Papa Lace.'

'The stones may be right,' said Poiret in a disgusted tone, retrieving another tight roll of banknotes from beneath her costume. 'But, in the meantime, I can pay you for your assistance.'

'How do we get to the citadel?' Alex asked.

'You have not yet told me your purpose,' objected Yeiwa.

'To stop what is happening.'

Alex told her succinctly about the sequence of murders, foiled terrorism and successful destruction fostered by the Castiles. While he spoke, he could see, in her eyes, a pattern of thought akin to his own, finding shapes and meaning in disparate events.

'I will help you,' she said simply, 'but it may be too late.'

'Because?'

'I came here to ask the stones what I should do. My father taught me to read them as his father taught him.'

Alex didn't believe in divination, but he knew that cards or bones or, indeed, standing stones could serve as a way of focusing the mind to reveal what it wasn't aware that it knew.

'What did they tell you?'

'I have seen darkness, storm and fire.'

Alex felt shocked at the precise correlation with the waves of terrorist destruction, but told himself that it was to be expected, that these ideas were not the Castiles' alone. He tried to get Yeiwa Egesho to elaborate – while Poiret became increasingly frustrated – but the *chefferie* leader insisted she had nothing to add.

'Fine,' he told her. 'You don't want Madame Poiret's money. What do you want?'

'I want my people to thrive in freedom.'

'So do we,' snapped Poiret, 'but you don't seem to be grasping that your Chief Castile doesn't want this. He wants to pull down, to devastate, to crush, to kill.'

Alex watched Yeiwa Egesho evaluate the harsh-tongued senior civil servant, then smiled as she said: 'You think only you can know what you know, but I have feared this day since he came.'

'Why?' barked Poiret. 'Don't say: "because of the stones".'

'Then I will say nothing,' said Yeiwa.

'Do you have any technology in your *chefferie*?' Alex asked. 'Comms devices, computers, internet access?'

'None of that wants to work any longer.'

'Since when?'

'Failures in cascade,' she told him. 'Except the fixed-line telephone.'

'Are there any other populations on the island?' Alex asked. Yeiwa gave him a concise reply, then he asked her to describe the topography. She did this with admirable precision. 'So,' he resumed, 'we need to hike round the citadel, via your *chefferie*, to the access level on the far side. Or do you have transport?'

'We have electric buggies if the charging stations have functioned.'

'Will we meet opposition?'

'Dressed as you are, no, I think not. There is a small troop of trained guards. They have modern weapons and body armour and things I know nothing of. Madame Poiret?'

'Yes?'

'I will take your money because one never knows,' Yeiwa said with a smile. 'The stones have never been wrong but the reader of the stones is not infallible.'

Yeiwa led them out of the circle, up a brief rise and down the other side of a ridge to a community of white bungalows, laid out in a grid. Passing between the identical homes, she greeted several people who were out of doors. Some of them addressed themselves to Alex and the others in Creole, before realising that they were not who they appeared.

They came to a larger building with a double door. Yeiwa opened it and led them into a vestibule where an older man was sitting behind a wooden counter with an old-fashioned telephone in his hand. Seeing Yeiwa, he hung up and said: 'No answers from the northern *chefferies* but it is busy at the docks with a tanker off-loading.'

'I asked you to send a messenger. Have they returned, Bernard?'

'Not yet,' replied the older man, then he frowned, realising in his turn that Alex and the others were not who they appeared. 'What is this?'

'My name is Claudine Poiret and I am a representative of the French government, in charge of the relief operation to Haiti.'

'Why are you dressed like this?' asked Bernard.

'Yeiwa,' said Alex, 'how many people live in the north?'

'Fewer than a thousand.'

'How many people does Chief Castile employ all together?'

'Everyone works for Chief Castile but, since the completion of the construction projects, more and more are idle.'

'And there are about three hundred of you here in the south?'

'Yes.'

Alex lowered his eyes. He had an unpleasant idea he knew why no one was answering the old-school telephone calls to the north.

'Are there any natural springs on the island for fresh drinking water?' he asked.

'Yes,' said Bernard, 'but providing small amounts, a few litres a day. Without Chief Castile's desalination and rain capture, Haré would not be able to support such a large—'

'So,' interrupted Alex, 'your sisters and brothers in the north are supplied by a central source.'

'From the citadel, yes,' said Yeiwa.

Alex told her and Bernard about the plot he had foiled in northern France, one in which millions might have fallen victim to a pathogen in the Calais water supply.

'They wanted to poison people with the water?' asked Yeiwa.

'Deliberately infect them with something. A virus. And I fear the villages in the north may have suffered the same way.'

Yeiwa paled. 'Why a virus? Why not simply poisoned?' she asked.

'Because—' Alex was about to give a categoric answer, then he changed his mind. 'Yes, that's true. The point of the viral terrorism was that it could be mistaken for just another transgenic outbreak. Here, that doesn't matter. If I am right in what I fear, your neighbours may indeed have been poisoned. Who can show us the way to the main access to the citadel?' he asked. Yeiwa said nothing for a moment. Her face was ashen. 'Can you do it?' Alex prompted. 'In desperate times, it is always better to do something rather than nothing.'

'Yes, of course but, if you are right,' she whispered, 'this crime would …'

'I know,' said Alex, not needing her to find a suitable adjective. 'Let's go.'

81

Aurélien Castile's guards were nervous. Despite their practical training in weapons use, the Haitian gang members were psychologically unprepared for combat. Oppressing the cowed and unarmed villagers of Saint-Just was one thing. Shooting ranges and close-combat practice without a real enemy weren't really any different. In both scenarios, the stakes were low to non-existent.

Four out of the troop of six were standing in the shadows, inside the main entrance to the citadel, carrying handguns. Two of these were wearing hi-tech arm sheaths with close-combat capabilities. Members of Papa Lace's gang, they were conversing in Haitian Creole.

'What are we even supposed to do?' one of them asked. 'Who are we supposed to be fighting?'

'Whoever came down in that plane?' asked another.

'And we mustn't kill them?'

'No.'

A third guard was trying to use a fixed-line telephone on a panel on the rough rock wall, its wiring disappearing into a conduit in the concrete floor, sighing with exasperation.

'There are no answers anywhere.' He hung up. 'I have never known the systems to fail. It has to be deliberate.

'Not even the docks?' said the fourth man, flexing his fist, making the blades protrude from the black-clad knuckles.

'Not even. And you know Yeiwene Egesho left at dawn to drive north and has not returned? I spoke to him.' His eyes narrowed. 'There are four of us here. Baptiste is in the med-centre. Where is Amadou?' The other guards exchanged glances. 'I'll tell you where he is. Amadou has deserted. I bet he's sitting on the jetty in Saint-Just, drinking and fishing, like we ought to be. He is cleverer than any of us and … What's that?'

It was the hum and hiss of the tyres of an electric vehicle, carried uphill by the breeze from the east. They all froze.

The hum of the motor came closer. They raised their weapons, their faces revealing their anxiety. A buggy swung rapidly in through the wide entrance and, to their relief, they all recognised that it was Chief Castile's son Davide. He jumped out, looking like he wanted to give a show of energy and strength, but stumbled and almost fell, snatching at the frame of his vehicle for balance.

'What's happening here?' he shouted. 'Why did you not challenge me? Why are you all cowering inside?' The guards didn't answer. He came close to them, shouting in their faces, his breath on their cheeks, his bloodshot eyes horribly close. 'This is the moment of crisis. This is where you prove worthy or unworthy. And can you guess what I'll do to you if you're not worthy?'

'*Oui, monsieur*,' they all replied in a kind of terrified chorus.

He pushed two of them aside and made for the elevator, stepping inside and pressing the button for the control room.

'No one in or out,' he shouted, but the elevator doors didn't close.

'It's been disabled, Monsieur Davide,' said one of the guards. 'And your father told us to bring any intruders to him.'

'No one may enter for any reason,' Davide repeated, emerging and spinning the handle on the watertight door to the stairwell. 'From now on, we take no chances.'

He stepped through and – at least, this was what it sounded like to the guards – locked it behind him.

82

The road from the southern end of the runway towards the citadel didn't run straight. The landscape of Haré was too complicated for that. It went left and right, cut into the sides of the hills. Only when Mariam and Paul came within two thousand metres of their objective did they begin to think about cover and how they might manage to make a surreptitious approach.

'We've been too slow,' said Mariam.

'How do you mean?'

'Landing, searching, being too cautious.'

'That was good sense,' said Paul. 'We'll soon be visible from the citadel, too.'

'So, we can't approach in this buggy,' said Mariam.

'Why shouldn't a buggy be on the road?'

'Because the people in the citadel must know that everyone in the north is dead. Therefore, anyone driving a buggy on the open road must be an enemy, someone who shouldn't be alive.' Mariam pointed. 'Pull over there.'

Paul lifted his foot from the accelerator and the electric brake immediately slowed them to a gentle halt below a steep slope landscaped as agricultural terraces, separated from one another by low stone barriers to retain rainfall, growing purple sprouting broccoli, callaloo, okra and spinach. They got out, each carrying their FR-F2 rifle diagonally across their shoulders.

Mariam led Paul up a path between the terraces, brushing against the wholesome leafy vegetables. She paused to inspect the spinach up close, admiring the perfect shapes of the leaves, the absence of disease or predation. On the next terrace up, the okra was just as perfect, like a plantation at an agricultural show.

'The climate here must be ideal,' she told Paul. 'Protected from hurricane alley for all-year-round tropical cultivation.'

They crested the rise and had a view of the northern coast of Haiti and the open Atlantic Ocean. Then they turned right and followed the ridge through a dense stand of zombia trees, a kind of palm that only grew a couple of metres tall, with many short branches covered with spiny leaf sheaths. At the edge of the trees, with their view of the citadel backlit by the sun, they remained under cover in shadow, observing the road that they would have approached on, had they not abandoned it, thirty or so metres vertically beneath them, running for about a kilometre through undulating terrain. The tarmac forked into two near the opening, with a branch disappearing beyond the citadel to the right, the western side, again in shadow, and another tracking downhill to the east in the direction of the docks.

Having established a good sense of the topography, Mariam used the scope on her rifle to look for details of the citadel, first noticing the open terrace at the top with an antenna array poking high into the sky. She tracked her sights down the built-up walls, thinking that the structure was much smaller than she had anticipated when she had heard the words 'Haré Stronghold'. Then she began to visualise underground levels. She realised that what she could see was only the 'tip of the iceberg'.

Finally, her scope found what looked like the main entrance, a wide opening with a flattened arch, like an artificial cave.

'We can't get any closer without profiling ourselves against the sky,' she said.

'How dangerous would that be?' Paul was also using his scope. 'I can see no …' He stopped as two figures came into view in the arched entrance, looking small and insignificant against the wide, shadowy mouth. 'You see them?' he asked.

'I do,' said Mariam. 'They're in uniform.'

'Guards. They aren't carrying distance weapons, as far as I can see.'

'No, but ... Hold up. Look there, on the road from the docks. Can you get a clear shot?'

Yeiwa had found them two buggies. Alex was at the wheel of the first, with Poiret – dressed as Mama Cov – with one of the Goat-Men marines riding behind. Yeiwa was alongside Alex so that he could question her, trying to get as much information as he could on the short trip. She told him that the southern *chefferie* was much closer to the citadel than the northern settlements, a short EV drive round the base of the hill into which the multiple floors had been dug – a hollowed-out bunker inside a natural hill. Unfortunately, she had never been inside.

'What opposition will we face?'

'There are six armed guards,' Yeiwa replied. 'My brother Yeiwene has told me about them. We sometimes hear and see them practising with their weapons.'

'Do you know them personally, by name?'

'One is Baptiste, one is Amadou. They don't come from the island. They are from Saint-Just, from Papa Lace's gang. They were brought over not so long ago.' She frowned, trying to remember when. 'And there is the American manager, though people say he is a fair man.'

Alex stopped far enough away from their destination for the lie of the land to conceal their approach, the EV motors running extremely quietly, the wheels almost silent on the smooth tarmac. He looked up the towards the citadel, seeing the transition where the natural rock was surmounted by concrete and stone. Above the walls, he could see the antenna array protruding into the bright sky.

'Maybe that explains why Papa Lace was short of manpower in Saint-Just,' said Poiret from the rear.

'Perhaps,' said Alex, then he asked Yeiwa: 'So we are close?'

'Yes, round this bend there is the main entrance, wide enough for vehicles to drive into the hillside.'

Alex glanced over his shoulder to see Victor Abadie driving the second buggy in his dirty Fat-Cat suit, the other Goat-Man beside him in the front and the woman disguised as White Zombie behind. Alex made a couple of hand gestures, indicating that they should all get out and be prepared to fight.

83

'Was that someone else coming?' asked one of the two guards wearing combat sheaths. 'We'll stay here. You go look.'

The other two swapped a look.

'Or we all wait here and see what happens,' one argued.

Alex chose to approach on foot, clinging to the right-hand side of the road, his shoulder grazing the steep rock of the hillside, with the marines in single file behind him and Poiret bringing up the rear. Yeiwa remained with the vehicles.

Despite the care he was taking, Alex trod on a fallen branch of tinder-dry wood that snapped, the sound eerily loud in the quiet of the morning.

He froze and White Zombie, following too close behind, trod on the same long branch, repeating the dry, abrupt sound.

Alex extended his arm behind him, palm vertical, in a gesture meaning: *Halt*.

Up on the ridge, Mariam was observing the movement in the entrance.

'Four of them,' she said, her eye still to the scope of her FR-F2. 'They don't look happy, like they've not received their orders and are wondering what's going to happen next.'

'I see them. Do we fire?'

Mariam left a pause, then decided: 'Not yet.'

'Who was that in the buggy from the docks?' asked Paul.

'I'm pretty sure that was Davide Castile.' She sighed. 'But he was too quick for me to be sure.'

Victor Abadie picked his way up the line to Alex's shoulder.

'I'll go ahead.'

'I'll come with you.'

'You are more valuable, captain, and you aren't in great shape. Let me find out what's happening.'

There was logic in what Abadie said, despite the fact that Alex hated it.

'Go ahead.'

From the ridge, Mariam saw a heavily built figure wearing a dirty suit emerge from the shadows at the foot of the rock wall, stepping out into the middle of the road with his hands at the level of his shoulders.

'Who is that?' asked Paul.

'And why is he dressed like that?' she replied.

Alex edged forward until he could see what was happening through the dangling fronds of a tropical creeper that fell in thick strands with broad, dark-green leaves. He saw Abadie's submissive gesture and heard him speak, though the words were indistinct. Beyond him, two men in grey uniforms emerged from the mouth of a dark entrance into the hillside, holding handguns out in front of them. Each had a heavy truncheon in a leather holster on his belt. Abadie stood very still, then spoke in a louder voice.

'You have nothing to fear from me,' he said. One of the grey-clad guards replied in Creole. Abadie said: 'I'm not from here.'

'Who are you? Where you come from?' demanded the other in strongly accented French.

'From Saint-Just. I crossed with Papa Lace.'

'You are wearing my brother's clothes,' said the first.

'I didn't know that,' said Abadie. 'He lent them to me. He trusted me. You can trust me, too. I mean you no harm.'

'I don't believe you,' said the guard with an edge of violence in his voice. 'What's happened to my brother?'

'Everyone on this island is in danger. I'm here to help. I have information you need. Can you take me to Chief Castile?'

The man looked pained.

'Monsieur Davide says no one in or out.'

As the two guards broke away and spoke to one another in an undertone, without Alex noticing, Poiret had made her way up the line to his shoulder, hissing in his ear: 'I have more money. Let me offer it.'

'Wait. These disguises are working against us,' said Alex. He pulled off his oversized jacket, revealing his own much closer cut suit, dragging the dirty, baggy trousers over his shoes. 'Stay here.' He followed Abadie out onto the tarmac, taking up a position beside him. 'We are not your enemies,' he said. 'Your enemies are the Castiles. Trust me. Trust us. We can prove it. And we have money – more money than you have ever seen.'

Mariam adjusted her position slightly, making sure she had a steady base.

'Who is the second man?' asked Paul.

Mariam knew but she couldn't, right away, bring herself to say so out loud. She could tell from his stature and his gait and from something indefinable, something unique to him that she loved.

'It's Alex,' she said at last and felt a rush of adrenaline and relief. She knew in that moment that she had never believed that he was dead, that she had always been certain that he would come back to her and life would go on, together.

She concentrated on her breathing, not wanting to compromise accuracy with joy and excitement.

'Those guards in grey,' she told Paul. 'You take aim on the one on the right, I'll take the one on the left.'

'Got it,' said Paul.

A moment later, though, they needed a new plan.

Two more guards came out of the shadowy entrance, forming a line with the first two. One of them spoke better French.

'We have our orders. Chief Castile will look after us. He says that the end times are here, that only Haré is safe.'

Claudine Poiret stepped out from concealment, struggling to remove a roll of cash from beneath the voluminous Mama-Cov medical smock. She advanced on the guards, babbling the same words Alex had heard her use at least twice already: 'My name is Claudine Poiret and I am a representative of the French government, in charge of the relief operation to Haiti.'

Immediately, he saw what would happen next. She was speaking and moving too fast, making the guards nervous. As she released her hand from her smock, one of them stepped in and struck her on her right cheek with the back of his black-sheathed hand. There was a crackle of electricity and she dropped to the ground, falling in a slack heap.

'Two for me and two for you,' said Mariam. 'Fire.'

The sound of the FR-F2's was aggressively loud. Because of Alex's proximity, Mariam and Paul took great care, firing individual shells, not repeated bursts of ammunition, taking down the grey-clad guards, spinning them round with the impacts. One of them just had time to turn and attempt to flee back inside before Paul put a bullet between his shoulder blades, no doubt severing his spinal column and punching him forwards onto the ground.

Mariam sprang to her feet, taking three steps out of the cover of the zombia palms. She dropped her FR-F2 on the carpet of dead dry leaves and waved her arms above her head, calling out Alex's name.

*

Victor Abadie was crouching over the body of Claudine Poiret, his fingertips at her throat, feeling for a pulse. He glanced up at Alex: 'Thready. But there.'

The other marines came out of cover from beneath the thick dangling creepers. Yeiwa was with them, looking appalled and uncertain.

'Take Madame Poiret carefully inside,' Alex told them, his attention elsewhere.

His eyes were on the ridge from which the gunshots had come. Despite his excellent vision, he found it hard to pick out the two figures in camo fatigues against the backdrop of vegetation. One was standing very still, apparently aiming a weapon at them, but with one hand held up in the air to show that wasn't the case, that they were simply using the sighting mechanism as a telescope. The second figure was waving their arms over their head – smaller in stature but poised and athletic.

Something happened inside Alex's chest, a kind of swelling but also a concentration – of energy and focus and emotion.

'Mariam,' he said quietly to himself.

There was no point calling out. The distance was too great and time was short. By raising his right arm, bent at the elbow, moving his fist in a circle, he gave the tactical signal: *Rally*. He knew Mariam would understand and make her way down to join them. Then he gave a second signal, moving his fist forward and back as if banging on a door: *Attack*.

Despite the distance and the distracting foliage behind her, he saw her raise her own right fist in a gesture that meant: *Understood*. Then the tiny figure turned to her companion and they began to scramble down between the agricultural terraces.

Alex wanted nothing more than to stand still and watch their progress, step by step – or even run to meet them halfway – but he dragged himself away to see what was happening inside the entrance.

The space was illuminated by small white LED bulbs, maybe forty of them, each providing a pinprick of white light. Two electric buggies were parked over to one side, attached to charging points. At the rear, he clocked a wide roll-down steel door and a pedestrian entrance that resembled a hatch on a submarine, next to an elevator with open doors. He went and tried to open the hatch, but the wheel-handle wouldn't move. It felt like it was held by some kind of mechanical ratchet or lock, rather than a mag-catch. He hit the call button on the elevator without response.

He went to see how Poiret was doing. Abadie had her in the recovery position with a hand on her shoulder, making sure she didn't move. Her eyes were open. She spoke in a hoarse whisper.

'I'm sorry … impatient … as usual.'

'I have to get inside the citadel,' said Alex. 'I think the only way in is to climb the exterior to the upper terrace where we saw the antenna array.'

'Who … shot?' said Poiret, unable to form a complete sentence.

'Mariam,' said Alex. 'Tell her to come and find me.'

84

Todor Kaldonov was back on the dormitory floor, his forehead pressed to the glass of his son's room, trying to reassure Mitya by gesture that all was well and that soon he, his father, would find a way to release him from imprisonment. He couldn't see, but he guessed that Stoyan was doing the same thing, through the double-glazing of the internal window between the two rooms.

Kaldonov pulled himself away with reluctance, moving out of sight of his son's terrified gaze. He felt furious with himself, unable to dispel guilty memories of his first meeting with Aurélien Castile at Davos. It seemed ridiculous, now, that he could ever have been taken in. The man was a reptile – worse, a demon.

Kaldonov's anger became a furnace, but he knew he needed to control it. The remote systems for the internal door locks were accessible from the control room. He knew how to access them but he was worried about the Castiles' guards, six coarse Haitian men from one of the vicious gangs that had replaced civilian government in the nation descended from the world's first Black republic. They would no doubt stand in his way.

He went back to the window to peer into Mitya's room. The boy was lying on his bed, now, his face close to the night light. He looked sickly, his breath coming in short, sharp pants. Kaldonov realised with a cold surge of horror that he was suffocating.

*

Under normal circumstances – meaning properly equipped and in peak physical condition – the climb to the terrace on the top level of the citadel would have been easy. But Alex was weary, bruised and malnourished, his energy levels and mental focus compromised by the hangover from the alcohol and mad honey.

He made a good start, using the joints in the stonework of the arch round the main entrance to get up onto the rock above. He scanned for likely routes, his eyes dazzled by the sun, then set off traversing the almost-vertical slope to the east, finding abrasive handholds in the porous rock that grated his fingers.

Having climbed twenty vertical metres, he found himself pinned by an overhang and thought for a moment that he might have to go back and look for a different route. At that moment, a family of birds flew up, speckled like starlings, squawking angrily, emerging from a crevice. He managed to turn both hands sideways, wedging them in the cleft, gaining enough traction to physically commit to one huge effort and haul himself out from under the projecting rock, onto an easier slope.

The natural terrain levelled out and he was able to stand straight, one foot planted higher than the other, and take a breath. He looked east, across the vastness of the grey ocean.

There were an incredible number of seabirds in the sky, flying towards him, shooting past overhead as if engaged on some urgent errand, all different species, leaving him with a sickening premonition of disaster.

With renewed energy, spreading his arms and legs wide across the steep rock wall, he found enough purchase to inch his way up another twenty metres, closer to a parapet that ran the perimeter of the terrace. But the final part of his projected climb was impossible. There were no further handholds because the top five metres were smooth concrete.

Davide Castile was back in the medical centre, deep inside the citadel. The med-port in his abdomen was weeping blood again, mixed with an unpleasant yellow-green pus. He was sweating through his clothes.

'What are you doing here?' he shouted at the Haitian on duty, one of the team of six armed guards performing his civilian role. 'You should be in uniform.'

'*Oui, monsieur.*'

Davide watched him hurry away, then opened an eye-level cabinet, sweeping the contents out onto the counter below, looking for a stimulant. He found a bottle of tablets containing a mild amphetamine and swallowed three with a handful of water from the tap on the nearby sink.

Wary that oral ingestion would take a considerable time to affect his metabolism, he clumsily searched two other cupboards, eventually finding a cardboard box containing two pre-loaded syringes for intramuscular delivery. He tore the packaging from the first, punching it into his right quad through the fabric of his lightweight trousers.

Alex edged round to his left, painfully traversing a few metres beneath the length of the terrace, hot and sweaty, making it more and more difficult to get a good grip with his damp hands, but managing to gain a little height. At the southern end, with still four metres of concrete above his head, he saw that he was close to the outer edge of a kind of extended walkway built onto the natural summit, with a low parapet wall, only about thirty centimetres tall. He guessed it must be a kind of viewing area, looking south to the gently sloping grassland on which the circle of megaliths stood. Between this belvedere and the meadow below was a precipitous cliff of harsh rock.

Before he attempted the final effort, Alex looked east once more, seeing a dark line on the horizon, an inexplicable detail on the edge of the flat grey ocean. The line stretched as far as his eyes could see, north and south.

Alex tried to compute what he was looking at. He had deduced the fall of satellites and seen evidence of it with his own eyes. But no satellite impact was capable of generating a tsunami.

Something else – something dreadful – must have occurred, an earthquake or a vast volcanic eruption.

At the top of the citadel, he would surely be safe. But Mariam and the others were much lower down and would inevitably be swept away by the flood.

Kaldonov tried to summon the elevator to take him to the control room on the floor beneath the terrace, but it was out of action. He opened the door to the stairwell and took the first two flights two steps at a time. Soon, though, he was exhausted and had to continue more steadily.

The submarine-style hatch into the control room was open. He went straight to Aurélien Castile's four-screen desk, looking for some way of disabling the hygiene quarantine on his family's rooms. But he had no experience of how to navigate the unsmart controls.

A bemused looking guard, pushing his arms into the grey uniform of the Castiles' armed troop, entered the control room, his eyes wide, darting from side to side.

'*Qu'est-ce qu'il y a?*' Kaldonov asked in careful French.

What is it?

The man spoke too fast for Kaldonov to follow. He begged him to slow down. After several attempts, he understood. The man had been changing from his medical scrubs into his uniform in the guard room and had seen, on the closed-circuit relay from the ATLAS ring of fire, a vast wave that stretched the width of the horizon.

'How long?'

'I don't know,' said the man, looking terrified. 'Minutes?'

'Give me your gun.'

'No.'

'I won't hurt you.'

'No, I tell you.'

'All right.'

Using mime and as many useful French words as he could remember, Kaldonov begged the man to go downstairs and take his weapon and shoot out the windows to Mitya's room, then do the same to the window through to where Stoyan was trapped. The guard looked unconvinced. Kaldonov told him that he would help the man survive, that he was the only person who could fix the digital systems on Haré Stronghold, but only if the guard saved his family.

'Or give me your weapon and I will do it myself.'

At last, after a painful pause, the guard nodded.

'I will release them.'

'Go quickly. And give me that.'

Kaldonov pointed to a heavy truncheon attached to the guard's belt. The man handed it over then left by the staircase. Kaldonov heard his heavy tread, receding down the concrete steps.

Alex turned back from the approaching tsunami – maybe a matter of minutes away? – to the rock face. He used an upside-down handhold to lever his weight up far enough to put his right foot on a firm ledge about three centimetres deep. From there, he could reach a line of vegetation growing just below the stubby parapet. He tested it with his hand, making sure the tenacious plants were solidly anchored, then used them to swing his left leg up, hooking his knee over the coping stones and heaving his body up onto the smooth walkway, his cheek against the cool terrace slabs.

For a few seconds, he lay still, his heart pounding in his chest, feeling out of condition and wasted. Then he raised his head at the sound of angry voices, engaged in violent debate.

'You could have killed them with the ATLAS guns,' shouted Davide Castile. He was standing by an outdoor sideboard, under an awning, close to the open doors of an elevator, a hand raised to his brow to shade his eyes from the dazzling sun. 'When they landed the plane. Why didn't you?'

'Because you aren't good enough,' spoke a dry, unkind voice from a man in an electric wheelchair. 'Because Haré needs leaders, not followers.'

'You can't believe, after all that we've done, that either Jordane or Lamarque will accept your arguments, will work with you.'

'They have no choice. There is only Haré Stronghold left. Everywhere else, societies are breaking down. Life was already cheap. Now it is worthless.'

'Do you expect me to share power with them?'

'I no longer expect anything from you, Davide.'

For half a second, Alex wondered how it was that the two men could have failed to notice either him or the tsunami on the horizon, then he realised that it was because they were in shadow beneath the half-roof that extended out from the central building and the light beyond was dazzling.

He braced himself for action but, before he could move, a door opened from a stairwell alongside the elevator, revealing a man with sallow skin and a thick moustache, swinging a truncheon. He caught Davide Castile on the side of the head. Davide flinched away, falling, and the man hit him a second time on the way down for good measure. Then he dropped the truncheon and launched himself at Castile Senior, grasping the armrests of his wheelchair, pushing it in reverse towards Alex with the frail old man ineffectively waving his wiry arms and wailing for Davide to save him.

Alex rolled to one side, out of their path. The wheelchair's rear wheels caught the low parapet and tipped up, flinging the old man over the edge, his desperate voice thin and weak.

'*Non, non, ne fais pas ça ...*'

No, don't do that.

But it was too late. Two seconds later, Alex heard the thud of Aurélien Castile's body striking the rocks far below.

85

The monumental tsunami crossed the North Atlantic with extraordinary speed, its terrifying height fluctuating with undulations and ridges in the ocean floor. It thundered on, not as a single vast wave, but in gigantic ripples. Just north of Puerto Rico, east of the island of Hispaniola, it hit a feature of the seabed known as the Milwaukee Deep, the dip and plunge of the first impact causing a higher peak behind.

The captain of the *Pablo Adisa*, Rodrigo Diaz, saw it coming. He was travelling due east, on his way back to Nigeria with his payment of bullion from Aurélien Castile. He felt the tanker – vast though it was – dip into the trough that preceded the wave and recognised the tsunami for what it was, like a line of hills where there could be no hills. Then it was closer and seemed more like a gigantic grey wall, but a wall topped with foam that was travelling at great speed, crashing and tumbling, soon to engulf his ship that, until that moment, had seemed enormous to him, strong and stable and enduring.

No longer.

The wave hit and he had a kind of momentary out-of-body experience, seeing the catastrophe from high above. The *Pablo Adisa*, empty of cargo and very buoyant, was flipped end over end, then driven down beneath the uncountable tonnage of churning water. As his body hit the wall and then the ceiling, Diaz's consciousness returned to the bridge and an awareness that he had dislocated a shoulder and smashed the orbit of his left eye.

Then the underwater pressure and the multiple collisions with the seabed stove in the windows and he choked and drowned, thinking how, inevitably, the same terrifying tsunami would very soon strike Haré.

Though he knew that he was dying, that thought made him glad.

86

Mariam and Paul were in the cave-like entrance to the citadel. In remarkably few words, she and Abadie had shared all that they knew, now and then interrupted by Claudine Poiret who was, little by little, regaining her focus and authority. At the same time, the other marines had been trying to force the steel roll-down door and the submarine-style hatch to the stairs, without success.

'I'm sure Captain Lamarque is fine,' said Abadie.

'We have to get to him.'

Abadie gave two succinct orders to the other marines who assembled in the doorway of the lift.

'Continuous fire, describing a square.'

The noise from the three automatic weapons was deafening. The three marines emptied their magazines, then Mariam and Paul finished the job with their FR-F2s, blasting away a kind of trapdoor opening through which they helped one another to climb, Mariam and White Zombie going last because they were the lightest and the easiest to haul up into the lift shaft.

'*Qui êtes-vous?*' asked Alex, unsure what to make of his sudden ally. The man seemed not to understand. He switched to English: 'Who are you?'

'I know who you are,' said the sallow-faced man with the bushy moustache. 'You are Alexandre Lamarque. You are "the man who saved the world".'

Alex demanded: 'What is happening here?'

'You have to climb the array.'

'What?'

'I can't do it. I am too old and too tired.' The man groped in his pocket 'I am Todor Kaldonov. It is my fault that …' He stopped then began again: 'Castile tried to murder my family. I have to go. The guard might have been too late. Or he might not have done what he promised.'

'What guard?'

'Never mind.' Kaldonov held out a simple USB stick without biometric coding. 'You must take this and insert it in the slot in the array control panel.'

'What will it do?'

'It's a kill-switch for the Fire virus, the software meltdown. If you can place it in the slot in the control box, it will piggy-back on any wifi enabled device that comes within range and propagate.'

With the impact of the tsunami only minutes away, Alex wondered if he would have time.

'Where must it go?'

Kaldonov pointed to the box on the antenna: 'The only empty slot. Second from the end on the right-hand side, bottom row. Go.'

The lift shaft itself was unlit but it was easy to see because the doors onto the multiple floors above were all open – or perhaps, Mariam thought, there were no doors.

She was in the lead, climbing a ladder of square hoops set into the wall. She clambered out into a clean, dust-free corridor, opposite an open doorway. She looked in, recognising some kind of medical facility. It was untidy, with products strewn across a worktop and the floor.

As the others climbed out of the lift shaft, she listened, telling them to be quiet. Before embarking on the ascent, Poiret had removed her Mama Cov costume and tried to wipe the white pigment from her face. She looked terrible, clearly not fully recovered from the taser in the guard's combat sheath.

'Stay with Madame Poiret,' she told the two marines disguised as Goat-Men. 'Carry her if you have to.'

Then they all flinched at a muffled sound of gunfire from the floor above, echoing in the stairwell next to the lift shaft.

'That's where we need to be.'

Alex put the drive in the right-hand pocket of his jacket and began climbing the fixed ladder on the concrete housing that, he thought, must contain the elevator counterweights and motors. Davide was still motionless on the terrace beneath him. Kaldonov had disappeared into the stairwell, calling out: 'I must go to my family.'

'Bring them back up here,' Alex told him. 'As high as possible.'

To the east, the vast wave of the tsunami was much closer. Alex could both hear and feel a threatening bass rumble from the incalculable mass of churning water.

He began climbing the second ladder, up the antenna, heading for the control box, above which was tied a bunch of dried out rhododendron flowers, attached to the superstructure with garden wire.

Davide's mind was slowly rebooting out of stunned semi-consciousness. In his pocket was the second syringe of medical stimulant. Hidden from Lamarque by the overhang of the awning, he sat up and plunged it into his quad, feeling the chemical infiltrating his bloodstream, energising him.

He stood up, clinging to the sideboard for balance and support, then lurched out into view.

Several floors below, Mariam, Abadie and the marine disguised as White Zombie discovered the shattered windows of a dormitory and a touching scene in the bedroom beyond: two men and a child hugging one another. Standing awkwardly to one side was another of the grey-clad guards. Mariam raised her gun in his direction. He dropped his own weapon and put up his hands. One of the others, a man with a thick grey moustache, told her: 'I am Todor Kaldonov. I am not your enemy. Captain Lamarque is outside on the upper terrace.'

Alex clocked the movement in his peripheral vision and looked down.

'I tried to persuade you to join us,' said Davide. 'Humanity can begin again. You could shape the future in a way no one has since your namesake, Alexander the Great.'

'It doesn't matter what bright future you believed you were ushering in. The scars your actions are leaving are irreparable. Generations will have to go by before humanity recovers from the trauma of our losses.'

'Memories are short, Captain Lamarque. Work with me. I offered you an escape route into the future. It isn't too late to accept it.'

Alex swung open the door to the control box, scanning the contents, finding the sole empty slot on the bottom row, second from the right. He groped in his pocket for the drive, finding the *chevalière* ring.

If he was close at hand, I might have used the poison as a weapon.

The USB was half-caught in a hole in the lining. He dragged it out and engaged it in the slot, hearing a faint noise of some concealed mechanism humming into life and saw a red LED tell-tale blinking to indicate transmission.

Will the signal find a pathway off the island?

He jumped down from the ladder to the flat roof. Davide was waiting for him below. He had picked up Kaldonov's truncheon and assumed a fighting pose. Alex swung himself off the roof, avoiding the first attempted blow. A figure appeared in the doorway to the stairs.

'You,' said a voice that he could hardy hear over the onrushing wave.

A volley of automatic fire punched into Davide Castile, sending him jerking and broken into the parapet wall.

'Mariam,' said Alex.

She dropped her FR-F2 and they embraced.

At that moment, the tsunami hit.

EPILOGUE

The floods in the English Channel were catastrophic, but Paris was unscathed. Gloria, Emmeline, Marthe Hidalgo and Régis Petit emerged from the presidential bunker and returned to their homes, full of fear and doubt, unaware if the world would ever be the same.

In the geological depression of Al Jaghar in the Great Sand Sea, Faroukh, Zeina, Wael and Mourad were safe as well. Faroukh and Mourad were preparing to return to the capital, Cyrene City.

'There is much to do,' the prime minister said, 'if we are to rebuild.'

'The administration of government for the common good,' said Faroukh. 'Nothing else is of any importance.'

Wael offered to find Zeina a job somewhere on the civilian side of the base.

'I used to clean the PV panels,' she said.

'No, something better than that.'

In the Caribbean, death was everywhere, even on Haré.

Aurélien Castile had chosen his goldilocks island for its generous annual rainfall, crucial in an age of ever more violent and unpredictable twenty-first century weather, harvesting that life-giving precipitation into enormous underground cisterns, making the stronghold immune from drought. Blessed with the perfect geology for rainfall capture, tectonic and volcanic forces had also thrust the peak of Haré about a hundred and twenty metres above sea level. Better still, the citadel itself – a multi-storey bunker mostly concealed within the central hillside – was high enough to survive the tsunami almost entirely unscathed.

In his quarters deep within the stronghold, though, Johnson Pederson never woke. He slowly suffocated, as Aurélien Castile had intended, because no one knew to look for him and save him.

The northern *chefferies* were obliterated and washed away, together with Yeiwene and his friend, the two dogs by the fountain, the baby Mariam and Paul had left in its cot, crying but safe – for just a little while.

In Saint-Just, Papa Lace was picked up and drowned along with every single other resident of that miserable settlement. The same was true of all the other villages and towns along the Haitian coast, before the cataclysm drove on, devastating Cuba, Jamaica, Florida and Louisiana, finally exhausting itself in the Gulf of Mexico on the beaches of Yucatán.

With the first shock of impact, Alex and Mariam had felt the ground shake and taken shelter in the stair well, unable to speak because, for several minutes, the noise was deafening. Then the cacophony slowly faded and they re-emerged onto the terrace to a new and different landscape, the agri-terraces scraped away by the flood, the trees dragged out by their roots, the dirt and vegetation stripped, leaving only naked rock on the steep slopes.

The terrace was wet with salt spray, thrown into the air by impact, but the antenna array had survived.

For a time, they simply stood, holding one another in their arms. Then Claudine Poiret emerged breathlessly from the stairwell with Victor Abadie, wanting to know what had happened and what they had done.

Alex told her about having succeeded in placing Kaldonov's kill-switch in the solar-powered antenna array.

'And?' she demanded.

'And nothing. It's a transmitter, not a receiver.'

'So, are we completely alone?'

'There must be a comms office, a control room. If there's anyone left in the western Atlantic to send a signal, that's where we'll hear it.'

She saw the body of Davide Castile, riddled with bullet impacts.

'Who is that? What happened?'

'Madame Poiret,' said Alex. 'I'll brief you more fully later on.'

'Yes, of course.'

With an unusual display of tact, Poiret took Abadie back downstairs, saying: 'We'll look round, make an inventory of supplies and so on.'

Alex and Mariam righted the chairs at the outdoor table and sat down. Left alone, Mariam's story was easy to tell, most of it being dead time on board the BWB, except for sharing more detail of the terrible news from Saint-Médard, from Montparnasse and from Aswan. Then, for a few minutes, they simply sat in silence, grief-stricken for their fallen allies, family and friends.

Alex saw a speck of white crossing the firmament. He watched it patiently, expecting to see its orbit decay, to observe it falling. But it didn't.

So, not all of them have failed.

Alex related everything that he had seen and done since he had climbed into the Castile Energie Ae4 at Bamako airport in Mali.

'I left a message with President Manouche. I wonder if he took any action.'

'But where did the tsunami come from?' Mariam asked.

'By its direction, from the eastern Atlantic. I've read about the threat from volcanic eruptions in the Canary Islands, but …' He hesitated, then told her: 'It makes no difference.'

'No,' she said, 'but I wish I knew. Will Kaldonov's kill switch work?'

'He seemed certain, but only if it can find a way to migrate off the island.'

'What do you think has happened in Paris?'

'Poiret promised me to keep mother safe. Time will tell.'

He stood up and led her to the belvedere from which they could look down onto the pasture and the solar observatory. It had survived, somehow sheltered by the way the enormous wave had divided, each side of the peak. The body of Aurélien Castile, however, was nowhere to be seen.

'We've survived,' she told him. 'We are together. There will be time enough.'

Alex and Mariam resumed their embrace, standing in sorrowful triumph, for the time being alone on the terrace of their enemies' stronghold, survivors of Darkness, Storm and Fire.

ACKNOWLEDGMENTS

Thanks are due to the generous support of many writing colleagues – authors, festival directors, bookshop owners, bloggers and more – in particular my (alphabetical) early professional readers Lee Child, Anthony Horowitz and Lesley Thomson.

But there would be no books in this series were it not for the encouragement, business acumen and editorial expertise of Jason Bartholomew and Joanna Kaliszewska of BKS Agency.

Moonflower Books prove over and over that they are a gem of a publisher – thank you, Christi Daugherty, Jack Jewers and Emma Waring, and cover designer Jasmine Aurora

I'm not sure how many authors have cause to be grateful for the brilliant 'additional writing brain' that Flora Rees provides, but I am one.

Finally, it only remains to acknowledge the professionalism, creativity, love and support of the best and only Kate Mosse.

ABOUT THE AUTHOR

Greg Mosse is a 'writer and encourager of writers' and husband of international bestselling author, Kate Mosse. He has lived and worked in Paris, New York, Los Angeles and Madrid, mostly as an interpreter and translator, but grew up in rural southwest Sussex. In 2014, he founded the Criterion New Writing playwriting programme in the heart of the West End and, since then, has produced more than 25 of his own plays and musicals. His creative writing workshops are highly sought after at festivals at home and abroad. His immensely successful Alex Lamarque cli-fi trilogy from Moonflower comprises *The Coming Darkness* (2022), *The Coming Storm* (2024) and its devastating climax *The Coming Fire* (2025). He also writes the Maisie Cooper cosy-crime mysteries.

Also by Greg Mosse

The Alex Lamarque Trilogy (Moonflower)
The Coming Darkness
The Coming Storm
The Coming Fire

The Maisie Cooper Mysteries (Hodder)
Murder at Church Lodge
Murder at Bunting Manor
Murder at the Theatre
Murder at the Fair
Murder at Sunny View
Murder at the Wedding

Non-fiction (Orion)
Secrets of the Labyrinth

Piece Of My Heart by Penelope Tree

Fame. Money. Beauty. Sex. Love. Ari wants them all. And when she becomes the face of the 1960s, it seems like they're hers for the taking. Overnight, her life is transformed into a dizzying whirlwind of drugs, photoshoots, and parties, all with notorious bad-boy photographer Bill Ramsey by her side.

But in the fickle world of fashion, nothing lasts for ever – and addiction, Ari's eating disorder and her increasingly dysfunctional relationship with Ramsey send her life spinning out of control.

How much more of herself must Ari lose to keep the things she always thought she wanted?

Based on a true story, *Piece of My Heart* is a stunning piece of autofiction in the vein of Esther Freud's *Hideous Kinky* and Chris Kraus's *I Love Dick*.

About the author

Model, writer and activist, Penelope Tree was the ultimate Sixties It girl. Born to a Conservative MP and an American socialite, she was discovered at the age of 13 by the photographer Diane Arbus and became an overnight sensation after an appearance at Truman Capote's Black and White Ball. A career in modelling followed – as David Bailey's muse, Penelope appeared on the cover of *Vogue* and travelled around the world. Now a practising Buddhist and charitable ambassador, Penelope has two adult children and splits her time between Sussex and London.

SCAN ME TO FIND OUT MORE

MOONFLOWER

www.moonflowerbooks.co.uk

Pagans by James Alistair Henry

SCAN ME TO FIND OUT MORE

Britain, 2023 ... only in this Britain, the Norman Conquest of 1066 never happened. An uneasy alliance of ancient tribes – the Celtic West, Saxon East and an independent Nordic Scotland – has formed, but the fragile peace is threatened by a series of brutal murders.

As the threat rises, Detectives Aedith and Drustan must put aside their personal differences to follow the trail, even when they uncover forces behind the killings that go deeper than they could ever have imagined.

Set in a world that's far from our own and yet captivatingly familiar, Pagans explores contemporary themes of religious conflict, nationalism and prejudice in a smart, witty and refreshingly different police procedural that keeps you guessing until the very end. Perfect for readers of Ben Aaronovitch, Neil Gaiman and Terry Pratchett.

About the author

Screenwriter and editor James Alistair Henry first started writing while working as a bookseller. He joined the writing team for Channel 4's *Smack the Pony* and went on to write the BAFTA award winning *Green Wing*, ITV comedy *Delivery Man* and cult hit *Campus* as well as episodes for smash-hit children's television shows *Bob The Builder* and *Hey Duggee*. James lives in Cornwall with his wife, a writer and medieval historian, and their two children.

MOONFLOWER

www.moonflowerbooks.co.uk

The Fortunes of Olivia Richmond
by Louise Davidson

After a terrible tragedy, governess Julia Pearlie finds herself with no job, home, or references. When she's offered a position as companion to Miss Olivia Richmond, she's relieved. But Mistcoate House is full of secrets. And Julia has more than a few of her own.

As the danger grows, and the winter chill wraps around the dark woods surrounding Mistcoate, Julia will have to fight to uncover the truth, escape her past – and save herself.

Original and engrossing, this Victorian Gothic thriller is an outstanding piece of storytelling from an exciting new talent. Perfect for fans of Stacey Halls and Michelle Paver.

About the author

Louise Davidson was born in Belfast and has always worked in the creative arts in some capacity, from working as an assistant to theatre directors, to holding scriptwriting classes in prisons and teaching English and Drama to A-Level students. Louise lives in London with her husband and stepson. *The Fortunes of Olivia Richmond* is her debut novel.

SCAN ME TO FIND
OUT MORE

MOONFLOWER

www.moonflowerbooks.co.uk

The Lost Diary of Samuel Pepys by Jack Jewers

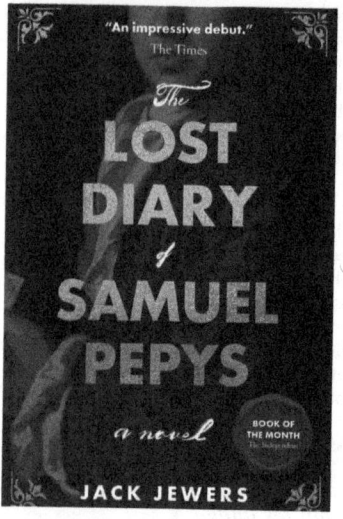

SCAN ME TO FIND OUT MORE

The diaries of Samuel Pepys have enthralled readers for centuries with their audacious wit, gripping detail, and racy assignations. Pepys stopped writing at the age of 36. Or did he?

This action-packed historical thriller picks up where Pepys left off as he is sent from the pleasures of his familiar London to the grimy taverns and shipyards of Portsmouth. An investigator sent by the King to look into corruption in the Royal Navy has been brutally murdered, and it's down to Pepys to find out why. But what awaits him is more dangerous than he could have imagined.

About the author

Jack Jewers is a filmmaker and writer, passionate about history. His films have been shown at dozens of international film festivals including Cannes, New York, Marseille and Dublin, and have received awards from the Royal Television Society and a BAFTA nomination for Best Short Film. The Lost Diary of Samuel Pepys is his first novel.

Praise for The Lost Diary of Samuel Pepys

'Book of the month ... A zestful imagining.'
INDEPENDENT

'One of the best historical fiction books of the year.'
THE TIMES

'Swashbuckling action-packed drama.'
WOMAN AND HOME

MOONFLOWER

www.moonflowerbooks.co.uk

Blue Running by Lori Ann Stephens

SCAN ME TO FIND OUT MORE

In the new Republic of Texas, guns are compulsory and nothing is forgiven.

Fourteen-year-old Bluebonnet Andrews is on the run across the Republic of Texas. An accident with a gun killed her best friend but everyone in the town of Blessing thinks it was murder. Even her father – the town's drunken deputy – believes she did it. Now, she has no choice but to run. Because in Texas, murder is punishable by death.

About the author

Lori Ann Stephens is an award-winning author whose novels for children and adults include *Novalee and the Spider Secret*, *Some Act of Vision*, and *Song of the Orange Moons*. She teaches creative writing and critical reasoning at Southern Methodist University in Dallas, Texas.

Praise for Blue Running

Book of the Month
INDEPENDENT & FT

'If there's one teen novel this year that readers will never forget, it's this one ...'
BOOKS FOR KEEPS

'Brilliant.'
HEAT MAGAZINE

'Gripping.'
GUARDIAN

MOONFLOWER

www.moonflowerbooks.co.uk

About Moonflower Books

The Independent Publishing Association's Newcomer of the Year 2023, Moonflower is a young, UK-based, independent publisher. Our award-winning books are the kind that make you sit up in your seat. Books that break the mould. That are hard to categorise. In short, the kind of books that deserve your attention.

moonflowerbooks.co.uk

MOONFLOWER